Somnus' Palace

Book One of The Sleepwalker Cycle

C.V. Vobh

SOMNUS' PALACE

Book One of The Sleepwalker Cycle

by C.V. Vobh

Cover illustration and design by Charles Utting.

eBook ISBN: 978-1-961425-07-1
Paperback ISBN: 978-1-961425-05-7
Hardback ISBN: 978-1-961425-04-0

Published in New York, New York by Thuban Books.

Copyright © 2025.

PART I
SLEEPING AND AWAKENING

CHAPTER 1
BEYOND THE THRESHOLD

Proto blinked and squinted at the light. Mist hung over his sight, and it clung there even after he rubbed his eyes. But a bluish hallway soon emerged from the bleariness.

It was long and straight. Silvery glow strips wove strange patterns along the walls at about chest height. Some white doors without knobs were scattered at random intervals. The faint fog in the air piled up and became opaque about a hundred yards ahead.

He looked down at himself. He was wearing his old high school track-suit—navy sleeves and pants lined with yellow, white chest, and, of course, the logo of the planet Saturn over his left breast. It'd made a strange school mascot. Having a ringed planet bouncing and waving its arms on the sidelines was more amusing than inspiring.

Where am I?

He didn't think he had amnesia. Twenty-seven years of life loomed clearly in his mind's eye. He recalled going to sleep—closing his eyes on the couch, hand still closed around his game controller. And he felt vaguely certain he'd woken up later. But what'd occurred after that point dwindled into mist. Much like this hallway.

He had a history of sleepwalking. It'd been a big problem in his youth. Once, his parents had spent all morning searching desperately for him, only to get a call from his friend's mom. Somehow, he'd been curled up sleeping in the back seat of their station wagon. But his sleepwalking had recessed with age, and now he mostly just woke on the couch instead of the bed, or vice versa. Certainly nothing like *this*.

He started walking down the hallway. The doors looked like the sort that would slide open as you approached. But nothing happened when he tried touching a few of them.

There were some intersections too, but he continued straight. He'd prefer not to lose track of where he started—maybe there was a reason he'd been there. That's how Proto was. He liked to keep his past close enough that he could get back to it.

After about five minutes, he reached a door that, unlike the others, was open. He heard a faint clinking from far within.

As he crossed through the doorway, the misty blue and silver décor ended. It was replaced by wood paneling and wallpaper of green and purple with interwoven gold vines. Old-fashioned gas lamps threw more shadows than they dispelled. The clinking grew louder as he advanced.

He emerged into a late-19th-century-style bar room lounge. The sides of the tables had exquisite inlays of medieval scenes. The chairs had cushions matching the wallpaper. Both were mahogany.

On one wall was a gigantic painting of a long-bearded old man with a thick tome in hand and a butterfly-winged fairy beside him. He was watching a young man work on the beach, as a late teenage girl reclined nearby and spoke with him.

On the opposite side of the room was the bar. Behind it stood a woman with her black hair up, except two long strands that framed her face on either side. Her eyes were similarly dark, but her complexion was powdery pale. She wore an elegant French waitress outfit of black and white. She had just finished polishing a glass and was setting it back with the others. *Clink.*

Her curved eyes caught upon him as she did so. "A visitor?" Her head tilted and she squinted at him. She seemed to be asking him an actual question, not just politely welcoming him. But he wasn't sure what to say other than the obvious.

"Yes?" he replied.

"Well, we'll see about that!" another voice jumped in. This was a man's baritone, booming and affable.

Proto turned and saw that a lean but strapping fellow of about forty had entered through a doorway under the painting. He had dusky hair midway down his back and wore a long robe matching the wallpaper. A nocked bow was embroidered in gold on his left breast.

"We're a private establishment, you know. Not just any old pub!" the man went on. "This is Somnus' Palace."

Proto rubbed an eye. He felt lucid, but everything around him seemed strange and hazy, like he'd just woken from a dream but the world was still sleeping. "And you are?"

"The man himself." He spread his arms forth winningly. "Somnus, in the flesh. So to speak. A pleasure . . . ?"

"Proto." This was all beyond strange, but the woozy warmth in his head obscured that fact.

"A pleasure, Proto. Please, have a seat."

He did so, following the man's hand to a barstool.

"Anything you're partial to?" asked Somnus. "I favor an old armagnac myself. That or absinthe. The richer, the deeper, the better."

"That sounds fine," said Proto. He was at that age where he felt he should learn more about drinks. At this point, he knew the difference between a vodka-tonic and a gin and tonic, but not much beyond that. He wished his friend Yemos were here to recommend a good bourbon.

The bartendress didn't ask him which of the two drinks he meant. She just grabbed a brown bottle and poured it into a small glass without measuring. She didn't ask him if he wanted it on the rocks. She held it toward him, the nails of her pale hand as maroon as her lips, and he nodded his thanks.

"As I said, we're a private establishment." Somnus sat on a nearby stool. "An employee lounge, one might say."

"Employees? Who's the employer?" asked Proto.

"The man himself!" repeated Somnus, smiling with his arms forth. "We'd give you a warmer welcome, but I regret to say most of my crew are out right now. They keep busy. It's always 5 a.m. somewhere, as they say."

What are you talking about? he wondered. "So . . . where do they work?" He tried to shake the bleariness from his head.

"That's a complicated question. Like asking a traveling salesman where he works. The world is our workshop!" replied Somnus. "Except it's not the one big breathing world you recall. It's the billion little worlds of a billion dreamers' dreams."

What the Hell? "Why am I here? Am I dreaming?" asked Proto.

"You could say that," said Somnus. "It wouldn't be quite right, but you could say that."

Proto frowned and pinched his arm. It hurt.

"Yes, not quite dreaming," smiled Somnus. "But the wheres and wherefores can wait. It's what we *do* that matters, don't you think?"

Well, he'd play along. "What do you do?" asked Proto.

"I'm glad you asked!" declared Somnus, slapping the bar. "To put it simply, we visit dreams. We try to be a good influence on people, try to guide people. And the only way we can reach them is through their dreams."

"Excuse me?" Proto squinted at the long-haired man and tried to parse what he'd just heard.

"We're visitors of dreams!" repeated Somnus. "People up there in the breathing world are all struggling with something or other. They all have hard choices ahead of them. We try to steer them in the right direction, by steering their *dreams* in the right direction. It's a little indirect. But that's why it works. And that's why it's fun! Don't you think, Lilac?"

The pale bartendress gave him a sidelong gaze. "I find fun is inversely proportionate to the number of people nearby. Living people." Her black eyes flicked now to Proto, one eyebrow arched curiously upward.

Somnus slapped the bar again and laughed. "That's why we keep her around! That, and the best cocktails this side of the Mists."

Proto suddenly was feeling disquieted. "Um." He looked at the bartendress. "What was that about living—?"

"So, as I said," interrupted Somnus, "we visit dreams and try to steer them in the right direction. We want a fair world! And we do what we can to make it that way, from this sleepy little corner of the cosmos."

"What does that mean?" asked Proto. "The 'right direction'? A 'fair world'?"

"What's right and fair? Ha! There's a question beyond my paygrade!" replied Somnus. "Let your inspiration lead you, I guess. Try and follow someone else's lead and you'll surely end up in the wrong place."

This was all weird and getting weirder. Proto sipped his drink—his armagnac. It had a round raisiny richness, with an odd note reminiscent of bleu cheese. Despite his bleary bafflement, he rather liked it.

Well, he would roll with this for now. He still was convinced this was a dream, despite the arm pinching. May as well enjoy it. "So, why am I here?"

"That's a funny question for *you* to be asking *me*, don't you think?" said Somnus. "I might ask why you roved so far along the borders of the dream realm that you managed to find this place! I might ask why you waltzed in here like you owned the Palace! But it'd hardly be in good graces for a bunch of visitors like us to question your reasons for visiting."

Proto wasn't sure why Somnus felt a need to answer questions in a way that just created more questions. But the free drink was good, and it smoothed over his vexation.

Footsteps sounded from the room's far side. Emerging from the shadowy doorway under the painting was a woman with silvery blue hair in a windswept bouffant. She wore a jumpsuit of grey lined with blue and purple, which followed her lithe curves. The overall look could be called cosmonaut-chic.

"So you're the one we've been hearing about?" she said to Proto. She looked at him like she'd been promised a pie and gotten a cow pie. "A visitor, huh."

"You all keep saying I'm a 'visitor,' and I 'waltzed in here,' and all that," replied Proto, trying not to let his gaze travel over her jumpsuit. Fortunately, her wide violet eyes held his gaze. "But as far as I can tell, I just woke up in a hallway here.

I don't know how that could've happened, unless someone carried me in here. And who would've done *that*, except . . . ?" He spread his arms toward them.

"I think you misunderstand us," replied Somnus amiably. He'd received a clear drink and placed an ice cube inside a moment ago, and it now was fogging up. Proto waited for him to go on, but he instead just sipped the drink. "Ah, that perfect savory note that seeps out of the bitterness as it cools. You can learn *so much* about life from a drink like—"

Proto shook his head in frustration. "Could you please just tell me clearly what I'm misunderstanding?" he broke in.

"You're going to be a *visitor*. You're going to visit people's dreams," the woman in the cosmonaut jumpsuit said flatly. "At least, you're going to try. Hopefully you figure that out faster than you're figuring all this out. Or else your visit here won't last long."

"Now, now," chided Somnus. "Let's remember that Proto just arrived here from a very different place. Let's reserve judgment for the time being."

"Let's get to it then," replied the woman. "The fastest way to learn to swim is alone in the deep end."

"Well said," affirmed the robed man. "Except Proto will not be alone. Since you'll be escorting him, Astrid, and making sure things don't go too wildly awry. As we discussed."

The silvery-blue haired woman—Astrid, apparently—scowled and pointed at him. "This counts as a visit for me. If I'm going to waste my day and my patience on this, it's going to count as a visit. With a Breath Token."

Somnus tsked. "The way you all talk to the Lord of Dreams! The Nightly Hunter! The Darkling Stalker! Try pointing at my brother Velnias like that. He'd haul you over the coals—literally! Try talking to *him* about Breath Tokens and true love and all that!" He sighed as she regarded him levelly, looking utterly unconcerned. "Yes, it will count, and you'll get your Token. As I told you, Astrid."

"Good. My Saturn Return is coming up, you know." She turned to Proto. "My name's Astrid. In case you hadn't picked up on that yet either."

"I'm Proto." Despite his bewilderment and concern, a warm tingling in his breast swelled into words. "Are you going to be my partner?" He smiled amiably.

She made a face like she was about to spit—then, thought better of it at Somnus' sharply inclined brow. "Here's how it works, Partner. I say, you do. When I say fetch, you fetch. When I say sit, you sit. Do that and you'll be my best friend; like a dog is man's best friend. Sound good?"

"Well. Arf arf, I guess," said Proto. Yes, this was clearly a dream. He probably could shake himself awake, but he was curious where this story was going. One thing he'd always liked about dreams was that he could act on his instincts, rather than repressing them the way real life required. He'd savor it while it lasted and see where things went.

"Arf arf? First's name . . . !" cursed Astrid. She turned to Somnus, who was sipping at his drink and smiling. "Do I really have to—?"

"Yes!" Somnus regarded her pleasantly. "Cheers." He clinked his cup against the glass that was being polished by Lilac—who frowned slightly—and watched the two new partners, waiting.

Astrid made a disgusted noise and turned around. "Come on."

Lilac was repolishing the glass that Somnus had clinked. "Ta-ta," she called flatly.

"Best of luck, Provisional Visitor!" called the Lord of Dreams.

Proto gave them one last look, then turned and followed Astrid through the doorway beneath the painting of the old man with the book.

Her grey jumpsuit was not quite skintight, so it shifted slightly over her form's curves with each step. Her silvery-blue hair swished back and forth. He followed her down misty blue hallways for several minutes, turning at a few corners. He would've sped up to catch her, but her pace suggested she didn't want him at her side.

"We're here," she declared abruptly, pointing at a blank door. Her other hand was on her hip, and her stare was both baleful and bored.

"Do you come here often?" asked Proto, offering her a winning smile. He raised his glass, which was still in his hand.

She mouthed his words as though parsing them. Then, she scoffed and turned around, tapping the door. It slid open. "We can make small talk if you survive day one, Dodo."

"An affectionate nickname?" he called at her back. "Already? Partner?"

Astrid said nothing, and all he saw was the shaking of her head as she vanished into blue mists beyond the threshold.

Proto's real life had been all too heavy lately. He'd felt so weighed down, he'd barely been going through the motions of life. But a dream was different. A dream had no consequences. Here, he felt light enough to live out the lively motions that emotions led toward. This was all fake, of course. But who could fault him for taking a break from reality? Especially when it felt so real?

He smiled and followed her beyond the threshold.

CHAPTER 2
BOTTOMED OUT, BOTTOMS UP

From swirling blue mists, Proto emerged into the woods in late Summer. Stars peeked through the canopy of leaves. A cool breeze rustled through the elms and ashes. Shadow-branches shifted on the ground.

The moonlight glistened on something in front of him—Astrid, he saw, still walking ahead of him. He jogged to catch up.

If this was a dream, it was a fresh and lifelike one. All five senses were registering, from the musky smell of fallen leaves to the chirping of crickets and the briskness of the night wind. All very real; except that, when studied closely, the details seemed to blur and shift. The horizon also trailed off into mist, as in some old video games. And the colors were dark and washed out, like someone had applied a filter called "2000s Horror Movie."

"So, that doorway we just walked through," Proto called to Astrid as he neared. "Was that like a dream portal?"

"Your powers of deduction astound me," she replied.

"Now look here." He adopted a mildly wounded tone. "I—"

"Shh." She pointed ahead, planting one hand on his chest to halt him. He looked down at her five fingers, long and skinny, then up at her face. He followed her gaze—and saw a glossy redness moving in the moonlight.

A red coat, he realized after a moment. The young man wearing it was stepping slowly and halting sometimes, like he were lost in thought and barely had any wherewithal left for walking.

"Alright. He's going to be robbed in a minute," murmured Astrid.

"Excuse me?" said Proto. "Are you . . . in need of a red coat?"

"We're not the robbers. We'll save that for another day," she replied evenly. "Today, we're his saviors."

"How do you know this? And how do you propose that we do that?" he asked.

She looked at him and held out an open palm. "Have you ever had a lucid dream? Have you ever tried to see what you could do in a dream"—within her hand, a knife swirled mistily into being—"when you know you're dreaming?"

She handed him the knife, which he blinked at and rubbed between his fingers. It felt solid and real, from the leathery hilt to the steely blade.

"We have the advantage here, usually, because we know the dream is a dream. We're in control. We can make things happen however we want." She waved a palm, and the knife wisped away to nothing.

"The one big limitation is this," Astrid went on, holding up a finger. "If we do anything too disconcerting for the dreamer—something that jars him too much, something that doesn't fit the story of his dream—he wakes up. And we get tossed back into that hallway." She thumbed over her shoulder. "And then we've failed. That's the art of being a visitor. We make dreams go the right way without startling people awake. Simple. Even for you."

"Such hostility!" he chided, watching the red-coated dreamer amble closer. "They say it's a sign of affection."

"Tell yourself that," she replied, "if it makes you feel better."

Proto shook his head grimly. "Cold."

"Anyway, Froyo, here's your chance to impress me," said Astrid.

"Froyo? Cold, like fro-yo? Is this really how it's going to go?" he said to her. And, for once, her lips curved up slightly.

Then, it was gone and she was pointing into the brush. He leaned and squinted.

And he saw it—a shifting silhouette behind the leafy branches. The robber. Harder to see, without a shiny jacket to catch the moonlight. But it was definitely a man's form, hunched and facing the path.

"Well, go to." Astrid watched with a hand on her hip, as the dreamer approached his would-be ambusher.

"Just . . . what? Help the red-jacket guy? How?"

"Use your imagination." She held out both hands. A baseball bat appeared in one and a pair of brass knuckles in the other. "Just don't do anything too jarring. Try to fit into the dream." The conjured weapons vanished as she brushed some silvery-blue hair from her face.

Proto felt nervous, but supposed he shouldn't. This was not only a dream—it was a dream *within* a dream. He'd play along for now. But if something went wrong, he'd just have fun with it. Why not?

Proto looked at his palm and focused. A pair of nunchucks appeared. He gave them a few test whirls. "Cowabunga," he admired.

Astrid eyed him disgustedly.

"Just kidding." He trained his mind upon the weapon and transformed it to an elegant cane. "Good?"

"Get going," she commanded. The robber had crouched as though on the verge of leaping out, as the red-coated dreamer drew near.

Proto leaned forward like a sprinter on the starting block.

The ambusher sprang from the brush straight onto the dreamer, who gasped as he was tackled onto his back. A balled fist smacked his face, leaving him in a glassy-eyed daze. "I'm gonna give you—" the attacker was saying.

Meanwhile, Proto had darted onto the path, cane raised for a swing. At the word "*you*," his wooden rod thunked loudly into the robber's head.

The man slumped forward onto his victim, like a bride collapsing into an embrace. The red-coated fellow stared upward in a stupor.

Proto glanced over at Astrid. She looked bored but less disapproving than usual. He grinned. "Here, let me help you." He extended a hand to help the dreamer rise.

Instead, the robber rose and turned to face Proto, who jerked backward in surprise. "That," said the man, rubbing his temple, "was uncalled for." He drew a handgun from within his coat and pointed it at Proto.

Fear surged through him and he stepped backward, raising a hand in pointless defense. He debated whether to run or reason with the man.

Then, he remembered: *This is a dream.* He took a deep breath. There were a million ways he could deal with this. But he had to think of something realistic, something plausible. Something that fit the dream, like Astrid had said.

He imagined into being a thick branch, lying on the path and barely visible in the shadows. Then, he started stepping backward.

"Oh, you're not going nowhere," the robber sneered. He advanced menacingly toward Proto, gun still leveled on him—and tripped over the unseen branch.

Rather than falling, however, he stumbled forward, speeding up to catch his balance.

Meanwhile, Proto's backward-stepping foot snagged on something. And now *he* was the one falling, gasping and throwing his hands back to catch himself. The cane went bouncing away as his hands struck the dirt, followed by his back.

The still-advancing robber hadn't gotten his balance back yet and, tripping over Proto's feet, plopped belly-first atop him.

Suddenly, everything was chaos. A whiskery face slammed into his, followed by balled fists smacking him. He threw up his elbows and shoved vainly, lurching side to side. He managed to get his palms against his attacker's chest, amid being pummeled, and pushed upward. But the angle was poor and he couldn't get the man's bulk off him.

A fist smashed into his cheek as he struggled. For being a dream, it felt awfully real—that momentary numbness, followed by a swelling pain.

Amid the barrage of blows, a lucid thought struck him. *This is ridiculous. I'm letting a dream kick my ass. Why?* He'd played along for long enough. Time to have some fun.

Proto tensed his muscles and gave a roar. A visible white aura rushed outward from his body, blasting the robber off him.

He rose to his feet, both arms flexed with balled fists at his sides. A golden glow had surrounded him, and his hair was billowing about his head.

Astrid hissed something from the nearby shadows. But he was too busy to try to decipher it.

Lying on his back a few yards away, his attacker now was staring in confusion and abject terror.

The red-coated dreamer was squinting at all this, seemingly still dazed. His head went tilted.

A mist swirled up from the ground and began rising.

"Look." The robber was trying and failing to keep a quaver out of his voice. He backed away slowly, leaning backward on his hands and feet. "Look, we all deserve second chances, right? 'Let he who has not'—what was—um, we've all done bad things, right?"

It was odd to think that this robber was just a figment of the dreamer's imagination. Then again, what did that even mean, when all of this was a dream invented by Proto's own mind? A dream within a dream.

Proto raised his hand. A golden radiance swelled around it.

The red-coated dreamer was watching with wide eyes. The mists had ascended to waist level now.

"No!" came Astrid's stifled cry.

But who cared? She would deal with it. Or he'd wake up, and that would be that.

The shining orb shot from his palm and struck the would-be robber. The energy discharged glowingly across his frame, and his back arched convulsively. He collapsed beneath the thick mists.

The dreamer was breathing heavily now. Strangely, the sound seemed to transpire their surroundings. It was everywhere at once.

So was the mist now, spreading and whirling with a life of its own.

Astrid now was diving at him. He held a hand up idly to block her.

Instead, she blasted into him with the force of a car. He flew through the air and landed twenty feet away, striking a tree trunk and halting against it, dazed.

Then, she was upon him, her fierce violet eyes glaring inches from his face. The mist was at their shoulders now. "Wh—what are you doing?" he asked.

"Ripping you a new one," she replied.

". . . how literally are we speaking here?"

Waggling her fingers above the mists, she smiled with her teeth bared. Then, her hand shot downward.

Before her hand made contact, abruptly, he felt like he'd been launched from a catapult. He rocketed out of the woods and into a grey void, swirling with mists lit with an eerie light.

Then, jarringly, he tumbled back into the blue hallway and did two full somersaults.

Astrid arrived an instant later on the same trajectory. She rolled right over him, and he felt every bit of it clearly. He felt his lips curve up even as he winced.

She grunted and lay prostrate for a moment, eyes closed. Then, "First's name!" she cursed, heaving herself upward. She spun to Proto and strode up to him.

He looked up at her fierce violet eyes, glaring down between the silvery-blue hair falling on either side. "This hurts a lot for a dream," he observed.

"Yeah?" She slapped him across the face. "Does it hurt? Partner." She turned and spat, this time not bothering to catch herself.

He frowned and rubbed his cheek. *Yeah, quite a lot.* "You put a lot of oomph in that. How long do bruises last in a dream?"

"You really believe that, don't you?" She stared at him. "You think that's why you're here. You think you're dreaming." In her smirk, there was a trace of—*sympathy?* "Boy, have you got a surprise coming."

Some concern tingled through him. He seemed to hear echoes of memories forgotten, just loud enough to be familiar, but too quiet to be understood.

He peered at Astrid, grumpily brushing her striped grey jumpsuit off. There was as much fire in her movements as in her glare. Her silvery-blue tresses fell tousled over the front and back of her shoulders, giving her a fey look.

The faint intimations of past events faded before the present. "Care to enlighten me over a drink?" he replied.

"A drink? You'll be lucky if Somnus doesn't dropkick you into the Mists," she replied.

Proto sighed with exaggerated exasperation. "I saved that guy in the red coat, didn't I?"

"No! No, you didn't!" She faced him squarely. "You want to know who he is in real life? He's a student. Graduating from university soon. He has an idea that could change the world. But he's afraid to go off and pursue it on his own. He's afraid to confront the unknown alone. He doesn't feel ready. He worries now isn't the time. But he also knows, deep down, there will never be another time, if he goes off and becomes some boring old consultant like all his friends."

"And so," she went on, "every few nights he has a dream of going off somewhere alone—the woods, an alleyway, an empty mall, whatever. And then something bad happens. He's attacked, or he has an accident, or something. He lives out his real-life fears in the dream. And the way the dream plays out affects how he thinks about real life."

"We try to steer the dream in the right direction, to help him make the right choices in real life. Like Somnus told you."

"So, yeah, he didn't die in tonight's dream. Great," she said. "Instead, he's convinced he *would've* died—but then some crazy deus ex machina figure appeared, powered up over 9,000, and blasted away the problem. Which was so blatantly, stupidly unrealistic that our dreamer was jarred out of his dream. And a very deep dream at that! This was easy mode!"

"You think that'll teach him something useful? You think he'll say to himself, 'Yes, now I'll pursue my dreams in a determined, passionate, and careful way. Because now I know that whenever something goes wrong, Goko here will just power up and spirit bomb my troubles to smithereens'?" she asked.

"No! What'll happen is, he'll wake up in a confused panic. He'll remember he was on the verge of death. And he'll feel that the only thing that saved him was something that *totally could never happen* in the real world. And the moral of the story for him will be, 'Stay boring, stay safe,' like Steve bloody Consulting Jobs," said Astrid. "Which is exactly the opposite of what we wanted."

"So, yeah, go get buzzed! Go get wasted!" she urged, waving a hand and looking upward. "And then buzz on out of here before you waste any more of our time."

"You know." Proto felt like the five year old who'd just pooped the pool at a birthday party. "It would've been nice to know this fifteen minutes ago." He still couldn't think of any good explanation for everything that'd happened, unless he were dreaming. And yet he doubted his own imagination could've come up with everything she'd just said. "Did you want me to fail?"

Astrid scowled. "Oh, please, don't try to shift your stupidity onto me. I told you to work *within* the dream's story. You didn't. And you knew it. Simple as that." She said this, but there was a pause and a brief pressing of her lips before she did so.

They walked down the misty blue hallways in silence.

When they arrived at the lounge soon afterward, Lilac was still polishing and clinking glasses. The two long strands of black hair framing her face swayed with her repetitive motions. A few used cups with dregs of green and brown were on the bar before her.

Nearby, Somnus was reclining on a padded chair with feet crossed atop another seat. His shoes were pointy and curled slightly upward. "Ah! Our Provisional Visitor returns," he declared, spreading his arms in welcome. A glass of mirky green sloshed in one hand. "How did it go?"

Proto took a deep breath and opened his mouth.

"He succeeded in keeping the dreamer alive and well," Astrid replied before he could speak. "He defeated the source of the dreamer's fears. Unfortunately, he woke the dreamer in the process. We discussed the issue, and he understands what happened and why. I expect he'll learn from it."

Proto blinked at her. Astrid looked straight-faced and dispassionate. She had one hand on her cocked hip, in what seemed to be her default pose. She didn't return his look.

"Ah. Yes, I expect he'll learn from this." There was a faint twinkle of amusement in Somnus' tilted gaze upon Proto. "Well, very good then."

"That said," Astrid went on, thumbing toward him, "Bozo here is also an idiot."

"Oh?" Somnus adopted a look of faux-surprise, but that hint of a smile didn't fade.

"You know he thinks he's dreaming?" she said. "Right now, I mean. Right here. He thinks this is a dream. Like, he thinks he dreamt up you and me and Lilac. And those 500 different drinks that Lilac has on the shelves." She waved toward the bar. "And everything we do here. Just one big dream from one big head."

"How delightful! You've got your work cut out for you, Astrid!" exclaimed the Lord of Dreams, casting his dusky hair over his shoulders. "Of course, he's *right*. You're dreaming, I'm dreaming, we're all dreaming, in a sense. What's real and what's dream—the breathing world or the Mists? And where do *we* fall between the two? The fact is, it's all *both* real and dream. As our philosopher friend here rightly observes." He waved his hand jovially toward Proto, as Astrid made a *psh* noise.

"That said." Somnus turned to regard Proto. Both his narrowed eyes and the teeth bared by his smile gleamed. His voice held a hint of dangerous zeal. "Sometimes, insight and idiocy aren't far apart. Chase the one too hard, and often you'll stumble on the other."

Meeting that gaze, Proto felt dwarfed by a sudden sublimity and power emanating from the Lord of Dreams. He couldn't avert his eyes.

And then it was past, as Somnus' stare drifted to his absinthe. "Yes. Rather like how a few of *these* bring insight, and a few more bring idiocy!" He sipped down the last of the mirky fluid. "Sometimes, they go hand in hand."

As Somnus turned to peer at Lilac's bottles behind the bar, Proto leaned toward Astrid and murmured, "I owe you one." He extended a hand toward her.

The corners of her lips tightened, but she took the hand and shook it. "Two," she muttered.

He looked down at their touching palms. "'Sometimes, they go hand in hand'!" he quoted.

She scoffed silently and swatted the back of his hand. "Idiot," she muttered, turning to find a seat elsewhere.

Proto felt a faint smile form as he followed her stiff strides. He'd been here barely an hour and already had some highs and lows. And he still wasn't sure how seriously to take all this. But he'd savor the emotional rollercoaster while it lasted.

"Excuse me, ah, Lord of Dreams," he said, drawing a quizzical look from the long-haired man. "Anything you'd recommend?" He waved toward the arrayed bottles.

"Ah! My favorite question," replied Somnus. He sized Proto up like a tailor at a suit shop. "Well, let's try out a few options. Lilac, why don't you pick something suitable to start with."

Her pale face tilted and her black gaze narrowed upon him. Then, she reached for the bottom shelf and retrieved something pink and effervescent. She coolly poured it into a hurricane glass over ice.

Proto's lips curved down grimly.

Astrid smirked. "Feeling bubbly?"

"When life gives you pink lemons, make pink lemonade," he replied, lifting the cup and scrutinizing it. An unnatural number of bubbles fizzed from the bottom to the surface. He lifted it toward his lips. It wasn't possible to smell sweetness, but somehow he already did.

"I forbid you to drink that. Why is this thing exposed in my presence?" Somnus strode up and seized it from him, holding it at arm's length with a wrinkled nose. He poured it down the drain behind the bar. "Let's try that again, shall we? Start with that one right there." He directed Lilac to something mercifully clear, covered in dignified foreign lettering.

Looking bored and disappointed, Lilac complied. She said something a moment later, but he didn't hear it, staring off into space and pondering this strange place.

Yes, there were highs and lows here, even while living the dream—literally. *But when life goes low . . .*

"Hey Slow Bro. Lilac just asked you a question," said Astrid.

"It's okay. He had his chance," said the bartendress.

. . . you go high, right?

"Not sure what you asked, but the answer's 'yes, more please,'" he replied.

Lilac raised an eyebrow, then doubled the size of his pour. She slid him the clear drink, which already was misting up around an ice cube at the center. "Bottoms up," she said flatly.

"Bottoms up!" He raised the glass before him, so all his world showed mirky through its white swirls; then, closed his eyes and tilted it back, savoring the bittersweet flavor of the moment.

Chapter 3
Attaboy, Partner

"Where are we headed, Partner?" Proto asked, watching Astrid's brisk strides from a few yards behind. "Another forest?"

She seemed to prefer this to walking two abreast. He'd considered complaining. But, observing the sway of her frame and, with each step, the slight shift and wrinkle of her jumpsuit around her curves, he decided he'd let her have her way.

"Follow and learn, Slow Bro," she replied.

"You already called me that one."

"Yes, that's how names work, Slow Bro."

Yesterday, after some time at the lounge, he'd been shown to his new room—a simple square that, like the hallways, had blue walls and a row of silvery patterns at chest height. They were strangely evocative, almost like script. He'd passed out quickly in his simple bed, already feeling half-asleep on his feet. Somnus had insisted that he try six different drinks.

When he'd woken and made his way back to the lounge, he'd found others there—a blonde woman in a Victorian robe, reading a thick book through a monocle, and a slim young man in a leather jacket. His hair was pink as that bubbly drink Lilac had poured, and it was pomaded to look like Elvis circa 1959. The lounge smelled of coffee and tea. Each of the two was holding a mug.

Before he'd had a chance to meet them, Astrid had appeared and swept him away for "today's visit," as she'd put it.

On the way there, she'd given him a briefing about the dreamer they'd be visiting. He was a late-middle-aged forest ranger, apparently. An ancient grove in the woods where he worked was being chopped down to build a condo development. He'd been advocating against it for years and suffered loss after loss.

"So, we're off to whomp some lumberjacks or something?" Proto asked. "Go all Avatar on a bunch of rapacious capitalists in giant tree-shredding machines?"

"Do you have one subtle bone in your body?" she replied. "You're really struggling with this 'work within the dream' thing." She turned and tapped a door, which slid open.

"Also, how do you make these doors open?" he asked, ignoring her insults. Like contrary winds, it was best to just let them blow by, rather than swinging back and inevitably whiffing. "They don't move when I touch them."

"On the off chance you're still here in a few weeks, maybe you'll learn." She strode beyond the threshold into the swirling mists.

He followed her silhouette through the passage. From ahead came the sounds of anxious debate and electronic beeping. The floor shuddered with a far off explosion.

Advancing to Astrid's side as she slowed and halted, he saw ahead what looked to be a spaceship's bridge. Men and women in jumpsuits rather like Astrid's were huddled over instrument panels with flashing lights. Some of them were running to and fro, tending to one emergency after another. Each had an emblem of a tree over his left breast.

At the center of the hubbub stood one man with a fist at his side, clenched so hard it was shaking, facing a huge glass wall. Beyond it loomed the starry expanse of outer space and a single planet, swarmed by a fleet of jagged-looking starships.

Country-sized explosions of orange-red were blossoming all over its surface as he watched. "Direct all fire toward the bomber at 2 o'clock," he ordered firmly.

"Aye, Commander!" answered a gawky but intense looking fellow in thick glasses. He tapped away at his panel.

"*Yes!*" murmured Proto to Astrid, raising a fist eagerly.

She made a disgusted noise, but her lips curved up—only to quickly return to a frown when she saw him looking at her. She waved him onward, and he stepped from the passage into the bridge.

Almost immediately, one of the crew members noticed him. "Commander, Ensign Shyteman is back!" she called.

Ensign Shyteman? He turned to Astrid. *You did that!* he mouthed. She nodded twice happily, and he sighed, then turned to face the Commander, who was regarding him intently.

"Ensign Shyteman reporting, Sir!" said Proto.

"The rear flux generator, Ensign. What's the situation?" demanded the Commander.

"The flux . . . " Proto stared for a moment.

"Stars above, Shyteman, the flux generator!" repeated the Commander with a handwave of impatience. "The prototype. The one *you* helped install."

Proto was clueless, so he just went with it. "Sir, still holding up! That blast a half hour past shook her up a bit, but the damage is superficial, Sir. She's humming again and ought to hold out for now."

"A half hour past?" The Commander stared at him. "We weren't in combat thirty minutes ago."

A mist started swirling up from the floor, just as it had in that first dream.

Uh oh. Think. Proto—or Ensign Shyteman, rather—stared back stupidly for a moment, as mist curled up around his legs. "Oh, you didn't hear it, Sir? The strain on our engines temporarily overloaded the flux capacitor. That's why electricals have been shaky. It wasn't enemy fire. Just strain, Sir."

The Commander stared, seemingly struggling to parse his Ensign's words. The mist kept swirling—but it gradually receded, till it was merely lapping at their feet. He nodded and turned to face the space battle again. "Very good, Ensign. We'll hold out for some time, Powers willing, so long as the flux capacitor continues—wait." He turned around again, frowning. "We were talking about the flux *generator*, not the flux capacitor."

The mist abruptly rose to waist level. No one seemed to notice it except Proto—and Astrid, who was hissing something to his rear.

"Uh! Just misspoke, Commander!" replied Proto quickly, lifting a hand above the mists to itch his head. "Ran the whole way here, got a little lightheaded. I mixed my words up."

"Ah." The Commander's lips curved up in a weary smile. "Very good, Ensign." He turned away, and the mists sank back to knee level.

As his gaze fell again upon the red-orange flowers of light blooming upon the planet before them, the Commander sighed, then looked at Proto again, as the crew bustled about and worked at panels all around him. "She's lost, you know. Centauri III. Yesterday, the new hope of humanity; today, a blasted waste."

Proto opened his mouth. He felt he should say something. But the mists weren't rising yet, and the Commander just looked thoughtful. He let his lips close and kept listening.

"Sir! Enemy bomber down!" called the gawky crew member with thick glasses. "Redirecting fire to their cruiser at 11 o'clock."

The Commander did not acknowledge this, instead continuing to stare upon the dying planet. "Have you seen the trees there, Ensign? The *trees!*" he spoke on, eyes shimmering as he waved toward the green-blue planet. "They really soar, with gravity at 0.8 g. And the bark's so red it's almost like blood. Something in the soil, I think." He sighed again and his stare fell to the floor. "Almost like blood. Or so it was. What life is left there will be gone in weeks. Radiation, blast clouds, and so forth."

"Ha! Got him!" cried the gunner in glasses, as explosions rocked a craggy ship to their fore, disintegrating even now. "What next, Commander?"

The Commander turned to Proto. "What do you think, Ensign? Will the flux generator hold up long enough for us to take down a few more? Or shall we start upon our collision course now?"

Proto stared, struggling to sift through his words. "Collision course, Sir?"

"You don't . . . ? Hm." The Commander regarded him sadly. "I'm sorry you have to hear it this way. But do you recall Directive 85-Q? And what we're required to do when there's a risk that a command vessel will fall into enemy hands?"

Proto pondered, wondering what to say to that.

The Commander stared for a moment, waiting, then smiled grimly and turned away. "I'm sorry, Ensign. I'm sorry, everyone," he murmured quietly toward the floor. Then, he raised his head and faced the violence outside. "Lieutenant, ready a course for that dreadnought at—"

"But Sir!" broke in Proto, still unsure what to say but feeling he had to speak now or never. "What about Directive 1-A?"

"Directive 1-A?" The Commander squinted as though trying to recall something. The mists started swelling up again, from knee height to waist height. "Odd . . . I can't seem to . . . " The mists were at chest height now.

"Yes, Directive 1-A!" blustered Proto. "'These Directives exist to serve life and humanity. All other Directives are subject to this one.' You remember, Sir?" The Commander's head tilted as he peered at Proto, who was desperately making this up as he went along. "If we self-destruct, what will happen to all the seeds and life samples from Centauri III that we have aboard? A world's worth of life will be lost forever. We need to survive to preserve it."

"But . . . " The Commander shook his head and held two fingers to his grey temple. The mists had risen to neck level now. "We tried, Ensign. We fought the battle and we lost."

"Maybe so," Proto replied. "But this is a war, not just one battle."

"So bloody cliché," Astrid muttered, but he ignored her.

"We have a chance here, Commander! We can plant those seeds again," affirmed Proto, struggling for a tone of bold certitude. "That's the thing about life. So fragile. So easy to lose so much. But all it takes is a few seeds to bring it all back again." Astrid scoffed again, but he ignored it and kept going. "Whether it's one little bit of woods or a whole world. All we can do is plant new seeds and wait. But as long as we do, in the end, that will be enough."

The Commander stared at him in silence. Nothing changed on his face. But after several seconds, the mists began to sink. "Yes. Quite right, Ensign. Forgive me, I lost myself," he finally said, then turned to the crew. "Direct all fire at that dreadnought! Give it every torpedo we've got. Then, Lieutenant, ready the warp drive. Set a course for our outpost at the Wise system."

"Yes Sir!" came the reply.

"Yes, that's what we'll do," murmured the Commander, staring again at the planetary bombardment before him. "Yes, indeed."

The dream was starting to shift strangely before them—first losing some details, then shrinking in their prospect, like they were staring on the world through a porthole window. Around their shrinking world was grey-white mirk.

Proto felt a hand seize and tug at his. He looked behind him.

Astrid's wide violet eyes were regarding him from behind her windswept tresses. "Time to go!" she whispered, pulling him backward.

"But what about—?" he started.

"*When* will you learn to just do as I say?" she interrupted, rolling her eyes and turning away. Suddenly, she was soaring into the encroaching mirk.

With an arm still in her grasp, he was yanked headlong from his feet. He literally flew in her wake.

And then they were emerging into the blue hallway—Astrid landing nimbly on her feet, and Proto tumbling head over heels beside her.

"Ugh," he grumbled, rubbing his tailbone. "I take it there's a reason that was necessary?"

"Yes." She delicately picked a violet nail, then turned and started walking away.

He forced himself to his feet and hobbled after her. "No comments, huh? No, 'Neatly done! Attaboy, Partner! Quick thinking!'"

"You want comments? Sure." Her silvery-blue hair swished behind her as she kept walking, not turning around. "You're more cliché and melodramatic than an offbrand comic book. You're lucky our forest ranger here was receptive to that stuff. Personally, I'd have crashed the ship in sheer disgust. Attaboy! How's that?"

He sighed and rubbed his new bruises.

"That said," she went on, "I admit that Directive 1-A thing was clever. A little goofy. A little easier-than-life. But it worked. You can spin a good yarn, Yoyo."

"Ha, 'spin.' Like a yoyo. Ba-dum-tsh!" he exclaimed, slapping his leg. "She does it again!"

"Don't get too excited," she replied. "Getting excited about minor success is the way of mediocrity."

"Like an arctic wind, she coldly snuffs out all warmth. Gone, that brief ardent flame!" declaimed Proto. "Once again, she is the Icebox."

Astrid gave him a frosty glower, then strode away. But she reached up to smoothe her hair as she did so.

When they emerged from the misty corridor into the lounge, the robed blonde woman was still reading through her monocle. She had three empty mugs of coffee beside her. She was holding a fourth below her lips and blowing steam from it.

"Things slow at the Shadowcaster today, Dahlia?" asked Astrid.

A couple seconds passed before the woman looked up and blinked. "Oh, you were talking to . . . ? No, not slow. Quite busy. But I finished an hour ago."

Astrid gave her a tilted gaze. "I could've sworn we were working the same hours last week."

"Yes, probably." Dahlia shrugged. "I stay up twenty hours and sleep seven each day. And somehow the math works, as long as I have enough coffee." She sipped at the steaming beverage.

"Brilliant," said Proto.

The woman squinted at him like a stink bug that'd just buzzed its way into being noticed. "You," she observed matter-of-factly, "are not like the rest of us."

"Nice to meet you too," he replied. "I'm Proto. But you can call me whatever you want. I'm used to it by now." He thumbed over at Astrid, who shrugged and nodded.

"Yes, I will then," said the blonde woman. "Sparky."

He looked at Astrid, who was beaming, and nodded grimly. "From Partner, to Yoyo, to a pet dog. How much further can I fall?"

"Much further," replied Dahlia. "Spunky."

This time, Astrid giggled.

"Two new terms of endearment in thirty seconds!" he admired. "Is that a record, Daisy?"

Dahlia opened her mouth as though to correct him, then frowned.

"No need to blush, Rose," he went on. "Embrace your creativity, Tulip."

"Is he always like this?" Dahlia asked.

"Yes," sighed Astrid.

"And you'd best remember it, Forget-Me-Not!" he admonished.

Dahlia eyed her coffee. "Lilac, I suddenly feel a migraine coming on. Could you top this off with rum, please?" She laid the mug upon the bar.

"How literally do we mean 'top off'?" asked the pale bartendress.

"Let's start with 'totally literal' and see where things go." The blonde woman idly flipped her monocle and caught it like a coin. "So, Somnus thinks this one has something to offer us?"

"Something altogether unapparent," shrugged Astrid.

"Good laughs and bad livers." Proto grabbed Dahlia's new rum and coffee from Lilac and slid it to her. "Cheers, Petunia."

"And migraines." Dahlia closed her book and drank deeply of her brew. "Stand by for another top off, Lilac."

"Leave some for the rest of us, Marigold!" chided Proto.

The women shook their heads at each other grimly.

Proto felt like he was acting out a caricature of himself—a version of himself who didn't worry about the 90% of things he wished he didn't have to worry about. One who lived life like a dream, following wherever instinct led. Well, so be it. This likely *was* a dream, if strangely long and elaborate.

But if it wasn't? If he'd permanently given his new companions the false impression that he was a vapidly playful simpleton?

Somehow, as the two women eyed him, then shook their heads again at each other—lips curving up, despite their best efforts—the thought didn't bother him all that much.

"Aha. I see what you're up to, Iris," he accused, seizing the now-empty rum bottle from the bar. He set it on its side before Dahlia, drawing a blink and arched brow. "Looking to play games, are we?" He gave the bottle a spin. It made several wobbly rotations on the smooth table before stopping just past Dahlia and pointing at—her book.

She inclined an eyebrow. "A fellow lover of literature?"

"Show your love, Pro Beau." Astrid lifted the book and bopped it against his lips—and rather roughly, at that.

"How was it?" Dahlia asked.

"She's a little . . . thick." He eyed the heavy tome and pursed his sore lips.

"Don't judge a book by her cover!" chastised Dahlia.

"We'll take it page by page," he replied.

Yes, he'd take things here page by page and see where it led. No grand plotting of his future. No musings on the arc of his life. Just living the dream by the seat of his pants.

"Look at that slaphappy look. I think he wants another one," declared Astrid.

"Wait till he meets her sister!" said Dahlia, lifting an even thicker volume from her bag.

"I am so ready for the sequel!" He leaned in.

Chapter 4
Alarms, Dreams, and the Lord of Dreams

The next day, Somnus' lounge was more crowded than Proto ever had seen it. But he'd never met anyone who was here now, except Lilac. The only other somewhat familiar face was the slim man in a leather jacket he'd seen yesterday. His pink hair was pomaded into a new shape today, rather more James Dean than Elvis.

Proto supposed he should wait for Astrid or Somnus to show up. He approached the bar and sat on a stool. "Morning, Lilac. You're here bright and early."

"It's equally bright and early at all times here," she replied. "Coffee or tea?"

"All business!" he lamented. "Like a robot. Programmed to do one thing, and one thing only: dispense drinks, and the best drinks you've ever tasted. No more, no less."

She eyed him flatly. "I've never even mixed you a drink."

He slapped the bar. "Then let's fix that! Give me a coffee Lilac-style."

She arched a black eyebrow. "I don't know what that means."

"Surprise me!" he urged.

She stared at him. "I don't have a style."

"Oh, come on now," he waved. "How about the way you—"

"That will have to wait," came a voice behind him.

He turned around. The pink-haired man was approaching and setting his empty mug on the bar.

"It's time for us to head out, if we want to make this visit," the man said. "Dream's started already."

Proto blinked. "No Astrid today?"

"Just Mayger today, no Astrid. She's with Dahlia at the Shadowcaster," replied the pink-haired man—Mayger, evidently. "I thought Astrid told you. I'm your substitute teacher today."

"Teacher or babysitter?" questioned Lilac.

"Ask me afterward," replied the man in leather.

"Everyone here has such faith in me. It's inspiring," observed Proto. "Also, what's this Shadowcaster I keep hearing about?"

"Well," said Mayger, striding toward the doorway under the painting and motioning him to follow. "You've probably wondered how we know what's going on in all these dreamers' lives before we visit them. That's what we see in the Shadowcaster."

"So, how does it—?" began Proto.

"I'll leave it to Dahlia to explain how it works," Mayger interrupted. "Or Astrid. Or anyone besides your humble substitute here."

"Alrighty then. What are we doing today?" asked Proto. "Any insights? Guidance? Warnings?"

"Be on your toes," suggested Mayger.

Proto sighed. He followed the lithe man through misty blue corridors for several minutes before they halted at a sliding door.

Mayger started to reach for the door, then turned to Proto. "Really. Be on your toes," he repeated.

Proto frowned. "Shouldn't I always?"

But the man already was walking through the opening door and into the mirk beyond it. He paused near the end of the passage. Blue skies and swaying barley loomed before him. Some shouting and clanging could be heard as well, but the sounds' sources were unseen.

Mayger extended an arm toward the scene. "After you."

Proto absently nodded and stepped across the threshold into the dream, scanning the sunny field.

The first clue as to why he should "be on his toes" was the dead horse lying to his left, with its belly hewn wide open and one of its legs severed.

The second was the roar that sounded to his right.

A huge bearded man in skins was drawing back a double-bladed waraxe over his shoulder. He was just over a yard away, and his menacing leer was directed squarely at Proto. Gleaming in the sunlight was an eagle-shaped brooch, affixed to the furry hide above his left breast.

Then, the half-moon blade was sweeping toward Proto's neck.

He gasped and flopped backward.

He was halfway to the dirt, with a broad blade whirring a couple inches above his nose, when he realized this was a dream and he didn't need to retreat—not even from a 6'5" howling barbarian wielding a waraxe in a berserker frenzy.

Still, he had to make this look convincing, in case the dreamer was watching. That would be difficult.

To be sure, Proto was mildly proud that, at age twenty-seven, he'd maintained the same lithe musculature he'd had as a high school athlete. Indeed, his old tracksuit still fit perfectly.

But lithe musculature doesn't help much when you're unarmed and facing a 6'5" barbarian with a waraxe.

Proto rolled aside and, seeing the corpse of another barbarian warrior, had an idea. He kicked back up to his feet, darted for the body, and reached as though to grab something from it.

Then, with a thought, he made a long knife appear in his hand, like Astrid had the other day. Continuing the fluid movement, he was back upright and wielding the blade an instant later. It looked like he'd grabbed it from the fallen warrior.

Meanwhile, Proto's opponent was grinning now with bared teeth, his axe gripped in two hands. "What will you do with that?" He inclined his head at the knife. It was quite long, at about eight inches. But it may as well have been a butter knife for all the good it'd do against that waraxe. "Cut my meat for me?"

The barbarian lunged abruptly forth into a sweeping arc.

Proto stepped back, letting it pass in front of his face, then dodged again beneath the next blow. He supposed he could parry with his knife. But it'd look so absurd—this dinky little food-chopper, halting that double-bladed monstrosity—that the dreamer may well be startled awake on the spot.

Instead, Proto artfully evaded a few more grievous deathblows, letting them whiff by mere inches away.

Then, smiling, he flung the knife at the barbarian. Guided by his thought, it spun twice in the air and struck squarely in the barbarian's right eye.

"Augh!" the huge man wailed, first stumbling backward, then crouching and putting both hands over his face. Blood dribbled through his fingers.

Well done, Proto inwardly complimented himself. He willed the barbarian to fall to the earth, done in by his fatal wound.

Instead, nightmarishly, the barbarian let his bloody hands fall and turned to face Proto, with the knife's hilt still jutting from his eye. His jaw sagged wide. His groans of pain became a bizarre shriek of fury.

Suddenly, he was charging with his waraxe raised. Blood streamed along both sides of his face and dribbled off in his wake.

WTF! Why isn't he . . . ?! Proto's thoughts didn't have time to register fully. He focused on an image of the barbarian tripping and falling and willed it into existence.

The barbarian did indeed trip. But somehow, he recovered and was back to barreling toward Proto an instant later. The knife in his eye threw off bloody sun-glimmers as he sprinted.

Why isn't it working this time!

Feeling a strange terror seep through him, Proto held up his hands defensively—a useless gesture, against this rampaging beast of a man and his mighty waraxe.

Just as Proto was gritting his teeth for impact, an even bigger form crashed into the barbarian's flank linebacker-style.

His foe was absolutely smeared. He hit so hard and skidded so far that he left a dust cloud.

"Woo! Woo!" howled the newcomer wildly—another barbarian, this one wearing a lionskin. Lifting a six-foot-tall greatsword over his head, he brought it smashing down upon Proto's hapless opponent. It squelched through the warrior at the waist, leaving him in two pieces. "Woo!"

Here's our dreamer, supposed Proto. He eyed the exulting victor and prepared to run away if necessary.

But it wasn't. After a bit more gloating, the barbarian turned to Proto. He squinted as though something were in his eye—and mists briefly swirled around them, causing Proto's breath to catch—but they faded a second later.

"You all right there?" The barbarian ambled up to him, his massive greatsword still dripping blood. "You almost got chopped down like a tree! Nice dodging though." He made some quick juking movements, accompanied by wind-whooshing sound effects. "And I like what you did with his eye." He pointed at the knife hilt jutting from the socket.

"Didn't work as well as I hoped," replied Proto.

"Ha! We're a tough lot out here." The man looked him up and down. "That livery you're wearing—I don't recognize it. You with some local lord?"

Proto looked down at himself. Somehow, his navy, yellow and white tracksuit had transformed to a tunic and leggings of similar hues. The icon of the planet Saturn was still on his left breast. *Odd. Did he . . . revise my outfit to match his dream?*

"Lord Somnus," nodded Proto, pondering just a moment before sharing the name. Why not?

"Hm. Sounds familiar. And you look familiar too." The barbarian peered at him closely, and the mist rose for a moment.

Then, he shrugged. "Anyway, as long as the Empire's trying to kill you"—he kicked the eagle brooch upon the dead barbarian—"and you're trying to kill them, you're a friend in my book."

"Likewise. You seem like a good friend to have." Proto reached down and grabbed the fallen barbarian's double-edged waraxe.

"Ah, now there's a man's weapon," admired the dreamer. "No one's going to keep walking with *that* thing in his head."

Proto took a couple practice swings. In real life, he'd have struggled with the weight. But here, it was effortless. He may as well have been swinging a spoon.

Meanwhile, the barbarian was gripping his greatsword eagerly and peering at some others wearing hides, who were fighting atop a hill some forty yards away.

"You need a hand with that bunch over there?" asked Proto. He wasn't sure yet what this dream was about, what the goal was, or how he was supposed to help. But it seemed likely that winning this battle and not dying was part of it.

"The more, the merrier!" The barbarian slapped Proto's back. "We're all going to die. But what a bloody way to go. Literally!" He barked a laugh and kicked the exsanguinating body.

"We're all going to die"? Well, this would be interesting.

"I'm Reks," the barbarian went on. "Happy to die by your side, friend. Come!" He roared and charged toward the fray.

Proto followed him, running with his new waraxe in hand.

As they approached the fight, it was hard to tell who was on whose side. But Proto eventually noticed that everyone wearing an eagle brooch was fighting someone without one. *So, we kill the ones with the eagles. Alright then.*

They fell upon the enemy with blades flashing. Blood splashed, men roared and cried, and they did red battle on the plains. When it ceased, the two new allies were still standing, together with ten others in hides. Among them were strewn dozens of corpses, most wearing eagle brooches.

"Ha! Traitors get what's coming," declared Reks, wiping his dripping greatsword on a fallen man's garb.

"Traitors?" questioned Proto.

"These are our kin. Men of our own tribe, who've sold themselves to the Empire. They care more about silver than our people and our ways." Reks kicked the silver eagle brooch that one of them was wearing. "In the end, they'll lose everything that matters. But they'll help the Empire destroy us first."

Proto wanted to ask what this Empire was. But someone in his place should probably already know that. He didn't want to risk waking Reks by asking strange questions. "How so?" he asked instead.

"They're getting close," broke in one of the nearby barbarians, pointing to the south. "Look right there."

From the hilltop, Proto could see many square masses of men in legion formation. Most wore identical steel armor. Those near the front rows held javelins and red tower shields. They were advancing slowly and inexorably. In their wake lay countless dead men in hides.

"The Empire. They use our people as skirmishers," Reks said grimly. "They pay our kin silver to run in front of them and die, since they know we're brave enough to do so. Their deaths are ugly and pointless. But it gives those boxes of men time to march up to us." He waved toward the square formations. "Once they're close, with those big shields and long spears and little swords, there's nothing we can do. Like battering at a prickly wall. We just hurt ourselves and die."

"That's what will happen to us today. It happened to my father, it happened to my brother, and it will happen to me," concluded Reks. "But when it does, we'll make a glorious end of it." He raised his weapon grimly, and his fellow barbarians did the same.

Proto blinked and shook his head. "You've already given up? You're not even going to fight this?"

"We fought as hard as men could fight," replied Reks. "And it led us here, where we have no hope but to die honorably. Doing so isn't giving up. It's acceptance of Fate."

"Fate?" Proto looked at the other men. They were nodding at Reks' words and eying the advancing formation eagerly. They looked ready to draw blood, bleed, and die. "I don't think so. It sounds to me like you've just decided to lose."

"Watch your tongue." Reks' face wrinkled with anger. "Each of us has bled a body's worth of blood in fighting the Empire. We fought in the old way, the beautiful way. And we've lost. The Empire and its boxes of men have won. Our time has passed. And we'll pass boldly with it."

Somehow, Proto knew that *this* was the problem he was here to solve—this attitude, this fatalism, this acceptance of tragic inevitability. This was what had to change for Reks to win this battle. But how?

"You're all good on horseback, right?" said Proto, struggling to recall what he knew of warfare in the Dark Ages. He was no expert on the subject. But he'd read enough Wikipedia articles and played enough strategy games to have a sense why battle formations like legions and phalanxes stopped working so well around that time.

"Of course we are. Far better than them," affirmed Reks, waving toward the advancing legion. "But try to charge them on horseback, and they'll just gut us on those spears. Believe me, we've tried!"

"And I assume you're all good archers too? And you have bows here?" said Proto.

At this, Reks' head went tilted. He frowned in thought. "I . . . " Mist started swirling up from the floor, quickly rising to waist level. "I'm not sure . . . "

"Since," Proto went on quickly, "you all hunt for food. So you all learn the bow in boyhood. Your people are famous for it, in fact." He was making all this up. But it seemed to make sense and he said it confidently.

There was a long pause, and the mists continued swirling upward till they reached Proto's neck. He tried to suppress a wince.

"Yes," Reks finally agreed. He sounded more like he was accepting Proto's statements than confirming them. "Yes, that's right."

Proto exhaled slightly as the mist sank to about chest level. "How many men and horses do you have here?"

Reks shrugged. "Maybe a thousand men, two hundred horses."

"Alright. I need you to gather all your horses," instructed Proto. "Put about a hundred of your best archers on horseback. Give them bows, leather armor, and nothing else. Have them circle the legion and loose arrows at it. Keep moving, don't stop. Don't let their skirmishers engage you. Just harry the main body. Do it long enough, and they'll eventually break formation. They'll try to chase you and block your path."

"That's when your other hundred horsemen charge," said Proto. "Give them spears and the heaviest armor you've got. Keep them out of sight till the formations start breaking up. Then, charge at the weak points. Try to scatter their troops."

"*Then*, do what you do best," concluded Proto. "Run in with those greatswords and battleaxes and cut them down in the chaos. Their long spears and little swords are no good, once their formation breaks down."

For all he knew, the advice he'd just given might be completely ridiculous. But this was a dream, and all that mattered was sounding convincing. He tried to keep a firm and confident face.

Reks stared at him. "Are you . . . a tactician?" The mist began inching upward again.

"Lord Somnus' head tactician," affirmed Proto.

He heard a scoff behind him and glanced. A slender man in hides and a helm was standing there. While steel hid most of his face, a bit of pink hair was visible beneath it.

"We've never fought this way," said Reks slowly. "And you would have us start today? Glory and death loom before us. Death like our fathers before us. You'd have us give that up to try this"—he waved a hand—"gambit?"

"Well, possibly dying is better than definitely dying, right?" replied Proto, glancing anxiously at the mists now creeping toward his chin. "Look, I know you love the way things were. The old way, the beautiful way. But time's like a clock, okay? You can't stop the hand of time. You try to, and you'll just get left behind. All you can do is follow it forward. And eventually it's a new day, and you're back where you used to be."

Where are these words coming from? The things he was saying felt familiar, like he'd heard them somewhere. *But where? Do I have amnesia?*

"Just when it seems like everything's lost, time brings it back again." The words flowed from Proto's lips before he'd even parsed them. "Maybe not exactly the way things were. But what you loved is still there—that beauty, that conflict, that glory. You can keep what you love, if you give up everything else."

"*You can keep what you love, if you give up everything else.*" He heard a different voice echoing this in his head. Why did it sound so familiar? Both the words and, especially, that voice?

"The way back is forward. The way to the old is the new," murmured Reks, rapt with thought. "Keep what you love by giving up the rest." After a moment, he nodded slowly, as one does when his mind is stretching to hold a new concept. "Maybe so."

The mist, which had been tickling Proto's chin, now started sinking.

There were no scoffs from the helmed barbarian with pink hair now. Indeed, his head had tilted curiously at Proto, like he now saw something different from what he'd thought he'd seen.

"Maybe so," repeated Reks, as the dwindling fog revealed his waraxe once again, gripped tightly in two big fists. "Yes, if we fight and win as you say, I think our fathers would be proud."

The other barbarians were all nodding and grunting their agreement now.

"Sound the warhorn, Calamis," commanded Reks. "Summon the men. We rally near Equilus. Half the horses are there already." He proceeded to give a series of orders.

Within a minute, the plan was underway. Barbarians were hying about gathering horses and armor, spears and bows. The Empire's troops were still advancing, but their pace was slow, and they didn't seem to be in any hurry.

"Well. That worked out nicely," commented Proto to the pink-haired warrior in the helm—the one and only barbarian in the area doing nothing to help prepare for the assault. "Didn't it, Mayger?"

The lithe man looked at him impassively. "Perhaps." He scanned the advancing legions, then the growing assembly of horses and riders. Some were equipping bows and leather, others spears and mail.

Suddenly, bizarrely, a sound halfway between a modern alarm clock and an air raid siren broke out. Mist began spiring from the ground in great geysers all around them. It obscured the horizon almost instantly.

"What the—? No! What is this!" demanded Proto.

Mayger tilted back his head and laughed uproariously. "Or perhaps not!" he cried.

The world began contracting to a sphere centered on Reks, surrounded by gloom and mirk. As the sphere of perception shrank, objects on its periphery fell into the void beyond it—trees, horses and men alike—and none came back.

"This is *not* fair!" objected Proto.

"Neither is life!" declared Mayger. "Not unless you make it that way." He strode calmly toward the mirk and withdrew a small clear vial from his pouch. He swung it at the mists, seemingly catching some within, and quickly corked the vial. Then, he stepped forth into the swirling obscurity and vanished.

Proto had no idea what the man was doing. But he had other things on his mind, with the world shrinking and blaring all about him. He stared at Reks. The warrior now looked distracted—strangely worried and grim, in a way that seemed foreign to the giant barbarian. He was hard to see through the mists. But he looked different now—slender, of rather ordinary height, and wearing—*is that a black turtleneck?*

And then, abruptly, Proto was hurtling headlong through the mirk, through the exit passage, and into the dim blue hallway. He stumbled again but managed to catch himself this time.

Mayger already was ten yards ahead and strolling away, brushing his hands lightly.

"What in the world was that?" demanded Proto.

"What did it sound like?" replied Mayger without looking back.

"Sort of like an alarm clock and—"

"Like Einstein and Sherlock, rolled into one!" praised the pink-haired man, throwing up his arms with exaggerated gusto. "What sounds 'sort of like an alarm clock' and wakes up dreamers? I'll leave it to you to put two and two together."

Proto watched him walk away and sighed. This place was like the A-Hole Olympics, and everyone he met was competing for gold. Everyone except Somnus, perhaps. But he'd probably be awarding the medals.

"By the way." Mayger paused and looked back at him. "That little speech you gave, about keeping what you love by giving up the rest, the way back being forward, and all that. I don't know where you got that from. But it was inspired. The way you turned him around was—well, impressive."

Proto opened his mouth and searched for words. By the time he'd found any, Mayger had begun to turn away. "Who was he? That dreamer. What is he in real life?" asked Proto.

"Mister Barbarian Swordsman? An artist. The paintbrush and pencil kind. Strange, isn't it?" replied the slim man. "He graduated from art school just as AI art took off. His grand career launch plans have flopped. He spends most of his time now playing an MMO. Guess what class he plays. Guess what weapon he wields." He walked away without waiting for an answer.

Lost in thought, Proto almost forgot to follow Mayger back to the lounge. He still didn't have much sense of the hallways' layout, and he'd prefer not to have to find his way back to the lounge. He jogged ahead to the turn Mayger had taken, caught a glimpse of him rounding a bend ahead, and managed to catch up.

"Another question," Proto called, stepping beside the pink-haired man. "Normally, I can control what happens in the dream. But there were a couple points today when the dream seemed to . . . *resist* that. I was fighting a guy, and I tried to make him trip, but it didn't work. And when I threw a knife in his eye, he was supposed to die, but he just wouldn't. For some reason."

"There's more than one reason that could happen," replied Mayger. "But 99% of the time, it's the dreamer. He's the master of his own dream. You can control what he's not controlling. But when he wills the dream in a different direction, it's awfully hard to overpower that. That's probably what happened here."

That made sense. Proto recalled how the *woo-woo*-ing dreamer had run up to slaughter his foe after he'd failed to do so. Reks must've wanted the scene to play out that way.

"Another question," said Proto. "What happens if you die in the dream? Do you die in real life?"

"You, meaning us? No, we don't die. Not in any permanent way. Or did you mean dreamers? No, they generally don't die. Not unless they're so shocked they have a heart attack or something," replied Mayger. "Or did you mean *you?* Would *you* die? I have my guesses, but no real basis to give you an answer. So I won't. My advice is, don't test it."

"Great. Helpful." Proto rubbed his neck where that waraxe almost had hit. "Which raises another question. Everyone keeps hinting that there's some difference between me and you all. What's the difference?"

"The difference is, we're visitors, but you're just visit*ing*," replied Mayger. "At least until your Saturn Return."

Proto stared. " . . . what?"

"The difference is," sighed Mayger, turning to Proto, "something you'll find out if and when you're meant to. Which, I can say with confidence, is not right now."

"Come on," he prodded.

"My friend," said Mayger, "we've gone well beyond this substitute's lesson plan. Ask Astrid sometime. Or, better yet, ask Somnus. Politely, and several drinks in, I'd suggest."

The leather-jacketed man led him into the wallpapered lounge, then promptly walked out the room's other doorway—the one that Proto originally had come from. Hanging over it was a tapestry of a vast and tangled tree, so tall it stretched into the heavens, while its roots crept deep into the netherworld.

This left Proto in a crowded barroom full of people he didn't know. He'd have found this awkward in real life. But in the dream, why not just walk up to a group and start talking? Nothing was permanent.

Let's see. A Velma-looking woman in glasses and a sweater was sitting with two whiskery black-haired men—identical twins—one in a suit and one in a sweatsuit. One of them was drawing a picture on a napkin and explaining something. A wiry guy was playing cards with two women. One was tall and full-figured and the other slight with a girl-next-door look. A mustachioed man in a three-piece suit had six empty glasses in front of him, and a hat hung from the opposing seat. He glanced at Proto, blinked and went wide-eyed, then looked away and didn't look back.

How about some cards, I guess? He started toward the last open seat at the card players' table, then decided he ought to get his drink first.

"Lilac!" he hailed the bartendress, who blinked and took a breath. "Lilac, Lilac, give me my rye back." He spread forth his arms winningly.

The pale woman stared at him. "You're hereby banned from ordering rye." She turned and started making another customer's drink.

"Come on now!" waved Proto. "It was a *double rhyme.*"

She did not look impressed. She measured out a double shot, her curved black eyes narrowed upon the spirit.

"Lilac, Lilac, make me a fried snack." Proto double finger-pointed at her.

"You should stop before the whole menu's off-limits," she replied calmly.

"Okay, oh Funless One," he exhaled wistfully. "I'll have whatever Somnus last had."

She opened her mouth and paused, before turning and grabbing a bottle of armagnac—then, pressed her lips and faced him again. "Didn't you want a coffee?"

Proto blinked at her earnest stare. "I . . . did," he recalled. He didn't really feel like a drink that'd make him focus and tense up right now. But something about her look told him he should accept this.

He mustered up some good humor. "You remembered!" He slapped the bar. "Very good, Madame Bartendress. You've passed the test. Prepare me my coffee Lilac-style, please, on the double. Don't make me wait for a thing like this!"

Turning away, she brushed one of her long loose strands of black hair from her face and let slip a scoffing laugh. But it quickly gave way to a focused look as she started preparing his coffee. *Lilac-style.* He smiled absently, his thoughts ranging afar.

"Here. It's ready." She set a black mug in front of him a moment later. A large crack had been repaired with white lacquer. The film atop the coffee also looked unusually white.

Lilac started to turn away, then looked back with wide eyes and warned, "It's hot. Give it a moment to cool."

"Will do." He blew lightly on the steaming beverage.

She stared a moment, then brushed a tress from her face again and quickly turned away. She reached rigidly for a glass and began polishing it, staring at it unswervingly. *Clink.* She set it down and started on the next one, going through stiff polishing motions.

Proto sipped the coffee and closed his eyes, inhaling. Beneath the creamy layer on top, the drink was black. It had notes of molasses and vanilla—fine and subtle—which somehow stayed sharply distinct rather than blending into mere sweetness.

"What do you think?" she asked,

He thought about how to put it. "Lilac-style. I think you've captured it exactly."

"But what do *you* think of it?"

He tilted his head at her. A faint flush bloomed in her cheeks.

"Coffee, eh?" A hand slapped Proto's back, scattering the reply he'd been piecing together. "All business, no pleasure for our Provisional Visitor."

It was Mayger. He was wearing a blue suede jacket rather than a leather one now. His pink hair now looked as spiky as a silent JRPG protagonist. But he was anything but silent.

"Alarm clock wasn't enough to wake you up, eh?" asked Mayger. "Who has *coffee* after a visit anyway?" He didn't seem to notice how Lilac's glass polishing went from stiff to stiffer.

"That alarm left me deaf, not well-rested," replied Proto.

"Well said!" came a booming voice from behind, prompting them both to turn around.

Somnus strolled up, his long robe swishing in his wake, and sat at a nearby table. "Yes, I recall when there were no alarm clocks. Just dreamers and the Lord of Dreams." He crossed his legs atop a nearby chair. "Ah, what happy aeons those were! Then, Electryone gave us roosters. And it was all downhill from there."

Proto questioned, once again, how his dreaming imagination could muster up a character like Somnus. Some people said you only use 10% of your mind for conscious thought. Maybe they were right. Maybe this was the other 90%.

"You should've seen the look on his face," said Mayger to Somnus, "when the alarm went off. Like a five year old whose candy just got stolen."

"Well, I don't blame him! That's how I'd look too!" exclaimed Somnus, throwing his hands up. "Alarm clocks. A sin against Nature, I say!" He shook his long dusky hair. "Anyway, how did it go otherwise?"

Mayger gave a fair account of what'd happened, and Somnus listened curiously. His ears perked at the part about "keeping what you love if you give everything else up." He eyed Proto at that point and opened his mouth as though to speak, then seemed to think better of it and let the pink-haired man finish.

"Well done, well done. You did your part, and the alarm wasn't your fault," said Somnus. "Hmph, an alarm! On your third visit! Lady Luck must be against you." He waved helplessly. "I'll have to introduce you to her. I think she'd like you."

Proto blinked. *Who* is *this guy?*

"Let it be a lesson, though," the Lord of Dreams went on. "Time waits for no man! And neither do *alarms.*" His lips curled.

Minutes passed, Proto finished his coffee, and they chatted. Meanwhile, Lilac swept about the bar, preparing drink after drink with her usual blank-faced efficiency.

"Well, I'm off. Much to be done," Somnus declared eventually, rising to his feet. "By the way, Proto. I had your drawers stocked with new clothes. I'd been waiting for you to ask about clothing, but it seems you just weren't going to! How long would you have worn that same tracksuit, I wonder?"

"If I had to wear one outfit forever," Proto replied, "it'd probably be this one." He looked down fondly at the familiar Saturn emblem.

"The Ringed One. Strange choice, but it suits you," said Somnus. "So, in your drawers, you'll find a few more of those—*tracksuits.*" He waved a hand at the word. "Plus a few tunics like that one you wore in today's dream. And even a fine robe like this one!" He tapped his purple and green raiment. "But in navy, yellow and white. And all with the Ringed One emblem."

"That's quite a haul," said Proto. "Thank you."

"Yes, well, we'll thank *you* to change clothes at the first opportunity!" retorted Somnus, striding away. "Good day." And off he went beneath the painting of the old man watching the two young lovers on the beach.

Something about what the Lord of Dreams had said bothered Proto. He realized what it was a few moments later. "Wait. He said 'the tunic you wore in today's dream,'" he recalled to Mayger. "Can you see into dreams from the outside like that?"

"'You,' meaning me and you? No," replied the lithe man. "But Somnus isn't me or you."

"What else can he do? What *is* he?" asked Proto quietly.

"All these explanations you want! You're drinking too much coffee," admonished Mayger. "Slow down! Enjoy the moment!" He sipped his drink. "For now, think of Somnus like Santa: 'He sees you when you're sleeping. He knows when you're awake. He knows if you've been bad or good.' And so forth. Except instead of being white-bearded, red-suited, and jolly, he's clean-shaven, fashionably bohemian, and jolly."

"Anyway, I"—a yawn interrupted the spiky-haired man as he stood—"will be back in a bit." He ambled out the door with the tree tapestry above it.

Clink. There was an unusual lull in customers requesting drinks right now. Lilac had returned to polishing glasses—quick, methodical, and precise as always. *Clink.* There was rarely much emotion in her black eyes. But they looked particularly hollow right now.

Proto felt warmth rush in to fill that void. "Molasses and vanilla," he found himself saying. "Creamy film on top, but black beneath."

Lilac looked at him as he raised his mug—that black mug with a white-lacquered crack. He didn't see any others here like it.

"Dark flavors, light flavors," he went on. "You kept them separate. You didn't muddle it all up into something sweet. What's already perfect doesn't need sweetness."

Her hands had paused mid-polish, as her pale face went tilted. Now, her black eyes blinked twice.

"So, to answer your question earlier," said Proto, holding out his mug, "I think I'd like more of it."

Taking a breath, she smoothed her black-and-white waitress outfit. "Well," she managed. "I suppose I'm not busy right now. I suppose there's more where that came from." She smoothed another nonexistent fold in her dress.

"Well, seconds then. Maybe thirds, maybe fourths! We'll see where things go from here, Madame Bartendress." He handed her the unique mug with a flourish and bow.

"Careful, or you'll be up all night!" Lilac chided, tapping his hand reprovingly with a finger.

"Yes, well, I've had enough of sleep and dreams today!" he replied, waving lightly at Lilac. "Who needs sleep and dreams when he has Lilac"—he blinked as she met his eyes—"style coffee?"

Her lips curved up. "And alarm clocks?"

Proto laughed as she turned around and started her delicate work. While she moved with her usual brisk efficiency, she seemed to bounce a little from step to step. Her light face never quite formed a sweet smile as she worked, but that just made the sparkle in her dark eyes all the more vivid.

Proto peered at his mug. It was half-empty or half-full, depending how you looked at it, but Lilac was on the verge of filling the other half. *We'll see where things go from here.*

CHAPTER 5
AND ... SHE'S BACK

"So, this time," said Proto, "I want to know about the dreamer *before* we get into the dream. Not some after-the-fact heartrending bio to make me feel worse about screwing things up." He was following Astrid down the misty blue hallways at a couple paces' distance, as usual.

She shrugged. "Okay."

He stared at her back. "Just like that? Okay?"

"Personally, I like not knowing," she replied. "Once you know about the dreamer's real life, you tend to think up an easy solution for his problems, and you try to steer the dream that way. But it doesn't work. Your easy solution doesn't work. And if you'd just gone into the dream without any preconceptions, you'd have found the *real* solution, lurking there in the dream. Something the dreamer sort of senses but hasn't quite worked out."

"Remember, they know their lives better than you do," she said. "If fixing their lives were easy, they already would've done it. Don't presume you know better. Especially from a one-minute bio."

Astrid strode on, as he slowed and pondered. This sort of made sense, though he struggled to fully wrap his mind around what she meant.

He also was distracted by the sway of her curved form in the tight grey jumpsuit. Its stripes of blue and purple glistened as she moved.

Proto shook his head and hurried to catch up. "If you don't like knowing, then why did you go to the Shadowcaster with Dahlia yesterday? Isn't that where you see the dreamers' real lives?"

"Because," she responded patiently, "*I* won't be the one visiting them. I was helping to pick our visitors for those dreamers. We're all good at different things here. We like to make sure there's a good match between our visitor and the dreamer."

"So," said Proto slowly, "you think I'm a good match for this dreamer?"

"With you, it was more a matter of picking the least bad option," she replied instantly.

"Yeah, I lobbed you a softball there," he sighed. But he felt better after hearing a stifled laugh from ahead. "Anyway, how about that bio?"

"You still want to know? Suit yourself," said Astrid. "She's thirty-two years old and a consultant in the city. Works sixty-hour weeks. She's had the same boyfriend for seven years. They both have a dream of moving to the country and starting a bison farm. But they also have a dream of getting married, and they have to get around to that first. And before that, they have to pay off their student loans. If they tried to do all that right now, it would leave them awfully poor. They'd really have to cut back. So they talk about the future a lot, but remain firmly in the present."

"Hm." Proto found himself thinking about his own job.

As a young boy, he'd dreamt of being a knight or wizard. As a teen, he'd dreamt of making video games involving knights and wizards. By his mid-twenties, he'd dreamt of sitting by the sea and fishing.

Instead, he did A/B testing for a marketing company, testing various versions of ads on customers and analyzing their reactions. It was not a job he'd ever dreamt of. But then, it also wasn't the sort of job one has nightmares about. It was what it was.

That was true of every part of Proto's life, more or less. Nothing to have nightmares about, but nothing worthy of dreams either.

Well, that *had* been true, anyway.

He strode along in silence for a moment. "Could I see this Shadowcaster sometime?"

"I suppose you can tag along next time I go."

"Awesome. Field trip time."

"Are we ten years old?" she said.

"Twenty-seven years young!" he replied.

She turned and regarded him with violet eyes, parting her lips to say something—then, resumed walking.

He wasn't sure what to make of that look. But she was always eying him like the guy pushing the door with the pull handle. So he didn't make too much of it.

Instead, he just followed her lead and admired the way her silvery-blue hair swished across the back of her jumpsuit.

Within a couple minutes, she tapped a white door, and it slid open. "Remember. You have to find a way to make us part of the dream. Sometimes, that's harder than others."

"Duly noted!" Proto brushed past her and through the doorway. He passed through the mirky passage toward an only slightly less mirky cityscape beyond it.

It was at once more and less than any city he'd seen. More dense with skyscrapers soaring higher than seemed possible, completely blotting out the sun and leaving the streets a shadowscape. Yet almost every building was in a dilapidated state of partial collapse, with rusted beams and girders exposed. Many buildings had large light-up signs and screens, but all were stained and dusty, and none were turned on. Everything was tinged brown and grey.

There was no one else in sight; indeed, no other *life* in sight, not even weeds. But he did faintly hear voices from around a corner ahead. He cautiously approached the intersection, keeping out of view behind the nearest building, and listened.

It mostly was a woman speaking and occasionally a man replying. "Let's hope it's right," he heard the woman saying. "Or else we've got some searching to do."

"Maybe," replied the man. "But not too much. Wouldn't want to be here after nightfall."

"Yeah, well." The woman sounded about ten yards away now. "We can't always get what we what."

"Can't and don't," the man agreed.

Yes, this woman was probably their dreamer. Proto pondered hiding or at least waiting quietly. But then what? Let them stumble upon him and be startled? Best to be open about it and get it over with.

"Afternoon," called Proto as they walked into view, prompting them both to whirl and face him. He looked at the mirky, sunless sky. "I think."

The woman had shoulder-length brown hair and big brown eyes, younger than her hardened face. She looked like she naturally had a curvy frame, but was so skinny that it didn't show through much. Her hand had fallen to the handle of something at her waist, as mists swirled up around her ankles.

The man instantly grabbed her arm, squeezing it slightly. She let loose the handle, giving him a narrow-eyed glance.

"Afternoon." The man's voice was wary but not fearful. He had dirty blond hair and was about five days unshaven. He stood a foot taller than the woman at his side. His pale eyes were as narrow as hers were wide. "You . . . out for a jog?" He waved toward Proto's tracksuit.

He looked down at the navy-blue Saturn emblem. "Good weather for a run." He shrugged.

"Then who's that?" asked the woman, pointing past Proto. "And why is she dressed like she just stepped off her starship?"

He looked behind him. There was Astrid, arms folded beneath her breasts in her grey jumpsuit. She was regarding all this calmly, as a breeze brushed through her silvery-blue hair.

What the hell. Now *she decides to show herself?!*

The mists had risen to about waist level. They whirled and crept upward with each passing second.

Proto thought for a split-second. "She's—"

"She can speak for herself," replied Astrid. "No, we're not here to jog. We're here for the same reason you are. Judging by what you were just talking about, for all the world to hear."

The man and woman looked at each other, their lips pressed tight. They seemed to be debating what to do.

"Don't worry." Proto held a reassuring palm above the mists, which were just below his breast. "We don't want to get in your way. There's plenty here for us all." He wasn't sure *what* they were here for. But he had a feeling this was the right thing to say. The mists, at least, had stopped inching upward. "In fact, maybe we can help each other."

The tall man looked at the woman, who was peering at Proto. He couldn't see her hand in the mists, but judging by her arm position, she seemed to be holding that handle at her waist again. "Maybe, maybe not. How do you plan to help us?"

"Well." Proto reached behind him and drew a retro-futuristic pistol from a holster at his waist, conjuring all this up with his mind on the fly. The gun was sleek and silvery with a few rings around it, but dull with grime and stained. He was careful not to point it at anyone. But even so, the dreamer stepped backward, eyes flashing, and the mists crept a little higher. "I'm pretty good with this."

"Did you dig that up at an old military research center?" The woman squinted at the weapon, her forehead furrowing. "Or a cosplay convention?"

"I wasn't the one who found it," replied Proto. "All I know is, it works."

"And what does she do?" The woman waved toward Astrid in her striped grey jumpsuit. "Fly your spaceship?"

"I tell him where to point that thing," replied Astrid. "It's most effective when there's a brain guiding it."

The dreamer's lips curved upward.

Oh, is that how it's going to be? Proto decided to go with it. "Exactly right, she's the brainiac here. A computer hacker. Don't let her near your terminal! Or your passwords, your identity, and your bank account will all belong to a Nigerian prince in seconds flat."

Astrid's violet gaze wrinkled at him behind her windblown hair.

"She doesn't look like it, huh? Total geek!" he went on languidly. "She's that rarity of rarities: the hot nerd. Which makes me an awfully lucky guy."

Astrid scoffed and tossed her hair back.

"You and me both, brother," said the blond man. He gave Proto a fistbump.

The dreamer couldn't quite scowl away her smile at him. "Well, anyway, you're right." The mists had dwindled down to ankle level. "There should be food enough for us all, and then some. And if we run into any Prototypes, we're better off with four than two. Assuming *you're* not Prototypes." Her expression was only half-joking.

Prototypes? It sounded like she expected them to know what that meant. He'd have to get them to explain without asking directly.

"I'm Genevieve. Or Jen," the dreamer continued. "And this is Archibald."

"Or Arch." The man inclined an eyebrow at her, and she patted his back with a smile.

Proto nodded at them. "This is Astrid, and I'm Proto."

The man and woman blinked and exchanged a glance. "Of all the aliases a Prototype might have," said Jen slowly, as the mists swelled up to knee level, "I suppose 'Proto' is about the least likely. Ha."

"True." Arch's eyes lingered a moment on Proto. "Anyway, we're headed that way." He pointed down the road, where the faint smog darkened to a haze.

"Somewhere specific then?" asked Astrid.

"Yep. Heard someone talking about a Sealed Door over there," replied Arch. Jen gave him a wary look but didn't say anything.

"Still sealed, after all these years?" Astrid's head was tilted at them. "But not for long, I take it?"

Good improvising, Proto mused.

"Not for long," affirmed Arch. Jen gave him a wide-eyed frown and opened her mouth, but he waved at her dismissively. "Jen, if they're with us, they're with us. Why keep secrets that we'll have to share five minutes from now?"

The dreamer sighed and rolled her youthful brown eyes.

"The secret of how you can open that Sealed Door, when no one else can, you mean?" asked Astrid. They both narrowed their eyes at her cautiously. She smiled. "Don't worry. Whatever you have, we don't need. We have what we need right here." She tapped her temple.

Yeah, she's good at this. Proto pointed at Astrid and nodded. "*Mad* hacking skills. If it's electronic, we've got access."

"Well, that's good. Because this will get the door open." Jen lifted a large key from a pouch. It was glossy and white, and its head was skull-shaped. "But it won't disable any security systems. Maybe you can help with that."

"You find me a terminal, I'll take care of it." Astrid flicked back her hair cockily.

"Where'd you find a treasure like that?" Proto pointed at the key.

Jen tilted her head and scrunched her eyes at him. The mists abruptly began rising—knee level, waist level, chest level—and gyring violently. "Where I found this, you mean . . . ? The Skeleton Key . . . ?" She seemed to be holding it up and staring at it, but it wasn't even visible beneath the mists.

Uh oh. Astrid was glaring at him, her violet eyes seemingly aglow. *What did I do?*

"The only other Skeleton Key I've heard of," said Astrid hurriedly, "was in the glove compartment of an old wrecked car. Friend of a friend said his cousin found it there. Looking for an old gun or something." She was looking and speaking at Arch rather than Jen. "Talk about luck."

"That's how it goes in the City," nodded the dirty-blond man. "Slave away till you get lucky or die trying."

"Ugh. Are we going to talk about this right now?" said Jen. "We're here in the City because—"

"*As for me,*" Arch broke in, "I got lucky." He reached around Jen's shoulder and drew her in close with a mollifying smile.

And, judging by her curved-up lips and silence, she was mollified.

Meanwhile, the mists had settled down to waist level. Proto let out a quiet sigh as his heartbeat slowed.

As Jen and Arch continued leading the way, Astrid leaned toward Proto from several strides behind them.

"*Never* put the dreamer on the spot like that!" she whispered, her curved eyes fixed upon him. "Don't ask questions they might not have answers to. Don't ask questions that force them to invent a whole history on the spot. Surefire way to wake someone up. If you have to ask that sort of question, ask anyone besides the dreamer."

He nodded. "That's why you switched and talked to Arch instead of her."

She nodded. "I'm glad you have at least half a brain." It wasn't much of a compliment, but the slight surprise in her violet eyes was.

"I get by, thanks to my better half," he replied suavely, extending a hand to her.

She reached to take it, then swatted the back of his head and walked in front of him.

Smoothing his mussed-up hair, he started whistling Hurts So Good. And she just shook her head.

They walked a few more minutes through the urban mirk before they saw an old woman. She was wrapped in a brown blanket and huddled against the side of a building. She shifted as they drew nearer but didn't rise. The blanket was hooded over her, obscuring her face.

"Odd place to be sitting," mused Proto quietly.

"Not odd for a Prototype," replied Jen. "Alone. No companions. Not integrated in society. Just waiting and watching. The prototypical Prototype." Her hand was not on that handle by her waist, but it was close.

"Should leave us alone if we keep our distance," remarked Astrid. "Group of four with its wits about it. Not the sort of prey she'd be looking for."

Arch nodded. After a second's pause, Jen did the same, with only a slight and brief swelling of the mists.

And, indeed, the far off woman stayed in place. But, judging by the way her hood turned, her unseen eyes followed them as they passed.

They'd only advanced another minute when a little girl sprinted in front of them at the crossroads about thirty yards away. Her feet were bare, and she looked skinnier than she should. Her hair bounced behind her in a rudimentary braid. She glanced behind her fearfully as she continued running.

Astrid opened her mouth and started to hold up a hand, a look of infinite tenderness on her face.

"*Don't!*" hissed Jen, slapping a hand over Astrid's mouth.

Astrid stepped back and frowned at Jen, watching the girl shrink into the distance and disappear behind a corner.

"You think some ten-year-old girl just happened to be here?" asked Jen. "Miraculously surviving? Scrounging up food day by day? Odds are ten to one that's a Prototype."

"And there's a one in ten chance she's not. We're just going to accept that?" replied Astrid.

Jen sighed and shook her head. "She'd try to stab us in the back the first chance she got. And it'd rip my heart out to do what we'd have to do at that point. Best not to get involved."

Proto studied the woman. Her young eyes had fallen to the floor, as the corners of her lips creased. But she was the first to continue along the path a moment later, followed by Arch.

As Proto and Astrid resumed walking behind them, he leaned toward her and whispered, "You seemed awfully concerned about that girl, given that this is all a dream."

"Was I?" Astrid replied. "Or was I just doing exactly what the dreamer expected me to do? Was I just confirming what she already believed—that everyone around her is too naïve and softhearted to do what's best? That it's up to her to be the hero in her life story, making the hard decisions that others won't make? Did I make a mistake? Or did I allow the narrative to progress properly to its next step?"

Proto looked at her. As usual, she seemed entirely self-possessed. And the explanation of her actions made perfect sense.

Yet the way she reached out toward the little girl! That earnestness in her violet gaze! If that'd been acting, it'd been very good acting.

Ahead of them, Jen was walking a little stiffly. She eventually looked up at Arch. "What if that girl *was* . . . ?" she asked quietly.

Arch shook his head and put his arm around her, pulling her in. "We're doing the best we can. It's not our fault we couldn't help her. It's not our fault the world works that way. All we can do is survive and try to carve out some small space where things don't work that way."

Jen smiled up at him, brushing the corner of a wide young eye, and continued onward.

"He seems like a good guy," Proto murmured to Astrid, observing all this from behind.

"Probably is," shrugged Astrid. "Remember, though. He is *her*. Everything here is *her*. He's not real. Only she's real. Only she matters."

"Sounds like my ex-girlfriend's philosophy," replied Proto.

Astrid rolled her eyes, but not before a laugh escaped.

To be fair, that probably didn't do justice to the ex-girlfriend in question, Karen Black. About half of the most memorable moments in his not-so-memorable life came from the few weeks he'd dated her, the summer after high school graduation.

One of the most prominent was when they'd been watching T.V. on the basement couch at her aunt's house, and they'd held hands, and then their fingers had started playing over each other's hands, and then rather more than hands, and . . . well. Things had quickly gone where such things go.

The other most prominent memory was when she'd betrayed him and made a fool of him to half his high school class, shattering his inborn romantic nature, and leaving him as a boring striver who majored in statistics and set out to climb the corporate ladder at a marketing firm.

Indeed, he'd recently been on the verge of asking out a nice barista at Starbucks, after—against all odds—getting her to genuinely laugh while she was handing him his cold brew. Then, he'd frozen up for two seconds, as memories of Karen had popped into his head. And, before he knew it, the moment was gone, and she was talking to the next customer, and that was that.

Proto shook his head and forced himself back to the present. He quickened his pace to catch up with the lithe and silvery figure of Astrid, who now was several steps ahead of him.

They soon reached the building they'd been headed toward. It was relatively short and stout at about fifteen stories tall. The facade was a wreck. It was missing about half its bricks, and beams and girders were visible behind them. Some entire rooms were exposed.

"Is that safe to enter?" asked Proto as they approached and came to a stop.

"Nothing's safe. Everything's a gamble," replied Arch. "That's life in the City. Gambling and winning or losing."

"That's life, period," Jen flatly corrected.

"Maybe. But it's not like we've tried anything else," replied Arch. Mist was curling around their ankles now.

"Well, if we hit jackpot today, maybe we can change that!" Jen declared. "Go out in nature and *live the dream*, like you've always wanted."

"And if we don't hit jackpot? Not this year, or next year, or the next year?" he asked mildly. The mist had risen to around waist level.

Jen shook her head and made a disgusted noise. "Do we really have to go through this again?"

"Maybe another time!" suggested Proto, glancing nervously at those mists. They'd just passed his belly button. "Why don't we see what's past that Sealed Door and worry about next year later?"

At his interruption of their lovers' quarrel, Jen and Arch both had turned and blinked. But now they looked abashed.

"Agreed," said Arch, as Jen nodded. "Save tomorrow for tomorrow." The mist dwindled back down toward their ankles.

They walked into the building through a revolving door that was missing its glass and rusted in place.

It took some time to find the Sealed Door—which, unfortunately, was not on the first floor, nor the second or third. Their only light came from windows and holes in the wall, which made it difficult to explore the building's inner portions.

It felt like they'd been wandering for a half hour when they finally discovered the Sealed Door. But when they did, it was glaringly obvious what it was.

Like the Skeleton Key, the door was sleek white and metallic. It somehow was untouched by the years that had degraded everything else here. Beside it was an instrument panel with a multitude of buttons. This was grimy and rusted, but a couple small lights were glowing upon it—one green, one red—so it seemed functional. Beneath the buttons was a rectangular indentation with rounded edges. It looked like a laptop touchpad.

Above the door to its left and right were two silver objects pointed down at them. Their shapes were convoluted, but vaguely reminiscent of both security cameras and security guns.

Jen dug into her pouch again and retrieved the Skeleton Key. Its skull glimmered with the green and red light coming from the panel.

She turned to Proto and Astrid and smiled affably. "Here. You can do the honors. Just tap it to the rectangle on that panel."

Arch tilted his head at her. Then, he turned to face the two visitors.

Proto exchanged a look with Astrid. He glanced up again at those security cameras. *Or security guns?* "I'm good," he said. "Go ahead."

"No, I insist." Jen's eyes were even wider than usual. "How often do you get to use a Skeleton Key? You *have* to try it."

Proto frowned and stared at her. "I mean, I can just watch and see, right?" The mists had started rising again and were now at their knees.

Jen stared at him a moment. Her hand fell to that handle at her waist.

"You can't do it because I'm going to do it." Astrid seized the Skeleton Key from Jen, who blinked but didn't try to stop her. "These things are so cool. The programming that went into them . . . ! Even *I* admire it." She tapped the key to the panel, and some glowing text appeared: *Access granted.*

Astrid turned to Jen, who had just exhaled and loosed her grip upon the handle at her waist. "Now," said Astrid, her eyes narrowed upon the woman, "why don't you tell us why *you* didn't want to do that? Worried about what those things would do?" She pointed up at the security cameras. Or maybe security guns.

"No!" Jen held up a hand apologetically. "I had to. It was the only way to know for sure."

"Meaning . . . ?" said Proto.

"It's because Prototypes won't open Sealed Doors," explained Jen. "It's a quirk of how they're hard-coded. The Sealed Doors were made to take advantage of that quirk, back when the Prototypes had just started destroying things. That's why the Doors exist. So people could shelter in place during any Prototype outbreaks. Shelters." She smiled bitterly. "And then civilization was destroyed. So much for that idea!"

"You thought we were Prototypes? Even after all that?" said Proto, waving behind them.

"Maybe, maybe not. That's how it goes," sighed Jen. "They act as human as can be. They win your trust. Then, the moment you're vulnerable—the moment they can do the most damage—their programming kicks in. Their killer instinct triggers. If you wait for that to happen, you're dead. Because eventually, everyone is vulnerable. And they're very good at recognizing when you're vulnerable."

Proto struggled to piece together an understanding of the dream from these bits of information. "So strange, isn't it? One moment, normal; the next, killers."

Jen nodded. "The weirdest part is, they say the Prototypes don't even realize they're Prototypes. They're programmed not to. No matter how much evidence piles up, they'll never accept that they're Prototypes. Not till the moment they go haywire and kill everyone."

"Makes you wonder if they're thinking, feeling beings like us," said Astrid. "Or just well-programmed machines, going through the motions of life."

"Exactly! But whatever's going on inside them, it's not like us, I think," responded Jen. "Like, they all have the same life history. They wake up somewhere. They don't know how they got there. They have all these memories of a past life, full of other people. But somehow, they all find reasons not to search for those people. Which is convenient, since those people never existed! Instead, they just loiter around where they woke up."

"You'd think they'd realize, 'Huh. My bio looks awfully like the standard Prototype bio!'" Jen went on. "And yet they never do. It *never* occurs to them. Bizarre, huh?"

" . . . Bizarre," nodded Proto, his stare drifting from Jen to the door beyond her. Something about all this felt strangely disquieting for him. He shook his head and glanced at Astrid. She did not return his look.

"Anyway, now that the Door's unlocked," said Jen, receiving the Skeleton Key from Astrid, "just let me get it open here." She approached the panel. "Here, hold this for me." She tossed the key to Arch.

Astrid pointed at the panel. "Probably that button, then that dial, right?"

Jen's eyes widened, as the mist rose slightly. "You know your stuff. Took me a whole afternoon to figure that out."

Proto pointed at Astrid. "*Mad* hacking skills."

She neither responded nor even looked at him. But she did fold her arms coolly beneath her breasts.

Jen worked the controls. "And . . . go ahead."

Arch tapped the Skeleton Key to the panel again. Now, an electronic hum swelled, and the door began sliding open. It was thick—about a foot of solid metal.

"You have any idea what we'll find inside?" asked Astrid.

"Well, these places were like fallout shelters, but for killer robots instead of radioactive fallout," explained Jen. "So they have all sorts of survival supplies. Tools, water purifiers, weapons. But the big one is food. Always tons of food. And it's so chock full of preservatives, it'll last longer than the pyramids did. But you already know that."

"Nothing like some good hearty preservatives for dinner. Also"—Proto pointed inside the doorway—"*that's* cool."

Unlike the corridor they were standing in—indeed, unlike all of the ruined buildings and boulevards outside—the hallway beyond the Sealed Door was a luminous and metallic white. Leafy plants and vines were creeping all along the walls and in and out of apertures, somehow still alive after all these years. A soft glow of bluish-white diffused evenly across everything. It felt like a pocket of utopian sci-fi in a post-apocalyptic dystopia.

"This," nodded Jen, basking in that prospect, "is why I haven't left the City. Nature has its perks. But it has nothing like this. Wandering through grey decay, day after day—then, *this*. Sleek white perfection, flush with green life. Perfectly adapted to us: Food, water, supplies, furniture. Even books!"

As she spoke, she led them inside, gesturing with admiration at a well-stocked bookcase built into the wall. "And the best part is, it's safe in here. As safe as can be. Just seal up the Door"—she held up the Skeleton Key—"and no one will trouble you. You could hole out here for a year. Catch up on your novel reading. Live in someone else's world, and forget how ours has ended."

"Nature has its perks," she repeated. "But not that. You're never fully safe out there. You can never forget the world, because it's always all around you. The good and the bad. Here, we at least can have some perfect moments together." By the time she finished, she was looking up at Arch.

"Until our ancestors' food runs out," observed Arch quietly, "and we can't anymore."

Jen waved dismissively. "There's more than enough to last our lifetime. You know how many millions of people lived here? How many Sealed Doors there are? And how few of *these* there are?" She waved the Skeleton Key.

"Our lifetime? Maybe so," he replied. "But is that all we're worried about?"

Her lips pressed tight as she stared up at him. She was scowling, but Proto also saw a shimmer in her eyes. The mists were swirling upward from knee level toward waist level.

"So," said Proto with deliberate nonchalance, trying to steer the narrative back on course, "any guesses where we'll find that food?"

"Shouldn't take long. These City places are never too big." Arch walked ahead and turned the corner into a side room.

Jen didn't follow him. Instead, she led them into the main room ahead.

There were no windows, but upon one wall was a glorious vista of stars reflecting off the coastal waters. The painting almost looked real.

To their right was a spacious kitchen dining area with a pantry wing. It held a stunning variety of foods and foodstuffs. The logos still looked as vividly colorful as a grocery aisle.

To their left was a small and cozy living area. The far wall consisted of a television screen. Near it was a quaint rocking chair, and facing it was a couple's love seat.

Upon the love seat were two skeletons, a man and a woman. They were holding hands and staring into the black void on the screen.

The three of them blinked and stared in silence for a long moment.

"That's . . . romantic. Isn't it?" Jen managed a smile. But her young brown eyes were wide, and her voice failed a little.

She approached the couple slowly, walking between them and the empty screen. She looked dazed, like she'd just woken from a long dream and was wrapping her mind around the real world again. She leaned down as though to touch those clasping fingerbones.

Proto, who'd been absorbed in watching this, felt a nudge from Astrid. She waved him toward the food in the pantry.

He was heading that way, with Astrid behind him, when they heard the thud and cry. *What . . . ?*

By the time Proto had turned around, Astrid already had whirled into a sprint toward the hallway from which they'd entered. She rounded the corner, disappearing from his view.

A second later, he heard a gasp, not quite vocalized as a shriek, followed by rapid light footsteps. He rushed toward the sound, turning to face the side corridor where Astrid had gone.

At the same time, someone barely three feet tall shoved past him. He was sent stumbling. The sheer force was startling for one so small, if not preternatural. In light of all that, it took a second for what he'd just seen to parse in his eyes.

The first thing he realized was that this was the little girl they'd passed on the street. She must have followed them here. Judging by that fact—and her inhuman strength—she was almost certainly one of those "Prototypes" Jen had been talking about.

The second thing he realized was that she was holding a bloody machete in one hand and the Skeleton Key in the other. Even now, whirling toward her, he caught a glimmer of its white skull as she ran down the hall and beyond the doorway where the Sealed Door had been.

Strangely, though, she paused at that point and turned toward the instrument panel. Biting her machete between her teeth, she reached for the panel.

"What's going—?" Jen began, having just made her way to where Proto was standing.

"She's got the key!" Proto interrupted. He started toward the girl—then, remembering that gasp and half-shriek he'd heard, peered the other way toward where Astrid had run.

In the far shadows, he saw her curled on the floor, arms bundled around her legs. Blood was seeping across the carpet beneath her.

He felt a yawning pit open within him. He suddenly was falling into a sprint toward her.

"The key?" said Jen, blinking at the girl, who was still visible and fiddling with the instrument panel. "The Skeleton—?"

A siren went off, and the soft white glow became red. "Lockdown sequence initiated," spoke a woman's smooth recorded voice. "Door will be sealed in twenty seconds. Warning. No exit or entry without an authorized key." As the voice spoke, and the rest of them listened in bafflement, the girl turned and ran off. "Twenty. Nineteen. Eighteen," began the countdown.

"Oh, *Hell* no—!" began Jen, starting into a sprint toward the disappearing thief. Then, she froze in place. "Arch?" she called. There was no response. "Arch!" she shrieked.

It occurred to Proto, at this point, that he was in a dream. It occurred to him that he could Do Something. He could make that braided little thief trip. He could cause Arch to call back, "I'm fine! Go get her!" He could run to the instrument panel and disable this lockdown. He could punch a bloody hole in the Sealed Door with his bare fist. Hell, he could draw that sci-fi blaster he'd half-forgotten about and blast that fleeing Prototype to smithereens.

And yet, something told him to hold back. This was Jen's dream, not his. And something told him that she had dreamt herself into exactly the dilemma she needed to be in. It was not for him to save her from this choice.

"Sixteen. Fifteen. Fourteen," the recorded voice counted.

Instead, Proto grabbed Astrid gently but firmly beneath her arms. "I'm sorry for this." He began dragging her toward the doorway, as she cried out and held her leg. It'd been slashed badly and was spilling blood.

"Thirteen. Twelve."

Jen let loose an inarticulate wail. She turned away from the Skeleton Key's thief and ran past Proto, leaping over Astrid, toward the side room where Arch had gone. "Arch? Arch!" came her voice from within.

Proto was too busy pulling Astrid to focus on that. Her eyes and teeth were scrunched tight, and she was breathing heavily. She left a trail of blood behind her. But, fortunately, he managed to get her out the door and safely in the hallway several seconds later. "Eight. Seven. Six."

Where's . . . ? He leaned and looked inside the door. "Five. Four."

Arch's head and shoulders appeared—gashed and dripping blood, slumped with a slack jaw—followed by Jen. She was carrying him over a shoulder, strain on her red face. She rounded the corner and ran toward the door. At least, it was as close to a run as she could manage, hefting an unconscious man a foot taller than her.

"Three. Two," the recorded woman calmly said.

Proto grabbed Jen and Arch as soon as they were within reach and yanked with all his strength—and, to be honest, probably a bit more than that. This *was* a dream.

The pair flew across the threshold and toppled into a heap. An instant later, the Sealed Door slid shut.

They all sat there a moment, breathing deeply and saying nothing. By now, there was no trace of the girl. She and the Skeleton Key were long gone.

Jen didn't seem too concerned about that. Instead, she was leaning over Arch's unconscious brow and crying, one of her hands brushing through the hair on his temple. Her teardrops pattered his forehead, mingling with the blood there.

This was the first thing Proto noticed.

The next thing was that Astrid was still lying on the ground. Her small breaths caught in her throat as she inhaled, wheezing quietly. The gash along her leg was seeping blood upon the floor even now.

Fear tingled through him. He instantly crouched down beside her, placing a hand on her shoulder "Hey. You all right?"

Astrid's eyes, locked in a furrowed wince, flicked over to Jen. She was leaning close over Arch, her brown eyes shimmering wide, concern on her face, childlike in its innocence.

Astrid's violet gaze returned to Proto. Her cringing face went straight. The lines of pain beside her eyes and lips vanished. Absently, she waved a palm over the bloody gouge along her leg. It mended in a swirl of mists. So did her grey jumpsuit a moment later. She reached for Proto's hand on her shoulder, gave it a little pat, then removed it.

She sat up and leaned toward him, till her lips were merely an inch from his cheek. "Nice acting. But I think we're good now," she whispered, gesturing at the now-embracing couple a few yards away. She withdrew and brushed her hands off.

He frowned. He wasn't sure what he felt more—relieved or disappointed.

"That's a nice sight to wake up to," Arch spoke weakly, lying on his back and squinting upward. "But what are you so sad about?"

Jen gave a gasp of relieved delight at his first words and, after a moment of beaming down, embraced him.

"Wait." Arch's brow furrowed. "The key. Jen, that girl took the Skeleton Key. Whacked my head. That was the last I saw."

"Yes, she did," replied Jen. "Luckily for us, she didn't take what mattered."

"Well." Arch's wan face went a little pink. "That's romantic." He gave her a groggy smile. "But what will we do now?"

"We'll keep living." Jen gave him another hug, so her cheek pressed against his. "And not like this. Not here. We're going to find ourselves a future."

Arch looked up at her, his pale eyes widening. She met that stare with a steady smile.

"True love," murmured Astrid.

Proto blinked at her. "What?"

"I said, time to go," she muttered, rising quietly to her feet. She pointed Proto down the dilapidated corridor.

Looking there, then scanning all around him, he realized that the world was contracting to a sphere around Jen. Mists were encroaching from all sides.

Astrid grabbed him by a couple fingers, like something gross you have to pick up but don't want to, and tugged him along toward the impending mists. "She's where she should be now. Nothing good can come of us hanging around."

Calmly, she led him into the swirling mirk. As its opacity swept around them, he abruptly was hurtling through grey indistinction.

Then, he was back in Somnus' realm and stumbling into the dim blue hallway. Astrid already was ahead of him and striding away, serene as could be.

"Hey," he called, prompting a backward glance and inclined brow from Astrid. "Nice acting." He wasn't sure why he'd said that, but it seemed to have an effect on her.

She slowed to a stop. Her gaze drifted from the path before them but did not meet his. "I said 'acting,' but it probably wasn't the best word," she replied slowly. "You can feel yourself being pulled in a certain direction by the dreamer. Almost always, it's best to let yourself be pulled along. That's what I did back there."

"It's like a river—the current of the dream," mused Astrid. "Deep down, the dreamer knows best where the dream should go. She gives us roles so we can help her—help her steer around obstacles, avoid crashing, and so forth. That's why I let things play out that way. I felt what role I was called to play, and I did it."

"You and me both." Proto's lips quirked up.

Her head tilted and her eyes narrowed, like she weren't sure if he was making fun of her.

"Anyway," he went on before she could reply, "why'd you decide to start participating in the dream today? Instead of just standing there in the background and letting me take care of everything?"

"'Start participating'?" She smirked, one hand on the hip of her grey jumpsuit. "How can I answer that? Even your questions are wrong. You think you know little and know even less."

"And . . . she's back!" he sighed wistfully.

Now it was her lips quirking up, though briefly. "The answer is, this would've been an awkward dream for only one visitor. Doing it solo would've required a lot of skill and care," she explained. "Which is why I felt it absolutely necessary to join you."

"And the burns keep coming! She's like a flamethrower!" lamented Proto.

"Of course, whether you'll become a visitor has yet to be confirmed. So far, your track record is iffy, and your tracksuit is iffier," she went on, waving a hand, as he just nodded grimly and let her do what she did best. "You shouldn't wear the same thing every day, Hobo."

"What! The pot calls the kettle black!" Proto gestured at her jumpsuit. "Or grey, I suppose. And nicely form-fitting."

She blinked, then scowled and walked onward.

"By the way," he called to her. "I'm glad I heard her bio first. The solution was exactly what you'd expect. 'Should she keep burning out in pursuit of unsatisfying money? Or should she pursue her dream life with her love while she still has youth and time?' I mean, come on! I feel like that's the plot of at least a quarter of all movies."

"Yes, this was an easy dream," shrugged Astrid. "I gave you exactly what you were ready for."

"Also," he continued, ignoring her, "speaking of biographies, I think I'm going to write one. It'll be about all this. But don't worry, I'll change the details so no one's recognizable."

Now, it was her turn to ignore him.

"The lovable sidekick will be 4'6", 250 pounds, and desperately infatuated with a certain new visitor, but determined not to show it," he mused. "The key to authenticity is not changing too much."

She swung backhanded at his face.

She was awfully quick, but he'd anticipated this. He ducked just soon enough that her hand swished through his hair, mussing it into a weird shape.

Astrid turned and regarded him for a moment. Then, she beamed. She reached for his hair and messed it up some more, then nodded approvingly.

Turning around, she walked on.

"You know, this is the second time today that you've messed up my hair," he said, not fixing it. "You like the do?"

Astrid kept walking away. "Let's go, Fro-Bro."

"Oh, that's sharp."

She still didn't turn around. But he could hear the giggle from ahead.

"You've been planning that all day, haven't you!"

He didn't need to see her face. Like music, the sound of her laughter was enough.

Of course, her swaying strides in that sleek grey jumpsuit helped too. He jogged to catch up.

"By the way, that sidekick," he said. "I think her name will be 'Astird.' What do you think?"

She launched another backhand at his face, fully anticipated and narrowly dodged.

And now it was his turn to laugh—at the moment, and the day, and everything.

CHAPTER 6
APPLES AND ORANGES

Proto decided to change things up the next day. He tried on one of those yellow, blue and white tunic outfits that Somnus had arranged for him and looked in the mirror. He rather liked it.

One of his life goals was never to have a job that required him to wear encumbering clothes each day—above all, the dreaded suit and tie. No danger of that here. He could turn somersaults in this getup.

Let's keep changing things up, he mused as he left his room, and turned left instead of his usual right. It seemed like everyone else here knew every turn in every hallway—despite the fact that they were all misty blue with intermittent white doors. The only route he knew was the route between his room and the lounge, which Astrid had taught him. It was high time he started exploring.

That went well for about five minutes. He'd felt sure he was heading in the direction of the lounge the whole time. But somehow, he'd encountered no sign of it yet—just intersecting hallways of mirky blue. And when five more minutes passed without any luck, he began to get worried. Astrid wouldn't be happy if he was late for today's visit.

He'd just rounded a corner, briefly closing his eyes and sighing, when he bumped into something at once soft and hard. Or some*one*, rather, judging by the way she gasped and stumbled backward. He blinked away his reverie and looked in front of him.

It was Dahlia, garbed in her usual Victorian robe with her hair pinned up. She'd been holding a book in one hand and reading while walking. In her other hand was an unbitten apple.

"Sparky," she hailed him calmly, brushing a dislodged tress from her blue eyes. "You're always finding ways to manhandle my books. Try to keep your hands off, won't you?"

"Good morning to you too, Morning Glory," said Proto. "Sorry, I can't resist a good book."

"Well, try asking nicely, rather than getting all handsy," she replied. "Anyway, this is a book by Anne Bronte. I'm not sure it's a good match for you."

"I liked Wuthering Heights. Is Anne so different from Emily?" he asked.

Really, it was just by chance that he'd taken a course on The Nineteenth Century British Novel. Until today, it had contributed absolutely nothing to his life advancement. But apparently, his teachers had been right. You never know when knowledge will come in handy.

Dahlia tilted her head at him, so that stray blonde strand fell over her face again. Her eyes narrowed skeptically, like a teacher whose worst student had just aced a test, while sitting next to the smartest student. "There are differences," she finally replied. "Just like Louisa and Abigail Alcott. Or Athena and Artemis. Or, say, me and Astrid!"

He blinked. "You're sisters?"

"I'm speaking figuratively, of course," she answered with a dismissive wave. But, for some reason, her cheeks reddened slightly. "And personally, I don't think the differences are all that subtle."

"Well, all those Bronte books end in true love and happily ever after, right?" countered Proto.

She blinked. Then, her eyes narrowed. "So the differences don't matter then? I think it makes them matter all the more."

Well, it seemed he'd botched this interaction somehow or other. It'd been a good try.

He smiled and held out his hands mollifyingly. "This student defers to the scholar!" he replied. "Anyway, I should be off—"

"You were asking about the Shadowcaster, weren't you?" interrupted Dahlia. "I suppose I'll have to show it to you, won't I?"

"I—suppose," blinked Proto. "If you have time."

"Not really! But if I only did what I had time for, nothing would get done," she spoke with a melodic lilt, waving lightly. "Or, worse yet, I'd have to give up reading!"

It wasn't clear to Proto how this course of action would help solve that problem. But he would go with it. "We can't have that. Lead the way, Apple Blossom!" he urged, prompting an agreeable nod from Dahlia.

"Come!" She turned and was off in a flourish of robes. "Show some spunk, Spunky."

"You know," he mused, almost jogging to keep up, "you may be different from Astrid. But your taste for name-calling is awfully similar."

She shrugged and waved her apple. "Even apples and oranges have something in common."

"They're both fruit?" he said.

"They're both far above you and out of reach," she replied instantly. "But they'll come down on you if you wait there stupidly for long enough." She bopped him on the head with her apple.

He sighed, as Dahlia's thin lips bloomed into a smile.

She continued down the hall with Proto in her wake for a couple minutes before tapping one of the white doors, which started sliding open. There was nothing to distinguish it from the thousand other white doors here, except perhaps the larger space separating it from the adjacent doors. But inside was a room utterly unlike anything else Proto had seen here.

It looked like a cave, but with blue stone matching the hallways outside. A gravelly path wound downward along its periphery toward what vaguely resembled a symphony hall with an orchestra pit. But the seating was all stone, and the stage was dominated by a smooth wall of stone, somewhat like a movie theater screen. As for the orchestra pit, it was more of an abyss, and continual flames were leaping from it toward the high roof.

Between the fiery abyss and the screen-like wall was an altar, made of the same blue stone as the cave and polished to a shine on top. At its center was an empty slot.

Proto regarded all this with wide eyes. He felt like he should see the Devil, the Oracle at Delphi, or Plato any second now. But instead all he saw was Dahlia, strolling ahead and passing through a smoke cloud on her way down.

She inhaled and breathed out with satisfaction. "Much as I like the dusty scent of old books," she mused, "this has a warmer charm, I think."

At the lack of any reply, she glanced back and saw him still standing near the entrance. "What are you ogling back there? We're not even at the part where I take off my clothes!" She smiled as he coughed and blinked. "Just kidding. Maybe? My, it's hot!" She fanned her face with her book.

Feeling a little red in the face, and not just from the heat, he lurched onward and descended the path.

At the bottom, she approached neither the stands nor the stage, but a small passage leading away from them. He followed her inside. They soon emerged into a simple room with an indented nook in the wall and a hole above it, rather like a vending machine. Above it was . . .

"Is that a touch screen? For a computer?" asked Proto.

"Ah, technology. Many things get worse with time, but not everything!" mused Dahlia. "This is where we pick the dreamer. It's so *easy* now. Just type the name and some details from his dream—or the city he's from, or his job, or his girlfriend's name, or his car model, or his favorite color, or his deepest fear—and he'll pop up! As long as we have the data recorded."

"You don't even need a name! Which is nice, because my job introduces me to more new names each day than a 19th-century Russian novel." She set down her book and apple. "Here, let me show you. 'Prime Minister of . . .'" she began typing. "Hm, let's go with that one." She typed a country's name and tapped a button. A few pictures of vials appeared on the screen, each with a brief description. She touched one of them. "And . . . voila!"

A corked vial clinked down into the nook in the wall from the hole above it. Dahlia snatched it and held it up triumphantly. "The memories of a national leader!" Mists swirled within the vial.

Proto stared at it for a moment. "Ohh. *That's* what Mayger was doing with that vial."

"Mayger?" she repeated. "Ah, right. Astrid was here, so you were with Mayger, weren't you? Visiting that artist dreaming of going berserkergang! But yes, you're right," she continued. "Our visitors collect the mists that arise in dreams. And from those mists, we shadowseers can see the dreamers' memories here in the Shadowcaster."

"Shadowseers," he repeated, wrapping his mind around all this. "So, dream visitors like Astrid and Mayger collect dream mists in vials. Those vials—what, get sucked up into the system here?" He pointed at the hole, as she nodded. "And the visitors type in what they know about the dreamer. Then, when you want to view the memories of that dreamer, you type in a search with some info about him here, and the vial pops back out?"

"Exactly. It's like a social media search for dreamers!" she enthused. "Which, let me tell you, is *much* better than the old system. That was more of a library of dreamers, with our own sort of Dewey Decimal System, only more ridiculously complicated and obtuse. If that's possible. Do they still teach that thing to kids?"

"I think I learned about it in library class at age seven," said Proto. "But that was twenty years ago."

Dahlia tilted her head at him and opened her mouth, as that stray tress fell over her face again. She briefly looked . . . *sympathetic?* But instead of replying to him, she brushed the hair off her face and smiled. "Well. Why don't we give you that demonstration?"

He nodded, wondering about that look but deciding not to dwell on it for now. "So, we're going to see a Prime Minister's memories, huh?"

"Hm? No. I was just showing off." She pushed another button. A whooshing sound of suction came from the nook. She inserted the vial, and it was sucked back into the hole it had come from. "Today, we're going to view the dreams of . . . " began Dahlia, starting to type.

Then, she paused, pressing her lips. She glanced at Proto again, giving him that same look as a moment ago. "You know what?" She held a button, erasing what she'd been typing. "We're going to let Lady Luck decide today! It's a custom. Can't get lucky without trying, as they say. Here, let's do it together."

Proto blinked at her phrasing.

But she already was tapping a search bar labeled "ID," then hitting a seemingly random bunch of letters and numbers. They filled the bar halfway. "Alright, your turn." She stepped aside and held a hand toward the screen. "Say a prayer to Lady Luck, Spunky!"

He glanced at her, unsure if she was expecting him to say something aloud, but she was staring at the monitor. So he just drummed his fingertips over some letters and numbers, filling the remainder of the bar.

"Good enough." She swept him aside and stepped back in front of the screen, checking a box labeled "Select Closest Match" and hitting "Proceed." She waited a moment. "And . . . your lucky vial!" The glass clinked down into the nook.

She seized it and spun around, already striding out of the room. "Come! Time waits on no man, and neither do I. Except Somnus."

Proto couldn't help smiling at her belletristic energy. Dahlia *was* rather different from Astrid, wasn't she? She almost could be called . . . nice. As long as you played along with her chatty bookish hauteur.

He followed her back toward the stone chamber with the stands and the stage, lost in such musings, as she approached the altar beside the flames.

Then, she unbound her hair and started taking off her robe. And suddenly he was very much in the here and now.

"Is it just me, or is it *hot* in here?" she mused, fanning her face beside the raging abyssal flames. "What, did you think I was joking earlier?"

Beneath her robe was a sleeveless toga-like outfit. "Don't get too excited! This is where I stop." She cast the robe aside and approached the altar. "You go find a seat and enjoy the show. Not too much though." She waved him back toward the stone stands without looking.

This was the most flustered Proto had felt since that bleary moment he'd woken up in the blue hallway. "I'm all ears. And eyes," he managed. That robe of hers had hidden quite a lot on top.

She laughed delightedly. "This, Sir, is a ritual. Conduct yourself accordingly!" she chastised, as he seated himself midway up the stands.

He searched for a reply, but she already was uncorking the vial in front of her. And as the mists within began to swirl up, what words he had were lost.

The blonde woman leaned over the ascending mists and inhaled. Her limbs stiffened briefly, then went languid. Her head lolled back so her hair fell low and she was staring upward at the screen.

The mists rising from the vial seemed impossibly voluminous. As they rose and spread, they blocked some of the firelight flaring above the abyss. This cast shadows upon the screen-like stone wall.

Those shadows' forms were strange and almost recognizable. He squinted at the shifting shapes, feeling continually on the verge of identifying them, only to have them turn into something else.

Amid his rapture, Dahlia broke into speech: *"I see him!"* Her voice was charged with deep pathos and backed by a toneless power.

"I see him emerge into the breathing world with two wails and cries. He is the first. He is the smaller and the greater. His place is below and above."

"Seasons pass. He grows and thrives on the cherry blossom lane. Seasons pass. He runs suntanned and shouting through the streets in Summer. He slides and trudges and shouts through Winter's whiteness."

"Mars rules the Sixth House, and a fever almost takes him. But Venus and Mercury are watchful from the Fourth, and he is given a second chance."

"From youth to teen he passes. He practices the arts and studies the sciences. He reads of times long lost and dreams of their return. They will return."

She went on speaking about the unidentified man in this allusive and oracular way. She described his young adulthood, his schooling, his eventual job, and the life he led.

Setting aside her prophetic mannerisms, the life she described was fairly unre-markable. The events she recounted did seem somehow familiar—indeed, even the shadows on the stone wall seemed familiar—but not in any way suggesting they were important.

At least, not until she got to the later portions of her shadowcasting. And at that point, things became altogether unfamiliar:

"He stares on the victim. His eyes go wide, and his heart falls. He shakes the body. He calls his name. There is no movement. There is no response," spoke Dahlia.

"He walks with his love through the hidden garden. His brother stares, jealous, but says nothing. They see him, but say nothing. They speak of a dreamt-of future. It will never come."

"The World Rood grows on the horizon. It beckons them. When the flames fall, it will beckon them, and they will come."

"The flames will fall, and he will not fall. Not until he walks through the flames to recover their source. And in his dying will he turn undying."

"His name is Yemos!"

Proto's jaw dropped at the name, and the familiarity he'd sensed earlier suddenly became crystal clear.

Meanwhile, the last shadows of the remaining mist from the vial ascended above the stony screen. As though on cue, Dahlia's arched-back head went slack. Her shoulders slumped, and she breathed heavily for some time.

Proto was close to asking if she was all right when she finally turned around. Her blue eyes were wide and peering off in thought. Her finger touched her lip as she pondered.

"So," he said slowly. "That guy you were describing. I know him."

There was a slight pause, and then her brow rose. "My, don't you have interesting friends! Tell me about this hidden garden and the World Rood."

He shook his head. "I don't know all that crazy stuff. But Yemos—yes, I know him. He was the older of two twins. He lived on that 'Cherry Blossom Lane' you mentioned. So did I. And when he was young, he had a fever. I heard he almost died. I remember since I asked him to play for the first time soon afterward."

Proto had continued being friends with the rather dark and brooding but funny Yemos all through childhood. Maybe even best friends in high school. Unless you counted Yemos' twin brother, Mannus—a blond, boisterous, simple-hearted football player—who, like many twins, was Yemos' best friend by default.

The fourth in their little band had been Quart, an eccentric nerd with world-class talent on the saxophone. Their group used to meet up two or three times a week to play cards, paintball, Capture the Flag, and Smash, in the way that suburban high school boys do.

"Hm. How interesting!" replied Dahlia, yawning slightly.

He squinted and tilted his head at her. It seemed like she should be reacting more to the fact that, coincidentally, he knew the subject of her shadowcasting.

In response, she yawned again and stretched ostentatiously. This made all the clearer that her shapeless toga concealed quite a lot of shape. "Pardon my speechlessness. I'm still pleasantly woozy," she said. "I tell you, if you felt this way, you'd likely fall asleep on the spot! Or abandon me and go smoke a cigarette outside."

Well, the normal Dahlia was back. But the mildness of her surprise still seemed off to him. "So … wasn't that odd?" he said. "The memories we viewed happened to be from someone I know. Weird coincidence, right? You think it was just *luck?* Lady Luck, you said?"

"Who knows? It seems awfully unlikely to be pure chance," she said lightly. "I admire a man who ignores his low chances and throws the dice. But a one in seven billion chance is awfully low. Unless someone up there rigged the dice for you! And who but Lady Luck?"

He stared and pondered. This was all bizarre. And there was something else familiar in what he'd seen. He couldn't quite put his finger on it.

But there was no answer in her sky blue gaze, and he eventually shrugged. "Anyway, that stuff at the end. 'Walking through the flames' and all that. Do you know what that means?"

"Not a clue!" she waved. "But I admit, that was rather unusual."

"Because, unless we're being really metaphorical here," said Proto, "I think I would've heard if an old acquaintance of mine 'walked through flames' and 'in his dying turned undying.' Whatever that means."

"Mm. Perhaps," she replied. "Or perhaps it hasn't happened yet."

"What?" Proto abruptly was confused again. "I thought those shadows were memories."

"That's the simple way of putting it. But it's not quite right," said Dahlia. "It's more like the shadows are little excerpts from the grand story of all things. And they *roughly* match what the dreamer remembers. But only roughly. Sometimes, they include bits of the dreamer's future. Like when you try to grab a slice of pizza, but part of the next slice rips off with it!"

"I'm hungry," said Proto.

"You know, I am too. For you, it's sleep or cigarettes; for us, it's food," she sighed. "One craving isn't sated, so we sate the other. All too often, it's a woman's lot, isn't it? It's unfair, I tell you. You make us both unsatisfied and fat!"

At this point, even he was having trouble following her repartee. "Well," he managed, "let's go drown our sorrows then."

"Indeed." She lifted her apple and eyed it like it were Snow White's or Eve's. "I don't even want this anymore. I need meat. Care for an apple, Sparky?"

"Can I have the apple and the robe?" he found himself replying.

"What, Somnus' gift-tunic isn't doing it for you? You want this old . . . ?" She'd started holding the robe toward him. But now she trailed off, following his eyes down to her sleeveless toga, then back up.

She tilted her head at him. That tress came loose again and fell over her face. "Well." She smiled. "Yes, I suppose I've worked up a sweat. Yes, do be a dear and carry all this for me." She wrapped the book in her robe and handed it over.

"Come!" She spun toward the stairway and was off with a sprightly gait. "I'm going to get cold unless I start drinking straightaway. And we wouldn't want that, would we?"

"No apple?" he called to her, following her upward.

"Far above you and out of reach! Remember that, Spunky!" She tossed the apple over her shoulder surreptitiously.

He didn't see it coming till it was falling toward his head. He jerked aside at the last instant, so it glanced off and rolled down his cheek. But somehow, he managed to catch it.

She'd turned around and now was beaming as he rubbed his stricken head.

"Yes, it comes down on me eventually, doesn't it?" he mused grimly, as she giggled. "And yet!" He lifted the apple and took a bite, savoring the juicy goodness. "Our suffering bears fruit eventually," he spoke through a mouthful.

"Maybe so! But don't let that head of yours get too bruised," she replied. "One fruit's plenty, yes?"

He chuckled and bit the apple again.

They exited the Shadowcaster cave and strolled side-by-side toward the lounge.

As they walked, Dahlia started talking about Sir Walter Scott's works and asking Proto for his opinions. Lady Luck must've blessed him doubly today, because Ivanhoe was another book he'd read in his course on The Nineteenth Century British Novel.

The familiar clinking of glasses and quiet chatter signaled that the lounge was near.

"I've always wondered that," Dahlia was saying as they entered. "Do I strike you as more Norman or Saxon? I mean, one *wants* to say Saxon. One wants to be the hero. But, being truly honest, I—"

"Ah, our Provisional Visitor returns!" boomed Somnus from the bar. He extended his arms welcomingly. "Decided to change things up today, I see?"

"We took a spin in the Shadowcaster," replied Dahlia. "It was a good show. Maybe even a bit more than he bargained for!" She pointed Proto to a chair. "You can set my robe right here." She fanned her face and smiled lightly.

"That's good. It's best to mix things up a little, when you're starting out," replied Somnus, stirring his drink. "We all have to pick our own path. But I'm a firm believer in making an informed pick." His eyes gleamed. "I mean, who knows? Maybe you'll be a shadowseer!"

Proto often couldn't help but feel that Somnus was—well, not mocking him. More like he was making a joke directed at Proto and the world, with the goal that they both laugh with him.

"We'll see," said Proto. "Seemed a little hot for me."

"Indeed." Somnus' lips curved up. "Speaking of which." He turned to Lilac. "How about a hot buttered rum? I'm feeling indulgent today." He continued conversing with Lilac as Dahlia and Proto got situated at their table.

"Anyway, we were talking about heroes, yes?" said Dahlia to Proto, absently smoothing her toga. "It seems to me that, in the best books, it's often hard to tell the heroes from the villains. They both have reasonable justifications for their actions. And in that situation, picking the 'right' side isn't so much about sifting through their past deeds and assigning the blame. It's more about asking, 'Whose world would be the more fair and beautiful, if it won this conflict?' *That* side is the heroes. Or so it seems to me."

Proto marveled at the way she oscillated between bookish reflection, witty repartee, light mockery, and Sean Connery-esque innuendo. But one of Proto's friends had told him what it was like to date a librarian, and this all seemed par for the course.

"But I'm being boring now, aren't I?" Dahlia sighed. "Here, let me fix that." She waved Lilac over, and the pale bartendress soon made her way to the table. "I'll take a Long Island."

"Uh oh." Proto blinked and stared straight ahead.

"You don't approve? Only hard spirits for hard souls, is it?" asked Dahlia. "Or is a Long Island too 'Hi, I'd like to get drunk as fast and cheap as possible and I swear this ID is real'?"

"No. I forgot I still have my visit today. I was supposed to meet Astrid here. Hope I'm not too late," he sighed. "Better stick with coffee."

Lilac arched a black eyebrow. "Don't sound so disappointed."

"Disappointed? No, delighted!" replied Proto with exaggerated suaveness. "I feel like I looked for sunset and found sunrise."

"Psh!" said Dahlia. "Don't be a poetaster, Spunky."

"There are no sunrises or sunsets here, Drunkie," observed Lilac flatly. But her dark eyes sparkled.

Why does no one here call me by my name?

"Come on!" he complained. "You can't call me Drunkie when I'm the only guy drinking coffee."

"Speaking of having drunk far too much coffee," said Dahlia, "I'm off to pay a visit to the ladies' chamber. Pour heavy please, Lilac!" She strode away briskly under the tree tapestry doorway.

Lilac started walking away too, then turned back and looked at him. "By the way, normal-style or . . . ?"

He extended his arms reprovingly. "Do you really need to ask?"

"Noted." Her lips quirked up and she strolled off.

Proto found himself recalling this was all a dream less and less lately. Or maybe it was so ingrained now that he didn't need to focus on it anymore. He certainly wasn't acting with the self-conscious gravitas with which he'd approached real life. He idly wondered where his real life would've ended up if he'd let his heart lead him along from moment to moment.

Probably on the streets. He smiled away a sigh.

"Something funny, Slow-Show?"

He blinked and looked up. Astrid had just entered beneath the painting of the old man. Behind her windswept bouffant of silvery blue was a look of light displeasure.

He winced and tried to think of a good explanation.

But meanwhile, Lilac was just arriving at his table. "Your coffee. Lilac-style." She leaned and set the unique black mug with the white-lacquered crack before him.

"Ah." He inhaled the aromatic steam politely. "Bliss in a beverage! Contentment in a cup! Divinity in a drink!"

Lilac already was turning around to get back to someone else at the bar. But she spared a moment to raise her brow and smile at Proto. "Kind compliments from a clown."

"Well said," he acknowledged as she glided off.

"Enjoying a late coffee, are we?" asked Astrid, as his eyes flicked back to her. Her look of light displeasure seemingly had darkened. "Where were you? I was going to take you to the Shadowcaster like we talked about. But now we won't have time before today's dream visit."

Donning a mollifying smile, Proto opened his mouth.

"Oh, no worries! He already went," called Dahlia before he could speak. She'd just strolled back into the lounge, her hair still unbound and a bit tousled over her sleeveless toga. "We ran into each other this morning, so I took him for a spin."

She swept past Astrid and sat down on the chair across from Proto, where her robe was draped.

"Ah," replied Astrid. Her stare shifted back and forth between them, finally settling on Proto. "Well, it seems you're getting along just fine without me." She turned to Somnus at the bar. "Does he still need a mentor?"

"Of course he does!" boomed the Lord of Dreams. "I know you think he's quick, Astrid, but surely not *that* quick."

Astrid's cheeks pinkened. "I have no idea what gave you that impression. I don't call him Dodo and Slow Bro and Loco because he's quick."

"Loco? I don't recall that one." Proto tilted his head at her. "You *do* think these up in advance and save them, don't you!"

Normally, she'd have some witty and incisive retort. But in her current state, she just flushed further.

"Anyway," smiled Somnus, "don't be too peeved with our Provisional Visitor. For being late, I mean. He went exactly where he had to go this morning. It was predetermined. Inevitable!"

"Predetermined?" Astrid shook her head. "How could you possibly know that?"

"The way you all speak to the Lord of Dreams!" lamented Somnus. "How do I know? Well, maybe I saw it in the Shadowcaster!"

Now it was Dahlia's turn to shake her head. "That's not possible, because . . . "

"Because *what?*" Somnus' eyes gleamed wildly.

She stared at him a moment. "Never mind," she mumbled.

Proto felt like he had at age four, when his parents would spell words so he wouldn't know what they were talking about. He wanted to tell them, *"Hey! I'm right here! I know you're talking about me."* But they already knew that, and if they cared, they wouldn't be doing it.

Somnus pointed at Proto. "By the way! I've been meaning to tell you. I think I've found the perfect drink for you!" He turned to Lilac, whose head had swiveled over at these words. "The perfect hard drink, that is. I defer to Lilac on coffees!" He winked at her, as Lilac blinked and went rosy. "Anyway, I think he'll agree it's perfect. But I'm going to save it for now. See how things go for a bit longer. We'll find out if I'm right soon enough."

"How will we know?" asked Lilac. "Can't you just change your pick later?"

"Absolutely not, Madame Bartendress!" he replied, eliciting another blink. "No, because I'm going to tell you my pick right now." He leaned forward and whispered something in her ear.

Lilac eyed Proto as Somnus spoke. She shrugged and nodded ambivalently.

"Whisper whisper whisper!" said Dahlia quietly. Her lips were an inch from Proto's ear, and her hair tickled his cheek. "I'm always jealous when others tell secrets. I get my revenge by pretending to do the same. Whisper whisper whisper!"

He laughed helplessly, his eyes drifting across the room. Through tousled blonde tresses, he saw the vast painting and, beneath it, Astrid's violet gaze.

"Well. I, for one, have a lot to get done today," declared Astrid a moment later. "Why don't you take the day off, Proto? I think you have your hands full as it is." She turned and strode away, her grey jumpsuit shifting along her frame's curves with her stiff strides.

"I approve!" Somnus smiled like a father watching his teenage daughter stomp away. "As the Lord of Dreams, I'm the last to fault anyone for taking a day of rest."

"What do you know! It seems we can have that drink after all!" cried Dahlia delightedly. "Lilac, two old peated whiskies please. Hard spirits for hard souls." She spoke this gruffly to Proto.

"Two?" Lilac regarded Dahlia's half-drunk Long Island and Proto's half-empty coffee. "Do you think it's a little early?"

"Lilac," chastened Dahlia, raising a finger. "I'm never late, nor am I early. I order precisely when I mean to."

The bartendress rolled her eyes. "I'll conjure that right up."

"I suppose it *is* a strange mix," Dahlia remarked, turning back to Proto. "I never thought I'd be drinking fine whisky side by side with a Long Island."

"What about side by side with a friend?" he replied with a look of smiling elfin hauteur.

"Oh, that's quick!" praised Dahlia, squeezing his hand. "Aye, I could do that," she gruffly affirmed, then sighed. "I don't do a very good dwarf, do I?"

He shrugged and waved. "Maybe an ancient Roman dwarf, with that toga."

"Toga? This, a *toga?*" She cast an offended hand to her left breast. "Heavens, do I look like the sort to swill cheap booze in a smelly house full of beerbellies and floozies, while inexplicably wearing Roman garb and calling my decadence 'Greek life'? Don't answer that. Anyway, this is a *chiton*. Do call things by their proper names!"

"Like Sparky?" he replied.

"I call you Sparky because I sense the spark of life in you!" she admonished, full of faux-righteous indignation.

"Why Spunky then?" he pressed. "Actually, don't answer that."

Dahlia tittered, bouncing a bit beneath her chiton with laughter.

On they spoke for quite some time, borne along from moment to moment and drink to drink by—well, he wasn't quite prepared to say what. But it felt ardent and good. Warmth beckoned him toward more warmth, like a bird winging south for Winter.

Or was it more like a moth fluttering toward the flame? Or Icarus flapping toward the sun? Or Adam reaching for Eve's fruit?

"Even apples and oranges have something in common," she'd said.

True, he mused. *You should savor every juicy bite.* He felt a tingle of guilty pleasure.

Morning gave way to afternoon and weary evening. Judging by the bags beneath her eyes, she felt as exhausted as he did. The conversation smoldered down from bright banter toward warm contentment. But he didn't have the heart to leave just yet. And, as exhausted flames keep aspiring toward Heaven as smoke, they kept going.

CHAPTER 7
RIGHT CHOICES, WRONG CHOICES

"Ah! What a fine morning," Proto declared.

Astrid made no response. She was striding briskly several paces ahead of him.

"Look at those mists shining in the east!" he admired. "And in the west, north and south. Exactly how they'll be shining this afternoon, evening and night."

No luck. If anything, Astrid's pace increased. He nearly had to jog now.

"Look at that blue horizon!" he went on. "Like the sea and the sky, rolled into one misty—"

"Please stop," interrupted Astrid.

"Grump, grump, grump," he lamented. "Do you need a coffee?"

"What I need is to finish this exercise in futility as soon as possible," she replied.

"Well then, tell me about this dreamer! Maybe it'll speed things up. Give me some insights."

"You know I think you're better off without advance knowledge. Usually," she responded. "It prejudices your decision-making. It makes you think you know more than you do."

"Okay. But you have to admit, knowing her bio was helpful last time," he said. "In that dystopian city."

"Right, what do I know?" Astrid turned and glowered at him. "I've only been doing this since you were just a gleam in your distant ancestors' eyes. You'll probably take my place soon, given how much *you* know—"

"Call me Know Bro," Proto broke in, double-gunning her.

A laugh slipped out, and then she looked furious with herself. She stomped along in silence for a while.

"Soo . . . that bio?" he pressed.

"What, Dahlia didn't show you everything in the Shadowcaster?" she shot back. "I don't see why you need a secondhand, second-best version from me. You can get all you need straight from her mouth. Or what have you."

" . . . wait, what?" asked Proto.

Astrid flushed. "From her mouth, the Shadowcaster, whatever," she mumbled. "Don't pretend you don't know what I mean! You know everything else, right?"

He pondered, watching her stiff strides and searching for a response. But it turned out he didn't need one.

She sighed and rubbed her temples. "So, the dreamer. He's twenty-two years old. A recent college grad. He did fine there—fine, but not great—just like he did in high school. That's how he was in sports too. And that's how his career search is going. A couple job offers, paying enough to get by, but not much more. Same with his love life. He meets someone, goes on a few decent dates, things peter out, and they move on."

"There's nothing terribly wrong with him. But also nothing terribly right. He's an Everyman, but also a Nobody for that reason. And he hates it," she explained.

"As he sees it, everyone else has strengths and weaknesses. *They* play to their strengths. And they win at life that way. At least, they win at some things," she said. "But he doesn't have that option, because he's middle-of-the-road at everything. So he wins at *nothing*. He's convinced he'll lead a profoundly insignificant life. And he's wondering what the point is."

"Hm," mused Proto. "This sounds like a 'keep working hard and things will work out' sort of situation. Like Tom Brady. He was second-string for years, not very athletic, and then his first college pass was intercepted. He kept working hard. And look what came of that! 'If at first you don't succeed,' and all that."

"Great. I'm glad you know exactly what to do." Astrid tapped a white door. It slid open. "I'll be watching from afar if you need me. But I'm sure you won't, Know Bro."

He tapped his temple knowingly, and she just shook her head.

They walked across the threshold into a mirky tunnel. Sunlight glared from its far end. It clarified to motley colors as he neared and his eyes adjusted.

Squinting, he emerged, just as a far off man was shouting some announcement. A peal of trumpets ensued.

Proto was facing a medieval arena, with lords and ladies seated in the stands beside an open field, the sort where jousts were held—the "lists," he remembered those fields being called.

The onlookers were cheering uproariously as an armored man sauntered from nearby into the center of the field. The apparent knight waved to them in lordly fashion. Maidens leaned from the stands as though to reach him from afar. They called indiscernibly toward him.

Then, he dramatically drew his sword and held it high, so it threw off a host of glimmers. And the applause and cries redoubled.

As the noise eventually died down, the man he'd heard a moment ago made his next announcement: "From the Fief of Greymere, wearing the azure and or, Sir Griffyngale!"

The crowd erupted in a cheer, as trumpets played a fanfaronade. But no one walked onto the field.

Proto looked down. At his waist was a scabbarded sword. He was wearing chainmail with a tabard overtop. A coat of arms covered its front, with something birdlike to its side and glaring menacingly.

He smiled.

Stepping forth, he raised a palm and started waving.

"What are you doing?" hissed a voice next to him, as a hand roughly seized his shoulder and yanked him backward. He stumbled and almost fell, but a strong hand held him up.

Turning, he saw a knight in a mostly white tabard was grasping his shoulder. He had hair down to his shoulders and looked to be in his early twenties. His eyes were scrunched up with both annoyance and concern. "Blood in Heaven! I know you forget your age and forget where you are. But now you forget you're not Sir Griffyngale?"

Proto abruptly noticed that mists had swirled up to about waist level and were rising quickly. And now—glancing back at the field—he saw a knight in blue and gold striding forth and waving. A griffin adorned his coat of arms.

"Uh, pardon. I forget myself," Proto replied, rubbing his temple and looking down.

The knight's visible irritation melted to sympathy. "Look, I'm going to need you today, Sir Wyndsack."

Proto glanced over his shoulder. A tall page with long silvery-blue hair, face half covered by a droopy medieval cap, was wearing grey livery. The page's frame was disconcertingly curvy.

Wyndsack? he mouthed, arching an eyebrow.

"Sir Wyndsack," Page Astrid hailed him with a bow, in the not-quite-changed voice of an early teenage boy.

Proto nodded grimly—prompting a half-suppressed smile from the page—and turned back to the knight. "Yes. Yes, I'm feeling better now. Just lost my bearings for a moment."

"Very good. I consider myself blessed to have the hero of Luourcourt as my guide today. Even if he is older than the whole field put together!" The knight grinned at him warmly.

Proto looked down at his hands. He saw now that they were wrinkled and spotted. *Wonderful.*

"Yes, well, what I've lost in strength, I've gained in wisdom," Proto managed. "And don't you forget it!" Even his voice sounded old and raspy now.

"Ah, there's the Wyndsack I know." The knight slapped him on the back—gently, as though he might break. The mists had dwindled to their ankles now.

"That's *Sir* Wyndsack to you!" Proto wagged a finger.

The younger man nodded amiably and started to banter back. But the announcer broke in first. "From the Fief of Terneplain, wearing the argent and ermine, Sir Blancheblade!"

The knight took a deep breath and nodded at Proto.

Then, he turned and strode out toward the lists, waving and beaming toward the assembled lords and ladies. They clapped and cheered, and maidens reached and cried out vainly. He drew his longsword with a flourish and held it high for a moment. Several young ladies threw flowers and threw their hands to their breasts sighingly.

Proto leaned toward Astrid. "Of all the days for me to be an old man!" he grumbled quietly.

"Stay on track, Wyndsack," she replied. "This dream's not as easy as the last one."

"How would you know that?" he retorted lightly. "I think you're just making it up. Psyching me out!"

"You know best, Know Bro." Her face was calm and straight.

By the end of their visit to that decaying city, he'd felt that, against all odds, he'd managed to break through Astrid's shell and reach the person beneath. Today, though, he couldn't help but feel the shell had been repaired and hardened.

Many more knights were announced and marched onto the field, one colored tabard and trumpet peal after another. In the stands, groups of onlookers wore colors matching different knights. When the knight of the same hue walked out, they cheered especially vigorously.

The one exception was the knight in green—"Sir Bertilak," wearing "the vert on vert," as the announcer put it. No one in the stands was wearing green, and his applause was rather mild.

The crowd went loudest when a knight tabarded in black, Sir Malin, strolled onto the field. But they mostly were booing and jeering. Some young maidens were even spitting. He basked in their derision, holding up both arms and beaming at them. A few raucous cheers came from one wing of the stands, where lords and ladies in black were waving pennants bearing his coat of arms.

"Lords and ladies, vassals and knights," hailed the announcer. "Behold, our kingdom's finest! Our boldest and brightest! Those whose might and main have lifted them from high to highest! Here is the lifeblood from which our future will be born. Heaven grant that we not spill too much of it today—but, perhaps, not too little either!"

The crowd laughed and cheered wildly. Pudgy old lords with horns of ale in hand slapped each other's backs and shouted "hear hear." Some maidens flung their hands to their mouths and looked about worriedly. Others chortled with the fat old lords.

"Let the lots proceed!" concluded the announcer.

Three brown-robed monks processed onto the lists and approached the sixteen knights standing in a row. Two of the monks were young and hefting a large urn, one at each handle. The third was elderly and held a slate and chalk. One by one, each of the knights said a brief prayer and drew a slip of paper from the urn. Each showed it to the old monk, who wrote something on the slate.

Once the knights had finished drawing lots, the monk presented the slate to the announcer. He proceeded to describe the tournament's structure—a two-sided bracket with eight knights on each side, single-elimination. The fourth round would be the championship. The crowd looked bored, like they already knew all this. But they perked up when he started listing who was facing whom.

Most excited of all was Sir Blancheblade. At one point, he thrust his hand up in a triumphant fist—not when his own name or his opponent's name was stated, but when Sir Malin's name was announced immediately thereafter.

Proto knew enough about brackets to conclude that Sir Blancheblade must be eager to face Sir Malin. The fact that he was this dream's "black knight," literally, made this all the clearer. What was unclear was why.

Sir Blancheblade confirmed his suspicions a moment later. "I face Sir Malin in the second round! Could it be more perfect?" he cried. "I'll be warmed up but not too tired or, Heaven willing, too wounded. And Malin will make it, no doubt. Zounds, if Sir Griffyngale emerges without broken bones, he'll be blessed!

The second round." He marveled at his luck. "Win twice, and I'll win everything that matters!"

Proto had no idea why the young knight was so excited to face Sir Malin. But he felt he must say something, even if he didn't know why Sir Blancheblade bore this apparent animus toward the black knight.

He decided to play it safe and keep it vague. "Ah, the fires of youth. I suppose if that old squabble must come to a head, now's as good a time as any."

"'Old squabble'? What are you on about? I've never met the man." Sir Blancheblade stared at him, as mists whirled upward wildly. "I never even knew Baron Quagmarsh *had* a son. Not till he slew Lady Aureal's brother last feast day."

Repressing a wince, Proto—that is, old Sir Wyndsack—held up a palm and shook his head. "Yes, yes, that's the squabble I meant. By Heaven, boy, I swear, I need to watch my words with you!" He nervously eyed the mist rising toward his chin. *The way he said Lady Aureal* . . . He decided to take a risk. "But it's forgivable, I suppose. At my age, I know well there's no one testier than a man in love."

Sir Blancheblade's face went pink. "Yes, well," he mumbled, as the mists fell precipitously. "Still sharp as ever, when you want to be."

"Not sharp, just stating the obvious," wheezed Proto in an old man's voice. He felt he was on a roll now. "You'll win your bout and have Lady Aureal, if you listen to even half of what I tell you to do!"

"That's why you're here, Old Man." Sir Blancheblade slapped him gently on the back again.

"That's Sir Old Man, to you!" admonished Proto.

Sir Blancheblade chuckled. A moment passed in silence. "Yes, I'd waited so many years for the right day to seek Aureal's hand," he spoke softly, staring toward the stands. "And when she pledged her hand to the man who bested Malin here . . . well, could the Fates have spoken more clearly? This is my moment. This is what I've waited for. This is *why* I've waited."

"And why you've worked so hard," affirmed Proto, prompting a firm nod from the young knight. He felt he'd steered things on their proper course. The mists had sunk nearly out of sight. Sir Blancheblade's gaze gleamed with readiness and zeal.

It showed when he fought his first bout soon afterward. He faced Sir Suethart, garbed in purpure and tenné. Sir Blancheblade sallied forth on horseback with cavalier verve, his lance extending far and low, and blasted the opposing knight off his horse so forcefully he left an imprint as he skidded in the dirt. He did not rise.

Proto's lips curved up. He might've given that lance a little extra *oomph*. But just a little.

The victor tore off his helm and waved a fist triumphantly. The lords and ladies reciprocated with wild applause. So did many a maiden—including, in particular, one white-clad lady with Rapunzel-like hair. Her beaming was so bright and wide it could be seen even here, on the other side of the field.

When Sir Blancheblade rode round the lists in a victory lap shortly thereafter, she pointed a white lily toward him, then kissed it. He responded with a deep bow. She looked ready to swoon with happiness as he rode off.

Yes, this is all coming along nicely, mused Proto. *Hard work pays off and all that!* He would make sure of it.

The young knight dismounted and made his way back to Proto—that is, Sir Wyndsack.

Proto adopted a look of pride and wistful admiration. "My boy, I could hardly have done it better myself," he wheezed, patting the lad's back with his wrinkled hand. "He'll be feeling *that* the next few weeks!"

Sir Blancheblade beamed. "Just like you said. 'Hold firm. Aim just a little lower than seems right. And you'll strike true.'"

"That's my boy," praised Sir Wyndsack. "Your future's waiting right in front of you!"

He heard the sound of spitting to his rear. Glancing, he saw Page Astrid smirking beneath her droopy cap.

Whatever. Let her grouse. In the end, it's just jealousy.

Proto already had planned out the rest of the dream. The black knight would win his first match easily. In round two, when he and Sir Blancheblade were jousting, both would be knocked off their horses. There'd be a hard-fought sword duel. Sir Malin would attempt some treachery—feigning injury, he would throw a handful of blinding dust at his foe—but Sir Blancheblade would fight through it and prevail.

The moral of the story couldn't be more classic: The good guy wins if he works hard.

And Proto would make sure of that.

"Next!" called the announcer. "Sir Griffyngale, wearing the azure and or, will tilt against Sir Malin, clad in sable!"

The audience broke into a mix of cheers for the knight in blue and gold and jeers for the knight in black. But they soon started pointing and shushing each other, as the green knight stepped forth and raised a palm.

"Excuse me, my good Sir!" called Sir Bertilak toward the announcer. Sunlight glimmered on his armor's green accents. "Might I make a proposal to my fellow knights here?"

Taken aback, the announcer turned to the elderly monk—who shrugged and held out his hands—and then back to the green knight. "Speak on, Sir Bertilak," he urged politely.

"My good Sirs," began the green knight. "A year and three fortnights past, Sir Malin basely and ignobly slew my brother-knight, Sir Gruen, without warrant or just cause. I am bound by honor to seek retribution against Sir Malin. I would do so fairly today, when he is neither wearied nor wounded. I would face him in trial by combat unto death. Therefore, I pray you, Sir Griffyngale, give me leave to fight in your stead. And, Sir Malin, pray accept my challenge."

Sir Blancheblade's ruddy grin had blanched away during this speech. At the conclusion, he whirled wide-eyed toward Proto—who was speechless—then back toward the scene unfolding.

"Hold now, Sir Bertilak, hold," called the announcer, as the elderly monk leaned and murmured to him anxiously. "If you do this, what becomes of our tourney? What becomes of our bracket?"

"Fair questions. My proposal is simple," responded Sir Bertilak. "Should I prevail, Sir Griffyngale will advance, and I will fight again this round. Should I fall, Sir Malin will advance, and Sir Griffyngale will take my place against Sir Lackthew."

The announcer and elderly monk conferred quietly for a moment. "Your proposal is fair and we will allow it," the announcer finally responded, "if your good fellow knights will consent. What say you, Sir Griffyngale?"

Sir Griffyngale looked at Sir Malin—who stood about a half-foot taller than him, had arms like tree trunks, and was hefting his lance as lightly as a broomstick—then back at the announcer. "Much as I've yearned to face the dastardly Sir Malin, I cannot in good conscience prevent this duel of honor from proceeding," he declared, not quite hiding his relief beneath exaggerated reluctance. "By all means, Sir Bertilak."

The announcer nodded. "And what say you, Sir Malin?"

The black knight eyed the two knights and shrugged. "It matters naught to me. Does the reaper care which stalk falls first?"

The black-garbed section of the stands howled with approval, as maidens scowled and spat. Sir Malin favored them with a slight bow.

"So be it! Sir Malin and Sir Bertilak will joust," affirmed the announcer. "Ready yourselves, my good knights."

As Sir Bertilak mounted his horse and prepared, Sir Blancheblade stared in silence, pale eyes wide. His hands were clenched at his sides. "I knew something would happen. I knew I should've done something sooner . . . "

The mists were back and rising toward waist level. Proto felt anxiety fluttering through his breast.

As this had been unfolding, he'd tried to alter the course of events—first by having the announcer forbid this change in the bracket, and then by having Sir Griffyngale refuse to consent. But the dream had resisted him both times.

It must be like Mayger had told him. When the dreamer *"wills the dream in a different direction, it's awfully hard to overpower that."* But why in the world was the dreamer resisting the happy ending Proto was trying to give him?

He'd figure that out later. For now, he had to deal with this mist, which had swollen midway up his chest.

"Worry not, worry not, Sir Blancheblade," he coaxed his young protégé. "Ignore this spectacle. Ignore this grandstanding by Sir Bertilak. He's just a nobody, foolishly seeking a name for himself. Sir Malin will prevail, and you will face him next round." *I'll see to it.*

Sir Blancheblade nodded uncertainly. His gaze strayed from the two knights to that Rapunzel-haired woman in the stands—Lady Aureal, the maiden he loved, who'd pledged her hand to whoever bested Sir Malin.

"Yes. You're probably right," the young knight finally replied to Proto. Then, barely audible: "My moment will come." His knuckles were clenched white. But the mist had stopped rising.

The two knights, black and green, rode into the lists and faced each other from opposite ends. Their silvery mail and lances glimmered. Wind billowed through their helmets' plumes and their horses' hair.

"Blessings of Heaven be upon you, Sirs Bertilak and Malin," called the announcer. "On the herald's mark, sally forth."

A man with a horn stepped forward and cleared his throat at length. Lifting the horn to his lips, he gave a ringing peal.

The knights spurred their horses and were off. Soon, they were galloping at full tilt. Their horses champed madly as they neared each other.

Watching closely, Proto *willed* the proper outcome with all his might. He focused as intently as he'd ever focused. He visualized exactly how this should play out, how this *would* play out.

And it did. The black knight's lance crashed into the green knight's helmed head and smote it clean off his shoulders.

Proto blinked. *Yikes.* That had worked even better than he'd aimed for. He almost felt guilty—even knowing that this was just a dream within a dream.

Lords and ladies in the stands were wincing and shaking their heads. Some maidens had flung hands over their mouths. Others hurled curses at the victor. "You scallywag! You rapscallion!"

Meanwhile, the black-garbed section of the crowd was laughing uproariously and exchanging high-fives. Sir Malin rode about with his lance held high, pumping it up and down triumphantly.

As for Sir Blancheblade, he stared with his lips hanging apart. His eyes fell to the decapitated body. It had fallen from its horse and lay slumped near the middle of the field.

Proto slapped his back. "You see?" he told the young knight. "You'll have your chance. You've earned it. You've played things exactly right."

"I . . . just hope I win." Sir Blancheblade looked pallid.

"Oh, don't doubt that!" urged Sir Wyndsack. "Malin will be lucky if he fares better than that green knight." He waved toward the head, which had rolled to a stop far from its body. "You'll win."

Yes, I'll see to it. Proto smiled upon that helmed head with grim satisfaction, pondering how best to make Sir Blancheblade triumph.

He was so intent on this that he didn't notice the audience's sudden gasps and murmurs—not till the sound grew into full-fledged cries of horror. He looked up.

Sir Bertilak's headless body was rising to its feet.

"What is this ghastliness?" the announcer was crying. "What foul sorcery is this?"

Turning slowly toward its head, the green knight's body shuffled toward it.

Sir Malin had stopped parading about and had cocked his head at his adversary. He looked more bemused than fearful.

"Heaven be with us!" entreated the announcer, as Sir Bertilak's body reached and lifted its severed head.

The green knight positioned the helmet beneath his left arm and lifted its beaver, baring the face beneath. Then, he drew and brandished his sword.

"En garde," called the head to the black knight.

The announcer had fallen to his knees and clasped his hands together, facing Heaven and speaking an unheard prayer. The three monks were doing the same.

The lords and ladies in the stands looked torn between running away, holding absolutely still, and watching intently.

Proto looked at Sir Blancheblade.

The young knight was shaking his head—not with shock and aghastment, like everyone else, but a sort of somber emptiness. His face was blank. His features sagged.

He heard a chuckle behind him and looked back.

There was Astrid, not even wearing her page boy outfit anymore. With her arms folded beneath her breasts in her grey cosmonaut getup, she laughed derisively. Tresses of silvery-blue hair blew wildly over her face.

Proto's eyes widened. *What are you doing?* he mouthed anxiously, waving up and down at her outfit.

"It doesn't matter. We're past the point of no return." She pointed at the horizon, where grey mirk was rolling and burgeoning toward them—or, rather, toward the dreamer.

Proto spun back to Sir Blancheblade. But he didn't seem to have heard Astrid or noticed the impending darkness. Indeed, like everyone else, he was rapt with what was playing out in the field.

Sir Malin had hopped off his horse and unsheathed his sword. He sauntered toward Sir Bertilak as though slaying swordsmen carrying their own heads were just another day's work for him. For his part, the green knight also looked untroubled, to the extent Proto could see that severed head's facial expression.

The two knights faced each other from about ten yards apart. Each had his visor raised to bare his face.

"I will not insult you by asking if you yield," the green knight finally said—that is, his head spoke from beneath his arm.

Sir Malin smirked. "Bold words. I'll give you credit. A lesser man in your shoes might *lose his head* right now."

A few of the maidens *ugh*ed and rolled their eyes. The black-garbed section of the stands chortled and nodded approvingly at each other.

"Well, let's not draw this out then," replied Sir Bertilak. He strode calmly toward his opponent.

As the green knight approached, the black knight didn't move at first. But when his foe came within reach, he suddenly let loose a heavy blow, sweeping his sword toward the green knight's head-holding offarm—a cheap shot, perhaps, but a fast one.

Sir Bertilak was swifter. His longsword flashed into a parry and, almost before the ping of steel on steel reached Proto, was riposting toward Sir Malin's throat.

The black knight stumbled backward and managed, barely, to evade the attack. He parried two more slashes as the green knight pressed his advantage, then dodged a third.

Proto looked again at Sir Blancheblade. Like a tragic hero, he faced a grim scene that it was now too late for him to change, and he did nothing.

It occurred to Proto that *he* still could try to change all this. But Astrid had told him this dream was "past the point of no return." And something told him nothing good would come of doubting her further today.

The two knights had traded blows for less than thirty seconds when the green knight's sword slipped beneath Sir Malin's parry and through the man's neck.

After balancing in place for a moment, his helmed head started rolling off his shoulders. But Sir Bertilak caught it by the plume in his sword hand and set it neatly beside the body, which now had slumped to the ground.

Meanwhile, the black-clad lords and ladies were groaning and clutching their heads with both hands. The rest of the audience was simply dumbstruck.

The dark mirk on the horizon was nigh upon them now, swirling tempestuous on all sides. But no one seemed to see it—not even Sir Blancheblade. Indeed, he seemed to be staring into a void.

The dreamer's shiny-armored image had grown blurry and ambiguous. He now looked vaguely like a slouching young man in a T-shirt.

Sheathing his sword, Sir Bertilak strode up to the stands and bowed with a flourish. Then, "A favor from Milady Aureal?" he called.

The Rapunzel-haired lady lifted her white lily, almost in slow-motion, and cast it toward the green knight.

Strange shadows flashed everywhere as the stem and leaves and petals whirled through the air, like the world's light were whirling with that flower and being blocked by it. Those shadows darkened Sir Blancheblade's face, over and over again.

And when the lily struck the green knight's hand, mirk swallowed everything.

Abruptly, Proto was hurtling through grey obscurity, where shining white dots swirled in parallax.

Then, he was tripping forward and barely recovering his balance in a misty blue corridor of Somnus' realm. He heaved in a breath, then let it out slowly.

Ahead, he saw Astrid already striding away. Her grey form mingled with the far off fog.

Proto wanted to call her and ask her to wait up. But he didn't want to hear what her response would be.

Instead, he just forced down his dizzy daze and jogged till he'd caught up. He followed for a while from a couple steps behind.

"Your performance was pathetic," she finally remarked without looking back. Her voice lacked any warmth. "He would've done better if you weren't there. He had a chance of figuring this out for himself. You steered him away from that. He sensed, correctly, he was doing something wrong. You reassured him he'd be alright."

Proto didn't doubt she was right. She almost always was.

No, he was more focused on how much he'd come to like this place. For the first time, he realized he'd be sad when he left it, even if he was just awakening from a dream.

"Look," he sighed. "I get it. I'll tell Somnus to either find me a new mentor or kick me out of here, okay?"

She spun and fixed him with a violet stare. "That's not—!" She sealed her lips and took a deep breath through her nose, letting her shoulders rise and fall. "You misunderstand me," she finally said.

"Well, what's new?" grumbled Proto.

She didn't reply. She just stared a few seconds, then turned and resumed walking.

But that glower on her face did fade first. A trace of something else now showed there. *Pity? Remorse?* Neither seemed quite right.

They reached the lounge of Somnus' Palace minutes later without any further words. That quickly changed when they walked in.

"Ah!" boomed Somnus, extending his arms in welcome. "My favorite track-suit-wearing trainee!"

As usual, he was sitting at the bar with several glasses in front of him, most with only green or brown dregs inside. Lilac was standing nearby and polishing cups again. *Clink.*

"How was today's visit?" the Lord of Dreams went on. "I heard about your success in that rusty old city the other day. Some clever work by the both of you! How'd he do today?" he asked Astrid.

"You should ask him," she replied mildly.

Somnus' brow raised. "Then I suppose I shall. Proto?"

It was so rare these days to hear his actual name, he almost flinched at the sound of it. Or maybe he was flinching at having to answer the question.

Well, no point delaying the inevitable.

"I failed," responded Proto. "I tried to steer the dream in a good direction, and it seemed to be working. But the dreamer resisted it in the end. Very strongly." He paused here and almost stopped, but felt compelled to say more.

"I think he would've resisted what I was trying to do no matter what. Because I was wrong about how the dream should end. I came into the dream with some preconceptions about what this dreamer needed. And that's because I made the mistake of not following some advice that Astrid gave me. I won't make that mistake again."

"Hm." Somnus regarded him at length with his chin in hand. "Yes, well, we all fall short sometimes. Even the Lord of Dreams! Why, just last year—"

"He hasn't told you the whole story," interrupted Astrid.

"Oh?" said the robed man.

Proto wasn't sure what criticism was coming, but he didn't feel worried now. He just felt hollow. What would be, would be.

"He asked me to tell him what I'd learnt about the dreamer in the Shadow-caster," recounted Astrid. "I told him, against my better judgment. I knew it would prejudice his decision-making. I knew he was likely to fail as a result. But I thought it might be a useful lesson for him. And I suppose it might have been. But today's outcome was at least as much my fault as his."

Proto stared at her in silence. Her violet gaze was wide but unswerving. Some stray locks of silvery-blue hung over her face, but she didn't seem to notice. Her lips pressed tightly when she'd finished speaking.

"Ah," said Somnus. "Do you think you made the right choice, Astrid?"

She looked at Proto, then at Somnus. "I don't know yet."

"This might be for the best." Somnus turned to look at that painting of the old man, his long hair shifting atop his robe. "Sometimes, small failures breed great success. We'll find out, won't we?"

Astrid didn't offer any answer, and he didn't seem to expect one. Not right now, anyway.

Instead, he turned to Proto, eyes gleaming with sudden zeal. "And what about you? What about *your* choice?"

"I . . ." Proto wasn't quite sure what Somnus was talking about. He'd planned to say something about the dream they'd just visited. But he suddenly felt Somnus was asking a much larger question. And he felt utterly unprepared to answer it right now. "I guess I'll need to think about it."

"Yes, that's likely wise." The Lord of Dreams smiled and cast a hand lightly. "But let's not tarry on this. This *was* just a dream, after all! Dreams recur. Choose wrong, and you'll have another chance to choose differently. To a point. You haven't made any choices you can't take back. Not yet."

Those last words echoed through Proto's head. He found himself turning to look at Astrid.

On noticing his gaze, she scowled slightly and gave him a look that said, *Yes?* She ran a hand through those stray tresses of silvery blue, brushing them off her face.

After a moment, she turned away and blinked twice.

"In any event!"—Somnus slapped the bar amiably—"I'm feeling thirsty." He turned to Lilac, who was polishing her black mug with the white-lacquered crack. "Weren't you just cleaning that one five minutes ago?"

"Maybe." The pale and black-eyed gaze she gave him was cool and straight. But her ears looked faintly pink. "I don't suppose I was paying close attention."

"Ah." He smiled cordially. "Well, there's no such thing as too spic-and-span, is there?"

"Was there a drink you wanted?" she asked flatly.

The Lord of Dreams laughed. "Indeed! I'll leave it to you. Pick something—Somnus-style."

She eyed him like he was the drunk uncle blathering inappropriate jokes in a room full of children. But she grabbed and poured an old armagnac, and he *ahh*ed with approval.

"So," Proto said after a moment to Astrid, who still was standing nearby.

His voice seemed to startle her out of a reverie. "Yes, anyway," she said, fixing her already-fixed hair. "Be here bright and early. No more tardiness."

"Are you my fifth-grade teacher?" he asked lightly. "Miss Beatrice, is that you?"

"No, I'm much older than she is," replied Astrid calmly.

"You'd never know it!" rejoined Proto. "Why, you'd fit in with those young damsels we saw earlier. Casting flowers at valiant knights! *Swooning* at their wounds!" He held a wrist to his forehead and made as though to faint.

"If I ever do that," she replied, "you have permission to slap me back to my senses."

"Likewise," he declared.

" . . . what?" she said.

"What?" he asked innocently.

She gave him a violet stare, then slapped his cheek lightly. "That's for doing the fainting thing just now." She lifted her wrist demonstratively. "I slapped you back to your senses."

"Oh, that's not fair!" he complained, rubbing his cheek.

"Rules are rules!" she waved innocently. "Next time, it's a punch in the face."

"What? Is it that serious an offense?" he asked.

"You think that's serious? Don't become a three-time offender!" She held out one finger, then made as though to chop it off with her other hand.

His eyebrows raised. She nodded earnestly.

"Hm. I can't help feeling this game is rigged against me!" lamented Proto.

She giggled. "The best games seem that way at first."

"Is that so?" He eyed his violet-eyed mentor in her cosmonaut-chic outfit. One hand was resting on her waist as usual, but the upward curve of her lips and sparkle in her gaze were quite new.

"I *am* the mentor, yes? But don't take my word for it." Her stare caught his and held it for a moment, as a sun's gravity catches a shooting star.

Then, she was turning and strolling toward the bar. "Come to think of it, I'm thirsty too. Lilac! Give me something Somnus-style."

Lilac sighed and turned to Somnus. "Look what you've started!" she accused, as he chuckled jovially and drank.

Meanwhile, still standing in place, Proto felt a smile forming, as he mused on things faraway and right in front of him. "I won't," he murmured to Astrid's back. "That, I won't."

Chapter 8
Cosplay and Coffee

"Back in the woods? Another robbery to stop?" asked Proto, squinting through midnight's gloom into the foliage. Before he'd even finished speaking, though, he'd seen enough to know this wasn't the shadowscape of elms and ashes where his first visit had occurred. That dream had had a dark and washed-out and high-contrast look, like horror films involving camping trips in forests.

This place, in contrast, was fey and lush. A full moon breached the canopy ahead and lit the rich blues and reds of forest flowers. Elder and rowan trees cast swaying shadows on the underbrush, which was flush with bulbous plants and huge rounded leaves. Verdant aromas hung upon the midsummer breeze, not yet fraught with the musk of fallen leaves.

"Does this look like a robbery dream to you?" asked Astrid to his rear.

"Not unless the robber is David the Gnome or a gang of Smurfs," he replied.

"Your references make even me feel old."

"No? Teddy Ruxpin, maybe? 'Come dream with me tonight . . . !'" he sang.

"Please don't ever do that again," she said.

Needless to say, Proto had declined to hear the dreamer's bio in advance of this visit. He was going in blind—literally so, in this shadowy area where he and Astrid were standing. He advanced toward the moonlit clearing ahead.

As he crossed the threshold into the lunar glow, Astrid gasped behind him.

Then, she *bwa-ha-hah*ed uncontrollably.

He frowned. "I take it I've unintentionally amused you."

"Look at yourself!" she cried. "You pixie puff!"

He looked down. He was barechested and wearing a sort of leafy loincloth. Flowery accoutrements adorned his arms and legs. Feeling a prickle around his ears, he touched it and felt a laurel crown.

He also felt an odd weight on his back. Reaching back he felt—*sigh*—fairy wings. He gave them a test flutter, then grimly nodded.

"Wait, did you just *flap* those?" Astrid cackled crazily, as he continued to study his fairy garb sadly. "I take it all back! Stick with the tracksuit from now on!"

Proto was feeling this was all very unfortunate when, abruptly, he wondered: *If* I'm *wearing this, then what about . . . ?* He turned to face her, just as she was stepping into the moonlight.

Astrid was clad in a leaf bikini with a see-through cobweb robe overtop. A leafy tiara adorned her hair, which sparkled silvery in the moonlight. So did her giant violet moth wings. She seemed oblivious to their slow fluttering, as well as the rest of her getup.

Proto was proud how straight he kept his face, as he eyed her up and down. The lunar glow played along her frame and caught on every curve. Of course, her usual grey jumpsuit hadn't left much to the imagination. But this was something else altogether.

"I guess the wings match the eyes, huh?" he finally said.

She stared, sifting through his words.

Then, she looked down—and gasped. She threw her arms across her breasts and nether parts, like a nymph in a Renaissance painting.

"My . . . queen?" A smile spread across his face. "My fairy queen?"

She squinted intently at her outfit, such as it was, then cursed. "First's name! Why won't it let me change this?!"

"It's meant to be. Come, my lady of the woodland realm!" Proto held a regal hand forth. "We'll wander the darkling ways! We'll tarry in the shadowy bowers!"

"I'll burn this place down," swore Astrid, as her wings fluttered with fury. "I'm gonna go Gargamel on this dreamer!"

"Be at ease, my sovereign of the sprites!" he urged.

"I'll tear it all down Wooly Whatsit-style!" she raged, sparkling involuntarily.

"I *knew* you knew my references!" Proto offered her a high-five, but she just stomped past him—as best she could, wearing dewdrop slippers. Flowers sprouted up and bloomed about her feet.

"Stop that!" She tried to squish the new blossoms back into the dirt, but that seemingly just made them reproduce.

"You could always . . . soar above all this!" suggested Proto, holding a hand toward her violet moth wings.

She stared distrustfully at him, then gave her wings a little flap. Stardust fell from them and powdered the earth with a silvery shimmer.

She whirled around and went back to stomping. "I look like bloody Anima!" she grumbled. She headed toward the darkest trail in sight. But as she approached, blue will o' wisps flared up along the path, lighting her way.

"First's name . . . !" Astrid cursed again.

Proto decided he liked this dreamer.

They followed the fairy fires until they heard several voices ahead. Their banter sounded more "twenty-something city dweller" than "winged creature of the woodland realm." So, Fairy Queen Astrid and her fellow sovereign stayed hidden in the brush as they approached. That's probably what fairies would do, after all.

A brown-haired and goateed man in a turtleneck was complaining about a book he'd had to read. "Not only is it BS, he *writes* like he has a B.S. No offense, Himari."

"None taken, Sweetums," replied a slight young woman in a red dress. "Someone has to calculate the tip after dinner. And pay it."

"Zing!" he lamented. "But true, unfortunately."

"What, there's not a market for dissertations on Cervantes' Italian literary influences in writing Don Quixote?" asked a grey-eyed woman with blonde hair.

"Alas, so it seems," sighed the man. "How's the market for research on Shakespeare's boyhood religion and its manifestations in Hamlet's soliloquies, Helen?"

"Not rolling in the dough yet," she confirmed sadly. "Except at the bakery. Where I'm paid a fair wage, unlike Atlean University."

"That's why I date a B.S." The man snuggled Himari close. "Love you, Honey-bunches. Money-bunches."

"I like you too, Dimitri," she sighed languidly. "Sometimes."

The blonde woman, Helen, ran a hand through her hair and rolled her eyes. She looked a bit like Dahlia—if, perhaps, not quite as favored by the gods of beauty. Not a face to launch a thousand ships, perhaps, but enough to burn the topless towers of the local university.

Proto smiled and absently wished Dahlia were here. She'd understand that reference. And then she'd respond something something about "topless" and "beauty" and things that are "burning" hot, like the dirty old pedagogue trapped in a knockout body that she was. She'd probably like this group.

Proto and Astrid listened to their conversation for several minutes. It wasn't clear yet who the dreamer was. But Proto pieced together that this was a camping retreat for graduate student instructors at a local university—"GSIs," as they were called. In response to complaints about low instructor pay and lack of benefits, the school had added this retreat in a school-owned forest as a "benefit" and valued it at $2,500. The fact that it was BYOB just added insult to injury.

The three who'd spoken thus far were GSIs. But the fourth, Sancho, was a janitor. He'd been busy cleaning up Solo cups and vomit during the staff retreat last week—a night of free beer and bowling at a local alley—so they'd stuck him with the GSIs instead. This was a somewhat awkward pairing, but they were all doing their best.

It helped that they'd just finished drinking a few bottles of two-buck chuck. Which, of course, Himari had purchased. She'd offered Sancho a cup when she'd seen him sitting by himself earlier. One cup had become five or six. And so, when the three instructor friends had wandered off from the broader group into the woods, he'd tagged along.

"Are you sure you don't have one more bottle with you?" Helen was asking Himari. "I felt sure we had four!"

"Alas, we did," Himari sighed, holding up two sets of two fingers. "Trust the math major."

"Do you think there's a store nearby?" pressed Helen.

The others stared at her beneath the moonlit leafy boughs.

She fixed them with a tipsy smile. "Come on! We can make an adventure of it!"

"Maybe you could convince me, if Himari's buying mezcal. I'm into mezcal lately," replied Dimitri. "Are there any you'd recommend, Sancho?"

"I . . . don't know any," replied the janitor. "I mostly drink High Life. When it's on discount."

Himari slapped the back of Dimitri's hand surreptitiously and mouthed *come on!* at him.

His eyes went wide and he held his hands out innocently.

"Anyway," said Himari, "we should either find that 'store' or find our way back to the tents. Everyone's probably sleeping by now. Do you remember the way back, Dimitri?"

"Not a clue!" he replied.

"I think I do," said Sancho.

"Well, my friend, lead the way," directed the goateed man.

"I'll catch up in a sec," called Helen as the others walked off.

"Time to break the seal?" asked Dimitri.

"Be polite!" she scolded daintily. "Yes, and I'm sure I'll regret it."

The others shuffled off through the darkness, and Helen made her way into the underbrush. There, she broke the seal.

As she did so, she grumbled to herself—first inaudibly, then more loudly. "Hi, I'm Himari. I don't know why men throw themselves at me! All I have are beautiful black eyes, a size-zero waist, gracefully feminine mannerisms, and loads of money!"

She groused a few more half-discernible sentences. "Not her fault. Stupid. Unfair."

"I think we've found our dreamer," Fairy King Proto whispered to Fairy Queen Astrid. She nodded in agreement. "And . . . I think we're about to meet her."

Helen's return route through the foliage was leading her squarely toward the two of them.

"Greetings," hailed Proto with a palm raised, as she stepped in view.

She gasped and gave a little shriek, throwing up her hands defensively. The mist lapping at their feet abruptly swirled up to waist level.

Seeing neither a robber nor a murderer, but instead two winged fairies in leaf-garb, her grey eyes remained wide. But her hands returned to fastening her belt, which was undone and dangling. "What do you want?" she demanded tipsily, struggling to get the belt prong through the hole.

"A fair evening to you too, Helen," replied Proto.

"You know my name? Been listening in, have you? Creepster!" she accused. " . . . wait. Don't I know you? I feel like I met you once, but maybe I was really drunk."

Proto eyed the flush-faced and tousled girl up and down as she struggled with her belt. "That seems feasible."

"Well, anyway who do you think you are?" demanded Helen, finally fastening her belt. "Oberon and Titania? Are you from that cosplay convention?"

"You may call me Queen Moonwing," replied Astrid serenely. "And this is King Utterflutter."

Oh, Hell no. Proto frowned and opened his mouth.

But Helen already was replying. "Well, my good King and Queen, how can I help you? No—how may I be of service?" She smiled and slurred the words a little, doing something vaguely curtsey-like.

"Better to ask how we can serve you," replied Proto, feeling a rush of inspiration.

"Oh, I don't think you can help me," Helen sighed. "Not unless you can give me some two-buck chuck. Or mezcal. Or make that guy over yonder fall in love with me." She waved toward the path where Dimitri and the others had walked off. "Please don't tell him I said that. I might be a teensy bit drunk."

"Make him fall in love with you?" replied Astrid. "And how would you propose we do that?"

"I don't know. You're the fairies, right?" retorted Helen. "Cast a spell on him! Make him fall in love with the first girl he sees after waking up. Then, *I'll* go wake him up, and we'll live happily ever after."

"Hmm," pondered Fairy Queen Astrid. "It would rather offend my scruples to make someone fall in love against his will. Especially if he's already in love with someone else!" She furrowed her brow in faint reproof.

"But what if he's making the *wrong choice!*" pressed Helen. "What if you're really just helping him see the *true love* that's meant for him?"

"That's an awfully big assumption, don't you think?" replied Astrid.

"Oh, psh!" waved the blonde-haired woman. "Dimitri just thinks I'm too tall. Or maybe he likes dark hair. And dark subtle eyes. With that perfect curve, speaking of both innocence and sophistication. But I'm sure it's something superficial like that."

"I could give you dark hair if you'd like," offered Astrid.

"I need *fairy magic*, not hair dye!" cried Helen.

"Tell you what," Fairy King Proto jumped in. "My radiant Queen here will use her fairy magic to make you as fair as fair can be. Like her!" Astrid scowled at him, but he pressed on. "Flowing locks, silvery moonlit shimmers, the whole deal."

"Then," he continued, "we'll go ask your friend over there—Dimitri, yes?—what's the most beautiful thing he can think of. And *you'll* be standing there with us, all sparkly and done-up. And Himari will be there too, all sweaty and disheveled. And then he'll tell us the answer."

"Whatever he says, we'll give it to him, on the spot," declared Proto. "And if he says it's you, it's *you!* We'll hold a nice big fairy wedding for you. That's about the best we can do."

Astrid had arched an eyebrow skeptically at the start of this proposal. But by the end, she was nodding with a smile somewhere between queenly and puckish.

"Hm," mused Helen. The mists had swirled up from waist level to chest level as Proto spoke. "You're not quite like fairies as I imagined them. And I should probably be more flummoxed about meeting fairies at a GSI forest retreat. But I've had just enough wine not to worry about it! Let's do this."

"Very well!" Fairy Queen Astrid waved two moonlit fingers.

At once, a fey glamor transposed itself down Helen's frame, shedding sparkles in her hair and a glowing smoothness on her skin. Her outfit, essentially, remained the same outfit. But now it looked like it'd been handsewn by an expert seamstress to flatter Helen's frame, and not mass-produced in a sweatshop and purchased from a discount bin at the mall.

"Wow. I haven't felt this cute and glittery since senior prom!" marveled Helen, holding a tress in front of her eyes.

"You're welcome," nodded the Fairy Queen.

The dreamer and two fairies walked the wooded path that the three university employees had taken—correction, the three independent contractors unentitled to benefits. The fae royalty were attended by panoplies of stardust-shedding moths and ushered along by flaring blue will o' wisps.

"That's so cool . . . !" admired Helen, as one moth perched upon her finger. "Who would've thought the University Arboretum would hold all this?"

"Yes, *who* could conceive such a thing," replied Astrid drily.

"What?" Helen looked over with a blink. The mist had been sinking, but now halted and swelled a little.

"Wonders abound where we expect them least," said Proto, "is what my royal consort meant, I think."

"Ah. Yes, that sounds very fairy," agreed Helen.

There was something odd about this dreamer. Like she was half-aware this was a dream, and savoring it rather than recoiling back toward wakefulness.

"Still, I admire whoever up there came up with all this!" mused Helen, waving vaguely moonward. "Assuming it's not just random chance, like Himari the math major claims. Silly left-brained types!" She smiled upon the motley and abounding verdancy.

"I'm sure you do," replied Astrid, wrinkling her nose as flowers sprouted between her toes.

"'Such tricks hath strong imagination that, if it would but apprehend some joy, it comprehends some bringer of that joy'!" quoted the Shakespearean studies GSI.

"'Joy' may be too strong a word." The Fairy Queen removed a moth from her eartip. It fluttered away in shining curlicues, leaving sinking powdery trails in midair.

"Hm?" asked Helen, distracted by her rapture.

"'Joy' is too small a word for such great beauty," said Proto, "is what my eminent wife meant, I think."

"Ah. Well said," agreed Helen absently, admiring some bulbous fruits and flora.

Some voices were audible ahead. Three forms came in view, mere silhouettes in the meager starlight.

They soon turned to regard the three approachers, apparently hearing the twigs snapping and leaves rustling beneath Helen's feet. The two fairies made no such noise. Spontaneous growths of grass tufts cushioned their footfalls.

Meanwhile, the mists had sunk to about ankle-level. The white wisps looked natural in the fey and luscious woods.

"Hi all," called Helen to her peers. "Meet my new friends."

The two winged sovereigns of the fae stepped into the moonlight.

"What the F?!" cried Himari, stepping backward. " . . . wait. Don't I know you?"

"Right?!" Helen pointed at Proto. "We *know* you."

"You were named 'Porno' or something, right?" said Himari.

"Why does everyone get my name wrong!" lamented Proto, who had zero recollection of these two GSIs.

"That or King Utterflutter, your choice," Fairy Queen Astrid replied to Himari. "Also, hail, mortals." She gave them a regal wave.

"Yes, a fine eventide to you all," grumbled Fairy King Proto.

"Helen," said Dimitri, "who are these flapping pixies?"

"This is Queen Moonwing. And, as she said, this is King Utterflutter," replied Helen.

"Utterflutter," repeated Sancho. "Wasn't that in some cartoon?"

"Right?!" cried Fairy King Proto. "It's on the tip of my tongue!"

"So, yeah, this is Himari and this is Dimitri. We're GSIs at the university," explained Helen. "Which means we do hard labor for below minimum wage."

"Me too," said Sancho. "Except I'm the janitor."

"Yes, quite right, Sancho! We're all in this together," affirmed Helen.

"Except Himari," said Dimitri, "who makes more per day than us each week."

"Also true," acknowledged Helen.

"Really though, it's an injustice!" lamented Dimitri. "I'll be fifty by the time I have Himari's net worth."

"Remember that story of the ant who worked hard and the grasshopper who read Don Quixote all day?" said Himari.

"Hey now, we're in this *together!*" admonished Helen.

"I feel we've been forgotten," mused Fairy Queen Astrid.

"I'm sorry. We're being rude and nerdy," Helen apologized. "It's what GSIs do."

"Ohh." Himari had approached Astrid and was eying her up and down. "That cosplay convention! I had to miss it because of this stupid retreat."

"I went to one of those when I was fourteen," recalled Sancho. "My little sister was Sailor Mars."

"What were you?" asked Dimitri.

"I don't know. An off-duty janitor, I guess."

"Kawaii, neee!" Himari reached for Astrid's wing and felt it between her fingers. Sparkles rubbed off on her. "So realistic! Where did you find this powder?"

"You might say it's homemade," replied Astrid.

"It's the only way to get good things here, isn't it?" sighed Himari. "That, imports and Etsy."

"Or the only way, period, if you're in the humanities," remarked Dimitri.

"Are we still going on about my money?" berated Himari, hands on her hips. "Is it not enough that *I* buy the wine, *I* treat when we go out—"

"Alright, alright," said Dimitri with a pacifying wave. "So, what brings Your Fae Majesties to our humble arboretum?"

"We come with a question for you, Dimitri," spoke Astrid in a dulcet croon. "It's very important that you answer it truly."

"A question for me? Well, you're in luck," declared the turtlenecked GSI. "Answering strange and pointless questions is my entire career path."

"Very good," said Fairy Queen Astrid. "So, my question is, what's the most beautiful thing you can think of?"

The man tilted his head at Astrid and regarded her appraisingly—her leafy curves, her cobweb dress, her shimmering hair of silvery-blue.

"Besides my radiant Queen," added Proto drily.

The Fairy Queen rolled her violet eyes at the Fairy King, but couldn't keep her cheeks from dimpling.

Dimitri looked thoughtfully from right to left—from Helen to Himari—then back again, and back and forth. His brow went increasingly furrowed.

So did Himari's. Her hands were soon back on her hips.

Meanwhile, Helen was batting her silver-sparkling lashes at the goateed man, her hands clutched prayer-like to her fore. Her hair shimmered with Luna's eminence. Her faint smile seemed to glow with elfin mystery.

"Well, the answer's clear in the end," Dimitri finally sighed. "Much as I like La Galatea, I'd have to go with Don Qui—"

"*What!?*" interrupted Helen and Himari.

"'Donkey,' you said? Well, a donkey you'll have!" declared Fairy King Proto. He waved a hand with stardust in its wake.

Out of the foliage wandered a braying donkey.

"What the what!" cried Himari, as mists swirled back up toward their waists.

Fairy Queen Astrid had whirled toward Proto and was regarding him with blazing eyes.

"Has something got your wings aflutter, Dear?" he asked her blithely.

"'Donkey,' 'Don Qui'—really?" fumed Helen at Proto. "My love turns me down, and you make a cheesy pun?! Worst. Fairy. Ever!"

"*Your* love?" raged Himari. "Whatever, you can have him. But you might have to pull him out of Don Quixote's arms!"

"Speaking of which," mused Dimitri. "That donkey—it looks just like Dapple. Don Quixote's donkey."

"Stop talking about Don Quixote!" screamed Helen, holding up her glittery hands.

The donkey, disconcerted by her shriek—and, perhaps, by a slight nudge from Fairy King Proto—suddenly charged at little Himari.

The red-garbed girl gasped and stepped back.

Sancho dove at her, pushing her out of the donkey's path just in time. Instead, it ran right through him, knocking him splayed upon the dirt. He hit hard and skidded sidelong.

Himari gasped and regarded her wounded savior, her hand flying to her mouth. She darted toward his supine form.

Meanwhile, following the impact, the donkey had slowed to a stop about fifteen yards away and started nibbling some grass.

Dimitri regarded the beast thoughtfully, not seeming to notice the ailing janitor or his girlfriend leaning over him. "So . . . I do like the donkey. But, to be clear, I *was* saying Don Quixote."

"Screw you," Himari muttered at him over her shoulder.

Then, she returned to her tender ministrations over Sancho. He was moaning and rubbing his head. "There, there," spoke the smiling math major, gently brushing hair from his brow.

"Don Quixote, is it? Well, we're all entitled to our own choices." Proto waved a palm, conjuring a thick leatherbound tome in Dimitri's hands.

"What fine binding!" wondered Dimitri, flipping through the book. "Is this section-sewn? I think it's section-sewn."

"Happy reading," bade Fairy King Proto. "And keep the donkey too. Let none accuse King Utterflutter of parsimony!"

"Have a read *and* ride, why don't you!" suggested Fairy Queen Astrid. She made an upward-wafting motion.

Abruptly, Dimitri was floating from the ground and waving his arms. He landed backward on the dappled donkey.

Startled at the impact, the donkey hied away from the clearing down the forest trail.

The tipsy GSI blinked and looked back and forth. Then, he shrugged and opened his new book in front of his face, blocking out the sparkling image of Helen dwindling in his prospect.

"My hero," crooned Himari over Sancho, clasping a hand around his cheek. He looked dazed but not altogether unhappy with this turn of events.

Proto observed that mirky clouds were bulging toward them on the skyline. Ominous as they looked, he didn't have a bad feeling about it.

"You know," mused Helen to Proto and Astrid, "you guys are questionable fairies, but fun people. I'm tired of scholar types. Maybe love isn't waiting for me at the academy."

"Well, I'm afraid *he's* spoken for." Astrid wrapped a queenly arm around her Fairy King, who raised an eyebrow at his winged consort.

"Yes, yes, I know," waved Helen impatiently. She was looking afar, like a traveler about to depart. "No, I know exactly where to look for true love now."

"Where's that?" asked Astrid.

"Online dating!" declared Helen. "I'm off to take some hot selfies that totally don't look like selfies, and summarize myself in three witty sentences, while signaling my lack of serious interest and my worthiness of serious interest."

"That, or maybe the cosplay convention," pondered Helen. "Or both! After all, why not? *Why shouldn't I?*" she finished in an old-Bilbo-Baggins voice.

"Go put a ring on it," affirmed Proto.

The blonde GSI strolled away. "Thanks for your insights and magic and whatnot," she called behind her, as grey mirk weltered toward them. "It wasn't what I wanted, but it was exactly what I needed."

"That's what we're here for," declared Proto regally.

"Ta-ta!" called Astrid with a handcurl, flapping up a cloud of silvery dust.

"You're the one I'm meant for, Sancho!" declared Himari wildly.

Then, the bulging mirk blew over them from behind. And Proto suddenly was hurtling through grey ambiguity, as star specks whirled about in shining ellipses.

For once, he landed smoothly, starting his forward stride while the vague oblivion was still clarifying into physical reality. His foot landed just as the misty blue hallway of Somnus' realm became recognizable. Momentum forced him into a brisk walk before he'd gotten his bearings.

At the same time, Astrid apparated beside him and began advancing at the same pace. In fact, the timing of her footfalls precisely matched his.

After about ten steps at exactly the same time, with Proto exactly at her side, Astrid looked up at him and frowned. "Are you trying to do that?"

"Do what?" he asked innocently. "Is it so strange that we'd walk two abreast, my good Queen Moonwing?"

She widened her violet eyes at him and wagged a finger. "Oh, no no no no. What happens in fairy dreams, stays in fairy dreams."

"Keep it secret? But why, my fair Matriarch of the Moss and Queen of the Copses?" inquired Proto. "Conceal our frolic in the mystic forest? Our rendezvous in Utterflutter's realm? Our tryst amid the enchanted trees? Our bliss amid the sylvan bowers?"

"Excuse me while I puke," she replied.

"And . . . she's back," sighed Proto.

"It'd probably be rainbow-colored flower-fertilizer vomit," she grumbled.

"That'd go over well at a cosplay convention," he observed. "'Hot queen of the fae barfs in seven colors.' You'd be swarmed by neckbearded men with phone cameras in seconds."

"I could be the 'boring girl who does nothing,' and that would still happen," she replied.

He shrugged and nodded. "Those events always feel like a sausage platter with a severe mustard shortage."

Her scoff couldn't quite hide her laughter. " . . . are you comparing me to mustard?"

"Can I call you Honey Mustard? Dijon Darling? Horseradish Hottie?" asked Proto, as Astrid just shook her head and failed to suppress her grin. "No?"

"Keep it up, and your new nickname will be Split Sausage," she answered.

Proto covered himself protectively, then studied his own pose. "I look like you did when you saw what you were wearing. A leafy two-piece! You looked like Eve's fairy godmother. Or Tinkerbell at the beach."

"What happens in fairy dreams, stays in fairy dreams," she repeated firmly.

"Are you sure? You'd rule the cosplay convention circuit!" he pressed. But she just smiled and shook her head.

"Also, while we're on the subject, I have a question for you," Proto continued, as Astrid glanced over curiously. "Have you ever heard the word 'tsundere'"?

She launched a backhand at him. He barely ducked beneath it.

"What the hell! Just from that?" he marveled. " . . . guess I hit a nerve, huh? You're just proving it, you know."

He expected the next swat and ducked again, but this one came much lower.

Thanks to his evasive maneuver, she missed her intended target—which was very fortunate indeed—but instead hit his funny bone. A jolt of mingled pain, tickles and numbness thrilled up his arm.

"Augh!" He shook his arm in a vain attempt to restore feeling, as Astrid giggled. "If it's not split sausage, it's pounded meat, huh?"

She tossed back her silvery-blue hair and laughed musically.

"Anyway, *that* certainly hit a nerve," he grumbled.

"You deserve it for hurting my hand," she responded archly. "With that hard elbow of yours. Rules are rules."

"Once again," he replied, clutching his ailing limb, "I can't help feeling this game is rigged against me!"

"And yet here you are, still playing!" she observed. "Maybe the best games aren't the easiest ones?"

"Here I am, in a literal *dream realm*, with free drinks and half-hour workdays. And what do I do?" mused Proto. "I play on Nightmare Mode!"

"If you work at it long enough," she replied lightly, her gaze sparkling, "you get the best rewards that way. Right?"

Looking into her violet eyes, he searched for an answer there. But he couldn't see all the way down their depths. He just saw a dark reflection of himself within a dazzling circle, as when the moon eclipses the sun but can't quite hide it.

He opened his mouth to voice *that*—at least, as best he could. But another voice spoke first.

"What are you two doing over here?" asked Mayger. Today, his pink hair was pomaded like mid-1960s Clint Eastwood, and he was wearing a fringed leather jacket. "You were in the Zone of the Fishes, right? You take the long way back?"

"Where you headed, cowboy?" Astrid asked. She looked irked, like she'd just taken her first big bite of dinner when the waiter asked her an unnecessary question. "Holding a country music concert?"

"Stopping a stickup." He double finger-pointed at her. "I'm running late. Ciao."

"Try not to stain your coat," she called to him as he walked off.

"It's vinyl, it'll be okay." The slim man disappeared around a corner.

Astrid resumed leading Proto down the corridors. "What were you saying?" she eventually asked.

"Oh, I don't remember," he replied. This wasn't quite true. It was more like he'd only half worked out what to say, and he no longer felt up to it.

"Ah." She continued in silence until the entrance to the lounge came in view.

"I have a question," said Proto, his steps slowing.

"Hm?" She gave him a violet blink, childlike in its wideness.

"Why wasn't that dreamer bothered by all the magic and weirdness in her dream?" he asked. "I feel like it's exactly the sort of stuff that would've woken our other dreamers.

"Ah. Yes, that's probably right." Astrid's face fell back into frosty inscrutability, like a snowflake hitting the ground. "I told you we have to work within the story of the dream. If you think that means we have to stick to realism at its most boring, you've been learning the wrong lessons."

And . . . she's back. Again. He felt a rueful smile form.

She turned away. "I had a feeling that dreamer would allow some magic. I picked her today for that reason."

"Because that made it easy for me?" asked Proto.

Astrid looked back at him, her violet eyes gone wide again. But in a blink, they'd narrowed. "Yes," she responded, flat and cold as ice. "That's why."

She strode into the lounge, and he followed.

"I was rather fond of the breathing world, once," Somnus was recounting to Lilac, as she cleaned off her coffee machinery. "I used to visit folk up there all the time. They loved me! *Poets* invoked me! Would you believe it?"

"After hearing a story fifty times," replied Lilac, "one tends to believe it."

"Nowadays, if anyone *invoked* me, they'd probably toss him in the loony bin!" sighed Somnus, ignoring her. "Which, by the way, they named after Luna. Quite unfairly, I might add. She's so sweet."

Astrid slowed as she passed the tables, grasping a chair as though on the verge of sitting. Then, she turned and walked out the door with the tree tapestry.

Proto paused and stared after her, then sat in the chair she'd grasped.

"They'd probably put you there too," Lilac replied to Somnus.

"Yes. Unlike *certain others*, who are high on the bitter and low on the sweet." Somnus flung his hand idly toward the bartendress. "It's a good thing you brew coffee for a living, Lilac! Where else can one pour out such bitterness to such delicious effect?"

"Stand-up comedy?" suggested Lilac.

"Touché," allowed Somnus. "But yes, that's the thing about folk up there now. They all *think* too hard about everything. Like coffee's running in their veins!" he lamented. "They leave less and less time to be flesh-and-blood humans. At this point, it's mostly just when they're dreaming!"

"Speaking of which." Somnus turned toward Proto. "Welcome back! How was it?"

"Dreamy," shrugged Proto. He felt like he'd just woken from a good dream and realized it'd been fake.

"Well, that's the best kind, isn't it?" mused the Lord of Dreams, slapping the bar. "What'll it be?"

"I'll have a coffee. The usual way." Proto nodded at Lilac.

She blinked and nodded back, reaching for the black mug with a white-lacquered crack. She brushed one of her two loose black tresses off her pale face. It immediately fell back where it'd been.

"Coffee. Is *no one* any fun today?" lamented Somnus. "At least have a pastry with it!"

Proto wasn't in the mood for sweetness. "How about biscotti?"

"Naturally! The most boring of all cookies," sighed Somnus.

"They're my specialty, you know," Lilac noted.

"Oh, come on, don't retroactively make an ass of me!" protested the Lord of Dreams.

A minute later, the quiet bartendress set the steaming black mug and white biscotti in front of Proto. "Let me know how it is." She turned around. "I think they're a good pair." And back to the bar she glided.

She was right. She usually was, on the rare occasions that she voiced her thoughts. He dipped the dry bread into black bitterness and, biting down, savored it. It wasn't sweet, but somehow made the bitter sweeter.

Feeling the coffee waking him up, he closed his eyes and relished it. His mind went empty as he filled his stomach. Sometimes, all that one needs to feel better is some contrast.

CHAPTER 9
RIVERS, SEAS AND ODYSSEYS

The lounge at Somnus' Palace, of course, served food as well as drinks—real meals, not just biscotti and pastries. Behind the bar was a stairway leading down to the kitchen. A man in a black and white French waiter's outfit brought meals on platters from down there. At any given time, you could usually find at least one or two people eating in the lounge's side booths, with their ornately carved wooden inlays and cushions of purple and green.

Today, though, for the first time since the day he'd arrived at Somnus' Palace, the lounge was empty—that is, except for Lilac. She was busy preparing a batch of cold brew.

On seeing him arrive, she paused, then resumed doing the same thing more stiffly.

"Morning," called Proto.

"Good morning." Now she paused her work and regarded him as though waiting.

"So . . . where is everyone?" he asked.

"Everyone else?" Her lips pressed slightly. "I suppose they're all working."

"Ah." He looked around again.

"Astrid's helping Somnus with something, if that's what you're wondering. And Dahlia is busy all day in the Shadowcaster," she added. "Or was there someone else you had in mind?"

"Um." He scanned her face, but its pallor was inscrutable. "I guess I'm just wondering what I should be doing."

"I suppose you'll have to decide that." She started polishing a glass, glancing up at him after a moment.

He frowned and rubbed his eyes, feeling foggy with sleep still. "Did Astrid leave any instructions on what dream I should visit?"

"Instructions? You can't intervene in a dream on your own," responded Lilac. "You're still a provisional visitor."

"Ah. So . . . no work today?" asked Proto. "Just sitting here and drinking on my own, huh."

Lilac stiffened. "Yes, I suppose so. What else would you do here all day?"

Proto blinked. "I—"

"Enjoy yourself," she flatly urged. "I'll be over here working on my own if you need me."

"Um."

"If you need any coffee Lilac-style, just give a holler and I'll crank that out for you," she said.

"Um."

"Cups, cleaning, cocktails, and coffees Lilac-style," she went on, polishing a glass. "That's what I'm here for. I live to serve."

Proto couldn't help feeling that Fate kept pushing him in different directions. Or maybe each of the three Fates sought a different direction for his life.

Well, Fate was Fate, and here he was.

"Alright, Madame Bartendress. Then serve me you shall!" he declared. "Today, you're going to teach me to make a drink."

She arched an eyebrow but continued polishing. "Now you sound like Somnus. Haven't *you* advanced today! First, doing a visit alone. Now, you're the Lord of Dreams."

"Show due respect for the Darkling Hunter!" he chided. "Or was it Darkling Stalker, Nightly Hunter?"

"Creepy Stalker, Daily Tracksuit," she corrected. "Or were we still talking about Somnus?"

Proto recoiled like he'd been shot twice. "Straight to the heart!" He gave her the double-guns. "Now, that drink you're going to teach me."

Her pale face stayed straight, but her black eyes sparkled. "Tell me why I should partake in this exercise in futility."

"Because the best bartendress makes the best teacher?" he suggested.

"And you're a worthy pupil of the best?" she questioned.

"The sun warms even the lowliest gnat!" he answered.

She eyed him flatly.

He gave her the double-guns again hopefully.

"Stop pointing at me," she chastised. "You're like a traffic sign, you point so much."

He switched to two thumbs up—"No?"—then, two peace signs.

"I suppose," she sighed to hide a smile, "it's too late to claim I'm busy today."

"Meaning?" He beamed and waited.

"We're going on a trip." She bent down and started reaching for things under the bar.

He blinked. "What?"

"'Just bother Lilac till she gives in,' right?" she replied calmly. "Well, now I'm bothered. No backing out now! We're going to make a drink. And since I'm missing two ingredients, we're going to go get them."

"Me, back out?" He held a hand out like an orator. "And miss this odyssey? This search for the secret drink? This quest for Lilac's concoction?"

"You like to repeat yourself in different ways," she observed. "Do you impress yourself that much?"

"You bring out the best in me," he shrugged modestly. "Like a Muse! An inspiration!"

"I hope you're not pointing at me," she called from below the bar as she searched.

He pulled his fingers in just as she looked up, leaving him with two fists extended toward her. "Uh, just rollin' with the punches." He gave a little Rocky-esque flurry.

She shook her head grimly and continued packing.

"Dying to go, huh?" he said.

"Like I'm on death row. But, as they say, 'Suffering is the highest form of charity.'" The bartendress stood. In her hand was a picnic basket. It was embroidered with little lilacs.

Seeing this, Proto's eyes widened. His lips curved up.

"Don't say a word," she commanded.

Still beaming, he touched a finger to his lips and zipped them shut.

"Very good." She turned around and pointed toward the stairway. "This way."

She glided away and down the stairs, and he followed. "I didn't know your job took you away from the lounge."

"Right, I just bustle about making drinks, as others go do adventurous things. 'Lilac the homebody.' 'Lilac the domestic.' Is that the thought?" she asked calmly.

He blinked and searched for a reply other than "yes." But she didn't give him time.

"As a matter of fact, I get out more than any of them. And by out, I mean *out*," she went on. "Who do you think stocks that bar? You think Somnus just magicks it up?"

" . . . that might or might not have been my guess."

"Mm-hmm. Well, today, you're going to learn how little you know. Including how big this place is." She led him down many flights of stairs. Each opened into an unfamiliar looking area, completely different from either the lounge or misty blue hallways. The stairs eventually dead-ended into a sliding white door. "And what lies beyond it," she added, tapping the door.

Unlike the doors he'd seen previously, there wasn't just one door. Instead, a series of heavy doors slid apart in various manners.

"Are we robbing a bank vault?" asked Proto. "Or infiltrating a secret government facility?"

"We're going to the beach," she answered, as the last door slid open.

Beyond it was a mirky grey cave. A stagnant little creek could be seen ahead.

Proto stared. "Drat, I forgot my swimsuit." He snapped his fingers.

"All that about odysseys and quests," she sighed, retrieving a mini-flashlight from her picnic basket. She beamed it toward a tunnel across the creek. "And the excuses begin before we're even *out the door!*"

"I mean, this odyssey is looking a lot more literal than I—"

"Who's the homebody now?" interrupted Lilac, already several strides ahead of him. "Don't worry, we'll be back in time for hot cocoa. You can curl up by the fire in your flannel PJs."

"Pulling out the big guns, are we? Well!"—he sighed and entered the cave—"it worked."

"Go big or go home," she replied evenly, hopping over the creek and continuing into the tunnel.

He followed and ducked into the cramped passage. "I think I've seen this scene before."

"Oh?" She leaned around a stalactite, then squeezed between two stalagmites.

"Yes," he said. "This is where we have a near-death experience, I find out afterward we weren't supposed to be out here, and Somnus freaks out and considers banishing me."

"You should leave the prophecies to Dahlia," she replied.

"And take up what? Mixing cocktails?" he asked playfully.

"Let's start with one and see where things go," mumbled Lilac.

"What?"

"I said, let's start with one and see how things go," she calmly repeated.

"Ah, ye of little faith."

"'Ye' is plural," she noted. "'Ah, thou of little faith' is what you meant."

"Thank you, Miss Beatrice."

"What?"

"She was my fifth-grade teacher."

"Did she also make you cocktails and go on odysseys with you?" replied Lilac. "Because, if so, I feel I suddenly understand you much better."

Proto pondered how to respond to that.

He and his fifth-grade friends had been a bit young to realize it at the time, but by eighth grade, they'd all agreed that Miss Beatrice was by far the hottest teacher in the school. Even in her mid-forties, and well over thirty pounds heavier than she'd been a couple decades earlier, judging by an old family photo she'd had on her desk.

Incidentally, Miss Beatrice had come to a school reunion event about a dozen years later—looking much the same as she had as Proto's teacher—and, indeed, had shared a cocktail with him and his friends. It'd been much harder and drier than anything those early-twenties boys were used to drinking.

He decided, on balance, not to share this story with Lilac.

"I'm not sure what that's getting at, but it seems disturbing and inappropriate!" he instead observed.

"Yes, exactly. That's my general reaction to your banter."

He clutched his chest and jolted backward. "Straight to the heart!"

She pointed a finger at him with her thumb up, then made a *bam* sound and flicked it upward.

Down they wended along shadowy ways. They passed several more underground brooks before reaching a black river, which was much more substantial—hundreds of yards wide. At its side was a rowboat with a single paddle.

"Care for a dip?" he suggested.

"You forgot your swimsuit," she recalled. "And I don't have one either."

"Well, as long as we're in the same position, right?" he reasoned.

"You're suggesting we skinny-dip together? Sure, maybe," she shrugged. He was just getting excited and approaching the shore when she added, "But I should mention, touching that water will make you lose your memories of life. The more you touch, the more you forget."

He frowned and halted about five feet from the black liquid. "Well! Let's lay out our blanket, have a bite and enjoy the view."

"No, no," she said. "Into the boat with you. We still have to get our two ingredients. No stopping halfway there." She walked ahead of him and into the boat's front, grabbing the oar.

"Uh, you want me to do the paddling?" He'd only done it a few times, years ago, and that had been a kayak. But he felt he should make the offer.

"No, I'm not about to let you capsize me in the River Lethe," she said. "You get to hold the flashlight. And if you'd like to show your manly strength, you can push us out."

"Will do!" Cracking his knuckles, he began to push the boat, then eyed the ground. "This stone is wet. Is it safe to step on?"

"Your shoes will be okay. They won't forget anything too important," assured Lilac.

"Great. Thanks." He finished shoving and hopped in, just as the boat began drifting out. She handed him the light and began paddling.

She was good at it, he had to admit—deft, precise and efficient, as always. They soon were moving at a steady clip.

He eyed the water. It had appeared black from the shore. But now that he looked more closely, it seemed almost mirrorlike. Except the reflection was not the rocky ceiling overhead, but . . . *what?* He seemed to see forms moving down there.

Why did they seem familiar? Not the faces—he couldn't see any—but the overall pattern of their movements. Like shadows of a scene that he'd participated in. He leaned and squinted.

Just as he felt on the verge of remembering, a droplet of water hit his hand, churned up by the oar.

He blinked. "Hey! You splashed me."

Lilac looked back with some concern. Then, seeing him pointing at a single bead of water on the back of his hand, she rolled her eyes. "That's enough to forget what you had for breakfast two weeks ago. Maybe." She resumed rowing.

"Sounds good," he said, "Lily. Or was it Lobelia? Lisianthus? Also, where am I?"

She delicately touched a maroon fingernail to the black water, then flicked it at his face.

He dodged aside. "Bloody Hell! She plays for keeps!"

She already was turning away, but her shoulders shook with a suppressed chuckle.

He smiled, his gaze falling upon the water again. Sometimes, his whole life at Somnus' Palace felt like he were in rowboat and someone else were doing the paddling. And all he could do was banter from the backseat and enjoy the ride. Well, he'd enjoy it.

He peered out at the rippling waters again, both black and strangely deep at the same time—like a million mirrors of obsidian, forming and unforming, showing fleeting depths. Were those depths real? He squinted down at them, absently keeping the flashlight angled ahead.

Those shadow forms were moving there again. Were they memories the waters had stolen from others? Or were his memories being reflected back at him? *Or. . . both?* He strove to peer more deeply.

There, he seemed to see himself. He was lying down. Others were bustling frantically around him—some focused on him, others busy with other things. He was being moved somewhere. He was being placed inside something. It was closing.

A noise sounded from afar, but it was not part of *this* and it barely registered.

The shadowy scene was waning away now. He stared harder in frustration. It reminded him of when he'd woken from a dream and wanted to return to it. But, try as he might, he couldn't force his way back.

It was a little like this rowboat, he realized. To get where he wanted to go, he couldn't do the paddling himself. No, he had to be content to sit in the back and lightly coax along the paddler, and shine a flashlight on his destination. Trusting that part of him that wasn't quite *him* to take him where he longed to go. And he felt so close—

"Proto!" Two hands grabbed his shoulders and, just an inch from the water, yanked him back upward.

He blinked as one reality gave way to another. Before him was a fearful black gaze against stark whiteness. She blinked and peered from inches away, her long black lashes batting at him.

The oar, lying sideways across the rowboat, slipped off into the black waters. Lilac gasped and whirled away from him

The movement happened so quickly. Her arm shot out. It dipped elbow-deep into the blackness. It emerged with the oar, dripping dark water. It ran along her hand and wrist.

Eyes agog, he stared at her. "Lilac?"

Stiffly, she resumed paddling. "Try not to do that again. If you hadn't let that flashlight sink so low, I'd never have known till it was too late."

"Your arm . . . the water . . . " he began.

"It's fine. Forget about it," she said flatly.

"But won't *you* forget—?"

"No! Just forget about it." She kept paddling without looking back at him.

Proto pondered and was silent. He sometimes found his stare drifting to the river again. He was wary about peering too deeply now, but it was hard to resist.

"You're letting the flashlight drift again," noted Lilac eventually, glancing over her shoulder.

He met her gaze. It was as black and alluring and deep as . . . "Hm? What?" He realized he was staring. "Oh, the flashlight. Did you know your hair is very reflective?" He pointed it at a tress.

She rolled her eyes, dark and deep, and resumed paddling. He fixed his mind upon an image of those eyes and found it easier to resist the water's siren song.

They soon reached the other shore and disembarked.

Lilac proceeded into another cramped tunnel. He followed her, absently wondering just how far this trip would be and whether he should've brought supplies.

He needn't have worried. They emerged from the cave a few minutes later.

He found himself on a patch of grass atop a small bluff. One tree grew here—a sakura, which was in bloom. Pink petals blanketed the ground around the tree.

A slender path led down from the bluff to a beach—just a few dozen yards wide, a mere nook amid the craggy cliffs on either side. Ocean waves washed up quietly, wetting the white sands. Far away, mists roved upon the sounding sea.

Standing a bit rigidly, Lilac regarded the cherry blossom tree. Her eyes flicked briefly to Proto, then to the cerulean waters.

"I feel lucky to be here," Proto found himself saying.

It was true. He'd grown up on Cherry Blossom Lane—an aptly named street, which turned pink and white with the trees' petals every Spring around April. Growing up, the week that the trees were flowering had always struck him as the most beautiful time of the year. Seeing them, he'd always felt like something profound was at work, even if it was just the blossoming of trees.

Even after he'd grown up and moved away—to a neighborhood much less beautiful, but much more affordable to a guy in his mid-twenties—he'd made a point to run past his old house several times each year, during that week when the sakura trees were blooming.

Lilac turned to him with narrowed eyes, as though searching for mockery, but found only a smile. Her lips curved up a little. "My little shore upon the Sea of Dreams."

He approached the tree and felt its trunk, as though to confirm it were solid. He felt a sakura blossom fall on his head.

Lilac didn't quite stifle a laugh. "Don't you look lovely."

"Oh? Well." He took two flowers and set them in her hair. "Same to you. And more of it."

Her black gaze met his, and her lips quirked upward. Some of the flowers' pink seemed to have stained her cheeks. She stared as though considering something.

Then, she turned to the sea. "First things first." She started down the pathway toward the water. "We have to get what we came for."

"Shells? Seawater? Sand?" he asked.

"Bottles."

Bemused, he followed her down to the shore. She reached down and felt the lapping waves. He couldn't see her face, but her sable hair was billowing in the sea breeze.

"Did you know," said Lilac, letting the foam rush between her fingers, "when you visit a dream, you can take what you find there back with you?"

Proto tilted his head. "I . . . did not know that." He'd assumed things from a dream would vanish upon departure.

Something about this new revelation bothered him. But, watching the sea wash over Lilac's arm, as the brumy wind blew her clothes taut against her frame, he found it hard to focus on why.

"So, we could get the ingredients you need by visiting a dream?" he asked after a moment.

"Mm-hmm," she nodded. "But anything you take from a dream bears the imprint of the dreamer. Like if you took a lock of my hair, it would always be *my* hair. Not just shiny black hair."

"There can be no substitutes," he affirmed.

She didn't look at him, but her lips curved up again.

"So, we could get our ingredients from a dream," she went on. "The problem is, there's no way for us to visit *my* dreams. So if I want something that's truly my own, I have to come here. To my little nook of the Sea of Dreams."

"Come here and . . . ?" Proto regarded the lone and level sea, then Lilac.

"And"—she reached deeper into the ocean's blue, beyond where the eye could follow—"dream of what could be." From the foam and swelling waves, she retrieved a corked bottle. Inside was a reddish powder. She stood it on the hard wet sand behind her.

Proto stared at it. He felt he learned a little more, each day, how little he understood. He watched as she retrieved another bottle from the sea, this one with a tawny liquid inside, and set it behind her.

"These are from me. No one else." She peered at them thoughtfully. "I don't know if the difference is noticeable. It sometimes seems different to me. But maybe I'm just dreaming." Her voice lilted with a hint of irony.

"Only one way to find out, right?" replied Proto.

She nodded firmly. "Yes. Let's have a drink."

From her lilac-dotted basket, she retrieved a thin blanket, black with ornate white needlework along the edges. She laid it beneath the sakura tree and sat atop it.

Then, she made their drink, mixing in a bit from each bottle, among other things. She poured the resulting cocktail in two coupe glasses. It was brown with a hint of maroon.

"Don't tell me what you think yet," she said as he sipped.

"No?"

"No."

She unpacked their food and they ate beside the sea. The milk bread sandwich squares and neatly apportioned side courses were simple.

But perfection lies in making what's complicated simple, Proto mused, staring at the blue serene. *Without losing what matters.*

Sakura blossoms rained upon them as they savored Lilac's creations quietly.

White seagulls flapped across the sky and turned to black silhouettes against the sun.

"I sometimes wonder what it's like up there," she murmured almost inaudibly.

He looked at her, ready to say something about those winging birds. But her black gaze wasn't trained on them. She was facing the mists, forming and unforming on the far horizon.

He shrugged. "Nothing beats this." He spread his arms toward the scene all around them.

"Are you sure though?" She looked at him intently.

He blinked and opened his mouth.

She tapped one maroon-nailed finger to his lips. "No. Don't answer that right now."

"Okay. But *this* though." He lifted his drink and breathed in the aroma. "Trees. Flowers. The sea." He sipped it. "And something more. Something I can't quite put my finger on." He touched his finger to the back of her hand. "There's no imitating this. That, I know."

She looked at him, suddenly grasping that hand. She squeezed it. She leaned in toward him, lips parting, breathing in.

Then, she scrunched her eyes and turned away, releasing his hand. The breath rushed out. "I hope you enjoyed this."

"Enjoyed?" he began.

But she already was standing up. She smoothed her French waitress outfit of black and white.

He scanned her face for some clue what this was, and whether he'd had something to do with it. But her dark gaze was on those mists again—forming fleet beauties, then wisping away.

"I've left the bar unattended for long enough," she explained. But her wistful stare, trained upon the heavens, seemed to reflect far more than an unattended bar.

"Can't the kitchen make drinks too?" he asked lightly.

"Yes." She started turning away, then paused, lifting her drink. "But if 'there's no imitating this,' I guess that might not cut it." Maybe the pink on her ears was just the sunset, splaying across the west.

"Well," he mused, standing up, "it's been a dream."

She tilted her head wryly, then tilted her glass toward him. "To dreams?"

"Cheers." They clinked and finished off the last of her creation.

They gathered the supplies back into Lilac's basket and departed back into the cave.

As Proto followed her through the grey mirk, he found himself reminiscing on an oft-repeated conversation that he and his band of friends had had back in high school—he and Yemos, Mannus and Quart. They'd often mused about what they'd do once they had jobs and had real money. They'd all sworn not to waste it on the boring things that most adults spend it on.

Yemos had declared that he'd buy an old castle, or at least a small tower, depending on his wealth. Mannus had vowed to turn his house's basement into an indoor football field. Quart had promised to buy some dragon fireworks of the sort set off at Chinese New Year celebrations and Bilbo's eleventy-first birthday, and launch them in the badlands of South Dakota.

None of that had happened, of course. Yemos had bought a bourbon collection. Mannus had bought a sports car. Quart had eloped with a girl from Poland—which technically hadn't kept his promise, but, to be fair, at least wasn't boring.

As for Proto, he'd vowed to live in the sort of place that people dream of living in, before he was too old to enjoy it. Exactly what that place would be had been unclear—maybe some beachy southern isle, or maybe one of those mountainous Swiss villages with the colorful rooftops, or maybe Iceland or Japan. His friends had agreed that these were all fine options.

He'd always felt he'd betrayed his promise the most of all, by remaining in his boring hometown less than a mile from the house he'd grown up in, running by his old home on a near-daily basis. He'd kept his past close, as was his wont.

Now, though—glancing at Lilac, her black eyes sparkling against the gloom of the long and windy cave—Proto couldn't help but feel that, maybe, against all odds, he was finally fulfilling his promise after all.

Absently, he realized he was smiling.

With all this on his mind, it took him a while to notice that they'd been walking for some time and should've hit that black river by now.

"That rowboat," he said. "Why haven't we . . . ?"

"Because we're on a different path this time." Even as Lilac spoke, the white door back to Somnus' Palace came into view around a bend.

Proto looked at her. "We crossed a river that can make you forget everything, when there was another path the whole time?"

"Is that what you think? Even now?" She looked both amused and wistful.

"Not that I regret our odyssey, of course!" he reassured her. *Quite the contrary.*

She chuckled quietly. "No. You had to take the odyssey first. Once you reach a place here, you can come and go safely anytime. But there's always danger the first time."

"The black river, you mean?" he asked.

She shook her head. "Sometimes, the River Lethe. Sometimes, other things."

He opened his mouth to ask more, but held it back, feeling the moment beckoned something different.

"Well!" he declared after a pause. "Homebody that I am, I'll need a guide through all these perils."

"A guide?" She inclined her brow. "Well, I'm just a bartendress. But I'll be happy to accompany you."

"All the way to the destination?" he asked lightly. "Through peril and pitfall? Harm and hazard? Thick and thin?"

"Speaking one homebody to another"—she tapped a finger to the back of his hand—"as long as we stick together, I think we'll be okay." Her black gaze sparkled up at him.

Then, tapping the white door, she led him into Somnus' Palace and up the mirky stairway toward their destination.

Chapter 10
Apples and Kates

This morning, Proto took a left turn out of his room again.

The last time, he'd meant to explore a bit and find an alternate route to the lounge. Instead, he'd gotten lost, run into Dahlia, seen the Shadowcaster in action, and ended up skipping his visit that day.

As it happened, he ran into Dahlia again today—this time, quite literally.

He was rounding a corner, lost in thought, when abruptly a robed figure with a book in front of her face stood inches away. He managed to stop, but, rapt as she was, she plowed right into him.

"Oof!" cried Dahlia, bouncing off backward and dropping her book in surprise. She blinked at the sight of him. "Spunky, that was uncalled for! Behave yourself."

Feeling the full-bodied impact, Proto was reminded just how much shape was concealed by her shapeless robe. It made the pain a little pleasant.

"Well, anyway, don't just stare at me dumbly." She brushed a tress of long blonde hair off her face. "Pick up my book for me like a proper gentleman. Or, at least, your best impression of one."

Leaning down to lift the book, he read the cover: *The Taming of the Shrew and Other Elizabethan Comedies.*

He smiled involuntarily. He couldn't believe how lucky he was getting. One of the few literary courses he'd taken at his university was on Shakespeare. And this was one of the plays he'd read.

"Your book, mademoiselle." He held it forth with a bow and flourish.

"Well, you tried, anyway," she acknowledged languidly, flipping back to the proper page.

Then, she paused and looked at him. "Do you think I'm a shrew?"

"You, like Kate?" he replied, drawing on what he remembered of the play. "No, I don't see it."

She raised her eyebrows at him. Then, she removed her monocle. "Good! I think I have a little of her in me. But I do try to bury her deep."

"No, you're more a Viola or Rosalind," replied Proto, mustering up the only two names of Shakespearean comedy heroines that came to mind.

"Well, now you're just being nice," she replied, tilting her head at him thoughtfully. "But, more importantly, I'm beginning to think you actually know your literature. Last time, I'd thought you'd just gotten lucky."

"No, not for some time now," he said.

Her lips quirked up. "Behave yourself!" she repeated, bonking him on the head with her book. "There's that shrew for you."

"That's at least the fourth time your books have banged me," he noted, rubbing his head. "Talk about hard-hitting stories."

"True," she tittered. "Hard-hitting stories and powerful characters, I tend to fall for." She smoothed her rumpled robe. "Anyway, best learn your lesson and avoid a fifth time!"

"I'll try, but I'm not sure how much I'll remember after this concussion." He patted his skull.

She pursed her lips. "How could I help make this lesson more memorable?" Her blue gaze glimmered over a playful smile, framed by her long blonde hair.

Clusters of white flowers bloomed starkly against her black and red robe. Its looseness concealed what lay beneath, save the start of cleavage showing at the V of her neckline. "Maybe you're not a book learner?"

He blinked and considered how to reply.

"Ah, there you are," called a man from down the corridor—Mayger, Proto now saw. He was wearing a Steve McQueen bomber jacket, tasteful and understated, but his hair was in a pink pompadour.

Dahlia sighed and glanced skyward. "Searching for me, were you?"

"Not even slightly," replied the slender man.

"Ouch," frowned Dahlia. "Really now."

"I'll be overseeing our provisional visitor's visit today." Mayger gestured toward Proto. "Astrid is busy helping Somnus with something."

"Still? Seems like she's busy half the time with something or other," said Proto.

"I hope you're not too disappointed with the substitute." Mayger spread his arms forth winningly.

"He may wear leather, and spike his hair entirely too often, but he's a softie deep down." She patted Mayger on the pompadour. "He's just compensating."

"All too true," sighed Mayger lightly.

"He lets it show in his pink hair and his forgiving evaluations," Dahlia went on.

"All too true," the man repeated.

"You guys do evaluations of me?" asked Proto.

"Well, he does. And so does Astrid, Powers have mercy on you," said Dahlia. "There's a Kate for you!" she added in a murmur.

"I don't know any Kates here, but we should be getting to that dream," responded Mayger. "Sooner it's done, sooner I can go watch Grease."

Dahlia wrinkled her nose. "Philistine. Please don't let it influence your wardrobe too much."

"Too late," replied Mayger.

"Well, I'm all dressed and ready to go." Proto patted his blue, gold and white tracksuit with the Saturn logo.

Dahlia scanned him up and down. "You really ought to mix it up a little. How about a chiton? Do you have a chiton?"

"As long as you don't wear that robe Somnus gave you," said Mayger. "I'll give you a leather jacket if you promise never to wear that robe."

"I'll accept the jacket, as long as you don't borrow his hair dye," Dahlia told Proto.

"Do you have blue dye?" asked Proto.

Mayger shrugged and pursed his lips in thought. "That can be arranged—"

"That settles it. I'm going to join you on this visit," Dahlia broke in. "It seems someone needs to supervise the supervisor. Blue dye!" She shook her head grimly.

"You can join our visits too?" asked Proto. "I didn't know that was possible. Or allowed."

"It is if I allow it," said Mayger. "But giving a provisional visitor an audience is usually a bad idea. Best to avoid unnecessary pressure."

"Pressure?" retorted Proto. "I'm like braised brisket—best under pressure."

Dahlia scoffed a laugh out.

"So, come supervise!" Proto entreated grandiosely. "As long as you don't mind watching me fail miserably."

"Not at all, Braised Brisket! I could use a good laugh," she replied.

"There's that Kate again." He wagged a finger.

"Indeed. Rather shrewish of me," acknowledged Dahlia grimly. "But who knows? Maybe you won't fail utterly and lamentably. Maybe…you'll get lucky!" Her eyes sparkled like the bare sky.

"Well, I'll allow you to come then," said Mayger. "But who *is* this Kate? She sounds like Karen only meaner. Should I avoid her?"

"*Meaner than Karen? Not possible,*" Proto was about to respond.

Then, he realized Mayger was referring to "Karen" in the abstract, and not to Proto's first major girlfriend, Karen Black. She'd won him over, head over heels. In more than one way, she'd been his *first*.

Then, a few weeks into their relationship—when he'd been midway through making her a mixtape summing up his feelings for her, as one does at that time in life—he'd found out she'd told the world she'd only pretended to like him so he'd give her a Muse concert ticket.

That was the extent of Proto's experience with teenage romance.

"Avoid her? Probably, unless you want a bruised head," he replied instead, rubbing his skull again.

"I always wear protection." Mayger patted the pomaded pink solidity atop his head.

"You would," said Dahlia. "Anyway, shall we? All this foreplay is killing me."

"Come!" Mayger waved ahead and strode down the misty blue hallway.

"That's more like it. Straight to the action. In medias res!" declared Dahlia to Proto. "What can I say, I have classical tastes."

"I could tell by your toga," replied Proto.

"I *told* you, it's a chiton." She banged him on the head again with her book.

"Now I'll definitely need that help remembering," he mused, rubbing the location of his second bruise.

"Focus on your visit, Sir! I'll be watching closely." She donned her monocle and winked. "Also, remind me to get you a chiton."

Then, she lifted her book and resumed reading as they walked. Somehow, she managed to follow Mayger without once looking up until he turned to a sliding white door and tapped it.

The door slid open, and Mayger waved Proto onward. "After you."

Nodding, Proto started to head inside the mirky corridor, then paused. "Anything I should know before we go in?"

"Probably," shrugged Mayger. "But don't ask me what. I wasn't there for the shadowcasting. I'm just the substitute."

"Perfect." Proto advanced into the grey passage.

"Oh. It's *that* one!" he heard Dahlia call from outside the passage. Her voice sounded vague and faraway, almost like he was underwater. "Well, won't this be interesting!"

He wanted to turn around and ask what she was talking about. But, even now, he was crossing the threshold into the dream realm, and another voice was intruding on his attention.

"They're saying the invasion will come next week, you know."

Proto felt momentarily bleary and disoriented, like he'd just awoken from sleepwalking and found himself in an unfamiliar room of an unfamiliar house (which, indeed, had happened to him once).

Specifically, he stood in a small dining room with a quaint Victorian table and sideboard. Seated at one of several exquisitely carved chairs was Yemos—Proto's boyhood friend, who had lived down the road on Cherry Blossom Lane.

Proto generally had seen Yemos every month or two. The man always had weathered the years well—he'd barely looked a day older in his mid-twenties than at eighteen, apart from his neater hair and increased musculature.

So it was puzzling and disquieting for Proto to see a man with Yemos' face looking almost forty, with hints of grey along his dark brown temples. Some lines of care showed on his forehead. His elbows were resting on the table, and his interlocked fingers were in front of his face. He was wearing a mildly futuristic military uniform.

It occurred to Proto that there was nothing stopping a dreamer from imagining himself older than he was. It certainly was no more farfetched than imagining oneself as a starship commander or a fairy.

And, given how Dahlia had reacted—"*Oh, it's* that *one!*"—he felt sure that Yemos must be the dreamer. She'd seen him in the Shadowcaster, after all.

"But you'd already heard that, I'm sure," Yemos went on, looking up from his brooding.

Proto searched for a response. The problem was, he not only didn't know the question's context; he had no idea who *he* was in this dream. Looking down, he saw that his hands were worn and thickly muscled. He also was wearing a military uniform similar to Yemos'.

Proto looked over his shoulder. There was no trace of Dahlia or Mayger.

Well, he'd just have to ad lib for now. "Yes, not long ago," he nodded. He pulled a chair and sat down.

"If I were you, I'd leave the city by tonight. Gonna get awfully congested once the news gets out," said Yemos.

"And what about you?" asked Proto, scanning their surroundings and struggling to piece together what was going on.

"Well, that's the big question, isn't it?" replied Yemos.

Proto didn't know what to say to that. So he just leaned over the table and tried to look suitably thoughtful.

As he did so, he caught a glimpse of movement to his side—his face, passing in front of a mirror within the sideboard's china cabinet. Blond hair, narrow blue eyes, a chiseled jaw, and a mature face still fresh with vigor. It was the face of Yemos' twin younger brother, Mannus.

Proto had been close friends with both, though a bit less with Mannus. The younger brother often had hung out with a different crowd, especially after he'd started playing college football. But he'd always been a nice sort. If he'd been in a 1980s teen movie, he would've worn a varsity jacket, sauntered around with a tousled blond smile, and protected the protagonist from bullies.

"So you haven't decided yet," replied Proto—that is, Mannus. This seemed like a safe reply.

"I should think not," said Yemos. "Or else you'd be the first to know. For obvious reasons."

Proto wanted to roll his eyes. *Not so obvious from where I'm sitting!* Instead, he said, "Well, why don't you tell me what you're thinking about all this?"

"About the same that I was thinking last night," said Yemos. "Options 1, 2 and 3 are all equally unappealing."

This was getting ridiculous. How many times would he have to prompt this guy for a more detailed explanation?

"Remind me," said Proto-Mannus, "which options were 1, 2 and 3."

"Do I really have to say it again?" sighed Yemos, as mists swirled up to just below the tabletop. "Alright."

"Option 1 is, Ausrine and I run off together. We escape the invasion. We avoid dying in defense of a government that's betrayed us. The problem is, given her health condition, she needs weekly treatments. And the only places that offer those treatments, I'd be caught in a heartbeat and court-martialed as a deserter. So there's nowhere to run."

"Well," said Proto slowly, "that seems to rule out option 1, doesn't it?"

"No, it doesn't," frowned Yemos, as the mists rose to chest level. "Since Ausrine could still get that surgery. Simple procedure, and the problem's gone forever. We could run wherever we wanted and live a happy little life together, in some nook in the middle of nowhere."

Proto resisted the urge to reply and waited.

"Of course, if she gets the surgery, she can't have kids. Which has always been her dream, even though she's denying it now," added Yemos. "She's urging me to do this. She'd rather be the one who has to sacrifice here." He shook his head.

Proto nodded. "Option 2?" he asked after a moment.

"Option 2 is, I accept that promotion I was offered last week. I get transferred to the command center at Vesper. By the time the invasion comes, I'm long gone. Safe in the best-defended place on the continent."

"The problem is, then Ausrine is stuck here for the invasion," said Yemos. "I mean, she *could* leave. But all the other cities where her treatment is available are sealed off, without me there to give her access. So she'd need to get that surgery, then find some little village to run to. And if she's doing that, we may as well choose option 1 and run away together."

"In other words," concluded Yemos, "under option 1 or 2, it ends up being Ausrine who has to sacrifice."

Proto studied the look on Yemos' face—wistfulness, mingled with . . . *self-disgust? Tiredness?*

"So," Proto said, feeling a sudden rush of certainty, "we both know neither of those is really an option."

Yemos grimly met his gaze. "Yes. Yes, I came to the same conclusion overnight. Option 1 is the closest thing to a happy ending. But it's still wrong, I think."

"Then what's option 3?" asked Proto.

Yemos looked at him. "Are you really asking me to tell you?"

The mist crept above Proto's lips. He felt a rush of dizziness as he inhaled it, like carbon monoxide were replacing the oxygen in his lungs. Except instead of passing out, he was on the verge of waking up.

Anxiously, he tilted his head back above the mist. Time for a gamble.

"Let me make the sacrifice," said Proto—that is, Mannus. He wasn't sure what that would entail. But something in Yemos' tone made him sure this was right. "I'll do it."

Yemos smiled sadly and placed his head in his hands. This had the effect of hiding him almost entirely, given how high the mists were.

The voice that eventually emerged from that grey obscurity seemed far away. "I'm glad you're offering. It reassures me that my brother is the man I've always believed him to be. A man who's worthy of the life that lies before him."

Proto was close to responding when he noticed the mists beginning to sink. He paused and waited as Yemos' hair came back into view, followed by his downcast eyes, then his rueful smile.

"You would take my place. You'd lead the missile defense," said Yemos. "Yes, I know you're more than capable. And I know the Commander would let you. He's always liked you. The men like you. And you're one of them." He looked away, as the mists continued receding beneath the table. "No. You're who they *want* to be."

Proto-Mannus waved dismissively. He felt he'd gotten a vague sense of the background story now. "Whatever. I don't know about all that. But it should be me. You and Ausrine go off and have your happy ending. You have to help her. I'll be just fine here."

Midway through this response, Yemos had looked at him sharply. The mists abruptly had swelled back upward. "'You and Ausrine.' The way you say that." He squinted at Proto. "You have a noble heart. But there's noble, and then there's . . ." He shook his head.

The mists kept rising, as Proto searched in vain for a fitting reply.

"I know why you're offering this, and I'm not going to accept it . . . !" came Yemos' voice, as though from far away.

Proto stood and took a deep breath while he still could, watching the mist swirling up toward his lips. He struggled to figure out why Yemos would react this way. But his mind was a blank.

"Mannus?" called Yemos, unseen and barely audible now.

And the pale mist kept ascending, from breast level to neck level. Proto stood on his tiptoes.

There was a knock at the door. Proto blinked. Yemos didn't say anything, and his facial expression was hidden beneath the mists.

Then, abruptly, the dark-haired man was standing and striding down the hallway toward the door. He didn't meet Proto-Mannus' gaze as he did so.

Not sure what to do, Proto followed him. Meanwhile, the mists sank to chest level.

Yemos reached and opened the heavy industrial-looking front door.

Outside stood a woman dressed neatly in a little hat skewed sideways and her Sunday's best. On her face was a prim and genial smile, and swept over one shoulder was long blonde hair. It was Dahlia.

"Good *mor*ning!" she declared sweetly. "It's just a blessed day, isn't it?"

Yemos sighed and gave Proto-Mannus a glance.

"Finally some sun," agreed Proto. "Let there be light, huh?"

"I *know*, right!" agreed Dahlia eagerly.

Yemos gave Proto-Mannus a baleful look, then faced the visitor.

"So I'm here, first of all, to wish you the very best on this downright mi*ra*culous seventh day," said Dahlia. "Second, there's a question I wanted to ask you."

Miraculously, during this exchange, the mist had begun dwindling—first slowly, then rapidly. It now was at their ankles.

"Let me stop you right there," Yemos broke in. "I have a lot to think about today. And, no offense, but I'm just not going to add this to the list."

"I understand!" replied Dahlia chippily. "Everything has its time and place. So, let me ask you instead, if you could find it in your heart of hearts, to consider a small monetary contribution—"

"Oh, for Heaven's sake," grumbled Yemos impolitely.

Dahlia tilted her head at him and smiled. "Exactly!"

Then, she looked over Yemos' shoulder at Proto. "What about you back there? Care to make a contribution? You'd help feed the hungry. Including myself." She beamed sunnily. "Or, better yet, you could just buy me lunch."

Yemos turned to Proto-Mannus and gave him a disgusted and envious smile. "Even one of *them!* Some things never change, eh?" Slapping his twin brother on the back, he walked back toward the other room.

Dahlia winked at Proto. "I'm free this afternoon!" she declared cheerily.

Proto pointed at her. "We'll talk in a bit."

She nodded happily and waved, as Proto closed the door and headed back to the other room.

Inside, Yemos was staring out the window at an enclosed garden. "It's funny," he said to his brother—that is, to Proto. "I spent years on this garden. Literal years of spare time. Spare life. And here's what they went toward: Hedges. Rare plants. An apple tree. A tire swing used by no one. Except me." He smirked sadly.

"Hey," said Proto-Mannus, improvising a little. "I'll have you know I've used that swing."

The mist swirled up a few inches, but Yemos smiled. "Oh? Snuck a ride or two? In that case, it all feels worth it."

A quiet moment passed. Proto felt sure the issue they'd been discussing—Yemos' three options—was central to resolving this dream. But, given his close call with the mists a minute ago, he was reluctant to raise the issue. Not yet, anyway.

"What do you think our odds are?" he asked instead. "To turn back the invasion, I mean."

"Well, I'll tell you this," replied Yemos. "Win or lose, there won't be a city left here. Win or lose, this will become a ghost town—all too literally. We had dreams for this place. They won't come to pass. Win or lose, this will be a place of fire and ash. It's just a question of who's burning amid the rubble and who's limping away from it." He smiled ruefully. "And apple trees and tire swings? They'll be memories. If we win."

"Alright, that's enough of that," Proto broke in, holding out a palm. "You're right, of course. But there's no point dwelling on the inevitable. Have a drink or something."

Yemos raised an eyebrow. "Eat, drink and be merry, for tomorrow—"

"For tomorrow, we turn back an invasion and achieve glorious victory. Or not," declared Proto. "We'll make it or we won't. We'll do our best, and in the end, things will get sorted out."

"That's well and good," sighed Yemos. "But some decisions still must be made before tomorrow."

"Where are the drinks?" asked Proto firmly.

Yemos chuckled and thumbed toward a closet. "Get me a bourbon, will you."

"Sure, if mine's on you," replied Proto, strolling to the closet and opening it.

Behind the door stood Mayger, poised stiffly in a gap in front of the shelf. The space was so tight that his pink pompadour had been flattened against the door.

Bloody Hell!

Proto resisted the urge to turn and check if Yemos was looking. Doing so would only increase the likelihood that he'd glance over and see what was right in front of him.

Mayger slowly reached for a brown bottle and handed it over, followed by two glasses. He gave a thumbs up.

"Nice selection here," called Proto as he closed the door.

Yemos looked up as his brother approached the table. He gave a guffaw of disbelief upon seeing the bottle. "The sky's about to fall, and *that's* what you pick?" The mists rose. So did Yemos, who started toward the closet. "Are we really related? Do I even know you?"

"Oh, for Heaven's sake!" replied Proto nervously, waving the bottle in Yemos' face. "Armageddon's here, your brother's sharing a drink with you, and you're whining about his tastes in bourbon?"

"Alright," laughed Yemos, "alright." He sat back down, as Proto poured two generous glasses.

They sipped in silence. After a few minutes, the lines on Yemos' brow started smoothing. His breaths grew longer and slower.

"Good call," he eventually remarked, lifting his glass.

"Like a charm, huh?" agreed Proto.

The dark-haired man nodded, eying his whiskey. "It makes some details blurry. But that just forces you to look at the big picture."

Proto wasn't sure what that meant. But he felt the time was right now. "So, as I was saying earlier, you should let me take your place—"

"The answer is no," Yemos replied firmly. "You're not going to make my sacrifice for me, any more than Ausrine is."

"Yemos, I can lead—"

"No," he interrupted. "Yes, you could lead them valiantly and well. But no, you will not."

The dark-haired man looked out the window again. "No, when the fires fall, and the lights streak across Heaven, and the redounding blasts rock the earth, and all is pandaemonium, I'll be in its midst. And you will not."

Resolution showed in his eyes. But was this really the right resolution?

Proto shook his head. "You're being fatalistic. Be creative. There must be other options."

Yemos smiled sadly. "Sometimes, life calls for a tragedy. And trying to avoid it will just make it worse."

A darkening in the window caught Proto's gaze. Grey clouds were bulging and weltering toward them from afar. *"The point of no return,"* Astrid had called it when those clouds arrived.

"I—" Proto started.

"Don't argue. I need you to promise me something important. It's about Ausrine." Yemos' dark gaze had taken on a narrowed zeal. "I know you feel the same about her now as a decade ago. Even if you're too noble-hearted to say anything. And I've always wondered what would've happened if *you'd* gone on that first trip with her, instead of me."

This was getting weird. Proto felt he like he was watching a train derail. But what words could stop a train from derailing?

"I need you to promise me, Mannus, that you'll take care of Ausrine like your own family. Whether as a sister or . . . " Yemos shook his head. "Just promise me, okay?"

Proto-Mannus stared back. With strange and abrupt certainty, he sensed that his response here would determine something very important—something whose consequences would redound far beyond this worn man facing him.

He had no idea why that'd be the case. This whole dream of an impending invasion was a fiction. Why would it matter what relationship two of his childhood acquaintances had with this Ausrine? Assuming she even existed?

The sober and cerebral part of Proto told him that, most likely, Yemos had been carried away by fatalistic hysteria. He'd been swept away by a delusional belief that he had to undergo some tragedy; that he had to lose his love; that his brother was meant to succeed in his place. The rational part of Proto told him that Yemos probably just needed to calm down, put things in perspective, and keep seeking solutions for whatever real problems he faced.

But that wasn't the part of Proto that spoke. "I promise," he replied.

Yemos smiled grimly and clasped Proto-Mannus' hand. "I knew you would, brother. And I know you'll keep your promise."

He turned to stare out the window. The burgeoning clouds were close now. They'd darkened since a minute earlier, and flames now fringed them. The sky itself was reddening ominously.

"Something is coming," spoke Yemos, sounding far away. His military uniform was blurring away, and the world was turning shadowy. "Something beyond what you or I understand. We're just players on a stage. But I'll play my part. I'll play my part."

Proto stared. What was he talking about? This was unlike any other dream he'd visited. What were those fires lacing the heavens?

But even as he pondered this, the dark mirk bulged and sweltered into the quaint little dining room, obliviating the hues and forms of the dream.

And abruptly, Proto was hurtling through grey obscurity, as flecks of starlight spun in silent parallax.

He lurched back into being in the misty blue hallway of Somnus' Palace.

"Oh!" cried Dahlia as she apparated beside him, flinging a hand out as she stumbled forward in her Victorian robe. Apparently, she'd lost her Sunday's best along the way.

Catching her balance, she clasped her hand to her bouncing breast and took a deep breath. "Well, that was exhilarating, wasn't it?"

Mayger, in contrast, had landed smoothly and stood a few steps ahead of them. He was looking thoughtfully at nothing, his hands in the pockets of his bomber jacket.

"Nice move back there," Proto told Dahlia. "'It's just a *blessed* day, isn't it?'" he mimicked cheerily.

"Wasn't it though!" she cried. "I was near-drowning in mists when I decided I'd better do something. Thank Heaven it worked."

"Thank Lady Luck," corrected Mayger, glancing skyward.

"Luck, you think?" She turned to him, hands on her hips. "Funny how I, the shadowseer, had to help out our provisional visitor. I wonder, where were *you?* His mentor. Supposedly."

"Stuck where I couldn't do anything," said Mayger. "In the closet."

Dahlia tilted her head at him. She smiled.

"Don't even," said the pink-haired man.

Dahlia beamed. "I said, where *were* you, not—"

Mayger took Dahlia's book out of her hands and bonked her lightly on the head with it.

"An attack! On a lady!" she cried, seizing the book. She started to swing it toward Mayger's pompadour, but made it bounce backward as it struck the springy pink form. "Deflected? What is this fell sorcery?"

"I always wear protection," repeated Mayger, patting his pink head.

Dahlia tilted her head and smiled again.

Mayger pointed at her. "Don't even!"

"Hm. Is that a lump?" said Dahlia, rubbing above her forehead.

"Now we have a matching set," noted Proto, patting his own head.

"We *do*, don't we?" she enthused. "Well, as they say, life's best pleasures are shared. And books are a close second."

"Dare I ask what's number one?" said Proto.

"Apples!" she replied instantly, retrieving one from her robe's pocket. She tossed it far above him and out of reach, then snatched it just as it was about to land in his waiting palm. She winked at him.

"Not oranges?" he replied.

She waved dismissively. "One taste will disabuse you of that notion."

Now it was Mayger tilting his head and smiling at them. He looked thoughtful. "Speaking of pink lumps on heads," he said after a moment, "that closet door messed up my hair. I'm going to stop by my room. See you two in a bit."

"Yes, you're looking a bit flat," affirmed Dahlia, smoothing her robe and not looking very flat at all. "Off with you!"

Mayger chuckled quietly and strode off, hands in the pockets of his bomber jacket.

Part of Proto was pondering what'd just happened in that dream—the fiery skies, Yemos' ominous speech, and the bizarreness involving his brother and Ausrine.

Is something going to happen to Yemos? Or is it broader than just him? Why is it him in particular that's dreaming this? Is it tied to me? Could it really be coincidental?

But, as important as these questions felt, it was getting hard for Proto to focus on them, now that he found himself alone with a certain shadowseer.

She was intently regarding him and twirling a strand of blonde hair around her little finger. He felt like he was that lock of hair.

"So!" She preened, eying the provisional visitor. "Back to our conversation earlier."

"Which one?" asked Proto. "About braised brisket or blue hair dye?"

"About making lessons memorable." She planted her hands on her hips. "What, had you forgotten already? Today hasn't been memorable enough yet?"

"Either that, or that book of yours banged the memory out of me." He pointed at his head where The Taming of the Shrew had made contact.

"Ah, well as long as that's taken care of." She aloofly turned her nose up and sauntered away. "One way or another."

Proto blinked and eyed the eccentric bookish blonde.

About ten yards later, she turned and waved him onward. "Hint: Chase chase chase!" she called.

Lips curving upward, he obliged and jogged toward her.

She put a hand over her mouth in gasping mock-horror. "You'll never take my apple!" she cried melodramatically, then turned and fled, lifting the sides of her robe like a long dress.

Laughing, he sped up as she turned left at an intersection, vanishing from view. "You can't hide!" he menaced. "The apple will be mine!" He followed her around the corner.

There stood Somnus. His head was askew, and one hand was on the hip of his green-and-purple robe. He regarded Proto with bemusement.

Dahlia stood calmly beside him. She looked as reflectively detached as a librarian. The only hint of their pursuit was a single dislodged blonde tress over her forehead, which, even now, she was brushing aside.

"'The apple'?" questioned the Lord of Dreams. "Are you hungry, Proto?"

Proto felt his face turn red as an apple. " . . . yes. Sure worked up an appetite during today's visit."

"I daresay." Somnus' lips quirked upward. "Well, you'll get your fill soon enough. Whether it's apples or oranges, or coffees and cocktails." His eyes glimmered with strange zeal.

"For now, though," he went on, "I need to steal Dahlia for a bit. Something odd is going on up there in the breathing world—something quite serious, I think! In fact, I think you and that Yemos fellow saw some traces of it just now. So, in short, I'll need our good shadowseer's help with the Shadowcaster."

"As for you, Provisional Visitor, you're off-duty for the day. And as for that appetite, why not have a snack at the lounge? It's on me." The dusky-haired man smiled amiably.

Proto often struggled to muster up a reply when Somnus was speaking. By the time he figured out what the man was getting at, he was always about two seconds too late to reply to it.

"Yes, go have a snack! Meanwhile, here I am, at Somnus' beck and call," pouted Dahlia. "Never mind Miss Shadowseer's appetites!"

"Soon enough, soon enough," assured the Lord of Dreams, turning and walking away.

"Here, promise me you won't eat this." Dahlia tossed her apple to Proto. "I'll share it with you later. If you can stave off your appetite till then!"

"Looks tasty." He lifted it toward his mouth.

"Don't eat the forbidden fruit!" she chastised, wagging a finger. "Not without me, anyway."

"Life's best pleasures are shared," agreed Proto.

Dahlia tilted her head at him and smiled. "I think we're on the same page." She waved farewell with her book.

"Are we coming?" called Somnus from down the corridor.

The blonde woman turned and bustled off in her Victorian robe. "Don't get your knickers in a twist."

"The way they address the Lord of Dreams these days!" lamented Somnus, shaking his long-haired head.

"It's high time you updated your titles," she replied archly, catching up with him down the hall. "How about Prince of Pests? Or Baron of Bothers! Viscount of Vexation! The Nabob of Nags!"

"Nabob!" he mused. "I've been around aeons, and I daresay you're the first to call me 'nabob.'"

They disappeared around a corner, and their voices faded. This left Proto alone with his thoughts.

And Dahlia's apple, of course. He studied it—firm and large, ripe and juicy. On its shiny smoothness, he could see a silhouette reflection of himself.

"Admiring some fruit? Or yourself?" called a voice down the hall-way—Mayger, Proto saw as he looked up. Somehow, he'd already reshaped his hair into a spiky punk do. He was wearing a denim vest with torn-off sleeves. "Same difference, maybe?"

"A little bit of both." Proto tossed the apple far above him and out of reach, then caught it. His smile probably looked giddy and vapid, but he didn't feel like suppressing it.

"Well, if you're not too busy with that, some friends and I need a fourth for cards," said Mayger. "Care to join?"

"If I can eat and play at the same time, sure," replied Proto, pocketing the apple. "I'm starving."

"Is there any other way to play?" replied Mayger. "Let's go grab some caviar and mozzarella sticks."

And off they went down misty halls of blue.

Buoyed by the events of the last hour or so, Proto felt he was floating along, light and airy as a dream. He got along well with Mayger's friends, Jet and Jag—the two whiskery black-haired identical twins he'd seen previously in the lounge. And he played well at cards too. Lady Luck was with him today.

Yet, the whole time, he felt he was only half-there. The rest of him was somewhere warm and vague, yet slowly clarifying in his mind's eye; still faraway, yet closer by the day.

Chapter 11

Cracks

or, Black and White and Red All Over

As Proto strolled down the misty blue hallway toward the lounge, it occurred to him that it'd been a while since he'd seen Astrid. They'd visited that fairy dream with the GSIs in the woods. He thought it'd gone well—at least, as well as an absurdist romantic comedy could go. But afterward, she'd disappeared on him, and he hadn't seen her in the multiple days since then.

Nor did he see her upon entering the lounge. It was relatively empty, though Lilac of course was present at the bar. A few customers were lined up there to order.

The pale bartendress looked at him as he entered. He raised a hand and opened his mouth to greet her. But before he could get a word out, she'd quickly turned away and strode toward the coffee machine. Her loosely tied black hair swished behind her as she stepped.

He let his hand fall and his mouth shut. *Well, good morning.* He ambled over to a small table and sat down. He generally didn't like standing in lines, if he could wait nearby instead.

Absently, he peered at the vast painting on the wall, with the long-bearded old man and that butterfly-winged fairy watching the young swain and maiden on the beach. The sea in the painting looked misty. It reminded Proto of the Sea of Dreams that Lilac had shown him.

Come to think of it, the young man looked a bit like *him*, right down to the navy blue and yellow apparel—though, of course, he wasn't wearing a tracksuit. As for the young woman, her appearance was harder to make out. She was looking away with windswept hair reflecting the sun. Its color was hard to discern, like that online photo of a dress that some people swore was blue and black, and others swore was white and gold.

"Not thirsty this morning?"

He blinked and turned. There was Lilac, looking down at him in her French waitress outfit with a little plate in two hands. Atop it was his usual black mug with a white-lacquered crack.

Maybe it was early morning bleariness, but he found this confusing, given that he hadn't placed an order. "That's . . . " he started, then dumbly paused.

Her face stayed straight as usual, but her ears went pink. "No point making you order if I know what it'll be, right?"

He glanced at the bar. The same customers who'd been waiting in line when he walked in were still waiting there.

A warm tingling swelled through Proto's breast. "Exactly right! I approve of this reasoning." He took a sip. "And this coffee."

Her black eyes sparkled. "As you should." She turned and primly walked back to the bar. There was a hint of bounce to her step, which translated through her skirt's frilly lace.

After a moment, his gaze drifted from her back to that painting again. Something else about it seemed familiar, but he couldn't quite put his finger on it. Not even after several minutes of sipping his coffee and waking up.

"May I join you?"

Proto looked over from the painting. Lilac was standing beside the table again. Her two hands were clasped, and her white-stockinged legs were touching at the knee.

He crooked his head and held out his hands. "Leaving your station unmanned?"

"Yes. I'll be five full yards away," she acknowledged in a surreptitious half-whisper. "I won't even be able to reach the coffee machine!"

"Well. Partners in crime then!" he declared. "Have a seat, co-conspirator."

She daintily sat down and faced him with a glimmering gaze. But she remained silent.

Proto tried to think of things to say. But he found his mind kept wandering to the business of the day. "Has Astrid been around? I'm supposed to meet her here for today's visit."

"Oh, Astrid. She left a message for you," replied Lilac. "She's busy again. She says that you can take another day off, like the other day. An 'odyssey' day." Her lips curved up. "Or, if you wanted, you could take on an optional visit that she has to miss. But she didn't think it was necessary for you to go."

"An optional . . . ?" Proto began, then frowned. "Wait. I'd be doing this visit alone? Even as a 'provisional visitor,' or whatever you called it?"

"Well, yes. This isn't an interventional visit. It's an *observational* visit," she explained. "In other words, this isn't a visit where you have to steer anything the right way. You just watch it and report back." She glanced away. "If, of course, you decide to. You're not required to. It didn't sound like Astrid was too concerned about it." She looked back at him. "How's your coffee, by the way?"

He gave it two thumbs up, then extended his index fingers toward her and made a firing noise. She wrinkled her nose and shook her head at him but smiled.

She seemed to be waiting for him to say more, but he was lost in thought. Astrid's absence was beginning to worry him. As well as their visit to the fairy forest had gone, somehow, things had veered off course during their brief exchange afterward.

It had seemed trivial at the time—maybe some accidental snub that'd soon be forgotten, or maybe just his imagination. But now he was concerned that Astrid was avoiding him.

Sometimes, when things veer slightly off course, you can end up very far apart, if you don't course-correct quickly. Proto was starting to worry that he should've corrected course much earlier—back when Astrid had strode wordlessly out of the lounge, leaving him behind.

"Where is she today, anyway?" he asked absently.

"Hm?" Lilac's black eyes were fixed intently upon him. "Oh, Astrid? I'm not sure. But she said she didn't need anything from you today."

"Ah." Proto suppressed a wince. That didn't sound good.

As he brooded, Lilac's lips pressed in thought. "Which means," she finally said, "you'd have time for a day trip. An odyssey, even. But no rivers of forgetfulness, I promise. Just a little peril and hazard." She beamed faintly, like a crack of sun between two clouds.

"Hm?" He'd been pondering how Astrid was a bit like a geode—hard and rough on the outside, but fey and pristine inside. There were some gleaming cracks in her craggy exterior. They showed sometimes when her violet gaze went wide. But the instant she turned away, those shining glimmers from the depths were gone.

Lilac blinked at him. "Oh, I just said . . . never mind." She smiled forcedly toward his coffee. "How do you like it?"

"Oh, I like it here." There was much more he could say, but his mind was elsewhere right now. "I'm starting to think being a visitor suits me."

"Ah." She took a deep breath and let it out. Then, her two small fists went firm, and she smiled again. "Well, if you want more coffee, let me know. An odyssey takes lots of energy."

"Oh, is today's dream a long one? Did Astrid tell you what it was about?" He very much hoped this visit went well. He felt he was at a point of inflection with her. If he messed up today too badly, things suddenly might become irrecoverable. *But* what *might become irrecoverable?* "Does it involve a long trip?"

"No, I meant—never mind," said Lilac. "I just mean, with how hard you work, you might need two coffees! And maybe a cocktail afterward." Her black eyes sparkled.

"Think I'm good for now," Proto absently replied. "Probably should pass on cocktails before a visit!"

"Oh, no, I was saying . . . " Lilac stared at him and trailed off. "Anyway."

"So, did Astrid tell you where my visit is today?" he asked.

Her lips pressed faintly. "The optional visit is at H4 in the Zone of the Ram."

He nodded. He knew what that meant now. The identical twins he'd played cards with, Jet and Jag, had explained room names and locations to him the other day. The system was surprisingly simple. The trickiest part was that the doors seemed unmarked. But in fact, the silvery glow strips on the walls beside them had slight variations to identify which rooms were which.

He'd also learnt that there was no secret method for opening the white doors, which slid open at Astrid's and Mayger's touch but not his own. The doors simply were designed to open only at the touch of a visitor. Not a "provisional visitor" like himself.

"Sounds good," replied Proto. "By the way, uh, do I need someone to open the door for me? I'm not a visitor yet. As far as I know."

Lilac shook her head. "Since it's an observational visit, the door should provide observational-level access. Meaning non-visitors can enter unattended. Like, say, you and me." Her eyes flicked up and met his. "No invitation is necessary or anything."

"Hm, helpful to know," he replied.

She stared a couple seconds as though waiting for him to say more. "Astrid hadn't taught you that yet? That non-visitors like you and me, or both, can enter some rooms? Like this one?"

"Nope," he sighed. "But I guess I haven't seen her in a few days. I'm starting to think she might be avoiding me."

" . . . are you concerned?" asked Lilac.

"I'm starting to be," said Proto.

"Yes," said Lilac after a moment. "It's probably concerning to go for days without a mentor."

"Without a mentor?" he said idly. "Oh, no, Mayger does a good job as substitute."

"Ah." Lilac's face went blanker. She looked more like she had when he'd first met her.

He hardly noticed. He had a sinking feeling that he'd messed up a few days ago and was struggling to think of a way to fix things. He sipped his coffee and pondered. "By the way, how long do I have to get to this dream?"

She checked her watch—a simple black and white circle, but with cat ears—and inhaled sharply. "About two minutes."

He blinked and leapt to his feet. As he did so, his arm swept across the table, swatting the black mug with the white-lacquered crack. It flew off the table and struck the floor, fracturing into two pieces—a new crack, not the one that'd been repaired already. His remaining coffee splattered across the tiles.

Lilac looked at him with wide eyes.

"Oh." Frozen in place, Proto stared. He started to reach for the mug's pieces, then stopped, unsure what to do.

She faced the broken mug. "You'd best get going," she said emotionlessly. "You'll be late."

"I . . . don't have to," he replied. "Here, let me help—"

"No. Go. I insist." She leaned and grabbed the remnants.

He stared at her, mouth open to speak. But already she was gliding away, one black mug piece in each pale hand, her long black hair swishing behind her.

Pressing his lips, he forced himself away and into the hallway, jogging to try to make the dream in time.

It was only now that he realized he might be leaving more behind than the lounge.

Never had this dream felt realer. Real life involved making choices. And, in the end, failure to choose was also a choice.

"You haven't made any choices you can't take back. Not yet," Somnus had told him days ago. But what about now?

As he ran toward the Zone of the Ram, the blue corridors looked mistier than usual. But maybe that was just the dismal bleariness within him, translating itself outward upon the world.

Sometimes, late at night, you get the weary feeling that everything is wrong, and staying awake longer could only make it worse, and the only possible respite is sleep's dark oblivion. That's how Proto felt right now, racing toward the dream realm. But he would find no respite there—no, he was going there to study how the world could go more wrong.

At least he made it to H4 in Zone of the Ram without having to backtrack. And a good thing too. If his count was right, it'd been nearly two minutes since he'd left the lounge. But somehow, that just made him feel worse, like a warm breeze after being submerged in cold water.

He tapped the door. It smoothly slid open, seeming slower than it ever had before. He slipped in as soon as he could fit and jogged in through the passage. The world beyond was so mirky that he couldn't make out what loomed there—not till he had stepped across the threshold.

He found himself upon a barren plain. The dirt was reddish-brown. Clouds of mist were drifting all about him. But there were gaps between them, almost like tunnels, forming and unforming as the mirk moved.

Against the black void overhead sparkled a sea of stars—not the sparse dots that blink feebly in cities, but the shining galaxies and nebulae that glitter over deserts and tundras. Their light was enough to give the world color, but only twilit greyish hues.

So . . . where to? He supposed one direction was as good as another. But he was uneasy with the idea of striding through these mists. They didn't look harmful—just wisps of whitish grey. And the mists that woke you up in other dreams weren't just roving clouds like these. *Still . . .*

Focusing, he tried to move the mists, the way he could control other dreams. But it had absolutely no effect.

Frowning, he held out a palm and tried to conjure up the first thing he could think of—caviar and mozzarella sticks, the meal he'd eaten with Mayger, Jet and Jag the other day. A silver platter instantly appeared atop his hand.

Interesting. This just reinforced his concerns about touching those mists, whatever they were. If the rest of this place worked like a normal dream, why didn't those mists? He idly cast the platter aside, and it dissipated before it hit the ground.

At the same time, a snippet of sound broached the mists—a girl singing. Listening closely and catching a few more snippets, he managed to discern where it was coming from.

It seemed clear that that was where he ought to go. The problem was, a wall of mist loomed between him and her. Probably multiple walls of mist. And there were no apparent tunnels toward her.

He moved toward the edge of the mists, where the white wisps were dwindling from semilucency to nothing. Cautiously, he leaned about a foot away and took a slight breath.

Instantly, he felt lightheaded and the world went mottled red-black, like when you stand too quickly and verge on fainting.

Reeling, he stepped back swiftly and took several breaths. He bowed his head and tensed his muscles so blood would flow back to his brain. Neither seemed to help much, but the dizziness eventually faded.

Well, that's odd. It was clear now that this was a different sort of dream. What *were* those mists?

There was that voice again. It was barely audible now—probably not even recognizable as a girl singing, if he'd not heard it earlier.

Grimacing, he scanned for the nearest tunnel heading at least slightly in her direction, then took off toward it.

He'd always been a good runner. He didn't even need to speed himself beyond his natural limits to make it through the tunnel before shifting mists sealed it off.

"Good thing I wore my tracksuit, huh!" he murmured to the misty wastes. It felt satisfying finally to reply to the thousand remarks about his outfit. He rubbed the Saturn logo fondly.

The voice was still far away, but at least it was discernibly a girl singing again. He searched for more tunnels leading at least somewhat toward her, and this time there were three.

He started toward one of them, then paused and conjured a glass bottle. "Lady Luck guide me!" he invoked, only half-ironically. He spun the bottle on the ground. It ended up pointing at the leftmost tunnel. "Thanks!" he called toward the heavens, already running toward that tunnel. "I hope."

One way or another, this turned out to be a good choice. After winding away from the singing for a minute or so, the tunnel curved back toward it. Soon, the song was growing perceptibly louder by the second.

"In every petal, You are there," he heard her singing.

Judging by the sound, she must be no more than ten yards away now, just across the wall of mists he was facing. No tunnels led toward her. But after a moment of staring vainly at the mirk, he noticed part of it thinning to a gauzelike wispiness. On the other side, he could see a girl's figure and the redness of her hair.

"In every vein of every leaf," came the girl's voice.

After an instant's deliberation, he decided to take the chance. He darted toward the thinning wall and leapt, closing his eyes.

As he entered the mists, a giddy daze swept over him, despite the fact he was holding his breath. It felt like he'd been launched tumbling through the air. As a result, he lost his bearings and stumbled to his hands and knees on the other side of the mists.

"In seeming chaos—" the girl was singing, when she abruptly cut off at the sound of Proto scuffing the dirt and exhaling.

Long red hair fell loose around her face, which was dusted faintly with freckles. Her eyes were shamrock-hued and had a fey curve. Her gossamer tunic of green was loose but clung to her frame, which was slender even for her youth—maybe eighteen years old or so. Clasped in two hands were a bunch of blood-red wildflowers.

"You . . . " She squinted at him. Her green gaze had the blazing sheen of starlight.

Then, she smiled blithely. "Hello there."

It occurred to Proto that he should be doing something to fit within the narrative of this dream, rather than standing here dumbly and weirding out this girl.

"Finally! I was worried I'd never find someone out here," he ad libbed, exhaling with relief. "My car broke down back there. I tried to find my way back to the road, but I got lost with these mists."

She tilted her head at him. "Why are you saying that? We both know this dream for what it is."

He blinked. This dream was getting stranger by the second.

"I'm impressed you made it here," she went on. "We're awfully far into the Mists! They drift far across the dream border around here."

He stared blankly for a few seconds. "I . . . don't understand what that means."

"That's okay! You don't need to," she answered cheerfully. "But would you like to walk with me? I'm headed this way." She waved directly toward a wall of mists.

"Um, I would. But if I tried to walk through those mists, I think I'd wake up," he replied.

"Yup, you would. *If* yours truly weren't here!" With a sprightly whirl toward the mists, she waved a hand. It glowed red as she did so.

Instantly, the mists parted into a tunnel before her.

"After you, Sir," she gestured with a curtsey—then strode in front of him as he approached. "Just kidding! Try to keep up." She giggled over her shoulder at his bafflement.

"The way you cleared those mists," he said slowly, following her. "I tried to do that earlier, but it didn't work. Could you teach me how?"

"Nope, I don't think so," she winced and smiled. "But feel free to visit anytime if you want a walk through the Mists! It gets lonely out here."

"But wait, how do you know I can't move the mists like that?" asked Proto.

"I can see it all around you. Wrong aura." She pointed at him. "As Gramps would say, 'You don't have the proper affinity for that.'" She wheezed these words out in an old man's warbling tones.

"But we're all different. Your aura's very interesting!" she politely hastened to assure him. "It matches your outfit." She tapped the tracksuit's Saturn logo.

"That's the first nice remark about my clothes in a long time," he replied.

"Don't let it go to your head, Mister!" she chided lackadaisically, waving toward him. His tracksuit abruptly transformed to a jester's outfit—navy, yellow and white, complete with a Saturn logo. "Your aura matches this one too."

He scanned his garb, then nodded grimly at her. She giggled.

"I'm going to guess," he replied to the freckled redhead girl with blood-hued flowers, "going way out on a limb here, that your aura is red."

"You can't see that. How did you . . . ?" she began, tilting her head at him—and then her cheeks went red, as she ran a hand through her hair. "Oh, we're going to go there, are we Mister! You'll be seeing a lot more red soon!" She held a glowing palm toward him.

Suddenly the mists were swirling around him on all sides, forming a tornadic cylinder. Eyes wide, he stood straight and stiff as a board, holding his breath.

Just as abruptly, the mist dervish disappeared, leaving him with the spritely girl.

She was beaming. "Oh, that face!" She opened her eyes bulging-wide and stood shiveringly stiff on her tiptoes, then fell into laughter. "*So* perfect!"

"Now that you've tornadoed me," he replied, "maybe you can tell me your name. I'm Proto."

"First-name basis, huh?" she giggled. "Fair enough! I'm Mercune."

"So, Mercune. This is your dream we're in, right?" He gestured at their surroundings. "Or are you a visitor?"

"Well, yes and no. I'm dreaming, and you came into my dream," she said. "But when you're this far into the Mists, it sort of stops being your own dream and becomes everyone's dream! Kind of." She shrugged thoughtfully. "As for whether I'm a 'visitor,' I don't know what that means. But I take it that's what you guys call yourselves."

"Um, yes," he said.

"Yeah, I've had a few other 'visitors' like you. They sneak into my dreams and try to fit in, and I play along like I don't know what they're doing. It's kind of fun freaking them out! Like this." She wafted a palm upward.

Mists began swirling from the dirt toward Proto's waist. His eyes widened.

She tittered and waved, and the mists dissipated. "But yeah, anyway, you're the first to stop by while I'm in the Mists. This is serious business! No play out here. As you can see."

" . . . this is utterly bizarre," observed Proto.

"Oh?" She planted her hands on her hips. "What's bizarre is that some cabal of creepsters goes around dreamstalking young girls like me!"

"Somnus does call himself the Darkling Stalker," he acknowledged with a shrug.

"Yep, Creepola!" she declared. " . . . wait, Somnus? I know that name. He's one of Flua-Sahng's sons, right? She says he's funny. And he wears fancy clothes and drinks too much."

"That about sums it up," affirmed Proto.

Mercune heeheed. "That's cool though. You're the first other person I've met who talks to the Elements. Or, I guess, 'Daemons' is what they're called in dreams like this. You call them 'Elements' when they're up on the breathing world. And they're 'Mists' when they're in the Mists. They're 'Daemons' when they're in between."

Proto struggled to sift some sense from this word stream. "The first *other* person who talks to them, you said?"

"Yep!" As she spoke, she waved a glowing hand, and the mists before them parted. He followed her into the new tunnel. "Even Gramps has never *talked* to them," she went on. "The brilliant scientist Fyrir! The man who unearthed the Fossil! The man whose genius will power a new world!" She rolled her eyes in smiling teenage fashion.

"Fyrir?" repeated Proto, staring at her. He *had* heard of a scientist with that name. Who hadn't? The man had been all over the news recently. He'd uncovered some weird red rock that served as an energy source—nearly limitless and pollution-free.

The Fossil, Fyrir had called that rock. Proto didn't know why. He assumed it was something about how this Fossil was going to make fossil fuel obsolete. There had been a bunch of news stories with cheesy titles like *This Rock Rocks* and *Forget Fusion, We've Got a Fossil*.

"'Gramps,' you said. Are you Fyrir's granddaughter?" he asked.

"Well, technically no. He adopted me. But he's old, so I call him Gramps," she explained. "These days, I'm sort of his assistant."

Proto arched an eyebrow. "You're a scientist?"

"Hey! I'll have you know, he says I have a *talent for physics!*" She wheezed the last part out in an elder's warbling voice. "But no. My interests lie elsewhere." She waved with queenly dismissiveness.

"How do you 'assist' him then?" asked Proto.

"I do lots of stuff! Like this." She pointed gun-like at the mists and, with a murmured "*pow!,*" flicked her hand upward with recoil. Something invisible shot through the mists, clearing a path. "Also, I taught Gramps what the Fossil was."

" . . . and how did you figure that out?" he asked.

"Figure it out? How would I do that? I'm just a girl with some gifts! And a talent for physics." Mercune flipped her red hair archly. "No, I know what the Fossil is because Flua-Sahng told me. And she should know! It's her own Fossil."

Proto shook his head, struggling to follow all this. "Wait, this Flua-Sahng. You mentioned her earlier. You said she's like Somnus, right? She's one of the—Elements? Or Daemons, you called them?"

"Yep! The Mother of All! We're tight, Flua-Sahng and I. Not to brag!" said the perky redhead. "She's so sweet though. Big softie. Always going all starry-eyed and talking about Fate and true love. And she knows about everything! But I guess that's not surprising, since she sort of created everything."

"Sort of created everything?" repeated Proto. "What does that mean?"

"Well, I could try to explain. But, better yet, why don't you *ask her!*" She swung a red-glowing hand dramatically, clearing the thick mists before them.

There, eminent amid the mists, stood a lady. She wore radiant raiment of starlike leaves. Behind her sunset-colored tresses was a queenly gaze of green.

This must be Flua-Sahng. Everything about her was strikingly beyond the human, from her poise to her beauty. Yet equally striking was how much she looked like the redhead girl at Proto's side.

"Good *mor*ning!" sang Mercune, waving childlike at the being before them.

"Hail, Mercune," greeted the shining being. "It's always a pleasure. But I see you've brought a friend today."

The gaze she leveled on Proto was daunting. But the smile on her face was friendly and strangely wistful. "Is this how one dresses to visit the *Queen of Heaven?* As a jester?"

Proto's eyes went wide as he abruptly remembered the outfit that Mercune had summoned up for him.

And yet there was an odd wryness to Flua-Sahng's smile, like she were sharing a private joke that he should understand but didn't.

"Oh, that's my fault!" explained Mercune. "Here's what he was really wearing." She gestured toward him, and in a blink, he was wearing his tracksuit with the Saturn logo again.

"Ah, athletic garb," observed the Queen of Heaven. "With the emblem of my long-lost husband, no less. Much better."

Her lips quirked upward as she spoke, but Proto's mouth still went dry. "This, uh, wasn't a planned visit. Milady."

"Milady, now? Not Queen of Heaven?" She sighed and smiled. Again, that look on her face made him feel like he was missing something.

"This guy's a visitor. He visits dreams," explained Mercune. "He says he's friends with your son, Somnus."

"Indeed. I wonder when Somnus planned to tell me!" The Queen of Heaven crooked a finger.

Mists suddenly swirled around Proto and bore him toward her. He lurched to a stop a couple yards from her.

"Oh, Somnus. Using a Spirit bound to the breathing world as a *visitor!* Against the rules!" The Mother of All shook her head. "Maybe he thinks you'll fit one of the exceptions. The big softie. Luckily for him, and for you, so am I."

"But that's no excuse for him not telling me!" she went on. "I'll have to berate him next time he visits. Which is *awfully* rare, given how often he 'visits' everyone else! It's offensive, really," she pouted. "After all I've done for your lot!"

Again, that wry hint of a smile on her face! . . . That, or he was just getting giddy and imagining things. He felt faint beside her celestial majesty. "I'll tell him next time I see him," he managed.

"Yes, pray do so, Proto," directed Flua-Sahng. "He'll likely be five drinks in and require a reminder who I am. Then again, he's hardly the only one." Her lips curved upward wryly. "In any event, Mercune, we should get down to business, shouldn't we? I'm afraid our friend here must leave for this part."

"Aw. Can't he stay a few minutes? The show's about to start!" lamented Mercune, pointing at the sky. It'd been reddening afar as they spoke. Now, lights were streaking across the ruddy glow.

"I fear he can't." Flua-Sahng eyed the far off radiance. Some sadness glimmered in her green gaze.

"Aw," repeated Mercune.

The Queen of Heaven smiled down at her. "Come, we must keep some things to ourselves, mustn't we? Somnus' crew see shadows of the future, and they use that knowledge to guide dreamers. That's enough. If they saw the future whole, as we do, they could use that knowledge to change Fate. And we can't have that, can we? Right, Proto?"

He blinked, unsure what to say, as the redhead girl sighed melodramatically.

Flua-Sahng gave her a motherly shoulder pat.

"Well, before he goes, can I give him a gift?" Mercune entreated the Queen of Heaven.

The Daemon tilted her head in amusement. "Please do. But be quick, child."

The girl dashed up and handed him a dull red rock, about as wide as her palm. "This stone is very special. I lost it for years, then found it miles and miles away! Weirdest thing ever," she explained. "I plan to give it to my daughter. When I have a daughter."

" . . . and you're giving it to me?" asked Proto.

"This is a *dream*, silly!" she retorted. "It's not like I lose my real one by giving this to you. I'm just being polite. And this is what I happened to have in my pocket."

"Ah." Proto turned out his empty pockets. "I'd be polite too if I could. Now I feel bad."

"No worries! The company's enough for me," assured Mercune.

"Wait. Is this rock the *Fossil?*" Proto vaguely remembered that it'd been a red stone.

"Of course not! Does this look radiant red and teardrop-shaped?" she replied. "But it's still a special rock, I'm pretty sure."

Meanwhile, the red radiance on the horizon was spreading across the sky, like some vast fire were approaching. The streaking lights overhead were larger and brighter now. Squinting, Proto seemed to see that they were . . . *manlike?*

The redhead girl faced the impending pyroclasm and sighed. "Are you *sure* he can't stay and watch?"

"Come now, I must leave something special for my seers like you, yes? We mustn't make old news of ourselves!" reasoned Flua-Sahng with a playful smile, as Mercune shrugged grudgingly. "In any event"—she turned to him—"it's time for you to be off. Be well, Proto! We'll meet again! Try to remember me." She flicked her fingers at him lightly.

He squinted at the Queen of Heaven, and his lips parted.

But, as Mercune handcurled farewell, Proto abruptly was swept away in grey mirk. He hurtled through an oblivion bristling with swirling points of starlight.

As he did so, he felt something dissipating from his right hand—that red rock he'd been given. But instinctively, he focused on maintaining it instead—that not-quite-smooth hardness, pressed against his palm.

"Did you know, when you visit a dream, you can take what you find there back with you?" Lilac had asked.

The dwindling of the rock reversed. Its solidity once more pressed against his clasping hand.

Then, he stumbled forth into a misty blue corridor of Somnus' Palace.

Standing just a few steps in front of him was Astrid. Violet gaze widening, she stepped backward as he lurched toward her.

His hands, extended for balance, narrowly missed her retreating torso.

"Watch where you're groping, Dodo," she frowned at him, planting a hand on her hip and regarding him disdainfully.

"Hello to you too," said Proto. "Yes, I'm fine, thank you. Doing well! Yourself?"

"Wait, did you just swing a *rock* at me?" She eyed the red stone in his hand. "Do you collect stones? I could totally see that."

"Hey." He pointed at her. "This stone is *very* special." He pocketed it in his tracksuit.

"Don't be a ditz," she chastised. "Anyway, I see you didn't take the day off. That's good. My opinion of you just went up a notch. I thought you'd pick the coffee and cocktails."

"A spontaneous kind comment? From Astrid the Horrid?" marveled Proto.

"You've gone from 3 of 10 to 4 of 10," she shrugged.

"Booyah. Climbing higher by the day." He offered her a fistbump.

She eyed him grimly and came no closer, like he were the dirty guy sleeping on the subway.

He changed his fistbump to two hopeful thumbs up.

"Getting excited about minor success is the way of mediocrity," she observed.

"And . . . she's back!" he announced.

Her lips curved up. "So. Your first solo visit. Purely observational. But still a solo visit."

"I know, right? That's a big deal, right?" he enthused.

"Sure. We all do it, but it is a turning point in life," she acknowledged. "Sort of like using a toilet solo for the first time."

"Great. Well, thanks for letting me savor that for thirty seconds," said Proto. "Now, if we're all done shitting on my small triumphs . . . ?"

She couldn't quite suppress her laugh. "Anyway, Mister Solo, what'd you see on your first solo dream?"

"It was odd," he replied. "I, uh, met Flua-Sahng."

Astrid's eyes flicked to his face. On seeing that he looked serious, her gaze went wide and her lips fell apart. "You *met* the Consort of the First? That Flua-Sahng? A dream of her, you mean."

Proto had never seen a look like this on Astrid's face, perpetually cool and collected as she was. "Uh, the real thing, I think. Somnus' mom, right?"

"That's the one," affirmed Astrid faintly. "But I don't see how that's possible. She would've been in the Mists, and there's no way . . . "

"Yep! Very misty. Mercune, the girl who was dreaming, led me through the mists to Flua-Sahng. Somehow or other, she could clear the mists," replied Proto.

"*Clear* the Mists?" repeated the silvery-blue haired woman. "Do you even know what that means?"

"Uh, evidently not. She just sort of waved her hand, all red and glowy, and the mists parted," he said. "Anyway, we chatted awhile. Then, when Flua-Sahng was going to show the girl something from the future, she shooed me away. I guess only seers are allowed to see the future there, not us visitors. And Mercune was a seer."

Astrid was so nonplussed that she didn't even remind him he was just a provisional visitor. "See the future . . . ? And not in the Shadowcaster . . . ?"

Proto shrugged modestly. "Don't ask me, I'm just the messenger. From the Queen of Heaven. On his first solo visit."

"This girl—Mercune Mirin, wasn't it?" said Astrid, ignoring him. "Her last shadowcasting was odd. A lot like how you and Dahlia described the shadowcasting for that friend of yours, Yemos. Ominous. Hinting at some dire future."

He nodded. "This was similar. The sky went red, and there were streaking lights. Something was coming. But then Flua-Sahng sent me away before I could see it clearly."

As Astrid stared in wordless thought, he found himself recalling the words of Yemos at the end of his dream: *"When the fires fall, and the lights streak across heaven, and the redounding blasts rock the earth, and all is pandaemonium, I'll be in its midst."*

"Well," she finally said, "this is something I'll have to discuss with Somnus. I, or maybe we."

"Do you think it's something serious?" he asked.

She paused before responding, pressing her lips. "Something I should discuss with Somnus," she finally repeated.

"This seems different from what we normally do here." Proto felt his mind stretching to fit these recent events. "We help steer individual dreamers in the right direction. But *this*—whatever this is—seems like something much bigger. Are we supposed to steer big things like this too?"

Astrid paused again, then shrugged away her brooding expression. "We do what we do, and it doesn't matter what others 'suppose' about it. And the future of humanity and individual humans is the same thing."

"So . . . that's a yes?" confirmed Proto. "Only cooler and more philosophical?"

"Yes."

"That's very Astrid of you."

"There can be only one." She archly flipped her hair back.

Proto smiled. "So. While you were busy being too cool for school the last few days, what were you doing? Helping Somnus save humanity, one human at a time?"

"No, that's what I do on normal days," she responded casually. "This was more pressing."

"Yes, that's very Astrid of you," he affirmed. "You're even doing the 'Hi, I'm Astrid and you're not' pose."

She frowned and looked down at herself, so her silvery-blue hair fell over one shoulder. One of her hands was on her hip, which was cocked out with her weight on her other leg. This amplified the curve of her frame, which the stripes on her jumpsuit followed very distinctly.

"Hi, I'm Astrid and you're not," he repeated, gesturing at her.

Her lips forced themselves up against her will. "There can only be one," she repeated. "But maybe next time, you can tag along."

"Lady Luck favor me, maybe!" he replied.

She pshed and rolled her eyes.

"Or, better yet, *Flua-Sahng* favor me!" he added.

She scoffed a laugh out and started to walk away, then slowed and glanced back. "Come on. I guess I should hear what my mentee has been doing."

"Even the way she initiates small talk is cool as ice!" he admired.

She shook her head and kept walking. But he could see her cheek dimple upward.

"Just coolly flip your hair next time, okay?" he suggested.

She obliged. "Like that?"

"And all is right in the world!" affirmed Proto.

They headed back to the lounge and found it still was relatively empty. Even Lilac was absent.

One of the kitchen cooks, Paunch, was manning the bar instead of her. He did his best with coffees and cocktails—which really wasn't bad, in Proto's experience. But he was no Lilac.

Proto therefore decided to stick to spirits today. He asked Paunch for some armagnac that he'd heard Somnus praise a couple times.

As he did so, Astrid loosed a disappointed sigh.

He raised an eyebrow. "I'll . . . be sure to leave some for you?"

"No," she wistfully lamented. "I was looking forward to making fun of your tastes."

"Ah." He beamed. "Yes, Astrid, tell me what you think of the Lord of Dreams' favorite drink!"

"Can't you get that fizzy pink drink again?" she urged.

"Again? Now we're just making things up?" he chastised. "False accusations, is it?"

"Lilac poured it for you. I'm going to count it!" she replied.

"Well, I'm going to pick your drink today." He turned to Paunch. "She'll have one absinthe. That kind." He pointed. "One ice cube, no sugar."

"I'm impressed you got that right," she acknowledged. "One ice cube, no sugar."

"I handle the coolness, you supply the sugar." He gave her the double guns.

She flicked his ear.

The bartender poured the last of the bottle into a glass and started to throw it away.

"Hey, hold up. Could we borrow that bottle?" asked Proto, then turned to Astrid. "There's a game we have to finish playing."

She put a hand on her hip and gave him a baleful violet gaze. "You brag about going solo all day, Mister Solo, and suddenly you want a second player?" She shook her head and picked a violet nail. "You pay visits to Flua-Sahng! The First's Consort! I think I'm quite unnecessary here."

"Aw. You can throw away that bottle I guess," he sighed to Paunch, who nodded and released it down a trash chute.

"Of course, I said unnecessary," Astrid quietly went on with a smile. "Not unwilling."

"Wait! Wait!" Proto entreated Paunch. But the man shrugged empty-handed.

Astrid tilted back her head and laughed musically, her silvery-blue hair spilling down her shoulders.

Proto just smiled and admired.

At some point recently—he wasn't sure when—Somnus' Palace had stopped feeling like a dream to him. Indeed, life here could hardly feel more vibrant and *real*. And what felt like a dream now was that pale half-semblancy of reality that he'd been living in before this.

But maybe the real change wasn't in where he was, but who he was. Here, he relished life like a dreamer in a dream, uninhibited by fear of real consequences. Yet by doing so, he made this life *more* real.

Maybe the old world up there wasn't such a bad place. *"I was rather fond of the breathing world, once. I used to visit folk up there all the time. They loved me! Poets invoked me! Would you believe it?"* the Lord of Dreams had said.

Maybe keeping it real and living the dream were one and the same, he mused. He felt a little giddy.

"What's that big clown smile for, Bozo?" Astrid asked Proto, who suddenly realized he'd been staring at her this whole time. "You off in dreamland? You care to join me back in reality here?"

"Yes and yes." He raised his glass. "Cheers to that."

"What the F does that mean," she scowled. But she smiled too and clinked his glass, and they drank away their cares.

CHAPTER 12
HAPPY ENDINGS

"More caviar and mozzarella sticks, please," called Mayger, placing the table's third food order that afternoon.

Paunch rolled his eyes and waddled to the stairway down to the kitchen. He'd been at the bar for the last couple days—the longest that Lilac had been away, in Proto's experience.

Together with Proto and Mayger sat Jet and Jag, the whiskery black-haired identical twins. They all were playing Euchre.

It was a local favorite where Proto was from. He'd probably spent at least a thousand hours playing it with Yemos, Mannus, Quart and others, back in high school and college—before he got busy with his A/B testing work, and Mannus got busy with football and the football crowd, and Quart got busy in Poland with his girlfriend. So Euchre's popularity in Somnus' Palace was a pleasant surprise.

For once, I feel like I'm better at something than others here! mused Proto as they played.

Well, most others. His partner, Jet, was an excellent player.

Luckily for Proto, the well-dressed twin flatly had refused to partner with Jag.

"'The twins will want to be partners, obviously.' Every bloody time," Jet had replied, after Mayger proposed that arrangement. *"Well, not this time. I'll take the new guy."*

This had worked out just fine for Proto. Jet was a disciplined and rational player who card-counted. Jag, in contrast, made key decisions by flipping a coin with Lady Luck's image on it.

Jet and Jag were opposites in all sorts of ways, despite being identical twins. Jet wore a suitcoat, and Jag wore a sweatsuit. Jet drank champagne, and Jag drank moonshine. Jet was a dream visitor, while Jag did oddjobs outside of Somnus' Palace. Jet trimmed his whiskers daily, while Jag shaved fully once a week. Jet preferred caviar, and Jag preferred mozzarella sticks. That's why they always ordered both.

It's like the twins had been created from the same blueprint, except whoever made Jag had read it upside-down.

"I'm feeling it." Jag's eyes were narrowed eagerly upon his hand.

"Not surprising. That's, what, round four?" Mayger gestured toward Jag's transparent drink.

"Third round drinking, fourth round losing," corrected Jet.

"No. Luck is what I'm feeling," declared Jag.

"What were you feeling the last three games?" asked Proto.

"Sadness," Jag instantly replied, prompting laughter. His modesty made all his faults forgivable.

They were gambling on the game with Breath Tokens—metal coins with Somnus' face on them, blowing out a puff of breath. Proto had seen them around, but he hadn't understood what they were for, given that food, drinks and lodging were free.

"Well, what if you need a favor from someone? What if you need someone to cover your shift? What if you want someone to go fetch you something from the Sea of Dreams?" Mayger had explained when Proto had asked what they were for. *"Breath Tokens. We trade them for favors."*

This explanation wasn't quite satisfying for Proto. Why did anyone care about these tokens in the first place, such that they'd do you a favor in exchange for one? It was just a hunk of metal. True, it could buy you favors, which made it valuable. But that was just because everyone here simultaneously accepted the fiction that the tokens were worth something.

Then again, that was how fiat currency worked too. So he'd ultimately just shrugged and accepted it.

It's not like it mattered for Proto's purposes today. Jet was spotting him the Breath Tokens for each game, and Jet was getting all the winnings. This had proven to be a good deal for Jet. His stack of coins had doubled since that morning.

"By the way," Jag remarked. He threw a card onto the table without looking, as Mayger clapped a hand over his forehead. "I really like your tracksuit, Proto. I may just have to expand my wardrobe." He pinched his grey and dark green sweatsuit and shook it a couple times. "I've been through a lot with this guy. It's time I gave him a break."

"Please don't," replied Jet. "No offense, Proto."

"Wait. Jag, did you just renege?" asked Proto. "That's a spade."

"Huh. Looks like I did," the sweatsuited man replied. "Good game."

"No." Mayger tossed his cards onto the table and pointed at his partner. "*Not* a good game."

"What can I say? Lady Luck wasn't with me today," lamented Jag.

"Judging by how things went," said Jet, "I think she was with Proto."

"Who isn't, at this point?" muttered Mayger wryly.

Proto blinked and wondered if he'd heard the man correctly.

The pink-haired man turned to Paunch at the bar. "Could I get a latte? Five shots, please. One for each hour of sleep I missed last night."

"Another coffee for me too," added Proto.

"What about you two?" Paunch asked the twins.

Jet waved it off. "I'm good. I slept eight hours."

Jag waved identically. "I'm good. I slept eighteen hours. One for each shot I took the night before."

Yes, that was Jet and Jag for you.

"Here are your winnings." Mayger handed two Breath Tokens to Jet, one from Jag's pile and one from his own.

Jet took them and promptly slid them to Proto. "Yours. Good game, Partner."

Proto's brow furrowed. "But . . . I didn't gamble anything. It was all you."

"No, it was not all me. I had an excellent partner." Jet held his hands forth toward the tracksuited Provisional Visitor. "Also, you have exactly zero Breath Tokens. So I feel both compelled and honored to give you your first. And second."

"For what though?" waved Jag. "It's not like he needs them."

Mayger and Jet simultaneously turned to face Jag, whose eyes abruptly widened. He said nothing.

" . . . what do you mean?" asked Proto.

After a moment, Mayger smiled and rolled his eyes. "What he means is—as we were discussing while you were in the bathroom earlier—a few people here would jump at the chance to do *you* a favor, I think. No Breath Tokens needed. Say, a certain bartendress, a certain shadowseer, and—"

"What's this about a shadowseer?" came a voice nearby.

Proto turned and saw that Dahlia was approaching. She was wearing her chiton, that white toga-like outfit she wore at the Shadowcaster. It was loose enough to hide her frame, but not its bounce as she moved. Blonde hair spilled over her breasts.

"Speak of the devil," observed Jag.

"And she's sure to appear!" finished Dahlia. "My, was it hot down there." She fanned her pinkish face. "Sinfully hot!"

Eying her up and down, Proto couldn't help but agree.

"So. This shadowseer has had a long day and would like to play. Who's going to make room for her?" Dahlia smiled sweetly. "No, not you, Proto," she added, as he started to rise. "I'm counting on beating you."

"Okay. But we can't kick out my partner, since we're on a winning streak." Proto gestured toward Jet.

"That's fine!" she waved. "Jet and Jag can play as one person. They're basically one person anyway, right?"

"Sure, if Goofus and Gallant were one person," said Mayger.

Jag shook his head. "If I had a Token for every time someone made that comparison . . . !"

"You'd have almost as many as your brother," said Proto.

Jag sighed.

"Maybe Mayger was calling you Gallant!" Dahlia placated soothingly. "Don't say anything, Mayger."

The lithe man's mouth clapped shut.

"Now." She turned back to Jag. "Shoo shoo." She waved him out of his seat and promptly sat, smoothing her chiton around her frame. "Are you ready to win, Mayger? I know it will be odd for you, but it's important to try new things."

"Nice to partner with you too," he replied. "I'll try not to hold you back too much."

"Every Sherlock needs her Watson," she waved magnanimously.

"You hear that, Sherlock?" Jag slid his chair up an inch away from Jet.

Frowning, Jet turned and pushed the chair a few feet away.

"Hey. How can I flip my lucky coin from back here?" Jag protested.

Jet ignored him and faced Dahlia. "We're playing for Breath Tokens. You don't have any to bet, right?"

"My partner can spot me," Dahlia declared dismissively. "Every Elizabeth Bennet needs her Mr. Darcy."

Mayger itched his pink pomaded hair. "Me? Your Mr. Darcy?"

"Only for financial purposes," she replied smoothly. "Be like Jet. He's spotting Proto, yes? Obviously, Proto doesn't have Tokens."

"Obvious? Why's that?" Proto pulled his two new Breath Tokens from his pocket.

Dahlia blinked. For once, she seemed speechless.

"Probably," said Mayger after a moment, "since you were hiding those in your pocket, unlike the rest of us." He gestured at their Token piles.

"Or she just thinks you suck at Euchre," said Jag. "That's why I don't have Tokens."

"Your foppish modesty is endearing, Jag. You're the Edward to your brother's Edmund," declared Dahlia. "Not that any of you will understand that reference. Except Proto, who has maybe a 25% chance."

Proto smiled and said nothing. As they say, better to stay silent and seem a fool than open your mouth and prove it.

"Alright! To business! Team Jet-Jag against Team Glorious Victory. May the best woman prevail!" declaimed Dahlia. "Partner, you deal first."

"Is that how I'm going to be addressed this whole game?" replied Mayger.

"Yes, Partner," she immediately answered. "I'll have you know, you're my first pink-haired partner."

"I haven't had any partners much like you either," responded Mayger. "But you knew that."

"We *all* knew that," smiled Dahlia.

Unfortunately for Team Glorious Victory, Proto continued his winning streak with Jet, who allowed Jag a total of three coin flips the whole game. Somewhat miraculously, each decision made based on a coin flip ended up being the right one.

So it came about that Dahlia was starting to hand over two Breath Tokens from Mayger's pile when she suddenly paused. "I forget," she idly remarked, "were we playing for clothing or Tokens?" She batted her lashes questioningly at Proto.

"Tokens," replied Mayger, straightening his black leather jacket. "Definitely Tokens." He took his two Tokens from Dahlia and handed them to Jet.

"I wasn't asking you." She rolled her eyes. "Who knows, maybe *I'd* spot *you!* Except I'd need two to spot, wouldn't I?" Her gaze glimmered at Proto as she adjusted her chiton beneath her.

"Ah, the stash grows," admired Jet, plinking the coins into his pile.

"Keep that up, and soon you'll have as much as Astrid," said Mayger.

"If soon means a century from now, maybe," replied Jet. "If Lady Luck is with me."

"She's with Proto," corrected Jag.

"What's this now?" asked Dahlia with raised brow, eying the tracksuited provisional visitor. He shrugged and spun a finger at his temple. She narrowed her eyes at him in exaggerated suspicion but smiled.

"What'll you do if you hit 777,777 and I'm still under 10k?" Jag asked his brother.

Jet paused before answering, glancing at Proto. "If you keep flipping that coin, you're bound to catch up," he finally answered. "Who knows, maybe I'll buy a century-long vacation. And then we'll be even again." His lips curved up wryly.

Proto couldn't help but notice that there had been a lot of pauses and glances at him during this conversation. But before he could dwell on that further, his coffee arrived.

It was Lilac. In her hands were two coffees, one in a standard glass and one in the black mug. It now had two white-lacquered cracks, but otherwise looked the same as before Proto had broken it.

"Ah, welcome back. We've missed your coffee. And you," Mayger greeted her. "I'll take the broken black cup, since I'm now flat broke."

Her black gaze fell on the pile of Breath Tokens in front of Mayger, then flicked to the empty space in front of Proto. "It looks like he's the broke one." She gave the black mug to Proto and set the other in front of Mayger.

As the pale woman did so, her eyes briefly met Proto's.

He opened his mouth but couldn't think of anything to say—at least, not with everyone sitting here.

"He's hiding two in his pocket!" protested Mayger.

"I don't care what Proto's hiding," Lilac replied calmly, turning and gliding away. Her black hair swished behind her.

"As I said," grumbled Mayger to Proto. He sipped his coffee without elaborating further.

"So, are we all ready to play again? Sufficiently coffeed up, you two?" Dahlia asked Proto and Mayger.

"Start shuffling and maybe I'll be ready," yawned Mayger.

"Always ready, never sufficiently coffeed," replied Proto.

"Good philosophy!" praised Dahlia. "Why aren't you my partner?"

"Let's win, Partner." Jet fistbumped Proto.

"I'll help you carry those home." Proto pointed at Jet's Breath Tokens. "I've been lifting."

"Enough of this cock-a-hoop showboating!" chided Dahlia. "Get dealing, Pinkie."

"I don't respond to that name," said Mayger.

"You'll get a new name when you win, you bohemian clothes dummy!" she retorted.

Eying his black leather jacket and turtleneck, Mayger nodded grimly and started dealing.

Team Glorious Victory did better this game. They soon were one point away from winning at 9, with Team Jet-Jag three points behind at 6.

At this point, Mayger needed a bathroom break after that coffee. The others decided to avail themselves of the opportunity too, except Dahlia.

"They say woman was made by taking a rib from man," she noted. "Myself, I think she took half his bladder. I swear, you're like cheap water balloons. Always ready to pop at inconvenient times."

"At least we can laugh and stay continent at the same time," observed Proto, walking away.

"Inappropriate!" averred Dahlia with righteous indignation. "Harassment even!"

Proto laughed and stayed continent, at least until reaching his destination.

He was the first of the three men to finish doing his business. Upon returning, he found Dahlia shuffling the cards.

"Finished stacking the deck, Daylily?" he greeted her. "I'm going to insist on cutting at least five times, Delphinium."

"We're back to that again?" she lightly sighed. "Your sophomoric name-calling won't do any good, you chuckleheaded Romeo. I have you exactly where I want you!"

"Losing horribly?" he said.

"Behind me," she affirmed. "Or as the 6 to my 9. I'll take either one." Her blue stare sparkled.

He blinked and searched for a suitable reply. "Or . . . you're on top?"

"Why not all three?!" she cried delightedly, even as Jag grabbed his chair and started sitting.

"What's that?" asked the disheveled twin. "On top of what?"

"Oh, I was bragging about winning, and Proto confirmed that I was winning," she explained. "I'm just riding high! So to speak." Her lips curved up.

"Ah," said the sweatsuited man. "What happened to all that modesty stuff?"

Dahlia laughed. "You know Jag, you are absolutely right. From now on, I'll be humble as . . . a missionary!" Her gaze glimmered at Proto.

The other two were now returning to the table. "What are you doing in my seat?" Jet calmly asked his brother.

Proto hadn't noticed until now, but Jag indeed was sitting across from him.

"Deciding if I'm going alone." Jag flipped a coin and it came up heads. "Yep, going alone."

"Excuse me? No, no you're not!" replied Jet with alarm.

"Too late!" cried Dahlia. "A card laid is a card played . . . or something like that. No takebacks!"

Proto frowned and laid his cards down. In Euchre, "going alone" meant that Jag would play the round by himself without Proto's help. But if he won every trick alone, he'd get 4 points instead of 1, winning the game.

"This isn't happening!" Jet insisted. "Get out of my seat."

"Sorry, Bro, but someone has to save your winning streak," Jag languidly replied.

"Well, this game seems likely to have a happy ending," said Mayger to Dahlia.

"Quite! I'm almost not ashamed to call you Partner," she said. "But, as a wise man once said, count no Mayger a winner till he wins. Count no girl happy till her happy ending comes." She glanced at Proto sidelong, lips quirked up.

Unfortunately for Team Glorious Victory, their name proved inapt once again. Jag flipped his coin before every single trick and, miraculously, ended up winning them all.

"Well then." Jag turned and beamed at his twin. "About that winning streak."

"I'm almost not ashamed to call you brother," Jet allowed.

"That was almost a compliment!" observed Jag.

Meanwhile, Mayger sighed and started cleaning up the cards.

"Game over. Two Tokens to continue," said Proto, holding out a hand.

"Continue?" Mayger yawned and handed over two Breath Tokens to Jet. "What say you, Partner?"

"I say this pink-haired partnership is at an end!" fumed Dahlia.

"Indeed!" came a booming voice from beneath the vast painting.

Proto turned and saw that Somnus was striding in.

"I'll be needing your help at the Shadowcaster, Dahlia," the long-haired man went on, his green and purple robe swishing around his ankles as he approached. "And, Mayger, why don't you come too. That way I won't have to repeat this to you later."

"Repeat what?" grumbled the pink-haired loser.

"How about, 'Yes, my Lord! May I ask how I could help you?'" admonished Somnus. "First's name, I'm the Nightly Hunter! Not your mother waking you up early on a Saturday morning."

Jag leaned and checked Jet's watch. It looked tastefully understated and ludicrously expensive, like most things Jet wore. "Oh. Uh, I should probably be off too."

"Probably fifteen minutes ago, yes?" agreed Somnus, turning to the sweatsuited twin. "As you know, I hate watches and clocks, so I don't fault your tardiness too much. I've just learnt not to give you time-sensitive tasks."

"Thanks, Lord of Dreams," replied Jag.

"You see?" Somnus turned to Mayger. "Simple politeness. Be more like Jag."

"Four words I never expected to hear," declared Jag.

"That waggish modesty!" admired Dahlia. "You should learn from him, Sparky. . . . Just that part though."

"Well, good game, Partner. I'm off to count my fortune." Jet fistbumped Proto.

"Modesty does more for a man than a fancy watch and nice clothes!" called Dahlia at Jet's back. "And annoying Euchre skills."

"I guess you're on your own, Proto. You and your coffee," observed Somnus, eying the black mug. "Your colleagues should return later. Till then?" He shrugged.

"Till then," finished Proto, "work hard, keep clean, and always stay focused?"

"Always focus? Heavens, no!" rejoined Somnus. "Rodents and vermin always focus. What separates man from beast is that his mind and spirit wander far from the here and now. It's out there that he finds what's true and inspired. Man is man because he *dreams*. Focus when you must, but dream when you can."

"Very wise, Lord of Dreams," Jag complimented.

"Truly a font of spontaneous wisdom, from which we're blessed to drink abundantly," concurred Dahlia.

"Jag, have a Breath Token," said Somnus, flipping one to him. "And, Dahlia, lay it on a little thinner, I'm trying to lose pride."

"That's my first Token all day!" Jag celebrated.

With the game over and Team Glorious Victory in no mood for another round, Proto's fellow players soon left the lounge, followed by Somnus.

"By the way," called Proto to the departing Lord of Dreams, "your mother says to visit more."

"What? I can't hear you," Somnus called back. "Also, tell her she needs better drinks. And ask her about the last time she visited here. In case she's forgotten, it was December 31, 1999. Ask our bartendress how many Sea of Dreams runs she made afterward to restock!"

"What?" replied Proto.

"I said, I can't hear you!" the robed man replied.

Then, he was gone, leaving Proto on his own with his coffee.

Clink.

Well, not quite on his own, was he?

He looked over at the bar. There was Lilac, quietly polishing glasses, one after another. *Clink.* Her two loose strands of black hair on either side of her face swayed back and forth as she leaned. They made her pallor even paler, together with her black eyes.

He remembered when he'd first seen the depths of that dark gaze. He looked down at his Lilac-style coffee, and his lips curved up.

He recalled her sitting with her lilac-covered picnic basket, watching the Sea of Dreams, as sakura petals drifted over her and him. Her black gaze had reflected that whole moment, and it'd sparkled.

Today, though, she looked more like the blank-faced bartendress he'd met on his first day here. Her downward black stare was a void.

Moved by an instinct, he rose and approached the bar with his mug.

Amid her polishing, she didn't seem to notice him until he stood a few feet away. Or maybe she just had more important things to do.

"Very Lilac-style," he said to her, holding up the black and white-lacquered mug.

"The coffee or the cup?" she asked impassively, continuing to polish.

"Disappearing on a mysterious journey for days," he answered.

She finally looked up at him and raised her brow.

"And returning with fresh coffee in a fixed cup," he went on. "Thereby making everything right in the world, Madame Bartendress!"

She stared at him a moment. Then, she turned and walked away, descending the kitchen stairs.

He winced. "A spirit she comes, a ghost she goes!" he called hopefully as she disappeared.

He stood there a full two minutes before he finally sighed. *I tried.* He decided to go lie down. Lifting his black mug to his lips, he sipped the last dregs of coffee inside.

But when he lowered the cup, Lilac was ascending the stairs. She had a milk bread sandwich cut into four squares on her plate, similar to the ones they'd eaten by the Sea of Dreams. She set it on the bar and began eating.

He wasn't sure what to say and decided to let her go first. But she didn't say anything, so neither did he.

"Would you like half of it?" she finally asked.

"Would I." He immediately took a bite of one of the sandwich squares. It was delicious—as elegantly balanced and tasteful and understated as everything that Lilac made and did and said.

He allowed satisfaction to close his eyes and curve his lips upward. When his eyes opened, she too was smiling.

"I hope I'm not eating your lunch," he remarked through a mouthful.

"Not at all," she replied. "I don't have the biggest appetite."

"Lucky me, huh?" He took another bite.

"I don't know. Do you think so?" She regarded him earnestly. "I've certainly wished I were different."

Proto—realizing that they were talking about more than food now, but not knowing exactly what—said nothing. He looked into her eyes, but they were faraway.

"I think that's why I chose this job when I arrived here," she recalled. "I wanted to savor everything. That's how other people were. Taking it all in and loving it." She waved toward the tables where Proto and his friends had been seated earlier.

"I couldn't, though," she said. "It always felt like I didn't have room for it all. I had to keep things at a distance. I couldn't get too close, because I could only allow things inside in little bits."

"But then I found a solution. If I made things for others to savor, I could share in *their* happiness. Even from afar." Her black gaze, still afar, was sparkling.

"'Is that my happy ending?' I've always wondered. 'Sharing from afar? Or is there something more for me to share?'" Her black eyes fell to Proto's black mug. She clasped its handle.

He stared at her a moment, then clasped her hand around the handle. "I'm sorry for breaking this. That isn't what I meant to do. Far from it." He hoped his face conveyed what words couldn't.

"There's no need to apologize. This is mine," Lilac mused, running a finger along the mug's old crack. "And this is yours now." She traced her fingertip along the new crack. "You've made it yours." She lifted the cup and his clasping hand to her breast. "Yours to do with what you will. And it will only become more yours by doing so."

He blinked at her curved gaze. Like a star before a black hole, he felt himself yearning forward.

"Yours to break and mine to mend." She handed him the mug, and suddenly he was set free. "But try not to break it too badly. Most things can be repaired, but not everything." Her black eyes fell to Proto's pocket. "Not everything."

His lips pressed. He felt like he'd died and every bad thing he'd ever done was under review. "I promise I won't—"

"Don't promise you won't break it again. You don't know that yet." She looked down at the black mug wistfully. "But if you have to let it down, try to do so gently, and it won't shatter. I promise."

He opened his mouth. "I . . ."

She put a finger to his lips. "No, you've said enough. You're good at speaking up. I know when to stay silent. Between the two of us . . . well. Now *I've* said enough."

He met that sparkling black gaze for a moment. Then, he found himself leaning toward her.

She took a deep breath, eyes uncertain—then clasped the mug he was still grasping and held it up between them. "Not today. You'll know when." Her black eyes sparkled with moisture. But she was smiling too.

Then, squeezing his hand briefly, she turned and walked away.

Proto wasn't sure where she was going and when she'd be back. But that wasn't for him to know today. Of that, he was sure.

He went to his room and lay on his simple white bed. His eyelids sagged shut. And soon, dreamy figures moved before his inward gaze.

One of those figures was pale with long black hair and gliding deftly across his prospect. But there were others too. There were others.

These were mere memories—perhaps memories of a dream!—and yet nothing had ever felt so real.

He had a choice to make. Of that, he was sure. But how much longer did he have? *"You'll know when."* Would he be ready? Would he make the right choice? *Was* there a right choice?

CHAPTER 13
PROTOS, KIMONOS AND PHOTOS, OH MY

Proto woke in his simple white bed in his blue room at Somnus' Palace, exactly where he'd fallen asleep. It occurred to him that that'd been true for weeks now.

For most people, that would not be terribly significant. Proto, though, had been prone to sleepwalking and often had woken away from his bed—say, on the couch or the carpet. Somehow, being here in Somnus' Palace had put an end to his nightly ventures.

He wasn't sure what that meant. Maybe it supported his long-running theory that this was all a dream. You generally don't dream of sleepwalking, even when you're doing it. That would explain why he hadn't done it in weeks.

On the other hand, most dreams don't last for weeks either.

Blearily, he shook away these dream-addled thoughts, donned his tracksuit, freshened up and headed to the lounge.

He smiled faintly upon seeing the room. It felt like a part of him now, and he felt like a part of it: the wood paneling; the dark green and purple wallpaper with interwoven gold vines; the old gas lamps; and, of course, the bar, with its elaborate wooden inlays of medieval scenes.

No one stood behind the bar. Scanning the room, he didn't see Lilac—or Astrid, Dahlia or Mayger for that matter. But he did find Jet and Jag sitting at a table, so he approached them.

"Have a seat, Partner!" hailed the better-dressed of the twins.

"Quick game of Euchre? Think we can find a fourth?" asked Proto.

"Lilac, you want to play?" called Jag. "With you, I might have a chance against these two."

Proto looked where Jag was facing.

There, emerging from one of the booths, was Lilac. He must've missed her earlier since, for the first time since he'd met her, she wasn't wearing her French waitress outfit.

Instead, she was wearing a yukata—a light summery robe. It was mostly white with black edging, but its belt was fraught with blue and yellow primroses.

"No cards for me! Or Proto." She approached their table.

"What? What's this now?" asked the sweatsuited twin.

"Somnus gave me an assignment for Proto," replied the black-haired woman.

"Ah. To be continued, Partner." Proto fistbumped Jet, then faced Lilac. "So, where's today's visit?"

"No visit. You'll be going somewhere new today," she said.

"Oh. Am I meeting Astrid somewhere? Or is it Mayger?" he asked.

"Nope!" responded Lilac, as Paunch emerged from the same booth. "Thanks again for covering the bar today," she said to the aproned man.

He waved dismissively. "Could do with some change. And less food."

"I hope Paunch doesn't lose too much paunch!" she said lightly.

"Oh, he can afford to lose a bit." He patted his belly.

Lilac turned to face Proto, whose head was tilted in bemusement. "Ready to go, Provisional Visitor?"

"I . . . suppose I am!" he declared. "Should I pack anything?"

"I've taken care of that. I always do." Indeed, Lilac was holding a bag at her side—well, something baglike, but it had a woven basket base.

"Well, alright then! Let the mysterious journey commence," he declaimed. "Lead the way, Liliana Lightrobe!"

She looked down at her white yukata. Then, she flicked his ear and walked toward the kitchen stairs.

"I do feel somewhat underdressed though!" He snapped the elastic cuff of his tracksuit against his wrist.

"You're just starting to feel that way today?" she replied evenly.

"Ouch," frowned Proto, rubbing his Saturn emblem.

"It's okay, Partner. I'll hook you up later," said Jet. "New suit, new man. Same card skills."

Proto fistbumped him again and followed Lilac down the stairway.

"Down into the mirky stony depths, is it?" he called to her ahead. "Back to the treacherous river of forgetfulness?"

"No. Maybe tomorrow!" she replied calmly.

She left the stairs before reaching the bottom floor and passed through a tall doorway.

Following her, he found himself entering a grand foyer. Mists hung about the dim blue walls and ceiling, similar to the corridors upstairs. But here, the silvery patterns on the wall crept all about the chamber in an ornate swirling pattern, forming a shape like the Milky Way. At its center was an image of Somnus' face, blowing out a puff of breath—the same image that was on the Breath Tokens.

People were strolling to and fro in twos and threes. They wore diverse clothing from various historical periods, like an acting troupe practicing several plays at once.

Once again, Proto marveled at how much bigger Somnus' Palace was than the single floor he'd come to know. Maybe he should take more breaks from cards and cocktails to explore like this.

His robed guide swished and shuffled around the passersby and led him outside. They passed through a misty courtyard with twelve fountains, some shaped like animals and others like people. He realized after a moment that they matched the twelve zones of the dream visitor floor upstairs—the Zones of the Ram, the Bull, the Twins, and so forth.

Following her out of the courtyard's grand gates, he emerged into nature—a few half-bare trees growing amid the sparse grass beneath mirky skies of grey. The scenery terminated in a cliff about fifty yards way.

Lilac glided toward the precipice. "The Mists," she said simply, pointing below.

Sprawling below them was a barren plain fraught with drifting mists. It looked familiar.

After a moment, Proto realized that the dream where he'd met that redhead girl, Mercune, had occurred somewhere like that plain. Maybe the same place.

Beyond those crowds of mists, he could see some shadowy figures walking about. The way they ambled aimlessly reminded him of how sleepwalkers were depicted in movies. Maybe sleepwalkers really *did* look like that. He had no way of knowing despite being one.

A memory suddenly flashed through Proto: Somnus, eying him with his usual look of ironic mirth, the day they'd met. *"I might ask why you roved so far along the borders of the dream realm that you managed to find this place! I might ask why you waltzed in here like you owned the Palace!"*

" . . . is this where I arrived here?" he asked.

She nodded twice at him.

"I don't remember that," he said. "Is that normal?"

"I don't know what would be normal. I don't know anyone else who arrived the way you did," she replied.

Vaguely, Proto recalled something Lilac had said a while back—something about choosing her job after she'd arrived here.

"What about you?" he asked. "This wasn't how you got here?"

She looked at him and silently shook her head.

He wanted to ask more. But something about her wide black gaze made him keep quiet. He had a feeling that if he descended now into those dark depths, he would not be prepared to climb back out.

Instead, he pointed toward the horizon. "Those people down there look like they're sleepwalking."

"That's a good way of putting it," she agreed.

"You know, I have a long history of sleepwalking," he noted. "Never know where I might wake up!"

"That, I don't doubt," she replied drily.

His lips quirked up. "Well, anyway, that all stopped when I got here. Haven't sleepwalked once here."

"That's not surprising," she said. "After all, this is all just one big dream, right?"

"I'll prove it someday, Lilac! Or, should I say, *Dream-Lilac!?*"

"And I'll prove I'm not a figment of your imagination!" she replied evenly. "But maybe I can be the Lilac of your dreams."

His eyes widened at the pale lady whose black stare suddenly was square upon him. His lips parted.

Smiling, she placed one finger on his lips. Then, she turned and faced the Mists.

Proto forced the dazzle down. "Those people down there. Are they dreaming?"

"Yes. Their dreams have taken them near the border of the dream realm and the Mists," said Lilac. "The part where the dreams of many begin to meld."

"So . . . they're dreaming of this?" replied Proto. "Wandering around a barren plain?"

"Not exactly," she said. "Think of it like . . . being inside a cruise boat. You can wander around inside all day, in your own world with its own people and stories and things. But from the outside, all people see is a big boat drifting forward."

"It's like that," she explained. "Each of these dreamers is inside a dream, like a cruise boat, in his own little world. But *you're* seeing it from the outside, drifting around."

"What happens if they touch the Mists?" he asked, recalling his dream with Mercune.

"They wake up," she replied. "Or, if they can't wake up, like if they're unconscious, the Mists bear them away, further into the dream realm and away from the border."

"Ah." Proto stared at them and pondered. "So that's what I was doing when I got here. Sleepwalking aimlessly on that misty plain."

"Well, no. Not aimlessly. That's the thing about you," she replied. "Somehow, you made your way *through* those Mists all the way up to Somnus' Palace."

He looked down. The manifold pathways amid the Mists wound about in a veritable labyrinth—except, unlike a labyrinth, those pathways constantly were forming and unforming as the Mists drifted, making it impossible to memorize the layout. "How did I do that?"

"First knows," she shrugged.

"So . . . are we going down there?" he asked.

"Really? That's so you." Her lips curved up. "You find out you miraculously made it through the Mists. And your *very first thought* is, let's go back into them!"

He smiled at first. But then, something that subconsciously had been bothering him since he got here abruptly surfaced. "Lilac, how long was I wandering on that plain?"

She looked at him for several seconds. "I don't know exactly how long. You should ask Somnus."

He recalled how Yemos had looked middle-aged in that dream of his. He'd assumed his twenty-something friend had simply dreamt of being older. But was it possible that all those years really *had* passed?

"Anyway," Lilac broke into his brooding, "that's not why we're out here." She turned from the precipice and headed toward a rocky pathway leading downward along the cliffside.

"Why *are* we out here?" he asked, following her.

"Be patient!" she replied archly. "It wouldn't be much of an odyssey if you knew where we were going before our journey even began, would it?"

"Actually, isn't that exactly how the Odyssey goes?" Long ago, his dad had read him a children's version probably a dozen times.

"Proto, this is your day with Lilac, not your day with Dahlia," replied his date. "Try to be witty in ways I'll understand."

"Noted. Apologies."

"Accepted."

She glided gracefully down the stony path until they reached a yawning cave mouth. Retrieving a flashlight from her basket-bag, she pointed it inside and flicked a switch.

The cave shone pink. From the dusty floor to the craggy walls to the stalactite-ridden ceiling, the whole thing was pink. And not just the vaguely pinkish-peach hue of flowstone, but the pink of Barbie's convertible or a Florida man's polo shirt.

Proto laughed.

"Is there something funny, Proto?" asked Lilac.

"Nope! Just looking forward to the bright prospects ahead of us. Very bright."

"Are you making fun of pinkness, Proto? I'm going to tell Mayger!" she threatened.

"Please do. Once for every time he's remarked on my tracksuit," said Proto. "But yeah, after so long at Somnus' Palace, it's weird not having everything be blue."

"It's because we're not in Somnus' domain anymore," replied Lilac.

Proto stared at her. "Whose domain are we in?" He felt like every day, this little world he'd woken in became a little larger.

"You'll see!" She glided onward into shadowy pinkness.

"Well, can you tell me anything?" he entreated. "Like, why are we venturing into a cave that looks like She-Ra's castle?"

"Why are all your references from the era of VCRs and latchkey parents?" she asked calmly.

He clutched his chest and held out a hand like Bon Jovi. "Shot through the heart!"

She'd been joking, of course. But there was also something about the way she'd said that. . . . How long *had* he been wandering that misty plain?

"Anyway, old man, we're here to get Breath Tokens," she went on.

"Why does Somnus send out his bartendress as his coin carrier?" he asked.

"Since I'm one of the few people here who has absolutely no interest in collecting them," she replied.

"Why not?" he asked.

She stopped and stared in silence. "Because I already have everything I need here without Breath Tokens," she finally answered. "Or at least, if I don't, Breath Tokens aren't what will fix that."

Proto tilted his head at her. "You . . . don't need any favors, you mean?" He lifted one of his two Tokens from his pocket and held it up.

She stared at him and the coin blankly. Then, she blinked and made an *ah* sound. "Correct, favors aren't what I need."

Sometimes, Proto felt like everyone here was required simultaneously to be truthful and avoid telling him anything. But he didn't say that out loud.

"What Lilac needs, she takes! She doesn't ask for favors," he instead declared.

The black-haired bartendress shrugged agreeably, and he followed her into the mirky pink.

After a few minutes, a shimmering of the flashlight's beam ahead revealed a river. This one was not like the last cave's river, black and slow and somber. No, its waters ran crystal-clear and tinkly as they rippled. It also narrowed enough here that they could leap across it—though it looked oddly deep, bottomless even. And very sparkly.

"I take it that touching that won't make me lose all my memories," observed Proto.

"No, you'll just grow fairy wings, and flowers will blossom beneath your feet," she replied.

"Well, wouldn't be the first time," he mumbled. He assumed she was kidding but wasn't quite sure.

She suddenly looked excited. "Wait, do you cosplay?"

"Yes, I dress up as a French waitress and serve coffee and cocktails," he said.

She flicked his ear, then pointed at the water. "Careful, or I'll slip this in your next cocktail!"

"Well, I'll make you share it with me!" he threatened.

She stared at him. Then, she removed a glass jar from her basket-bag, delicately filled it with the water, and corked it shut. "It's a date!"

He blinked.

She winked.

He stepped backward away from her.

She flapped her arms.

He ran and jumped over the river.

She laughed delightedly and leapt after him. In her robe, she seemed to glide through the air like Princess Peach. Or Princess Toadstool, rather.

. . . Man, I'm old.

They wound through cavernous coral hues till a stone cliff loomed before them, about fifteen feet high.

"Might have a hard time climbing in that thing," remarked Proto, gesturing at her yukata.

"It's okay. I have a big strong man to help me." She retrieved a rope from her basket-bag and held it out to him. She smiled sweetly.

He raised an eyebrow.

"Well, a male, anyway," she acknowledged. "So, all you have to do is climb to the top and tie the rope to the pointy rock you'll see up there," she instructed. "A big, pink stalagmite, but wider on the top, so the rope won't slip off. It sort of looks like . . . you know, just tie it. Then, toss it down. Okay?"

He eyed the vertical cliff face. "Have we thought through our alternatives?"

"Of course," she immediately replied, lifting the glass jar she'd filled with water. She flapped her arms.

Proto stared. Then, he turned and started climbing.

Her laughter sounded behind him.

The pink cliff was not exactly sheer, but it was no rock-climbing wall with handholds either. Fortunately, he was in decent shape, his strength-to-body-mass ratio was pretty good, and he was flexible.

"Good thing I wore this tracksuit!" he called down.

She flicked his calf. "What's next, Mount Everest?"

The climb got harder. He often had to stretch to reach the next handhold or foothold. At a few points, he had to make a sort of half-jump from ledge to ledge, or shift his weight far over empty space, such that there was no way of turning back. He'd inevitably fall if he messed up.

Once, as he made such a maneuver, he found out too late that the stone he'd reached for had a jagged edge. Even as it cut him, he had to put his whole weight on that hand for a second to avoid falling. When he managed to find a foothold and release the sharp rock, warm, stinging wetness dripped across his palm.

But exhilaration surged through him too. The top of the cliff now loomed almost within reach. This was a challenge he could surmount. Last time, he'd had to cross the River Lethe, the forgetful black waters, to reach Lilac's little beachy paradise. This time, it was The Cliff. Here he was, just inches from surmounting it. What awaited him beyond?

Proto clasped his bloody hand around the top of the cliff and heaved himself overtop. Lying on his back for a moment, he loosed a long sigh of satisfaction.

A rope plopped down atop his belly, startling him out of his contentment. "Heads up!" called Lilac after it'd landed. "Flashlight's next."

He scrambled up in time to see her winding up and tossing the flashlight. As it spun through the air, its beam whirled in wild ellipses across the cavern walls. He barely caught it in his torn-up hand, then almost bobbled it.

"Nice catch, Sausage Fingers," she noted calmly. "Now, go tie the rope."

Grumbling and pondering where to wipe the blood from his fingers, he scanned for that stalagmite she'd mentioned. He beamed the flashlight back and forth.

And there it was: pink, jutting straight up, and wider at the tip.

Smirking like a twelve-year-old boy, he approached and began uncoiling the rope.

From behind the pink pillar emerged a ghostly fairy.

She was human-sized and semilucent. He could see her body and see through it at once. She had red and purple butterfly wings and a matching little dress. Her pale hair was pinned up with sprigs of mistletoe. She looked like Tinkerbell as painted by a pre-Raphaelite.

Proto blinked at her.

She flapped her wings at him.

A glittering dusty breeze wafted from her wings and swept over him. She beckoned alluringly with her finger.

Much as he might've liked to oblige, he'd read enough fairy tales to know this probably wouldn't end well. He resisted the temptation, girding his superego against the urgings of his id. He thought of ice-cold baths and that wrinkled old lady from The Shining, and he resisted.

But that all changed when he inhaled.

It didn't seem like much, that drifting haze from her powdery wings, dispersing through the air. But when he breathed it in, that cloudy eminence seemed to come aglow.

And he *felt* it. Suddenly, it wasn't just sight that his mind was translating into physical attraction. It was *all* the senses.

He found himself ravished by her aroma. It was unlike anything he'd ever smelled, yet had something of many scents: Roses. Honey. And something almost . . . *human*, but not quite.

He'd always laughed a little at the notion of animals being irresistibly drawn to each other by body smells, dignified as "pheromones." But now he understood. Oh, yes, he understood.

"Proto!" called a voice behind and below these lofty heights. "I'm waiting down here!"

There was a feeling too—not just the pseudo-feeling we call emotion, but the reality of *touch*. He felt like unseen hands were massaging him everywhere at once, always gently, but firmly enough to release everything pent up inside. Yet they'd stop any second, too early, unless he continued to come where she was calling.

The fairy crooked her finger at him, drifting backward as she flapped. He stepped forward obligingly, happily, and stepped again.

He felt his world had widened five times over. And his old world now felt unbearably small.

"Proto!" called Lilac earnestly.

A memory flashed through his recollection: *"This is mine. And this is yours now. You've made it yours. . . . Yours to break and mine to mend."* She handed him the mug, and suddenly he was set free.

He looked down in a giddy daze, half-expecting to see the mug there. Its absence made him sad. The whole world seemed foggy, like he were driving a car in the Winter, and the windows had steamed up with breath and heat.

He turned and scanned the bottom of the cliff. There was Lilac, looking up with wide, blinking eyes.

Upon seeing him, she let loose a sigh and planted her hands on her hip. "Well? Having trouble finding that *gigantic pink pillar*? Do I need to characterize it further?"

"Uh, no. Sorry. Just a sec." It was a dullard's reply. But the fog in his head was clearing.

By the time he turned back toward the pillar, it was dawning on him that he'd just been remotely roofied with some sort of pixie powder. And the red-and-purple-winged culprit was fluttering away even now. She disappeared into the shadows of one of four tunnels ahead.

He wondered whether he should chase her or something. But to what end? Demand an apology? Tell her that her lust-dust had just whirled his world and shook his rook?

Let her be. Do what you came here to do, his inner voice commanded.

And Proto obeyed, approaching the tall pink stone and tying the rope.

"Incoming!" he called to Lilac, then tossed the coils down to her.

She'd hiked up her yukata to near waist-level, rolling and tying it. She began climbing deftly from foothold to foothold, only occasionally grasping the rope and pulling herself up a couple feet where necessary.

As she did so, another voice in Proto wondered what would've happened if he'd come where that fairy had called him. *Shall we . . . spread our wings and find out?*

He told that voice to shut up.

We'll keep her waiting in the wings, the voice replied.

"A hand, please?"

He looked down.

Lilac's head and shoulders were above the cliff, and she was holding out a hand. Her bared legs were splayed wide on far apart footholds. Their pallor shone even in the indirect dimness of the flashlight.

The bottom half of the yukata was bunched up about her midsection. Long black hair fell over its front and back. Her hair really was thick. It both was darker and reflected more light than seemed possible.

And then there were her black eyes, those shimmering pools, those dark depths—glaring with annoyance at him.

"Well!?" she demanded, waving her open hand.

Blinking, he grabbed her hand and hauled her overtop, a bit harder than he'd meant to. She was also willowy and light. And she'd sprung upward herself to give some added momentum.

As a result, she ended up being heaved over the cliff's edge and tumbling toward him. He caught her—but not his balance.

Back he fell, pounding onto his rear and then his back. She came with him, managing to catch herself on her hands and knees. This left her crouching over him.

Her black hair was spilling over him. In its shadowy midst, he could see her gaze, glimmering dark amid the darkness.

Was it a void that he was drawn to fill? Or was it a black hole, immeasurably vast and adding him to itself?

Either way, he found himself drawn toward it irresistibly.

She tore her gaze away and stood, brushing off her hands. "I'm supposed to test you. But sometimes, I feel like *you're* testing *me!*" She ran a hand through her hair. "My patience, I mean."

"Um." Her yukata was still hiked up to waist-level, and she was standing almost directly over him. "Please, keep testing."

She tilted her head at him. Then, she followed his gaze to herself.

She stepped away from him, ears flushing pink, and let down her robe.

Forcing down a smile, he sighed wistfully. "Is it just me, or did this room just get darker?"

She swatted his arm as he rose to his feet.

"This flashlight's low," he observed, shaking the tube. "Could you maybe just . . . ?" He grabbed his pantlegs and pulled them up a little.

She swatted the back of his head.

"Now I'm seeing stars." He rubbed his head. "Actually, no. That's just light spots from the extreme white brightness of—"

"Last time I went high," she broke in sweetly, balling her fist. "Next time I go low!"

He looked down at his pants, then back up at her.

She smiled.

His eyes widened. His hands covered the front of his pants. "Lilac, Lilac, please don't strike that!"

She stepped forward, eyes sparkling. "Lilac, Lilac, here comes a light smack!" She raised her fist.

"Lilac, Lilac—what if I fight back!" He raised the flashlight menacingly.

"Lilac, Lilac . . . something something sliced sack!" She drew a butter knife from her basket.

Proto turned and ran away.

Lilac laughed delightedly behind him, as the flashlight in his hand beamed all over the pink walls.

"By the way." He paused his retreat. "I should mention. When I first got up here, there was some sort of fairy ghost. She seemed to be, uh, beckoning me."

"Oh? Was she?" Lilac sounded utterly unsurprised. "Well, we'd best get going then." She strode toward the tunnel through which the fairy had flapped off.

Proto frowned. He had not told Lilac which of the four tunnels it'd been.

"A ghost fairy, was it?" Lilac calmly continued. "Next you'll be telling me she lured you in with scents of roses and honey, I suppose!"

He stared at her. *"Sometimes, I feel like* you're *testing* me!" she'd said.

"That's the tack, is it!" Lilac went on archly. "Make me feel jealous. Mm. You should ask what *I* saw when *I* first came here!"

"Should I?"

She nodded. "Here's a hint. Fairy wings. Nice hair. Nice body. And no tracksuit!"

"Oh? What was his name?" he asked.

"'His'?" she said.

Proto blinked.

She winked.

And on she glided.

"So. That comment about the tracksuit," said Proto after a moment.

"Oh, I like your tracksuit," she assured him. "Like I like your mussed-up hair and frequent screw-ups."

He frowned. "Well. That's reassuring."

"I hope my polite hinting isn't too subtle. Have you considered a yukata?" She gestured at her robe and her belt of blue and yellow primroses.

"Yes. The more flowery, the better," he confirmed.

"Perfect! I have a spare belt." She retrieved it triumphantly from within her robe. It was covered in lilacs.

He nodded grimly as she wrapped it around his waist, sizing it up, then tied it around his tracksuit.

She nodded in satisfaction at her work. "What do you think!"

He eyed the thing. "Oh, what have I done."

Her eyes sparkled. Then, she pulled what looked like an off-brand Polaroid from her basket-bag. "Proto, Proto, how about a photo!"

"Wow." He fixed his apparently mussed-up hair. "Do I have a choice?"

"Not today!" She beamed. "Proto, Proto, how about . . . a kimono!" She reached inside her basket-bag excitedly.

"In there? There's no way . . . " he trailed off.

She pulled out a doll-sized kimono.

He looked down at it, then back up at her.

She placed the kimono on his thumb.

He stared at it. "Did you plan all this? What sort of mastermind . . .?"

"Proto kimono photo time!" she cried, leaning in next to him with her little camera raised. She made a cool face and a peace sign. He gave a thumbs up with his kimono thumb. And she snapped the picture.

The paper slid out and started slowly clarifying. "Hang it somewhere nice!" she enjoined, handing it to him.

"You want me to have it?" He watched the memory take shape on the paper. The lighting wasn't perfect. And the photo wasn't exactly high-resolution. But no camera could've missed how those black eyes sparkled.

"Sure, there's plenty more where that came from." Lilac strolled ahead. "If you want it."

She stepped into the shadows of the fairy's tunnel. And he followed her lead, beaming it bright.

As the tunnel ahead broadened to a chamber, she flapped her arms. And his light cast a titanic shadow fairy against the far wall, fluttering its shadow wings.

"Now I reveal my true form!" she declared in a menacing baritone. She flapped her way around the corner ahead.

"You won't escape me, Shadowfairy Lilac!" Proto vowed, racing after her with a smile and pumping flashlight, as he rounded the corner. "I'll—"

He cut off. In front of him was a shadow fairy.

Well, no. It was a fairy standing in the shadows—the same fairy that'd almost lured him in earlier. She now looked fully corporeal, not half-transparent. Her fey beauty and charm now had a note of queenliness. Indeed, a tall throne stood behind her. It looked like it'd been formed from stone flowing like water, churning and foaming, and abruptly frozen in place.

Nearby, Lilac stood calmly in her kimono, serenely brushing a strand of black hair from her face, looking for all the world like she'd been painted there by some classical artist.

"Greetings, manfolk. My name is Anima," hailed the queenly fairy. "I had hoped that you'd chase me. But perhaps not quite like that." She eyed his getup.

Proto looked down at his tracksuit, complete with a big lilac-covered yukata belt and—*sigh*—the doll kimono on his thumb.

Why does this keep happening to me?

"Yes, that's mine!" replied Lilac mildly, clasping his lilac-covered belt. "I'm afraid he's tied up."

"Shame," yawned Anima.

"I wonder where that chase would've led," mumbled Proto, eying the lithesome queen as she fluttered.

"Nowhere good!" Lilac tugged him backward by the lilac-covered belt.

"Oh, all over this cave, and ultimately back where you started. And *she*"—Anima gestured toward Lilac—"no doubt would've moved on by then. No one can catch me! People only reach me here by chasing something else. Or someone."

As she spoke, Proto surveyed the room—a sort of decorated grotto open to the outdoors. Both sunlight and a burbling brook flowed in from outside.

Beyond the entrance, he could see grass and trees. Flowers grew in colorful multitudes. Frolicking in their midst were dozens of fairies.

"Speaking of which," said Lilac, "we're here on an errand for Somnus."

Anima sighed. "Yes, yes, the Breath Tokens. It's vexing how he ignores me except when he needs something, and then he sends others to come get it!"

Something about the way she spoke reminded Proto of Flua-Sahng—that redheaded and radiant Queen of Heaven he'd met in Mercune's dream. Maybe her regal bearing or something.

"What would you do if Somnus came?" asked Lilac.

"Lead him on a merry chase, then fly away and take a nap," she replied immediately. "Then, if he still wanted anything, he could come visit my dreams and ask me about it!"

"I can't imagine why he doesn't visit more often," mused Proto.

"Quite!" pouted Anima. "The problem is, no one seems to understand what *fun* is. The fun lies in the chase, not the catching. People get so good at getting what they want, they miss what they need!"

"Fun?" asked Proto.

"Me." Anima was enswathed again in cloudy radiance. Her lips parted, and her eyes widened. Pink, shimmering eyes, rapt upon *him*. And that aroma! Roses and honey and . . .

"So. The Breath Tokens," Lilac flatly interrupted.

"Alright, alright!" sighed Anima, turning away. The spell over Proto abruptly broke. "This way." She fluttered out of the grotto into the grassy paradise outside.

They followed her about a hundred yards, as motley birds and fairies and butterflies winged by. Ahead, dozens of silvery sacks were hanging from the boughs of a hawthorn tree on silken strings.

Anima crooked her finger at a straying fairy and issued a command. It gathered some of its brethren and flapped over to the tree. Together, they untied two sacks and carried them back to the waiting trio.

They dropped the two sacks directly at Proto's feet.

He looked down at the hefty bags, then up at Lilac. "By the way. Why did you need me here?"

She looked down at the hefty bags, then up at him. She smiled cheerfully.

He sighed.

"You brag to the world that you've been lifting," she recalled. "And then you complain when I give you the chance to show it off?"

"You'll certainly have your chance to show off!" observed Anima. "This is a double order."

Proto managed to heft the two sacks in one hand. "Okay, where's the other half?" He stretched his other arm behind his head, absently flexing his bicep.

Anima laughed. "That may be more impressive minus the tracksuit."

"Always the tracksuit!" he lamented. "No comments on my flowery belt?"

"Your friend is fun, Lilac. He reminds me of myself," remarked Anima.

"Is it his whimsical flightiness? Or the fact that everything's a joke to him?" asked the bartendress.

"Both! Well said," concurred Anima. "Also, I get the sense that he likes a chase almost as much as I do. Though I suspect he chases more than he's chased."

"Oh, it's quite a bit of both, I think," muttered Lilac.

"What's that?" asked Proto, who was busy shifting a sack to his other hand. This weight was killing his left arm.

"Nothing!" she replied, turning to Anima. "Well, we're off, before Proto's arms fall off. Thank you as always."

"Anytime!" Anima touched her lips and briefly glowed again. "Really, *any-time*."

Proto forced his stare away and started to follow Lilac.

Dazed and bedazzled, and straining with the bags, it took him a moment to realize they weren't returning to the grotto. Instead, they were wandering further into fairyland.

"Taking a detour?" he asked.

"Giving your arms a much-needed workout!" she answered.

He eyed his bicep and nodded grimly.

"No. Your arm is good." She patted his muscle kindly. "We're just taking another route. Like I said, you have to take the odyssey first. But once you do, there's an easier route home."

"That does sound like the Odyssey," he noted.

"Remember, Proto! Lilac, not Dahlia."

"My bad." He scanned the luscious flowery fields. "So . . . is our odyssey over then?"

"Not quite!" She pointed toward a circle of standing stones atop a hill on the horizon. It looked like Stonehenge, only not half-fallen. "We're headed there."

"Ah. Is it time for our druid ritual already?" inquired Proto. "Has the solstice arrived? Is the sun transitioning from Gemini to Cancer?"

"Here, have an hors d'oeuvre and keep quiet." She reached into her basket-bag and handed him a wafer with pear, bleu cheese and honey.

"Will do." He bit off half and, closing his eyes, savored it.

"Yes, make it last," she instructed. "No seconds till we're all set up!"

"Can this odyssey last forever?" he asked through a mouthful.

"That's entirely up to you," she murmured, looking heavenward. The sun beamed down upon her pallor, and she beamed back.

Outside of Somnus' Palace, the sky had looked universally mirky and mysterious. But here, it looked as celestial blue as the grass was elysian green.

"I guess there's no rush, is there?" Proto felt a little giddy.

"Nope. Only Paunch and Somnus are waiting for us," she replied. "I don't care what one of them thinks. And the other could use some time away from the kitchen."

Proto swallowed again, savoring the dreamy flavors. "If he's not careful, he's going to find himself out of a job. Replaced by Lilac!"

"Which one of them?" Her black eyes sparkled. "The one who cooks delicious food? Or the one you dream of?"

He looked at her: That dark gaze glimmering light. The paleness of her face around her quirked-up lips. The black hair pouring down the white and blackness of her robe. Indeed, she was black and white from head to heel, except those blue and yellow primroses on the belt that held it all together.

He found his lips falling apart.

Before he could decide what to do or say next, she slid another hors d'oeuvre into his open mouth—a bacon-wrapped water chestnut.

He blinked but, obviously, couldn't say anything. Instead, he just started chewing.

She nodded in satisfaction.

About twenty seconds later, she glanced at him but found him still chewing vigorously. She giggled.

Meanwhile, they reached the standing stones, looming large and mysterious. Lilac opened her basket-bag and pulled out a thin blanket fraught with primroses, lilacs and other little flowers. She lay it across the grass.

When Proto finally swallowed that bite, he loosed a long sigh of wistful satisfaction.

Again, she peered at him a moment, then smiled. "Yes, that's enough of an answer for today," she murmured.

"So . . . is there more where that came from?" He leaned and tried to look inside the basket-bag. From this angle, it looked nearly as dark and obscure as the depths of her eyes.

"What do you think?" She reached inside.

CHAPTER 14
FRIENDS AND

Time passed. Proto's daily visits with Astrid and occasionally Mayger became routine for him, but that didn't make life dull. On the contrary, it just freed up more of his focus for all the little human things along the way: humor and friendships, and meaningful moments.

And the occasional weirdness—for example, when that mustachioed man in the three-piece suit, named Wentsworth, came up to him and declared, "Your secret is ours, Proto! You can count on us!" He was a shadowseer who was obsessed with H.P. Lovecraft, according to Dahlia. And as far as Proto recalled, those were the first words the guy had ever spoken to him.

All in all, it felt a little like high school; or, rather, as if working life had continued like high school. A working life where those around him behaved like humans, rather than soulless corporate robots mimicking humans. It felt like a family; not just a business calling itself a "family" to guilt employees into working longer hours and happily obeying its parental authority.

Then again, maybe this was just another example of how Proto's change in mentality had made life better. Maybe *this* sort of life had always been there, waiting for him, if he'd just gone out and made it his.

In any event, his present life was good. As for the future, Dahlia's shadowcasting had continued to show ominous but ambiguous scenes. That strange redness of the skies, streaking with lights, was appearing more and more often.

What this meant, no one knew—at least, no one Proto talked to. They carried on their lives the same as always. Those fiery skies became like fire alarms at college dorms. They made you lose some sleep at first, but everyone got better at ignoring them after a while.

Thus was Proto sitting calmly with Jet and Jag one morning, sipping from his black mug, when Lilac arrived at the table with a platter full of pastries.

"Who's *that* for?" Jag leaned toward it like a cat toward sushi.

"Hello to you too," she replied.

"Who baked this exquisite spread?" asked Proto. "This confectionery cornucopia?"

"That's better." Lilac held out the platter to let him take a pastry, then the others. "Save some for Paunch. Or soon you'll look like him."

"Not me. I can't gain weight from eating." Jag patted his belly. "Special talent. Jet can confirm."

"I'd give up my taste in clothes, my Breath Tokens, my diligent competency, and my Euchre skills," Jet nodded, "if I could have his special talent."

Proto supposed he had a bit of that special talent too. To be sure, he'd always exercised—mostly running and skiing—but not enough to earn the lean muscularity he'd somehow maintained since his high-school-athlete days, given all the greasy fast food he ate. Sometimes he woke up feeling sore, like he'd done a killer workout the day before, when in fact he'd just lounged around. This was odd, but he wasn't complaining.

Meanwhile, Astrid had approached the table, holding what looked to be half a freezer cheeseburger. It looked like she had something to say, judging by her focused face, but she didn't want to interrupt.

At least, not yet. She now was planting a hand on her hip, cocking her head and exhaling.

"Even Paunch's sweets aren't this good," observed Jag through a mouthful.

"You should make more full meals, Lilac!" urged Jet. "It's been years."

"Oh, I don't think it's been that long." Lilac glanced at Proto. "Anyway, my range is nowhere near as broad as Paunch's. Mostly just Provencal and Tuscan cuisine. And Kyoto, modern and traditional. And British meatpies. And—what?" She frowned at Proto, who'd begun laughing, followed by the others.

Well, almost all the others. Astrid was rolling her eyes. She took a bite of her burger.

It occurred to Proto that he hadn't had a burger in a long time. Quadruple smashburgers had been one of his go-to lunches, back at his marketing job in the breathing world. He had good memories of sitting back in one of the restaurant's padded booths, taking his first greasy bite, and letting his mind go warm and hazy. It was a good thing he'd gone running so often—he'd devoured those juicy, savory burgers all the time. In fact, eating one of them was among his very last waking memories, right before he'd gone running and . . .

Proto blinked. *Right before what?* He'd seen the outlines of a memory in the corner of his mind's eye. But when he'd focused on them, they'd disappeared.

"What about you, Astrid?" Jag was asking, as she took another bite. "Do you cook?"

Astrid, still rolling her eyes, froze and glanced at Proto. "A little," she mumbled through her mouthful.

"Like, what cuisines?" asked Jet.

" . . . I can make eggs a few ways. Scrambled, fried or . . . what's it called. Sunny-side up," replied the jumpsuited woman. She brushed her bouffant off her face.

It was silent for a moment.

"So, Lilac, tell us about food in Kyoto," urged Jet.

"Sure." The pale woman began rattling off appetizing facts, absently running a hand through her long black hair. "So, I love kyou-zushi and all that," she concluded. "But after a while, sometimes, I just want a meatpie. And, luckily, they have *excellent* meatpies at those covered arcades—"

"What's this about meatpies?" Dahlia now was strolling up in her flowery Victorian robe, her blonde hair flowing all over her back. "I make a mean meatpie! And cream pie."

Astrid scowled, taking another fierce bite of her burger.

"Do you?" replied Proto to the curvaceous bookworm. "You find time to cook between shadowcasting, reading every book in the world, playing cards, and outdrinking everyone here? Besides Somnus."

"Besides Somnus," agreed Dahlia. "But yes, how could I *not* make time for cooking? The way to the heart is through the stomach!"

Astrid scoffed audibly.

"In fact," the shadowseer went on, "I made Somnus install a cooking range, using those abyssal flames by the Shadowcaster. And *my*, does it work well! It gets hot down there. But a little heat never bothered me."

"Well, Madame Bartendress, perhaps a cookoff is in order!" declared Proto.

Lilac sized Dahlia up. Then, she shrugged agreeably. "Always happy to support amateur competition."

Dahlia's brow rose. Then, she turned to Proto. "If there's a cookoff, I'll be needing a nickname too. What, will it be Dahlia vs. *Madame Bartendress?* Unfair! Prejudicial! I won't have it."

"Very well, Madame Shadowchef!" said Proto.

"Mm. Very sinister," observed Dahlia. "I'll take it!"

"You can leave me as 'Astrid,'" the silvery-blue haired woman abruptly broke in. "But I'll be competing too."

Everyone blinked and stared at her.

"I thought you said . . . " Jag began after a moment.

He cut off at the sight of Astrid's fiery violet glare. Her fingers had clenched halfway through her burger.

" . . . Very well, Madame Silverwear!" Proto threw up his arms. "A three-way it is!"

"Silverware? Why . . . ?" Jag's eyes followed Jet's finger to the silvery grey she was wearing. "Ah."

Astrid's face was flushed. But maybe that was just because she was realizing what she'd gotten herself into.

"A battle for the ages!" enthused Jet. "Rule number one is, we get to try everything."

"No, that's rule number seven," noted Somnus. He'd just walked in beneath the painting of the old man. "Rule number one is, never give up on something genius because of the rules."

"Well, Lord of Dreams, this cookoff is genius, so we're doing it even if it breaks your rules," replied Jag.

"You think I'd stop this?" asked Somnus. "And ruin the best cookoff since Louis XVI? What sort of Jacobin do you take me for?"

Jet held out his arms welcomingly. "I don't know what that means, but it's good to have you with us."

"I thought it was funny, Somnus," consoled Dahlia. "Let them eat cake! Baked by me."

"Oh, that's sharp, Dahlia!" chuckled Somnus. "I'm glad one of you understands references from before the days of polyester and frozen food."

"Are you subtweeting me?" Astrid eyed her jumpsuit and freezer cheeseburger.

"I don't know what that means, but it bodes poorly for this cookoff," replied Somnus.

"At least your references aren't all from the days of shoulder pad suits and Thundercats," said Lilac.

"Now who's being subtweeted?" sighed Proto.

"Enough of these birdbrained neologisms! You're *visitors of dreams*, not teenage phone junkies," admonished Somnus. "That is, visitors of dreams, a shadowseer, an oddjob assistant, and a provisional visitor."

"Is that from top to bottom?" asked Proto.

"Hardly!" replied Somnus. "Visitors and shadowseers are very much on equal terms."

" . . . hey," said Jag.

"Hello to you too, Oddjob Assistant," said Somnus. "Speaking of which, Provisional Visitor," he turned to Proto, "you won't be a provisional visitor much longer. Your evaluation date is just around the corner!"

"Speaking of which, Proto and I should be off to our visit," Astrid broke in, finally saying what she'd come here to say. "We're now late."

"Well, why didn't you say so?" waved Somnus. "No points off for Proto. This falls on the mentor!"

Rolling her eyes, Astrid stuffed her remaining burger in her mouth, grabbed Proto's arm and dragged him away. She released him after they'd exited beneath the vast painting, then continued at a brisk pace, forcing him into a near-jog.

"What do you know! I'm going to be a visitor soon," declared Proto.

"Maybe. But that's not what Somnus said," she replied.

"What?"

"He said you *won't be a provisional visitor* much longer," she said. "That will be true whether he approves or rejects you. And if he approves you, then you'll have to decide what *you* want to do."

"So … what do you think my chances are, Miss Evaluator?" he asked. "I assume you have some insights on the matter."

She eyed him sidelong. "I've made my criticisms known to you. Consistently." At his look of distress, her face softened. "But maybe I haven't been as vocal about my other thoughts."

"Like what?" he said.

She said nothing, but stared at him with wide violet eyes. They looked young.

Then, she turned abruptly away. "You'll find out at your evaluation, I suppose!"

"Alright, alright, Miss Geode," he said.

She halted and faced him again. "What did you just call me?"

"Rough and hard on the outside. But something very different shows through the cracks!" he observed.

She blinked her violet eyes twice. "Oh, shut up," she finally said, turning away and showing him a grey shoulder.

He smiled. "Yep!"

"Also, you're ignoring the second part of what I said," she murmured.

"Huh?" Proto wasn't sure what she meant.

She shook her head. "Never mind."

"Oh. About me having to decide," he remembered. "Like, I could decide to be a shadowseer or something? Or a bartender?"

She looked away, her lips curved up. "Sure. Sure, those are possibilities."

"Yeah, not really feeling it. But we'll see." Proto walked a little further in silence, eying that look on her face. "It sounds like I might be misunderstanding something."

"What? You, misunderstand something?" Astrid replied. "Next you'll be telling me that Somnus overdrank and Mayger overdressed."

"Or Astrid gratuitously burned the provisional visitor," said Proto.

"Or Hobo wore his tracksuit!" She gestured at him.

He smiled and rolled his eyes. "So . . . what *am* I misunderstanding?"

She looked wistfully at him, lips parting, then faced forward again. "Tomorrow's winds will blow tomorrow."

"What?"

"I said, save tomorrow for tomorrow!"

And that was that. They continued in silence for a while down corridors of misty blue.

A quiet yawn from Astrid drew his eyes. He saw that her cheeks were sagging and eyelids were droopy. Another yawn followed about thirty seconds later.

"Someone need a nap?" he asked lightly.

"Someone needs a break," she replied. "Not all of us do just one thing each day."

"You've been helping Somnus a lot, right?" he said. "With whatever that situation is involving Yemos, the reddening skies, and so forth?"

"Yes. As I told you the other day," she answered.

Proto frowned. "*You most certainly did not tell me that, the other day,*" he wanted to say.

"Important business?" he instead asked.

"Oh, just about a thousand times more serious than normal dream visits. Which I'm continuing to do," she said. "And, in the meantime, I'm helping a provisional visitor lose his 'provisional.' Maybe. So, yeah, I'm staying busy."

"Well, why don't you take a break?" Proto reached into his pocket and held out the two Breath Tokens he'd gotten playing cards. "Have Mayger and Jet handle a couple days for you."

She stared at the Tokens. "Are you asking me for a favor? Or is this about the evaluation? I can't change what I already told Somnus."

His face flushed. "No. You just looked tired." The arm he was holding out sank. "I mean, I still owe you two, right?" His lips curved up as he recalled that first day.

"No. I was just doing my job," she said quietly.

He looked at her, hearing an odd note in her voice. Her lips were pressed in an expression of . . . *guilt?* Her eyes were narrowed upon the ground.

Proto adopted a playful smile. "I know you'd prefer that I remain in your debt forever—!"

"You know absolutely nothing!" she shouted.

He blinked and slowed to a stop, crestfallen.

She met his gaze. Her violet eyes were shimmering. Then, she quickly turned away and wiped her face.

What is going on . . . ?

He stared, unsure what to say. Her clenched fist trembled at her side.

Finally, she turned toward him and reached for his hand, grasping it—no, clasping the Breath Tokens. "Thank you, Proto." Her voice quavered.

"Proto?" he mused. "I think that's the first time—"

Astrid cut him off, rushing forward and hugging him. She buried her head in his shoulder.

Eyes wide and unsure what to do, he clasped an arm around her back. After a moment, he felt tears wettening his shoulder beneath his tracksuit.

Sometimes, Proto felt he'd come to know this place, bit by bit, day after day. Then, there were moments like this, when he realized all he knew was just one corner of a map bigger than he could see.

Then again, it also was moments like this—with violet-eyed Astrid pressed against him, arms thrown around him, feeling the swell of her every breath—that Proto realized he didn't need to know everything in life to live it.

She eventually withdrew. She wiped her face with her fist, still clasping the Breath Tokens, then pocketed them. "I'll ask you to forget that little episode." Her voice's calmness was belied by its hoarseness. And her puffy eyes.

"Yeah, I can't do that. And I wouldn't if I could," he replied. That brought a little red glower to her face. "But my lips are sealed," he quickly went on. "What happens in my dream, stays in my dream."

"Your 'dream.'" She rolled her eyes but smiled. "It had better, Utterflutter. Wyndsack. Shyteman."

"My lips are sealed, Miss Geode! Madame Silverwear! Astird!"

His mentor swatted his rear, eliciting a yowl. "That's what insubordination gets you!" She resumed walking down the corridor.

"Okay, but what do I get for being nice?" he grumbled, rubbing his backside as he followed.

Astrid said nothing and kept walking, apparently ignoring him.

Suddenly, she stepped in front of him and faced him, seizing both his hands. She peered at him with wide violet eyes. Her lips were pursed with thought. *Or . . . ?* She was leaning forward now.

Then, she tapped two fingers to her lips, and touched them softly to his cheek. "That. For now."

She turned and walked onward.

Proto felt his cheek tingling. He followed her with his eyes, the curves of her grey-clad figure swaying into prominence with each step. He smiled dumbly.

Then, he realized he should probably follow her with his feet too. He half-jogged to catch up.

A minute later, Astrid tapped a sliding white doorway. It slid open, revealing a mirky passage. "Let's see what you've learned."

"Hm?" He was still feeling slaphappy. "A test?"

She just gestured him onward. And on he walked into the swirling blue mists.

He emerged into the woods in late Summer. Stars peeked through the canopy of leaves overhead. A cool breeze rustled through the elms and ashes. Shadow-branches shifted on the ground.

Snapping twigs and scuffed grass behind him signaled that Astrid had arrived. He inhaled, savoring the musky scent of fallen leaves and the brisk night wind.

Wondering where the dreamer was, he scanned his surroundings. Everything looked a bit dark and washed out. The horizon trailed off into mist.

Somehow, Proto felt he knew where he should be going. He let instinct guide him, rustling and brushing through the foliage, until a dirt path appeared before him.

He started to step onto the trail, until a glimpse of red movement in the darkness made him hesitate. He stayed in the brush and peered down the path toward its source.

After a moment, a young man in a red coat came into view. He was stepping slowly and halting sometimes, like he was lost in thought and barely had any wherewithal left for walking.

Proto suddenly realized what was going on. He turned and looked at Astrid. But she just raised her brow and pointed toward the dreamer.

It was the same guy as in Proto's very first dream visit. The one who'd been robbed in the woods. Proto had jumped in to stop the robber and rescue him, but instead had woken him up.

Excitement thrilled through Proto. For once, his work here as a visitor reminded him of his day job, where he'd worked at a marketing firm doing A/B testing—that is, running sample ads with slight variations on test groups of customers, with the various ads known as version A, version B, and so forth. His whole job had been finding ways to make tweaks that resulted in better outcomes.

And that's exactly what he had to do right now. He had to find a way to make this dream turn out better.

With his mind racing, Proto peered at the red-jacketed dreamer. *So, if this dream is anything like the last one, this guy should get robbed any minute now.*

That earlier dream replayed in his head over the next few seconds: How the robber had sprung from the brush and tackled the dreamer. How Proto had darted forward, cane in hand, and smacked the robber to the ground. How the robber had stood and drawn a gun on him. How they'd ended up struggling on the forest floor. And how Proto couldn't beat him—not until he'd turned himself into some sort of anime superhero, startling the dreamer awake in the process.

In retrospect, this seemed to be one of those situations where the dreamer was firmly steering the dream in a certain direction—the robber would win. Proto had been able to change that only by doing something totally unrealistic. And that had sent the whole dream swerving awry, irrevocably off-course.

How can I beat that robber without waking this guy up? Maybe if I hit him harder at the start? What if I draw a gun? He's not gonna get up from that, *right?*

Somehow, it didn't feel right. *"Do you have one subtle bone in your body?"* he recalled Astrid asking him, on one of those early visits. He stared for another second at the red-jacketed dreamer.

Then, Proto smiled. He stepped onto the path. "Hey there," he called to the dreamer.

The dreamer stepped backward and raised a hand defensively. Mists swirled up from the leaf cover to knee level. "Who—?" His eyes flicked back and forth, like both his mind and feet had been wandering and left him somewhere unfamiliar. "I mean, uh, hi." He eyed Proto like he might draw a jackknife and spring forward at any moment.

That, at least, was something Proto could keep from happening.

"This will sound weird," said Proto, "but any chance you want some company? I'm kind of lost out here. Trying to find my way back to a campsite."

"Uh. I guess that's fine," the man slowly replied. He glanced down at Proto's waist, as though checking if there was a gun or knife there.

Proto made sure there wasn't. "Great." He gestured forward along the path, and the dreamer fell into stride beside him. "I guess I should've asked, is this the right way?"

The dreamer tilted his head thoughtfully, as the mists rose a bit more. "Yeah. Yeah, I think the camping grounds are this way," he finally nodded.

"Good."

They walked for a while down the leafy moonlit trail. The world emerged from far off mists as they moved, like it were being created from that ambiguity on the fly.

Meanwhile, the robber never appeared. It seemed Proto's sudden appearance had satisfied this guy's psychological need for someone unexpected to show up.

"So, uh, how'd you end up lost in the forest after midnight?" asked the red-coated man.

"I wish I had some cool story," replied Proto, improvising as he spoke. "But I actually just sleepwalk. I was camping with some friends out here. Went to sleep in my tent. Woke up in the middle of nowhere."

"No joke?" The man stared at him. "Is that normal for you?"

"I wouldn't say normal," said Proto. "Not these days. But I used to do it all the time. Definitely not the first time I woke up outside." All of this was actually true. "Once, I woke up in the back of my friend's station wagon."

"No way." The guy's lips curved up. "The kind with the backward seats?"

Proto nodded. "The best kind."

"Man. Even sleepwalkers can see how cool those are," the man mused. "I'm Emil, by the way."

"I'm Proto."

Immediately after saying that, he wondered if he should've used an alibi. What if he eventually woke up and met this Emil in real life? What if Emil looked up Proto online and found out he was *real?*

Proto felt like he'd just broken the time-space continuum and was about to start disintegrating Marty McFly-style.

But he didn't. They walked onward.

"So, I take it you're not a fellow sleepwalker?" asked Proto.

"Nope. Just an insomniac," said Emil. "May as well get some exercise while I'm failing to sleep."

"You could always try doing that while sleeping. Kill two birds with one stone," suggested Proto. "Might wake up in some weird places though."

"Say, a station wagon," chuckled Emil.

"So, what's keeping you sleepless?" Proto didn't miss the irony of asking a dreamer this question.

"Eh. Got some big decisions coming up," the man said. "Just graduated the other day. Now, I have to decide what to do with my life."

"Well. What are the options?" asked Proto.

The mists swirled up to belly-level as Emil glanced at him—perhaps wondering what, exactly, he was doing talking to a stranger in the woods at night about his potential career paths. "One option," he finally said, "is to accept a consulting job offer I got recently. The other is . . . something different."

"Different?" repeated Proto.

"Oh, I have an idea for something. Very secretive." Emil grinned and rolled his eyes self-deprecatingly. "But I mean, realistically, there's zero chance—"

"This consulting job," interrupted Proto, feeling a sudden sense that this conversation was on the verge of swerving off-course. "Is it like your dream job or something?"

"Heh. Who would say *consulting* is his dream job?" asked Emil. "I mean, call me a nerd and a geek, sure. But 'consulting is my dream job' takes it to a whole new level."

"Fair," grinned Proto, absently noting that the mists were sinking now. "But probably a dream salary at least."

"That's the tradeoff, isn't it?" sighed the red-jacketed man. "Salary. Reliability. Some certainty about my future. Just do what I'm supposed to do, and life will go right. Or at least, life won't go too wrong." He seemed to be half-talking to himself by the end.

A quiet laugh slipped from Proto before he could catch it.

"Hm? What?" asked Emil.

"Oh, nothing. 'Do what I'm supposed to do, and life won't go too wrong,'" repeated Proto. "That sums up 27 years of my life. And look where that left me!"

Emil looked at him. "Sleepwalking in the woods in a tracksuit?"

"Nope! At a reliable job. Working 8 to 6. And using my spare time and money to play video games," replied Proto. "Where I could pretend to lead the interesting life I'd chosen not to live."

Emil eyed him sidelong, as the mists swelled back up to waist level. "You and our whole generation."

"Yeah, for the most part," he agreed.

They walked in silence for several seconds.

"And yet here you are, sleepwalking in the woods," the red-coated man observed.

"Here I am!" nodded Proto. "I've messed up more the last few months than in ten years before that. For every time I've made the right decision, I've made a wrong one. Maybe two or three."

"What changed?" asked Emil.

"It's complicated," mused Proto. "For a while, I thought it was just a change of mentality. I'd started living life like a dream. Like it wasn't quite real. Like you could take risks rather than avoiding them."

"But . . . ?" the man said.

"But everything just ended up feeling *more* real." Proto had only half-worked out what he was saying as it came out. "When I took risks, and things went wrong, I felt it more than ever. It *hurt*. And when things went right—well, I have more memories these last few months than in ten years before that."

"So what do you think now?" asked Emil.

"I think," said Proto slowly, "the reason that approach worked for me—the reason my life has been a dream lately, and not a nightmare—is that I've made friends who've helped make it that way. Friends and—well, anyway."

Proto was not sure why he was saying all this right now—thoughts he'd been hesitant to think, much less voice aloud. But somehow, it felt like the time was right.

"It's funny though," he went on. "Sometimes, I feel like all my friends have some secret that I'm not in on. And they're all leading me along toward doing something for reasons they're not telling me. And I wonder, 'Can they be trusted? Or should I back away from it all?'"

"But then, another voice in me says, 'Dude. *You* can't be trusted. You *failed* without them. Your life sucked. Who cares if they're concealing something? You *need* them. You should be asking yourself, how can I make my future *with them* as good as it can be? Because there's nothing worthwhile left of you without your friends. Friends and . . .'"

Proto's lips pressed together. He suddenly was acutely aware that he and Emil were not the only two people in this dream.

"'Friends and . . . '?" repeated Emil.

Proto firmed himself up. "Friends and—"

"*There* you are!" called Astrid, strolling into view from around a bend. "Bloody hell, Proto, we thought a bear ate you."

"Did I ever tell you I sleepwalk sometimes?" he asked her.

"Oh? Gonna have to tie you down, huh," mused Astrid.

"I suppose you will!" he replied enthusiastically.

She tilted her head at him. Then, frowning and glancing at Emil, she flicked Proto's ear.

"So. You came for me!" he observed merrily.

Astrid rolled her eyes. "That's what he said," she mumbled.

"... wait, what?" Proto beamed. "Am I dreaming? Who is this standing before me, looking like Astrid, yet speaking such words? This must be ... Nastrid."

She swatted his head, mussing up his hair.

Like a fly hit by a hand in midflight, he kept going. "What's next? Will pigs fly? No point rolling in dirty filth anymore—leave that nastiness to Nastrid!"

This time, she swung low.

But he'd come to expect this. He had a hand in place as he dodged aside, so her fist slapped him a high-five. "Oh yeah," said Proto like the Kool Aid man.

Astrid's violet eyes flared with fury. But her lips curved up too.

Meanwhile, the mists had sunk so low they'd almost disappeared. And Emil was barely suppressing laughter. "Friends and," he murmured.

Astrid blinked and looked at him, apparently remembering where she was. She flushed faintly.

"A ... friend of yours?" Emil asked Proto.

"Emil, meet Astrid," he replied. "She may look like a 1960s Russian cosmonaut Bond girl, but she's our Astrid."

"A pleasure!" She clasped Emil's hand. "As for Slow Bro here, his tracksuit and dumb grin may make him look like a mafioso's loser son who's had too much hard seltzer. But he's our loser."

Emil looked back and forth at them and chuckled quietly.

Astrid ran a hand through her hair, glancing at Proto before looking away. On her cheeks was ... *a blush?*

"Anyway," said Proto, his breast swelling with a tingling warmth, "it seems I'm not lost anymore. But if you still want to hang out, you can come to our campsite. Play some cards or something."

Emil started to laugh it off, then tilted his head at Proto's serious face. "Really? I mean, I guess it's a weekend, right?" He shrugged. "What do you play?"

"Euchre?" suggested Proto.

"Never heard of it," replied Emil. "How about wild rummy?"

"*Yes!*" cried Astrid. "I haven't gotten to play that in fifty years!" Then, she blushed again as she realized what she'd just said.

Meanwhile, Emil blinked at her, as the mists swirled up to their knees. "Uh, ha. Yeah, it's an old game. Must be older than you look, huh!" he joked.

"1960s Bond girl," shrugged Proto.

She flicked his ear. "Older than that!"

Emil smiled, apparently having concluded this was some inside joke. "Well, lead the way, Nastrid!"

She spun to him, her violet glare wide, as Proto cackled.

Then, her lips curved up too. She turned and led the way.

After a few minutes, they reached a campsite. It had a food table, a still-smoldering fire pit, and a couple large tents a ways off. Astrid got a fire going, and they started playing atop a flannel blanket.

"Nice setup," observed Emil. "Wish I'd brought drinks."

"Here, we can share Proto's flask." Astrid reached behind a tree stump and retrieved a huge, canteen-like flask, blazoned with an ornate image of the planet Saturn.

Proto raised an eyebrow.

"Wow. Where'd you find that thing, Proto? Local temple holding an auction?" asked Emil. "Also, does that match your tracksuit?"

Proto gave a sidelong glance to Astrid, who was beaming. "I don't remember where I got it. I must've tested it out too much afterward, huh."

"Hope you don't mind strong whisky," said Astrid, pouring a dram into a red Solo cup.

"If I'm going into consulting," replied Emil, "I'd better get used to it."

They played wild rummy. Astrid was a master of the game—even after fifty years, apparently. Proto, in contrast, had to be reminded of the rules, so it took a while to get started. But things went smoothly after a couple rounds. Soon, it felt like their many card nights back at Somnus' Palace.

"This is fun," remarked Emil, sipping some whisky. "Makes me feel less bad about missing that other camping trip."

"Other camping trip?" asked Proto absently, focused on his hand.

"Yeah. Friend of mine, Yemos, invited me. Would've left with them yesterday," replied Emil. "He and his girlfriend and brother are going to see some huge tree you can walk inside. Big as a house in there. When it was discovered, they say there was a *Viking axe* inside. Which is pretty weird. And pretty cool."

"Wait, Yemos?" Proto stared. "With his twin brother, Mannus?"

"That's the one. What, you know them?" asked the red-jacketed man, drawing a bemused nod from Proto. "Small world. Yep, those two and Yemos' girlfriend, Ausrine. I feel sorry for Mannus—I was supposed to be the fourth wheel."

"How do *you* know Yemos?" asked Proto. Emil had just graduated college, which made him considerably younger than Yemos and Proto.

"Oh, we met last year at the university museum. Medieval weaponry exhibition," recalled Emil. "We were both admiring some huge halberd. At least, they called it a halberd—it was really a bardiche, I looked it up later. Anyway, we hung out a few times after that. And then he invited me on this trip. Thought I'd be interested because of that Viking axe. Which, of course, was right."

Proto exchanged a glance with Astrid. Her violet eyes were narrowed with thought.

It couldn't be a coincidence that Yemos' name kept popping up like this. Was this Lady Luck's doing? And if so, *why?*

"But I don't feel so bad now," waved Emil. "If I'd gone, I would've missed this."

"This excellent night of sleepwalking, old card games, old Astrids, and whisky from a chalice-flask?" asked Proto.

"That's the one," confirmed Emil.

"Many things have improved since the 1960s," remarked Astrid, "but not hair, jumpsuits and card games."

"Cheers to that!" Emil raised his red Solo cup. They tapped all three and drank.

"To Slow Bro, Red-Jacket Guy, and Nastrid!" declared Proto, raising his cup. Emil tapped it and drank.

Astrid flicked his ear.

"One of these times," observed Proto, rubbing his ear, "it's just going to come off."

"You're lucky! Could be worse," retorted Astrid.

Proto looked at her a moment. "And . . . Nastrid's back!"

Her face flushed. "That is *not* what I meant!"

Emil laughed quietly. "Friends and," he murmured.

Proto smiled. This was a weird night—befriending a random guy in a dream and playing dream-cards with dream-whisky—but a good night. And not just for the dreamer.

He glanced over at Astrid. Strands of silvery-blue hair hung in front of her face. One finger was over her lips in thought. She was peering upon her cards with narrowed eyes. They reflected the dancing flame in violet hues.

He felt that warm tingling in his breast again. *Yes, a good night.*

They finished their game—with Astrid narrowly beating Emil—and then basked in the flames' waning light and warmth.

"Suppose I should get going soon. But this was good," yawned Emil, stretching his arms, as the others nodded. "Had a lot on my mind lately. I'd been worried about striking my own path, going it alone. But maybe I don't have to do it alone. Maybe . . . " He shook his head after a moment and smiled self-deprecatingly. "That whisky's strong, Proto!"

Proto and Astrid exchanged their own smiles, which said all that needed saying.

The world had started turning faintly shadowy and translucent, taking on an air of half-reality. In the distance, clouds of whitish-grey were bulging and burgeoning toward them.

Emil didn't seem to notice. He was facing the starry heavens.

Suddenly, Astrid turned to Proto with wide violet eyes. She blinked twice at him.

He realized he had just clasped her hand. *Too much dream-whisky . . . !* He felt her slender fingers between his, smooth and cool with the night air. His thumb slipped over one of her violet nails. *And yet . . .* He gave her hand a squeeze.

She eyed his hand, then squeezed it back. Their intertwined hands glowed golden for a second. "You did it, Goko." Her lips quirked up.

As they stared at each other, everything around them was growing more ghostly and semilucent by the second.

Then, it went red—starting with the skies, and then everything underneath. All three of them looked up at a nightscape going blood-hued, drowning away the spangled stars.

As the heavens ruddied, lights started streaking afar like comets. But they didn't dwindle—they grew and persisted. Sounds reached them moments later, halfway between the wail of jets and the shrieking of raptors. The earth first shook, then heaved and quaked convulsively.

"What in the world . . . ?" wondered Proto, looking at Astrid. For once, she appeared as utterly baffled as he felt.

As for Emil, he looked the most dumbstruck of all. But his shadowy image was only half-there now.

One of those streaking lights struck the earth. A gigantic semi-orb of light spread into being around it.

Moments later, a tidal wave of flame was roaring toward them from the point of impact.

Gasping, Astrid threw one arm around Proto and flung out her other palm toward the impending pyroclasm. A violet orb surrounded them just as the flames struck. He watched fire rage around that violet semilucence, mere feet away.

Emil was in the inferno, but he did not react. Indeed, he just smiled wistfully. That was the last Proto saw of him before he wisped away to formlessness.

The whitish-grey mirk that had been rushing toward them on the horizon abruptly burgeoned all about them, immersing everything.

Proto couldn't see clearly. But he felt those mists lifting him and bearing him away.

After a moment, he found himself hurtling through the starry grey obscurity that they typically crossed when returning from dreams. But instead of emerging into the misty blue corridors of Somnus' Palace, he just kept flying through the void, tumbling toward oblivion.

He felt like he couldn't breathe, no matter how hard he tried. Pain jabbed through his lungs. But after a while, this stopped bothering him. As when a foot falls asleep, those prickling pains soon faded into warmth.

Through a bleary haze, he saw a hand with violet nails, extended toward him. He faced it—and there was Astrid. She looked like a swimmer who'd been holding her breath for longer than she could bear. Her face was furrowed with strain.

She waved that hand at him violently, desperately. He pondered it a moment. Then, he clasped it.

Squeezing his hand, Astrid turned toward a point of light in the distance. She began accelerating toward it, dragging him limply along.

The light grew before them, like a star transforming to a sun, until the brightness dwarfed all other things.

Then, abruptly, the world snapped back into being—a misty blue hallway, a white sliding door, and Proto and Astrid, heaving in breaths on the floor. Both did so for a full minute without saying anything.

As Proto got his lucidity and bearings back, he scanned his mentor—tousle-haired, staring wide-eyed at nothing. "What *was* that?" he finally asked. "Did he get woken up by a fire alarm or something?"

"No. Not a fire alarm," spoke Astrid numbly, staring afar. "He just *died*."

Proto stared. He felt like his world's floor had fallen out from under him. "And those red skies? Those streaking lights?"

She looked at him for several seconds, her lips pressed. "Let's go speak with Somnus."

Nodding uncertainly, Proto followed her back to the lounge. Many voices echoed down the corridor as they approached.

Upon entering, he found the elegant old chamber was more crowded than he'd ever seen it. All of Proto's friends were there, and almost all the other visitors, shadowseers, and miscellaneous assistants that he'd seen here. Hubbub reigned.

Many were talking to many at once. But at the center stood Somnus, and the largest crowd was gathered around him.

"So, what's going on?" Proto asked Mayger, who happened to be standing nearby. The lithe man had his pink hair slicked back and was wearing aviator sunglasses, but he'd lifted them off his eyes atop his brow. His face was furrowed and, for once, showed no trace of an ironic smile.

"I was just cast toward oblivion together with a dying dreamer," answered Mayger. "How about you?"

"Same, I think." Proto glanced at Astrid, but she was focused on Somnus.

"We're not the only ones, unfortunately," the pink-haired man observed. "Far from it." He gestured toward several other visitors nearby, rubbing their heads and looking shellshocked.

Proto stared. "What happened? So many dreamers dying at once. Nuclear war?"

"You'd think so, right?" said Mayger. "No. Something much weirder, according to Somnus."

Proto turned toward the Lord of Dreams, who was answering questions from at least two dozen people massed around him. For once, he neither had a drink nor was in the process of getting one.

"What about Uberta?" demanded Wentsworth, the mustachioed oddball who always wore a three-piece suit. "She was supposed to be back a half hour ago. Is she Lost? What are we going to do about it?"

Proto recognized Uberta's name. She was that Velma-looking woman with thick glasses and figure-hugging turtleneck sweaters. He'd played cards against her once.

"Yes, Lost, so it seems. And Annar too. And others," sighed Somnus. "As I said five minutes ago, before you got here, we'll find them all. I've been doing this for aeons, and none of my visitors has ever been Lost for good. At least, not unless he chose to be."

"Meanwhile," he went on, "we're all going to be practicing what to do if your dreamer dies. That is, if he goes to the Mists mid-dream, and brings you along with him. This is, alas, something that's likely to happen to more of you in the coming days."

"Why?" asked Astrid. She'd made her way through the crowd and now was facing Somnus directly.

"Ah. Welcome, Astrid. Glad to see you're well," replied Somnus. "I'll explain this again, for you and everyone else who's arrived in the last five minutes. In short, the world just ended."

"Well, no. It didn't end," he continued, as half his audience gaped, "although half of humanity thinks so at this point. But who can blame them? Winged figures with horns are screaming through the red heavens and raining fire upon them, wreaking worldwide ruin, as the earth convulses and heaves great cities to the ground. I'd likely reach the same conclusion."

Astrid tilted her head at Somnus. "... what?"

The Lord of Dreams sighed. "This is a long story, and if I try to tell it all right now, then before I'm halfway through, I'll have fifty more people in here demanding that I start over."

"In short," he said, "a scientist named Fyrir and some of his colleagues had been doing research on the Fossil of my mother, Flua-Sahng—that is, her remnants up there in the breathing world, from when she still had a corporeal form. Fyrir invented a device that used my mother's power to awaken my brethren, slumbering in the depths—the Elements—and prod them into a fury. They've erupted from the earth and are now destroying it."

Astrid blinked slowly and shook her head.

Somnus sighed again. "Yes, I know. I feel like I'm Oppenheimer trying to explain the hydrogen bomb to some Amazonian tribe. Or worse, Congress. Do you have time for twenty years of schooling?"

"... so, why aren't you up there, raining fire?" asked Proto. He'd made his way toward Somnus and was now near Astrid.

"Hello Proto. Good question. That's because, like my mother, I lost my bodily form up there long ago," replied Somnus mildly. "I'm left with my dream form, my Daemon form, which you all know and love. That's quite alright with me, since I spend my days visiting dreams anyway. And I'd sure hate to be up there right now!" As he said this, his eyes met Proto's and gleamed strangely.

Then, he was facing the crowd again and it was gone.

"So ... what should we do?" asked Jag.

"What we've always done!" shrugged Somnus. "What, you think this is the first time I've seen civilization rent? How about the fall of Rome? That was a long time coming. But I had a bad feeling once they started smashing my statues. Or, ugh, the invasion of the Sea Peoples. Any of you remember that? What a lovely little world it'd been, till they *utterly ruined* it."

"Anyway, what I've learnt is, a world in chaos needs guidance more, not less," concluded the Lord of Dreams. "We'll go on doing what we've always done. Which for you, Jag, means you'll do precisely what I ask of you."

"Or maybe not! Maybe this all is just a dream!" Somnus turned to Proto and smiled pleasantly. "Maybe you'll wake up, any moment now. Wouldn't *that* be lucky!"

Proto's face flushed. "This is bizarre," he found himself saying. "Elements? Fossils? Fyrir? Fire from the skies? Out of nowhere, everything's destroyed? Why didn't we know about any of this? What *is* this?"

"Yes, who ever heard of people losing everything without being forewarned and given a fair chance to avert it?" the Lord of Dreams retorted lightly. "Fate may be fair in the long run. But it's up to us to make each day that way. As much as we can. As I told you when you arrived here."

Proto didn't know what to say. He felt like a child whose understanding of the world was based on goofy remarks made by his elders playing with him, who'd just spoken to him seriously for the first time.

Then again, everyone else looked dumbstruck too. Even Astrid—whose habitual coolness rarely slipped for more than a second or two—was now staring with wide eyes, looking young and uncertain.

"I . . . guess it doesn't feel like a day for drinks, does it," observed Jet. He had a half-full glass of something brown in front of him.

"I don't know that I'd go that far," mused the Lord of Dreams. "When almost everything has changed, it's good to seek some sameness out. A world aflame still needs rest and sleep, drinks and dreams. And so do we."

"On that note, excuse me a moment." Somnus strode through the crowd toward Lilac at the bar, pointing her to a bottle. "Quickly, if you would. In about thirty seconds, people are going to start asking me questions I've already answered and demanding explanations I've already given. It will go better if I've had this."

Meanwhile, Proto stood there dumbly for a while. And when he finally found a seat, he stared off at nothing. He tried to wrap his mind around everything Somnus had just said—which, indeed, he soon had to repeat to the next crew of returning visitors.

But Proto's mind kept going back to the dream he'd visited earlier. "*Friends and . . .*" He recalled that wistful smile on Emil's face at the end. And he felt like the world as he knew it, much like that red-jacketed man, was wisping away smilingly into nothing, nothing at all.

CHAPTER 15
SAVE THE WORLD

A rapping at the door woke Proto, about an hour earlier than he'd have liked. He hoped it would go away if he said nothing and pretended not to hear it.

Fifteen seconds passed, and he started slipping back toward sleep.

"Proto, it's rude to keep the Lord of Dreams waiting!" boomed the man's voice outside.

"He does that to everyone," assured Astrid.

So much for that.

"On my way!" grumbled Proto. Clambering out of his covers, he opened his wardrobe.

He'd put off laundry too long. Now, most of his clothes were being washed. He currently had one wrinkled and dirty tracksuit, plus two tunics that were missing their leggings. And then there was the robe like Somnus'.

Yeah, not happening.

That left the chiton—the toga-like thing that Dahlia wore while shadowcasting. She'd kept her promise to get him one. His was dark blue and yellow, and a bit more shirt-like. But it still made him feel like he was an extra on the set of Jason and the Argonauts.

He started toward the door—then caught a glimpse of himself in the mirror and winced. He brushed his hair, then quickly brushed his teeth.

"First's name, Proto, are you putting on your makeup?" called Somnus.

"Can't forget the eyeliner and mascara!" he replied, as he finished shaving.

When he finally opened the door, he found not only Somnus and Astrid waiting there, but also Lilac and Dahlia. All of them had folded arms and baleful eyes.

The blonde bookworm, though, promptly gasped with pleasure. "You wore it! And you didn't even know I'd be here!" She pinched some of the blue fabric and rubbed it between her fingers. "Isn't it comfy? Don't you just feel . . . classic? Or maybe classical?"

"I feel tired." He rubbed his eyes.

"You'll want some coffee." Lilac handed him a travel mug.

"You know me, Madame Bartendress!" He sipped in satisfaction.

"Lazy as a bear in Winter," she nodded.

"You know me!" he repeated.

"You know what," mused Dahlia. She unsashed her Victorian robe, removed it and tossed it into Proto's room. This left her toga-like chiton. "Now I'm ready too."

"Anyone else? Astrid, you good with your spacesuit?" asked Somnus. "No more coffees? Bathroom breaks, anyone?"

"Are we in a rush?" asked Proto. "Also, where are we going?"

"To save the world. Where else?" replied the Lord of Dreams.

"One dream at a time," affirmed Astrid.

"Indeed!" said the robed man. "But it's not every day we visit a dreamer who's caused worldwide pandaemonium, *and* has the power to stop it."

"We're visiting the President?" asked Proto.

"Thank you, Jon Stewart," replied Somnus. "No. Fyrir! The scientist! The man whose genius set the world aflame!"

"Was that a timely reference? From Somnus?" asked Lilac.

"A broken sundial is timely twice a day," the robed man said.

"That doesn't even make sense," said Astrid. "Sundials don't have hands like clocks."

" . . . Astrid, do you *remember* sundials?" asked Proto.

"Like I said. Old lady." She flipped back her silvery-blue bouffant over her jumpsuit, looking no older than twenty-two.

"Ah, I'm going to miss you, Astrid," mused Somnus. "Who will remember the good old days with me? I'll have to—alas—visit my mother more!"

"She seems nice," offered Proto, recalling the red-haired Queen of Heaven in her leafy raiment.

"Oh, she has *lots* to say about you!" said Somnus. "Talked my ear off just yesterday, and half of it was 'Proto this' and 'Proto that.'"

Proto tilted his head in confusion. He didn't see how that was possible, having met her for only two minutes in Mercune's dream.

"Really, Proto?" muttered Astrid.

Lilac flicked his ear.

"Anyway, we discussed saving the world too," Somnus went on. "Which is good. I may be the Lord of Dreams, but this fiery worldwide pandaemonium is a bit above my paygrade."

"This calls for the Queen of Heaven?" asked Proto.

Somnus' lips quirked up. "She loves that nickname. You're going to give her a big head, you know! But yes, visiting Fyrir was her idea."

Something that Somnus had said a minute ago was nagging at Proto. He'd meant to ask about it, but it slipped his mind now.

"So," Proto said instead, "today we need not only visitors, but a shadowseer and a bartendress?"

"And a Lord of Dreams!" added Somnus. "Quite an expedition."

"*You're* coming?" said Proto.

"Indeed!" affirmed the robed man. "I may be a fifth wheel, but I roll with anything."

"What the F does that mean?" asked Astrid.

"It means," said Somnus, "you don't have to do an evaluation today."

"Your terms are acceptable," she said. "Welcome to the team."

"Hmph. You, welcome me?" He shook his head. "Like Steve Jobs being welcomed back to Apple. I *made* this place!"

"Is that two modern references from Somnus in one day?" asked Lilac. "Modernish."

"As I said, every sundial," he replied. "Now, let's get going before Astrid starts lecturing me on clocks, or Lilac starts brewing more coffee, or Dahlia decides she doesn't need her toga."

"It's not a toga!" said Dahlia and Astrid simultaneously.

Dahlia blinked, staring at Astrid. "I know that since I like old books. You . . .
"

"Old lady," affirmed the silvery-blue-haired woman.

"Please, you weren't even around for the Bronze Age," waved Somnus. "You're not even older than the pyramids! Or Stonehenge!"

"Stop bragging," chided Dahlia.

"Is that bragging or self-deprecation?" asked Proto.

"Must I choose?" asked Somnus.

"You all talk too much. Let's go." Lilac walked away.

The others agreed on that much, at least, and followed her down the misty blue hallway.

As they walked, Dahlia read a pocket copy of the Iliad, squinting at the tiny text through her monocle.

"Some light reading as we save the world?" Proto asked her.

"Why not? It's my Bible. I read it for edification. I swear my oaths upon it. You wouldn't *believe* all the things I've done while reading this!" Her eyes gleamed.

"Did you know I'm in that book?" remarked Somnus.

"Book XIV," replied Dahlia, without looking up.

"Oh, but that *was* fun," Somnus chuckled. "The Bronze Age was the time to live, I'm telling you!"

"Is that why you're here?" Lilac asked Dahlia. "To make Somnus feel timely and relevant?"

"Indeed! And she's seen the future. She knows what has to happen, and what maybe doesn't," answered the Lord of Dreams. "Handy to have her around when seeking a future where the world survives."

"I see the future, love the past, live in the moment, and wear a chiton," replied the shadowseer. "Who wouldn't want me around!"

"Wives with their husbands, perhaps," replied the Lord of Dreams.

Dahlia frowned slightly, then shrugged.

Proto began whistling Maneater.

Dahlia banged him on the head with the Iliad. Fortunately, the pocket edition didn't hurt too much.

"I feel like Somnus deserved that more than me." He rubbed his head.

"The Fates aren't always just, Proto," she replied calmly. "If you'd read this, you'd know that."

"So, Dahlia's here to tell the future and flatter Somnus," said Proto, turning to Lilac. "How about you?"

"I'm here to do what I always do," answered the pale woman.

"Kick ass and make coffee?" asked Proto.

"Yes. But I'm not all out of coffee." Lilac lifted a pouch of coffee beans from her pocket. "Somnus' idea."

The others raised their brows at Somnus.

"I had a feeling this would be a long dream!" he explained. "Look, no one ever says, 'I wish I *hadn't* been prepared.'"

They'd arrived at the sliding white door. Somnus waved his hand and it opened.

Proto frowned. "I can't even open it by touching it. And you can just wave your hand?"

"As I said, Provisional Visitor," replied the Lord of Dreams, "I *made* this place!" He strode into the mirky passage, and the others followed.

Proto heard the sound first—a soft electric hum, swelling and fading—then saw the light. It flowed from blue strips along the matte grey walls. They emerged into a futuristic room that looked like something between Star Trek and a Tesla car interior.

One wall was a giant computer screen, covered in text of various colors. One of Proto's programmer friends was always telling him that "Linux is best" and that "no GUI is as powerful and efficient as the command line." It looked like that guy's screen.

Ergonomic chairs sat in front of terminals around the room's periphery. At the center stood a large hexagonal table. A man on the other side of it was facing away from them, eying his watch and shaking his head.

At the sound of their footsteps, he turned around.

This was an old man. What little hair he had atop his head was white, as was his belt-length beard. He wore a white lab coat. His eyes were icy blue, but his cheeks had warm dimples. The glow of the computer screens gave him a faint aura. On the whole, he looked like an angel sent down bearing good news about the Theory of Relativity.

"Well. Hello there." He squinted at them. "Do I know you . . . ?" Some mist started swirling up from the floor.

"What? Have you not had your coffee, Fyrir?" asked Somnus amiably. Somehow, he was already wearing a similar lab coat. "You've forgotten our summer lab interns? *Again?*"

Fyrir winced. "Ah. I do apologize." He rubbed his temples. "Every year, I swear I'll do better. And then I don't."

Somnus introduced them one by one. "This, of course, is the one and only Fyrir. And, as you all know, I'm his humble assistant Somnus."

"Ah, right," murmured Fyrir half-audibly. "Yes, this is my assistant Somnus, of course. And this is Wraithing Research Center." He rubbed his temples again. "I do miss being forty. Or fifty, sixty or seventy, for that matter."

"Would you like some coffee, Sir?" asked Lilac, lifting her coffee beans. "I can brew it up."

"No, no, quite alright, Dear. We used to make our internesses brew coffee, but we've come a long way since then," said Fyrir. "Now, I leave it to my secretary." He looked around. "Where is that Moll? Probably off snatching a wink somewhere."

"I *love* inappropriate grandpas!" murmured Dahlia to Proto. "Will you be one someday?"

"Inappropriate, yes. Grandpa, to be determined," he replied.

"We'll work on that," she affirmed.

He blinked.

"Anyway, pardon me if I seem distracted," said Fyrir. "My Mercune is missing, and I'm beginning to get worried. Any chance you've seen her? Red hair, green eyes, freckles. Talks one ear off, and then the other."

"Oh, you're her 'Gramps,' right?" recalled Proto.

"Ah, you've already met!" observed Fyrir. "Not sure why I'm surprised. She's been introducing herself to everyone within a mile since she was a toddler."

"Yep, we met this morning." Proto felt a surge of inspiration. He decided to go for it. "She said she was going to . . . a cosplay convention."

Somnus raised an eyebrow at him.

"A cosplay convention? In Dubai?!" exclaimed Fyrir. The mists swirled up to waist level. "Is it safe?"

We're in Dubai? Proto knew roughly as much about Dubai as the Theory of Relativity. He stared blankly and searched for words.

"You know, don't answer that. I have to go find her!" Fyrir started to hasten away, then paused and frowned. "Ah, might one of you know where this cosplay convention is?"

"Yes, we all know. As you might've guessed." Lilac gestured at their outfits.

"Ah," said Fyrir. "That's why you look like a French maid, and your friends look like Antony, Cleopatra, and Jane Fonda as Barbarella?"

"A French waitress, to be precise," corrected Lilac politely.

"They're all alike, those cheese-eaters," waved Fyrir. "Anyway, yes, I was wondering where your lab coats were. But I wasn't going to say anything. Last time I mentioned our dress code to an interness, there were whole *news stories* about it!" He shook his head, then chuckled. "Now, we're in Dubai. Anyway, lead the way, Lily! Or Fleur-de-Lis, or whatever it was."

Lilac led the way, heading toward the building's entrance—or at least, did her best.

"What's this? Why are we headed to the underground levels?" asked Fyrir.

"Sorry, I'm new here!" winced Lilac. "Still learning my directions."

"Not at all. My Everleigh was the same way," waved Fyrir genially. "It's winsome."

"I *love* this guy!" whispered Dahlia to Proto.

"What, you're coming too, Somnus?" asked Fyrir, seeing the other white-lab-coated man had fallen into stride beside them. "Don't you have work to do?"

"And leave you with childcare duty?" asked Somnus. "You'll have your hands full with Mercune."

"Fair enough, fair enough," agreed Fyrir, as the mists dwindled away.

"I'm really quite old," grumbled Astrid.

"I know you are, Doll." Fyrir patted her back. A moment later, he fell back and murmured to Somnus, "The things the fillies wear these days, eh!"

"Oh, I've seen it all, at this point," mused Somnus. "You should've seen the Minoans!"

"Eh?" Fyrir cocked his head. "Were they on the cover of National Geographic?"

"Not exactly!" said Somnus. "Although the comparison is apt—"

"Let's go find Mercune," interrupted Lilac.

"Mm, quite right, Dear," said Fyrir. "Let's go see what this *costume play* rubbish is all about."

They left the futuristic building and walked the streets of Dubai. Lilac did a good job of striding confidently and nonchalantly, as though she'd walked this route a hundred times. Or at least, so it seemed to Proto.

Then, Fyrir paused and frowned as Lilac rounded a corner. "Eh? It's at one of the consulates?"

The pallid woman blinked and brushed a strand of black hair from her face. She opened her mouth, as the mist swirled back up to knee height.

"Probably the only place they can't ban it!" observed Somnus.

"Eh. Good point, good point," murmured Fyrir. The mists stopped rising.

They walked about fifty yards down the road, then Lilac halted in front of a stately civic structure. "Here we are!"

Fyrir raised an eyebrow skeptically, but followed her and the others inside.

The details in the building were hazy, like an old video game where you could only see about twenty yards before fog swallowed everything. They were approaching a security checkpoint with patdowns and bag checks. Mists lapped around their upper legs.

"Why is it like this?" whispered Proto to Astrid.

"Because Fyrir has no idea what to expect right now," she replied. "Remember, he's the dreamer. He's imagining all this into being. He's an eighty-year-old guy who's never been to a cosplay convention, trying to imagine one at a *consulate!*"

After passing through security, they followed colorful signs to a staircase with double doors at the top.

Lilac threw open the doors. Light beamed in through them, and Fyrir squinted.

Mists whirled and rose all about them. No image clarified beyond the doors. The light just kept coming.

"I . . . eh?" Fyrir rubbed his eyes. "Need my specs, I think . . . " He shook his head. "Odd."

"What is this—?" whispered Proto to Astrid.

"He's clueless!" she hissed. "*We* have to dream it! Quick!"

He blinked at her, as she faced the misty ambiguity and narrowed her violet eyes. It started clarifying into a vast exhibition hall with wandering shadowy figures, tables, display props, and portable storefronts.

"Where are all the cosplayers?" asked Proto quietly.

"I'm an old lady, I don't know this stuff!" she muttered at him. "*You* do it!"

"Uh, okay." Proto pondered, then focused on the scene before him.

Suddenly, about fifty of the shadowy figures came into clarity. They were all Dragon Ball Z characters in full, precise detail.

Lilac looked at him. "Are you kidding me?" She squinted intently at the exhibition hall.

The shadowy people began clarifying into a host of figures from a hundred different animes and video games, from Sailor Moon to Death Note to Final Fantasy VII. It was all rendered in exquisite detail.

A black-garbed shinigami ambled by. "Anyone have an apple?"

"Sorry, mine's spoken for." Dahlia held one up and smiled sympathetically.

"Drat." He walked on.

Meanwhile, Fyrir was rubbing his eyes again, squinting blearily at the motley assemblage. "Ah. Well, isn't that bright. Looks like a lively crew."

"That's actually quite impressive, Lilac," noted Astrid.

"This is going to be so fun." Lilac clasped her hands behind her back, stood pigeon-toed with touching knees, and beamed upon the scene in her French waitress outfit.

A herd of Pokèmon-dressed teens stampeded by. "Sorry!" yelled one girl as she bumped the Lord of Dreams. "They're handing out free foils!"

"Well, in that case, forgiven!" Somnus amiably assured her.

"Nice costumes!" the apologetic girl called backward as she ran away. "Professors Oak and Elm, right?"

"Every year, I swear," muttered Fyrir to Somnus, "we get older and our interns get younger."

Proto scrunched his gaze against the barrage of light and color. "Lilac, Lilac, give me eyes back."

She giggled. "Proto, Proto—hey, is that Frodo!" She pointed, and a hobbit-looking fellow waddled into sight.

"Oh, I *approve!*" declared Dahlia, leaning down and pinching his vest.

The hobbit gave her a smarmy smile. "Let's take a little trip 'there and back again,' lass, what do you say?"

Dahlia gasped and covered her mouth. "Hmph, I never!"

Then, she smiled and wrinkled her nose. "Well, maybe not *never*. 'This quest may be attempted by the weak with as much hope as the strong'!" She patted him on the head.

The halfling flexed and shuffled away.

"There's a girl who's got a couple things going for her, eh?" admired Fyrir to Somnus.

"So . . . why are we paused here?" asked Astrid.

"Oh, sight just got blurry for a moment," replied Fyrir. "Dry eyes, probably. Or a small stroke. In any event, let's get going."

They advanced into the cosplay convention. Costumed attendees wandered and glimmered and mock-battled all about them. But there was no sign of Mercune.

"I worry I might not recognize her," observed Fyrir, as a flock of girls wearing Angry Birds masks flapped by. "I fear I'll have to ask every young redhead here if I know her."

"Well, at least you won't have to do anything new," observed the Lord of Dreams.

"Eh! Eh!" the eighty year old chortled and elbowed Somnus agreeably.

"Hey, there's some red hair," pointed Proto. "See those three girls in . . . chitons?"

"Yes! I do!" cried Dahlia. She hied toward the white-garbed trio, followed by the others.

The red-haired woman was holding a bronze Greek helmet under her arm. Her two companions were a dark-haired woman with an elegant poise and a blonde woman in an especially figure-hugging chiton.

"Not Mercune, I'm afraid," observed Fyrir, sizing up the three women, who looked more mid-twenties than late teens. "Although I can't say I regret the trip."

"Yes, I think that's Athena," noted Dahlia sadly. She eyed the red-haired woman, then the dark-haired and the blonde. "And Hera and Aphrodite, I take it?"

"In the flesh!" they cried, posing with their arms thrown wide.

"Oh, but I love your shirt!" Aphrodite gushed to Proto, feeling the fabric of his blue chiton. "Is that Corinthian?"

"It is!" enthused Dahlia. "Corinthian is my favorite."

"Hm. Which of us is *your* favorite?" Aphrodite asked Proto. The three women posed again.

Proto pondered as all eyes turned to him. "Uh. I feel like nothing good can come of this choice."

"Still, you have to choose!" urged Somnus.

"Yes, stop being boring and homely!" chided Aphrodite, smiling and coyly slapping the top of his hand.

"Indeed, Proto!" agreed Dahlia.

Hera waved dismissively. "There's nothing less boring than what happens at home." She briefly clasped Proto's arm as she spoke.

"She's right, you know," agreed Lilac, snapping a photo with her off-brand Polaroid.

Athena rolled her eyes, with one hand resting on her cocked hip. "Why choose between a romcom and a sitcom, when you can have an adventure?"

"That's what I'm talking about," agreed Astrid.

Proto was getting more uncomfortable by the second about making this choice right now. He glanced back and forth between the three.

"Hmph! You'd think he's picking for real, the way he's ruminating!" mused Fyrir.

"What? I'm not picking for real?" replied Proto, stalling for time.

"Oh, don't worry too much about what's real," counseled Somnus. "You can always make things real. What's hard is dreaming them up in the first place!"

"Who do you think you are?" Athena asked the Lord of Dreams. "The god Hypnos?"

"Oh, I've *missed* that name!" cried Somnus. "Could you three call me Hypnos, please? Or maybe—Lord Hypnos?"

"As you wish, Lord Hypnos!" Aphrodite insinuated herself under his arm.

"As you please, Lord Hypnos!" Hera curled around his other arm.

"Command me, Lord Hypnos!" Athena held out her helmet beckoningly.

"Mm. Don't mind if I do," said Somnus. Some mists had swirled up, but he waved a hand imperiously and they dissipated. "Come, goddesses!" He strolled off with them.

"Hey." Proto frowned. "What about my choice?"

"Sorry, Mister, you took too long!" Aphrodite called over her shoulder.

Proto nodded grimly, as Somnus and his entourage ambled away. The others just stared.

"WTF," said Astrid. "Now what?"

"Ah, to be forty again," Fyrir envied.

"On the bright side, I got a good photo." Lilac handed Proto the mostly-developed slip of paper. It showed Hera clasping Proto's arm warmly, as Aphrodite looked away and Athena rolled her eyes.

"*That's* the moment you captured?" pouted Dahlia. "*She's* going to be the centerpiece of this memory? That's like . . . putting Tom Bombadil on the cover of Lord of the Rings!"

Astrid nodded in agreement. "Or like . . . putting Aki on the cover of You Only Live Twice!"

"Who should be on the cover? A Russian cosmonaut?" Lilac asked Astrid coolly.

Proto had no idea what they were talking about. "And you tell me *my* references are outdated."

"Ah, Aki. What a tart she was!" said Fyrir. "I remember seeing her at the theater."

"Me too!" recalled Astrid.

The bald old man tilted his head at her, as the mists swirled up a bit. "Eh, second-run?"

"Like I said," mused Astrid, turning to Proto, "old lady."

Proto shrugged. "I like my women like I like my drinks."

She raised an eyebrow and waved him onward, in a silent, *let's get this over with.*

"Balanced and tasteful and understated?" suggested Lilac.

"Full-flavored and sophisticated?" suggested Dahlia.

"Hard and fiery with rich undertones?" suggested Astrid.

"In sets of three or more." Proto double-gunned them all.

Dahlia giggled. Astrid and Lilac flicked his ears.

"Ah, we have a Sean Connery here!" Fyrir slapped Proto on the back. "My kind of man."

Dahlia nodded eagerly and gave him a thumbs up.

They wandered the convention looking for Mercune for a few more minutes before Fyrir *ah*ed and strode toward a young woman in a mech suit. "Shirley! Is that you in there?"

She stiffened, then nodded. "It sure is! What a nice surprise, Sir!" She pressed her lips and looked around, then approached them.

Fyrir turned to the others. "Lab interness. I remembered her name!" He tapped his temple, then faced the woman. "Shirley, wasn't today a work day? Also, have you seen Mercune here?"

"Sure, we were hanging out earlier," replied Shirley, ignoring the first question. "Then, Mercune went off to be a *VIP*." She rolled her eyes.

"Excuse me?" said Fyrir.

Shirley sighed and pointed at a big glowing sign saying "VIPs." Beneath it was a guarded doorway.

"What does that mean?" asked the elder.

"Vegetables In Pots," she answered grumpily. "Good to see you, Sir!" She walked away.

"I don't think that's what it stands for," observed Proto.

"Interns these days. Gen Z!" Fyrir shook his head. "I miss Himari. Now *there* was an intern!"

He led the group toward the VIP-labeled doorway, maneuvering through the crowds, and approached the guards in front. "Afternoon, friends. I'll need to get in there."

"Are you a VIP?" asked one of the guards, looking him up and down.

"In whose estimation?" asked the world-famous scientist.

The guards exchanged a glance. "Do you have a damn badge?" one of them asked.

" . . . no," said the old man.

"Then . . . no," replied the first guard.

"It's an emergency! My little girl is *lost* in there!" objected Fyrir. "I must go find her."

"Oh, a little kid?" The second guard blinked with concern. "I'll go in and get her. What's she look like?"

"Well, not a little *kid*, precisely," corrected Fyrir. "Late teens. Red hair—"

"Late teen girl in the VIP area at a cosplay convention?" the first guard interrupted. "Yeah, not an emergency. You can wait."

"But . . . !" Fyrir balled his fists in futile vexation, then exhaled and turned away.

Meanwhile, a fat gamer with a Bubble Bobble hat waddled up. He was followed by a bone-skinny, neckbearded guy in a T-shirt. It showed some pixelated girl on a beach next to a shipwrecked boy, and it said, "The only Princess for me."

One of the guards nodded and thumbed them toward the VIP doorway. They strolled right in.

Fyrir stared. "You can't be telling me that *those* are VIPs."

"Nope. Contest winners," replied the second guard. "See the badge the big guy had?"

"So . . . contest winners can go in? And bring their friends?" asked Astrid, drawing a nod from the guards.

"We're friends with, uh, that fat fellow!" Fyrir waved toward the pair who just entered.

The first guard scoffed. "Go win a contest, old man." He pointed at some tables across the room. There, various costumed gamers were playing cards, board games, and old video games against one another.

Fyrir stared at the tables, shaking his head. "To think!" he grumbled. "My research is changing the world! I likely have just a few years left! And how will I spend them? Entering *contests* against physiognomically challenged wastrels!"

"I'm sure Mercune will thank you," assuaged Dahlia. "The things we do for those we love!"

"Sometimes you have to give things up to keep what you love," said Proto.

Then, he wondered why he'd just said that. He felt himself flush as everyone looked at him. *What a weirdo.*

"Anyway," said Fyrir after a moment, "I guess I'd best go win a contest. Do you think they have Bingo? Or shuffleboard? I play a mean shuffleboard!"

"I don't know about that." Proto tried to think of something suitably old-fashioned that Fyrir might've heard of. "They might have Sudoku."

"Eh? Think one of my uncles was killed in the war at Sudoku," recalled Fyrir. "Or was it Sukumo?"

The others exchanged a glance.

"Maybe we can all try to win a contest," suggested Astrid.

"Good idea."

They headed over and scanned the contest tables. Things looked grim for Fyrir at first, as they passed from a Magic: The Gathering tournament to a Warhammer 40k game to a Smash tournament.

The old man squinted at the screen. "Is that yellow rat electrocuting the dago-looking fellow in red?"

But he perked up a bit after watching Cards Against Humanity for a few minutes. "The dames these days will play *this* with you?" he murmured to Proto. "Maybe the 21st century's not so bad!"

He really got excited, though, when they found a table playing wild rummy.

"Wild rummy!" the old man cried with satisfaction. "I haven't played that game in fifty years."

"I *know*, right?!" exclaimed Astrid.

The game was about to start, and it seemed clear this was fated. So, Fyrir and Astrid sat at the table and joined in.

There was a concession stand nearby. Fyrir waved over the vendor, who was dressed as Calamity Calamari, complete with an elegant cane-sword. The man touched his chest questioningly, then approached.

Fyrir held up a wad of bills. "Sir, she could use a dry martini." He gestured at Astrid. "And so could I. I'll have mine dirty."

The vendor looked back at the concession stand. There was a half-full bottle of vodka, no gin, no vermouth, and certainly no olives. "Shaken or stirred?"

"What do you think?" waved Fyrir.

The vendor rolled his eyes and went to pour some vodka.

"Another Sean Connery, I see," said Astrid.

Fyrir extended his hands in a *what can I say* gesture. "As for you." He sized her up thoughtfully. "Britt Ekland. Maybe Shirley Eaton. But with Holly Goodhead's spacesuit."

Astrid frowned, and Proto laughed.

The game went well for Astrid and Fyrir—especially Astrid. A couple teens at the table struggled to remember the rules, let alone strategize. One middle-aged lady dressed as a d20 was pretty good. But she was no Fyrir, and Fyrir was no Astrid.

The silvery-blue haired woman was preternaturally aware of what sets and runs lay in front of the other players. She also never made a mistake. As a result, it soon seemed clear she'd be the winner.

Meanwhile, she sipped her "martini," then a second. "You know," she observed, "I thought this was bad vodka at first."

"But now?" replied Fyrir, laying down a card.

"Now, I'm sure this is bad vodka," she replied. "Could you buy me another?"

"My kind of dame!" praised Fyrir. "You look like a Russian cosmonaut, and you drink like one too."

"That and more." She laid several cards down, as Fyrir blinked and chuckled.

Dahlia tilted her head bemusedly. "Is she always like this when she drinks and plays cards?"

"I'll have to practice wild rummy," mused Proto.

Dahlia flicked his ear.

"You too now?" he griped. "It's going to fall off!"

"We can make do without." Her eyes gleamed.

The game went on. Astrid was running away with it, with only Fyrir in touching distance.

"You know your rummy, Madame Silverwear!" complimented Proto, as she lay down several cards.

"Ain't it the truth!" She yawned and flicked a card on top of one Fyrir's sets. "You should've seen me in the old days. I was winning twenty Breath Tokens a day!"

The silvery-blue haired woman sounded a little loopy. Proto noticed she was on her third drink. Not that it had any impact whatsoever on her playing.

"What do you need all those Tokens for?" he asked.

"Oh, I don't know," she mused absently. "I've just always dreamt of having a little girl, and—"

She blinked twice, then gave Proto a violet-eyed glance. "What am I even saying? Too many martinis."

"Eh? A little girl, you said?" replied Fyrir. "My Everleigh said the same thing. We'd only had a pair of boys, you see. So when we found young Mercune on her own, found out that her parents had passed away—well, it seemed fated."

Astrid looked at him and smiled. "You'll have to introduce me when we find her."

"Oh, she'll introduce herself, I'll tell you what!" averred Fyrir, drawing a little laugh from Astrid. "Ah, feels like just yesterday she still needed a babysitter. What was that blonde's name, Spice Girl or something?"

Proto, meanwhile, was sifting through what Astrid had said to him. How was that an answer to his question? *Was* it? Or was that just her vodka speaking?

"Breath Tokens," mused Dahlia. "I don't even collect the things. But you're getting awfully close, yes, Astrid? When's your Saturn Return?"

The jumpsuited woman stiffened. "Not sure. I need to focus on the game."

Proto started to open his mouth to ask what they were talking about. But the look on Astrid's face told him to shut up, and it was persuasive.

Fyrir, meanwhile, was focused on his cards and apparently not listening. A grin was forming on his face, turning his many wrinkles into dimples.

It was then that Proto felt a strange tugging inside of him. It reminded him of standing in a lake and suddenly being pulled by the undertow.

"It's like a river—the current of the dream," Astrid had told him once. *"Deep down, the dreamer knows best where the dream should go."*

It might have been possible to resist that current. And yet something told him things were flowing exactly as they should.

Proto watched as, beaming, Fyrir abruptly laid down over a dozen cards and discarded the last one.

"Ha!" gloated the old man. "Oh, how I held out to do that!"

"That's not possible," objected Astrid, squinting at the cards. "That eight of spades. I'm holding the other . . . " Her voice trailed off. She glanced skyward, her lips curving up wryly.

"Ha! It seems everyone makes mistakes. Even Wonder Woman here!" declared Fyrir, patting her on the arm. "Wonderful playing, Dear. My, I haven't had such fun in years."

"You've clearly had a lot of practice," Astrid graciously observed.

"Indeed, indeed." He itched his long white beard. "Age before beauty, eh? But beauty's in close second."

Astrid laughed good-naturedly.

"Take lessons from him!" Dahlia murmured eagerly to Proto.

"Good game, Old Man," said one of the teen players. He'd checked out and started browsing Twitter midway through the game.

"Much obliged, Sonny," replied Fyrir. "Don't take the loss too hard!"

The teens walked off. "That beard! Like a village elder from Final Fantasy!" one of them remarked to the other.

One of the convention organizers approached Fyrir and pinned a badge to his lab coat. It had a picture of a Queen of Hearts atop a pile of cards, her mouth agape and her arms thrown up wildly.

"*Wild* rummy," explained the organizer.

Fyrir just shook his head.

"Who are you supposed to be, anyway?" the organizer asked, gesturing at Fyrir's lab coat. "Hojo? Dr. Mario?"

"Fyrir, the world-famous scientist," replied the old man.

"Oh yeah, that dude," recalled the organizer. "Cool beans."

They headed back toward the glowing VIP sign. Fyrir led the procession, marching boldly toward the two guards at the door.

"I already told you, you can't—" the first guard began.

Fyrir raised a finger sharply, cutting off the guard, and pointed to his pinned-on badge. "Now, out of our way, before I report you to the organizers," he admonished.

The guards squinted at the badge.

"Look at that! The old man pulled it off," mused the second guard.

"Alright. Get in there, Gramps," grumbled the first guard.

"There's one girl who can call me Gramps," replied Fyrir. "And you, my Neanderthalensian friend, are not her."

The guard tilted his head and struggled with the long word, as Fyrir led the others through the door. It emerged into a short hallway with another door at the opposite end, which they opened.

Beyond it was luxury. The room—nay, the chamber—sprawled before them, majestic and broad. The tables were marble. Each had a chandelier above it. The chairs were capacious and cushioned. There was, miraculously, no shortage of them.

Half-full glasses were all over the tables. They came from an open bar, where some steampunk alchemist was in the process of ordering—indeed—a martini with an olive.

Nerds with contest-winning badges sat beside beautiful cosplayers with millions of YouTube followers, regaling them with stories of their triumphs. A green-haired woman in a leotard listened attentively as a bony guy in a Hawaiian shirt described his strategy in Settlers of Catan. Four teens wearing 19th-century schoolgirl outfits flocked around some actor from a 1990s video-game adaptation, who was struggling to keep up with their questions.

"Waste of life!" declared Fyrir grimly. "If these crapshooting libertines spent half their time on science instead of dice, vice and devilry, we'd have a second Renaissance!" He shook his head at the Jenga table, where several realistic-looking demons carefully pulled out blocks, and scantily clad succubi gasped with delight.

"Science . . . and wild rummy? With martinis?" asked Lilac.

"Well, card games are different, of course," Fyrir stoutly explained. "Why, I daresay wild rummy made me a subtler thinker!"

"The difference between wholesome interests and wasteful obsessions is whether they existed before you grew up," observed Astrid.

"Spare me your harebrained philosophizing," waved Fyrir archly. "No one likes a Bond girl for her philosophy. All I'm saying is, there's a *reason* classic card games became classic."

"'And thus, a century and a half, they trod the footsteps of a calf,'" quoth Dahlia.

"Save your old poetry for the stacks, you double-stacked humanities major!" admonished Fyrir.

"Oh, can I call *myself* that?" cried the curvaceous bookworm.

"What do you think, Proto?" Lilac's black eyes glimmered. "What are your views on dice, vice and devilry?"

He looked at her, then at the enthusiastic succubi around the Jenga table. "I think . . . I'll go play with some old-fashioned, wholesome, classic building blocks."

Astrid and Lilac flicked his ears. Dahlia shrugged and nodded agreeably.

So did Fyrir. "Yes, well, I can't argue with that," he mused. "Spoken like a younger me!"

Dahlia gave Proto two eager thumbs-up.

"Speaking of classic competitions," said Lilac, "we'll have to get that cookoff scheduled. Assuming we save the world."

"Save the world?" Fyrir frowned and tilted his head. Mists started swirling upward. He squinted as though half-recalling something.

"You should try her cooking," Proto hastily jumped in. "She's a wizard in the kitchen."

"Indeed! Well, as I often say, a man needs two things in life," said Fyrir. "And both are in the kitchen." He wandered off to find Mercune.

"That guy!" Astrid smiled and shook her head.

"I *know*, right?" enthused Dahlia gleefully.

"Also, Lilac, is it really you who dreamt up this room?" Astrid eyed those succubi and blue-and-green-haired divas.

"I think Proto's having an influence," Lilac answered drily.

"No comment." Proto admired what looked to be two Tifas strolling by. "I have no comment."

Astrid and Lilac flicked his ears.

"Ooh, I *need* that crop top!" Dahlia looked down at her chiton and sized herself up thoughtfully.

They fanned out across the VIP room, searching for Mercune. Proto was about to ask some guys in Halo armor if any of them was a teenage girl, when he heard Fyrir's voice nearby.

"Ah! There you are, Mercune." The old man patted a tanktopped red-haired girl on the shoulder. She was sitting and watching some collectible card game, played by a guy in a red and white baseball cap beside her.

"Mercune?" repeated the redhead, turning around. She had blue eyes, a glib smile, and an unfamiliar face. "Nope, just a humble water trainer!"

"Ah," frowned Fyrir. "My apologies."

"It's okay, Professor. Here, have a rare candy!" She handed him some taffy and went back to watching.

The old man sighed, eying the wrapped-up treat. "I need a martini. A real one." He ambled toward the open bar—and Proto blinked at what he saw there.

Somehow, Lilac was now behind the bar and helping a bartendress in cat ears prepare cocktails. There was a line of customers, but with Lilac's help, it was getting shorter quickly.

Fyrir shuffled toward the bar, maneuvering past the line and chatting crowds. "Ahem, excuse me, Doll!"

"Back of the line, please!" replied the cat-eared bartendress, rushing past him with three bottles in hand.

"No no, just a question," he assured her. "Have you seen—?"

"Back of the *line*, please!" she interrupted, cracking an egg on the counter and straining out the yolk.

Fyrir heaved a slow sigh, then turned around and hobbled toward the back of the line. "Fifty years ago, they called me Sir!" he groused. "And coyly smiled!"

Clink. Lilac deftly slid a fresh batch of empty glasses into place behind the bar.

"One White Russian!" called the bartendress.

"Got you girl!" affirmed Lilac. "One White Russian."

"I think they're calling for you, Astrid," Fyrir grumbled to the Russian-cosmonaut-looking woman, joining her at the back of the line.

Astrid chortled quietly.

"You'd flick my ear if *I* said that," complained Proto.

She shrugged agreeably. "Life's not fair."

Lilac slid a White Russian to a short guy dressed as Oddjob.

"Thanks." He tipped his bowler hat to her. "Love the French maid outfit!"

"It's a French *waitress* outfit," corrected Lilac politely.

Fortunately, the line continued to move quickly. Soon, the last guy in front of them, dressed as a Viking in a horned helm, was walking off with a neon green highball.

Fyrir wrinkled his nose at the concoction. "Hmph. 'Don't judge a man by his hat,' eh?"

"If Somnus saw me make that," said Lilac, "he'd dump it on the floor and make me clean it."

"Ha! I knew I liked that fellow," declared Fyrir. "Suppose I hired him, didn't I." He frowned slightly, and the mists swirled up around their legs. "Wait, my colleague has you *making him cocktails?*"

"I liked the little guy's bowler hat," said Dahlia. "The smaller you are, the bigger you go!"

The cat-eared bartendress heaved out a weary sigh. "Alright, Pops, what'll it be?" she asked Fyrir.

"'Pops,'" muttered the old man. "First, a dirty martini. Then, a question, *Toots.*"

Astrid laughed quietly from behind him.

Then, quirking her lips in thought, she surreptitiously grabbed an empty vodka bottle from the bar. Bending down, she sealed some of the swirling mists inside with a conjured cork.

"What's that for?" asked Proto.

"This old man's something special." She smiled wistfully. "Should collect this while we can. I'll miss him when he goes."

Proto looked at those violet eyes, fixed sadly and happily upon the swirling mists. This was one of those rare moments when Astrid seemed as old as she claimed.

Meanwhile, the bartendress was sliding Fyrir his olive-garnished triangular drink.

"Ahh." He sipped it. "Delicious. *That* was worth the wait."

"That's what he said," the bartendress yawned.

Fyrir blinked, then turned to Proto. "I've changed my mind. What a fine establishment!"

Then, he faced the bartendress again. "So, I have a question, Kitty." She was, after all, wearing cat ears. "Have you seen a girl in her late teens with long red hair?"

"Actually." The woman tilted her head in thought. "Yes. Never stops yapping, right?"

"That's the one!" affirmed Fyrir.

"Yep! She was chatting with one of the organizers," recalled the bartendress. "They went off into the back rooms together. The Organizers Only area." She pointed at a door with two guards in front of it, both of whom were huge and wearing Calamity Calamari amulets around their necks. "Hm, they've been gone a while, haven't they?"

"Into the back rooms?!" cried Fyrir. *"Alone* with someone? An *authority figure?!"*

"Sorry Bro, your Princess is in another castle!" declared some mushroom-headed drunkard in a Middle Eastern vest. "Probably getting bowsered right now!"

Fyrir knocked the mushroom cap off his head.

"Bro!" complained the drunkard. He went to lift his mushroom cap.

Before he could do so, a plumber in overalls and a red shirt grabbed it and started chewing on it.

"Bro!" repeated the drunkard. "Stop eating my head, you mustachioed cannibal!"

"Look, I can break bricks now!" yelled the plumber, punching down a Jenga stack mid-game.

"What the F!" shouted the demon-dressed players, as the surrounding succubi gasped and stepped backward.

"Oh yeah?" The drunkard seized his mushroom cap and stuck it back on his head. "Well, I can dig quickly!" He grabbed the fallen Jenga blocks and started throwing them pell-mell.

One of them struck another nearby Jenga tower, which leaned and toppled.

"What the F!" shouted the demons again. They clenched their fists and advanced menacingly.

"I'm also very fast!" noted the mushroom head. He turned and ran away.

The demons gave chase. Meanwhile, several had formed a ring around the mustachioed plumber and now were shoving him around inside it.

The huge guards at the Organizers Only door exchanged a grim glance. "Time to do what they pay us to do!" They drew wooden Minecraft swords and approached the fracas.

Fyrir marveled at the sudden chaos. "Like 1939 all over again!"

"Let's slip in while we can!" urged Lilac, pointing at the now unguarded door.

Proto and Astrid smiled at each other. They'd pushed this scene along a fair bit.

Together, they hurried to the door and entered the Organizers Only area, leaving the hubbub behind them.

It was quite a change: one moment, dodging Jenga blocks and ornery demons; the next, walking a quiet office-building corridor.

Fluorescent lights shone palely on the white walls and blue edging. Intermittent doors led into offices, conference rooms and supply closets. They were strangely silent and free of people.

Then again, this was post-Covid, so maybe that wasn't so strange.

The office proved to be a labyrinth. They began hitting frequent dead ends, forcing them to turn back and try different routes. Worse, there was virtually nothing to distinguish one area from another, save the occasional abstract art hanging on the walls.

"Ugh!" sighed Dahlia, as they passed some splotch of red ink inside a picture frame. "Did this artist spill her cranberry sauce? Or forget her pads?"

"Well said, Blondie," chuckled the old man. "I've been saying it for sixty years. There's more art in pulp fiction and pin-ups!"

"I quite agree," affirmed the bookworm. "You know they once called Shakespeare low art? They *still* do it for Gone with the Wind!"

"Ah, that Scarlett. What a tart!" recalled Fyrir.

After a while of futile wandering, they started hearing screams and shouts, echoing off the walls from afar—then, not so far.

"Eh. That's a mite bit unsettling." The scientist squinted down a hallway, then frowned at Astrid. "Also, is that a vodka bottle you're carrying?

Astrid lifted it. "Cheers."

"You Russki vixen!" admired the old man.

After some long wandering, they felt a surge of hope upon reaching a sort of lobby area where two hallways intersected, with a couple couches and an empty reception desk. Any change from the endless corridors was welcome.

Then, better yet, they saw a sign labeled "Organizer's Office" just past the desk, pointing them onward into another corridor.

Their excitement curdled upon hearing a sudden howl from that hallway.

A demon from the Jenga game—no, several demons and a couple succubi—emerged from around a corner ahead, snarling and scrambling toward the lobby. They were wielding fiery objects in their hands—flaming bottles from the open bar, it looked like.

Proto and the others stood back in shock as the demoniac band rushed into the lobby, laughing maniacally.

One of them chucked a blazing bottle at a sofa. The liquor splattered across it, spreading a broad fire instantly.

"If we can't build, we'll destroy!" the thrower vaunted.

"Oh, my Mercune!" exclaimed Fyrir, clenching his long white beard.

Another demon grabbed a handful of Jenga blocks from inside his pocket, dark and glimmering like they'd been soaked in something, and hurled them at the couch fire. When they struck, the flames exploded into a torrid geyser, blackening the ceiling.

"We've been driven to this!" the hurler howled.

"You mephistophelian hooligans!" accused Fyrir, pointing at them.

The demons turned and fixed their fiendish stares upon the elder. "And who are you?" asked a bald one with a red and black face. "Professor Farnsworth? Egon Spengler?"

"That's *Doctor* to you!" fumed Fyrir.

The infernal fiends frowned at one another.

Then, they advanced menacingly, bottles flaming in hand, explosive Jenga blocks at the ready.

Proto and Astrid shared a glance and stepped in front of the others.

Mists instantly started swirling up. "Since when do lab interns care so much . . . ?" marveled Fyrir.

Proto—who had been on the verge of drawing some conjured weapon from his pocket—now hesitated, staring at that rising mist. It was at waist level.

"I won't have my interns pushing up daisies for my sake!" declared the labcoated elder, advancing beside them and clenching his fists. "Put 'em up!"

Indecision paralyzed Proto as the demons drew near. They bared their teeth and raised their flaming bottles.

And—what could he do?—he balled his fists and gritted his teeth. Astrid did the same.

Then, a blue bolt streaked across the room from an adjoining hallway. It struck the foremost demon in the temple. He plopped to the floor, unmoving.

"What the F?" exclaimed the demons.

One of them bent down beside their fallen brother and shook him. "Nick! Nick!"

The fallen demon snored and rolled onto his side.

"Who the F?" cried another demon, pointing at an adjoining hallway.

Rushing into the room, barechested with a winged hat and a leafy wand in hand, was Somnus. Behind him came Athena in her Greek helmet, followed by Aphrodite and Hera, their chitons billowing in their wake.

"Get 'em!" yelled the red-and-black-faced demon. He charged.

Somnus leveled his wand at his attacker, and a blue bolt crackled forth. It struck the demon square in the forehead.

He collapsed smilingly.

"You bastard!" screamed a succubus. She dove at Somnus with her claws outstretched.

Athena balled a fist and socked her in the breast.

The succubus squealed and fell, then started bawling. Mascara blackened her cheeks.

"Anyone else?" Athena curled her hand beckoningly.

The other demons backed away warily, clutching their burning bottles.

But some cackles and howls now came from another corridor. More demons marauded into view, rushing eagerly toward the chaos.

"Go on!" Somnus urged Proto and Astrid, waving them toward the Organizer's Office. "I haven't had such a good row since the Gigantomachy!"

The mists had swirled up to about belly level. But Somnus waved his wand imperiously, and they dwindled away.

"On our way!" Astrid darted forward, followed by the others, as Somnus and the three goddesses did battle.

"I knew I hired you for a reason, Somnus!" Fyrir called behind him.

"That's why they call me Lord!" replied Somnus. He loosed a blue bolt at a demon, then disappeared from view as they turned a corner.

"A bit full of himself, eh?" wheezed Fyrir, hobbling in a jog. "But for good reason."

They hastened along the hallway for several minutes. Echoes of distant cackles and shouting swelled and receded. Smoke wafted in from some intersections.

Proto was beginning to get worried they'd missed a turn when, finally, the end of the corridor came into view. There was an open door with a sign next to it, labeled, "Organizer's Office." It showed an arrow pointing down a staircase.

"About time!" The old man was panting and heaving. "I haven't run this far since Reagan was an actor!"

Sighing with relief, they all advanced toward the doorway.

"There they are!" came a howl from far behind them.

They looked—and a horde of demons was emerging from around a corner and rushing toward them. The fiends waved their Jenga blocks and brandished their blazing bottles.

"Quick, inside!" urged Fyrir.

They dashed past the doorway and slammed the door shut. But there was no lock.

Proto quickly scanned the room. It seemed to be a storage area for unused cosplay convention props and displays. In the room's far corner was a downward staircase.

"Here, help me!" Proto grabbed what looked like a life-size Iron Throne and, with Astrid's help, shoved it against the door. Lilac and Dahlia then wedged a DDR dance pad between it and a ceiling support column. Finally, together, they rolled what looked like a molten, red-glowing boulder from Hell on top of the pad.

And just in time—the door started rattling a couple seconds later, as the demons howled in frustration outside. But the makeshift boundary held.

"Nicely built," Astrid complimented Proto.

"Oh, it's just a . . . Proto-type," he modestly noted.

She swatted his head, mussing up his hair.

"Well done with that dance pad though," Proto complimented Dahlia and Lilac, as he vainly tried to fix his hair.

"You see, I told you it would fit there!" Dahlia nodded happily at Lilac. "Just have to squeeze it in there. And then it's perfect!"

"That's what she—" Lilac began, then rolled her eyes. "I'm not going to give you the satisfaction."

"Come on, this is tee ball!" cried Dahlia.

"Enough of this chickabiddy coquetry!" admonished Fyrir, shuffling toward the staircase. "Come help me find Mercune."

They hurried to follow, descending into dim obscurity.

Meanwhile, the door banged and shuddered behind them, but stayed in place, thanks to the red-glowing boundary they'd built.

The stairway was bizarrely long, with at least sixty stairs. When they at last reached the bottom, they found a long hallway before them. It looked strangely like Somnus' Palace, with drifting mists and ornate silvery glow strips. But, instead of blue, the walls were blood-red.

At the far end of the hallway was a door. Red radiance emanated from beyond it.

Exchanging a look, they advanced silently to the door. Pressing his lips and readying himself for anything, Proto threw it open.

There, poised regally and garbed in her radiant raiment of leaves, with long red hair flowing all about her, was Flua-Sahng, the Queen of Heaven.

Beside her stood Mercune, wearing red and purple butterfly wings and a matching little dress. Her red hair was pinned up with sprigs of mistletoe.

"Gramps! You came!" cried Fairy Mercune.

"Hello again, Proto," hailed Flua-Sahng. "Won't you introduce your friends?"

"'Hello *again*. . . ?'" Dahlia stared at Proto.

"*Really*, Proto?" asked Lilac.

"You get around, don't you, lad!" murmured Fyrir in admiration.

"Um." Proto stepped forward. "Astrid, Lilac, Dahlia, Fyrir: Meet the Queen of Heaven, Flua-Sahng."

"Indeed." Flua-Sahng tapped a nametag on her leafy garb. *The Organizer*, it said. "I should've asked for Queen of Heaven! Much nicer ring to it."

"And I'm Mercune Mirin!" The teenage girl strode up and gave Fyrir a hug. "But you knew that. Assuming that old memory's holding up." She beamed. "How's it going, Gramps? You playing hooky to hang with *me?*"

Clasping her shoulders, Fyrir just stared at her and smiled. Then, he wiped an eye. "Oh, how lucky I am to have you, Mercune."

"Aw." Now, she blinked twice and wiped an eye.

Then, she threw her arms around the labcoated old man, who clasped her tight.

Lilac sighed happily at the scene—then blinked and stiffened, facing Flua-Sah-ng. "I, ah, apologize if we seem distracted, Your Majesty!"

"Oh, no worries, Madame Bartendress. I'm enjoying this scene," Flua-Sahng assured her. "It's awfully rare I get a scene that's not about me!"

In the distance, they could hear the faint echoes of howling demons. But here they stood in peace and satisfaction, safe behind the boundary they'd built.

Proto glanced over his shoulder. Down the hallway, he could see clouds of mirk, slowly burgeoning and bulging toward them.

"Well. This was nice," he mused.

"Mm." Astrid eyed Mercune's fairy wings. "Do you think we helped save the world today?"

"Well." Proto glanced at her vodka bottle. "One dream at a time, right?"

Astrid seemed not to have heard. Her eyes were fixed upon the hugging girl and elder.

Proto smiled away a sigh, waiting for the impending mirk to swallow them up.

Then, he felt a hand squeeze his. He looked—and there was Astrid, her violet gaze upon him, grinning from behind a few stray strands of silvery blue.

Then, in a blink, she'd released him and was facing forward again.

"My oh my." Fyrir was wiping his eyes again. "I'm afraid I take you for granted, Young Lady!"

"What?" Fairy Mercune blinked. "What are you talking about?"

The old man gestured at his puffy cheeks. "A few hours without you, and I go all to pieces! What would I do without you?"

"Nothing, you old fuddy-duddy!" she retorted warmly. "Like a fireplace with no fire!"

"Well said, well said." He hugged her again.

"I'll tell you what," the Mother of All mused, smiling upon Mercune and Fyrir. "A pair like those two—why, you're lucky to see it once a millennium. Trust me, I know!"

Proto eyed the red-haired girl. "She reminds me of someone else."

"Oh?" Flua-Sahng looked amused. "I would *love* to hear you tell me whom, Proto."

He stared at her a moment. "... have we met? Before recently, I mean?"

The radiant woman laughed. "Oh, Proto. You're a rare bird yourself. You rather remind me of . . . " As she spoke, her finger stretched toward his breast, stopping just shy of his Saturn emblem.

"What . . . ?" He stared at her.

"Oh, never mind." Flua-Sahng smiled wistfully. "Just remember. When you think you've exhausted the Possibilities, there's always one more. Always. And there, the unattainable becomes attainable."

Proto tilted his head and regarded the Queen of Heaven in confusion.

But now the mirk was bulging over him from behind, swallowing him up and hurling him away from this scene. It dwindled into ghostliness before him as it spun to wispy nothing.

And now he was hurtling through grey obscurity, spangled with distant stars that whirled in parallax. Through the shining void he flew.

And then he landed mid-stride in a hall of misty blue, momentum carrying him several steps forward.

Behind him, Astrid arrived gracefully and caught up with him a second later, vodka bottle still in hand.

"Oof!" came Dahlia and Lilac behind them, bumping into each other.

"Well!" Somnus strode into sight from around a corner ahead. He was back in his purple and green robe. "I daresay I haven't had so much fun since Byzantium fell."

Proto exchanged a glance with the others. "What exactly were you doing, when you weren't rescuing us?"

"Oh, no no no," waved Somnus. "What happens in Greek goddess dreams, stays in those dreams!" He smoothed his ruffled robe.

"That was an awfully lighthearted dream," noted Proto. "Given that the world is being burnt and demolished up there."

"Yes, well, enjoy this while it lasts!" urged Somnus. "This was a dream untouched by the pandaemonium. There won't be many more."

"The world up there is broken," he went on. "Soon, *that* will be what people dream of—a world rent by quakes and blackened by fire, where man is driven back to Nature. There will be no cosplay conventions. They'll be mere references in old books that no one understands. And then those books will rot away, and they'll be gone. Believe me, I've seen it happen more than once! Astrid can tell you, she's seen it."

Proto looked at Astrid. But the silvery-blue haired woman just stared at the mists swirling inside that vodka bottle and smiled wistfully.

"Let this be a lesson," Somnus continued. "Sometimes, our world seems dull and empty, compared to what it could be. Then, some part of the world goes away forever. And suddenly, you realize what was always there and ready to make your life full, if you'd just made it a part of your life, before it was too late. Learn not to be too late!"

"So . . . does that mean we saved the world?" inquired Dahlia.

"We've made one dream a fairer place. We've thereby made the world a fairer place. Beyond that?" Somnus shrugged. "I'm just the Lord of Dreams. Go ask my mother!"

"As for me, I'm going to have an armagnac," he concluded. "Soon, there won't be many people making armagnac up there. Sad! But maybe some will dream about it still." He strolled away.

Disquieted into silence, the others watched him go, feeling like they'd just woken from some drunk dream into a very sober reality. They exchanged a glance—blank and bleary, unsure and wondering.

That is, all of them except Astrid. She was still gazing on that vodka bottle in her hands, full of swirling mists.

She suddenly looked at Proto, violet eyes shimmering wide, blinking twice.

Then, she strode away, her jumpsuited curves swaying into prominence with each step. She was nearly around the corner ahead when her hand reached up to wipe her face.

Proto stared after her for a moment, then looked back at the others, hoping to find some insight there. But Lilac's face was as studiously blank as usual. As for Dahlia, there was just a hint of a sad smile.

Sad . . . or sympathetic?

He wanted to say something, but nothing seemed right. He wanted to ask something, but he was afraid of the answers he'd get.

So, instead, he just walked back toward the lounge of Somnus' Palace. And they came with him, his friends, heading together toward the familiar and the unfamiliar looming just ahead.

CHAPTER 16
SATURN RETURN

Proto woke with a springtime feeling. If he didn't know better, he could've sworn he felt the warm sun beaming on him, and a soft breeze billowing in from somewhere.

Today was a big day!

Tossing off his covers, he leapt from the bed and opened the wardrobe.

He blinked at the shadowy nothing inside. That semi-dirty and wrinkled tracksuit he'd been saving? In the wash. The tunics? In the wash. Even the chiton was getting its first cleaning!

Of course, there *was* one thing in there, hanging in rumpled menace in a lonesome corner, like Strider at the Prancing Pony.

He'd forgotten to pick up his clothes after washing them all yesterday. There was just one exception, which he'd never worn in the first place.

One exception. This was like opening the pantry, seeing all the food was gone, and saying "one exception" was the dead fly in the corner.

How could he have forgotten? Now, it was too late. He *had* to wear it. He couldn't even call in sick today. This was his big day!

Proto slipped into his robe—the yellow, blue and white one with a Saturn emblem, otherwise identical to Somnus'. He stared grimly at the bohemian magus-looking fellow staring back at him in the mirror.

"I put on my robe and wizard hat," he grumbled groggily at his image.

Well, when life gives you rocks, you gotta roll. Maybe Somnus would approve. That'd be a very good thing, today.

For today was the day of decision—Evaluation Day! Today was the day that Provisional Visitor Proto might just lose his Provisional!

Or he might be banished back among those slumbering dreamers outside of Somnus' Palace, wandering the Mists, submerged within their dreams.

In any event, this was a big day!

Brushing his rumpled raiment, Proto strolled out of his room and recalled everything that'd happened lately.

Time had flown since they'd visited Fyrir's dream weeks ago. During that time, Proto had kept visiting dreams the same way as ever.

This had been disconcerting, given the fiery pandaemonium that'd recently engulfed the earth. He felt like a monk isolated in an abbey during the Dark Ages, living out his peaceful days, as the far world burnt and reeled, slowly recovering from the destruction of civilization.

"*Recovering*"—for Proto and his friends had, in fact, saved the world. Or perhaps the world had saved itself, and Proto and his friends had just enjoyed a manic romp through a dreamt-up cosplay convention. In any event, the world might be wrecked and burnt, but it wasn't going to end.

They'd learnt that several days after Fyrir's dream. Somnus had convened another impromptu meeting in the lounge. Evidently, the day after his dream, the old scientist had had some insight about how to protect the world against the fiery Elements raging across it.

Proto didn't really understand the hows of it. As Somnus had put it: "*Fyrir drew on the Fossil of my mother to create uncrossable Boundaries dividing the earth into Fragments, which, in turn, drained the power of the Elements. Their range of destruction was thus limited to little Fragments. And even now, they're crashing from the skies and burning out upon the earth. Many have been reduced to Fossils like me already. They no longer live in the breathing world. Only in dream and Mist, like me. This will cause problems eventually. But, for now, the world is saved.*"

Whatever. That was all way beyond Proto's paygrade. He was just a guy who visited dreams and delayed making big decisions.

"*The bottom line is this,*" Somnus had said. "*Many died, but many survive. Modern civilization as you know it is gone, but life will go on. Dreams will go on. Of course, the people up there won't be dreaming as much about little things like 'Will I fail my exam?' and 'Should I switch jobs to get a raise?' Not for a long time, anyway. But I've seen the world rent before. And I can tell you, while things will be different, they'll reorganize themselves back toward the familiar, eventually. As they say, different trees, same forest.*"

At this point, Proto had asked Somnus if all this could've been averted. He'd asked if they could've done something differently—if, by visiting the right dreams, they could've steered humanity away from this.

"*I don't think so. As my mother tells me,*" Somnus had responded with a sad smile, "*the future's not an endlessly branching set of possibilities. No, it's a set of roads. All we visitors of dreams can do is steer humanity between them. The roads are laid by Fate. And I think all roads led to this. Or something like it. Who knows? Maybe we avoided a dead end.*"

In any event, life in Somnus' Palace had gone on much as before. For the most part.

Astrid had acted odd for a while—first disappearing for a couple days, and then acting shaky and uncertain toward him in a most un-Astrid-like way. She'd even smiled and called him *Proto!*

He'd been on the verge of staging an intervention or something, when, abruptly one day, she'd gone back to normal. And he'd gone back to being Bozo, Coco, Dodo, and whatever other insulting double-rhymes Astrid could come up with. And all was well, and all would be well.

Wentsworth, the mustachioed man in the three-piece suit, had been despondent while Uberta was Lost in the space between dreams. But she'd eventually been rescued and now seemed fine, with only occasional shrieking nightmares of eldritch horrors.

Soon thereafter, the man had struck up a conversation with Proto while passing by—just the second time they'd ever talked, as far as he could recall.

"Queer, isn't it?" Wentsworth had mused. *"It happened just as Uberta imagined. Or foretold, perhaps? Lost in the space between dreams. The unbreathing realm. My Birdie!"*

"You know I was the one who found her? Me, not even a visitor! She called me 'my hero,' in that lovely midcentury American way. Probably the only thing lovely from midcentury America. Besides her." He'd shaken his head and smiled, twirling his mustache. *"Horribly unlucky, what happened to her. But when Lady Luck takes with one hand, she gives with the other, eh? Lady Luck or Fate. Or Aitvaras."*

At Proto's uncertain chuckle and sidelong glance, Wentsworth had inclined his head knowingly, leaning in close and murmuring, *"Ahh, yes, of course. Can't say those things here. Ears in all places, eh? My lips are sealed! But good comes of ill sometimes, eh? By the grace of… well, you know. Life is good. Cheerio, Proto."*

"Uh, cheerio," concurred Proto, who'd only understood about a third of that.

"Wear that morning suit again sometime, eh?" Wentsworth had called back to him. *"Those were the days!"*

"I'm saving it for a special occasion," Proto had replied, having no idea what a morning suit was.

"Ahh, yes, can't be showing your true colors yet, eh? Just a lad in sports kit, eh? Heh heh!" he'd chuckled. *"Oh, by the way, that ginger lass you visited is doing well! Says to say hi."* And off he'd strutted in his jaunty way.

Well, Wentsworth would be Wentsworth.

Indeed, the very next day, Proto found the man being scolded by Dahlia for letting some of Anima's fairies take vials of Mist from the Shadowcaster without asking Somnus first. Apparently, Anima used it to brew an elixir, or potion, or something—it was a bit unclear.

"Come now, no use crying over spilt Mist! Our visitors will collect more from around the world, and no one will know anything was ever missing," Wentsworth had argued in his defense. *"It's like the Victoria and Albert Museum when I was a boy!"*

Later, Proto and his friends celebrated saving the world with that long-awaited cookoff between Lilac, Dahlia and Astrid. They'd temporarily converted the Shadowcaster room to a sort of cooking arena.

Proto smiled. *That* had been fun. He started to recall it: That look on Astrid's face as her pan fire leapt higher than the abyssal flames. Dahlia's horror upon realizing she'd used salt instead of sugar on her sugar cookies.

Better yet, there was that outfit Lilac had worn. *"You think you're the only one who gets hot in the kitchen, Dahlia?"* she had coolly asked.

But no. He couldn't reminisce on all that right now. He'd save it for another day. Today, he had important business to focus on.

He was, after all, the man of the hour. And he'd best act the part!

Proto approached the lounge and scanned it smartly through the doorway. *Crowded, isn't it? And all for me!*

Everyone was in his or her usual place. Lilac stood behind the bar, wearing her yukata for the occasion, complete with the blue-and-yellow-primrose belt. Somnus sat across from her at the bar, together with several empty glasses with green and brown dregs. Jet and Jag were playing cards with Wentsworth and Uberta.

Mayger was watching the game from an adjacent table, with his black leather jacket on and his hair in a pink Elvis do. Across from him sat Dahlia in her Victorian robe, reading some old book called The Cypria through a monocle.

And then there was Astrid, suddenly standing right in front of him, directly beneath that painting of the two young lovers. She looked him up and down with wide violet eyes, her lips parting.

Then, she threw back her head and laughed maniacally, pointing at his Somnus-robe.

Half the room turned to face them, their conversations stopping.

Proto nodded grimly. *So, it's gonna be one of those days, huh.*

The Lord of Dreams himself looked over from the bar. His mouth fell open with delight. "Hold up everyone! Hold the phone! Press pause!" he cried, extending an arm grandly toward the doorway. "Look how our Provisional Visitor is *honoring* me today!"

The other half of the room obliged and looked over.

"What are you doing, Proto?" cackled Astrid, pointing at his fabulous garb.

Our poor Provisional Visitor scanned the lounge. So far, the rest of the room had managed to hold in its laughter, but looked like a volcano on the verge of erupting.

"Just saving the world, one dream at a time!" declared Proto in his best booming Somnus-voice. "Get me my absinthe, Madame Bartendress!"

That laughter erupted now—but it was laughter with him, not at him.

Well, maybe a bit of both. But that was okay.

"Couldn't have said it better myself," applauded Somnus. "Evaluation Day comes, and suddenly, he's the Lord of Dreams! Well said."

There was a general *hear hear*. Then, all went back to their revelry and merriment.

That could've gone worse, mused Proto, though his cheeks still felt red.

They grew redder still when Astrid gave him a quick hug. "Just kidding! I remember when all the guys wore robes! They come back every few centuries. You wear it well."

"Every few centuries," he repeated. "Well, maybe I'm behind the times, but I'm also ahead of them!"

"That's the spirit!" affirmed Astrid. "I started thinking that way a long time ago."

"Was that before or after the Industrial Revolution?" he joked.

"It was before B.C. became A.D., Proto," replied the silvery-blue-haired woman.

Not for the first time, he pondered the strangeness of his new life. "I need a drink," he concluded.

The jumpsuited woman laughed and waved him toward the bar.

From behind the ornate wooden bar, Lilac scanned his equally ornate robe up and down. "What will it be, Father Proto? Some wine and wafers?" Her black eyes glimmered.

"Lilac, Lilac, get me my armagnac!" he directed. "If I'm going to be Somnus, let's do this right."

"In that case," she replied, "I'll pour you three, plus an absinthe to wash it down."

"See to it, Madame Bartendress!" he commanded with his best Somnus-like airy nonchalance.

As he waited for his four drinks, his other friends congregated over. This was, after all, his big day.

Quite a crew at this point, mused Proto, scanning them all—Jet and Jag, Mayger and Dahlia, Lilac and Astrid, and, of course, Somnus.

"I *am* flattered though," declared Somnus, slapping the bar. "Here I was, thinking you just didn't like my robe. But no! You'd been *saving* it—for months—for your Evaluation Day!"

"Gotta dress for the occasion, right?" Proto managed.

Jag tilted his head. "Wait. At the laundry yesterday, didn't you say 'this better get done by tomorrow'?"

Proto eyed him sidelong. "Uh, is that what I said?"

Jet tilted his head. "Right. You said, 'I have nothing left. Well, nothing wearable.'"

" . . . I don't recall saying that," mumbled Proto.

Mayger tilted his head. "Right. You said, 'I'd rather wear Mayger's spike-shouldered pink leather jacket than *that*.'"

"I definitely don't remember that!" Alarmed, Proto glanced at Somnus.

"That doesn't mean it didn't happen," observed Astrid. "You do have a history of both amnesia and sleepwalking, yes?"

"Wait, Sparky, is that the robe you offered me last month?" asked Dahlia. "'If you need another grossly outdated frock,' I think you put it?"

"For Heaven's sake, people, do you *want* Somnus to fail me?" cried Proto.

"Have no fear, Provisional Visitor!" the Lord of Dreams replied. "Your fate is sealed regardless of their words!"

Proto sighed. Well, that was that.

Astrid patted him on the back. "Nice knowing you, Snow Blow."

Jet patted him on the back. "Nice knowing you, Partner."

Dahlia patted him on the back. "Nice knowing you, Spunky."

"Heavens, am I the only one here who calls you by your name, Proto?" observed Somnus.

"*Thank you!*" Proto threw his arms up in a hallelujah. "I'm glad this has been established before I'm banished back to the Mists. Or Sleepwalker Land, or whatever it's called."

Lilac patted him on the back. "I've never called you anything but Proto."

"You never call anyone anything," observed Jag. "You just give them good drinks."

"Jag makes a fair point," acknowledged Jet.

"Untrue," replied the black-haired bartendress. "You're Suave Dope and you're Slob Dope."

"Lilac wins!" decreed Dahlia gleefully. "You've been christened. Those are now your names."

"Very gracious of you, Dahlia!" said Somnus. "But I'm afraid Proto will be picking our winner today. And it won't be Suave Dope or Slob Dope. Not unless I've *severely* misjudged you, Proto."

Proto blinked and struggled to parse what he was getting at.

"But first things first," the Lord of Dreams went on, fixing him an amiable smile. "*Your evaluation!*" His voice now boomed across the room. All went quiet, eager to hear what would become of the Provisional Visitor.

"As I told you when you arrived, Proto, this is a private establishment. A sort of employee lounge. Members only!" recalled Somnus. "You've been evaluated over several months. Today, we decide whether to make you a member."

"Now, it's highly unusual to have a candidate evaluated by both our hardest *and* easiest evaluators. Lucky you!" declared the Lord of Dreams. "Under my own rules, I'm supposed to keep this process confidential. So I won't tell you which of the two was Astrid the Horrid and which was Mayger the Pushover."

The two veteran visitors frowned at each other, then at their boss.

"Not like our evaluations matter," waved Astrid. "The Dorkling Screwball was always gonna make the call."

"First's name, I should banish *you*, you grape-eyed tsundere!" retorted Somnus. Dahlia scoffed.

"Something funny, Blonde Bombshell?" inquired Somnus.

"No, Lord of Dreams," she replied politely. "I'm just eager to hear you pronounce your most esteemed judgment about this important matter."

"Well, keep your shirt on, if you can, and we'll get there." Somnus paused, then turned to Lilac. "Anything from you before I go on? Some remark about the 'Lord of Drunks,' perhaps?"

"My Lord, who am I to question your most wise choice of titles?" she piously replied.

Somnus sighed. "As you can see, Proto, insubordination doesn't factor heavily into evaluations. Or else this place would be a lot emptier!" He waved at the assembled crew.

"Just me and you, Lord of Dreams," affirmed Jag.

"Yes, precisely," sighed Somnus. "Which, alas, reminds me why leniency is best."

" . . . hey," said Jag.

"I'm starting to get lost," observed Proto.

"Quite. To the point then!" declared Somnus. "Proto, you passed. Huzzah."

Proto blinked. " . . . that's it?" He looked around.

Lilac politely tapped her glass to his. *Clink.* Some scattered two-fingered applause ensued.

"Well. Huzzah," mused Proto. "I guess."

"What do you want from me?" waved Somnus. "Proto, Proto, he's our man. If he can't do it, others can! But they'll complain about understaffing, and Breath Tokens, and, *ugh*, it's just not worth it."

Mayger patted Proto on the back. "Nice job, Snow Blow."

Astrid spun to Mayger. "Don't you dare steal that, you flamingo-headed backup!"

"The fact is, Proto," Somnus went on, "it's awkward complimenting a true friend. That's why we've all had such a hard time of it."

Proto surveyed them—Astrid and Lilac, Dahlia and Mayger—all shrugging, their lips curved up.

Lilac gave him two thumbs-up, then flicked her fingers forward. "Pew," she fired.

He clutched his chest recoilingly. Her black eyes sparkled.

"But, yes, we each find our own way in the end," smiled Somnus. "Speaking of which, it's time for you to choose *your* way. Today's real question isn't what we think of you. It's what *you* think of *us*."

" . . . what?" said Proto.

"And I'm dying to find out!" the Lord of Dreams went on. "I admit you've surprised me quite a bit, Proto, since you've arrived here. But I don't think you'll surprise me today. I'm good at judging these things. We'll see."

"And even if Somnus were surprised, he wouldn't admit it," noted Astrid.

"On the contrary!" retorted Somnus. "On the contrary! If you'll recall, I made a very specific prediction about Proto—the perfect drink for him. I'm on the record, right here!" He tapped Lilac's temple, and she frowned slightly.

"But first," the Lord of Dreams continued, his eyes gleaming with strange zeal, "there's something important I have to tell you, Proto."

Meeting that gaze, Proto felt dwarfed by a sudden sublimity and power. He couldn't avert his eyes. Meanwhile, the room had gone dead silent.

"Later today," Somnus said, "unless something very unusual happens, you'll have to leave this place. You'll return to the breathing world where you came from. Technically, you never were supposed to be here. You're *alive!*"

A strange uncertainty began rising in Proto's breast—that hazy, nagging doubt he'd felt in his early days here. It had dwindled for a while, like the mists in the dreams he visited. But now it was back and swirling higher.

"You got here through a loophole. You made your way here through the Mists while dreaming. Which, by the way, still amazes me," said Somnus. "Fair enough. But we do have to send you back to the breathing world, first chance we get. And that's later today."

"Today?" Proto stared. "Why?"

"Because it's your *Saturn Return!*" answered Somnus.

Proto blinked twice. He tilted his head.

"First's name, you wear a Saturn emblem, and you don't even know your own Saturn Return?" exclaimed the Lord of Dreams. "Ah, but humans these days are astrologically challenged, aren't they? Your Saturn Return, Proto, is when the planet Saturn returns exactly to the spot in the sky where it was located when you were born. It happens once every 29.5 years or so."

"Every 29.5 years?" Proto pondered the implications of this. "But I was 27 when I got here. It's been barely months since then. Certainly not two years. So how could my Saturn Return be today? I'm not 29.5."

"Oh?" Again, Somnus' eyes gleamed with zeal. "Are you so sure about that?"

Proto stared at him. He suddenly felt he should be remembering something.

Indeed, in the dark depths of his recollection, some shadowy scene was playing out. But he couldn't quite make out what was happening.

"Here, let me shed some light on things." The Lord of Dreams smiled sympathetically. "It's time you knew."

Uncertain, Proto opened his mouth to ask what Somnus meant.

But those words were washed away when, abruptly, memory flooded him. It was as real and vivid as a dream. He lived it once again. He *remembered!* He—

—was breathing heavily but felt good. He'd almost skipped running today. But, as usual, he was glad he'd pushed through it.

The traffic, though, was beginning to annoy him. He turned down Cherry Blossom Lane to get away from it, absently noting a yard sale sign on a telephone pole. Soon, car sounds had faded, and he was immersed in familiar sights—houses and yards he'd come to know intimately in childhood, in that exquisitely detailed way that children memorize their early surroundings.

Yes, this was better. Peaceful, pastoral even. His tracksuit let through just enough of the brisk breeze to stay cool. And that breeze often bore with it pink petals, some of the first to fall from the many cherry blossom trees reaching over the road.

Ah, there was Yemos' house. Hadn't seen that guy in a while. He'd have to message him, maybe set something up.

More car noises behind him, loud ones. Maybe a motorcycle, or something without a muffler. He sighed and pushed his earbuds in deeper.

He'd been good about running lately. Maybe he'd medal at that race next week. He'd gotten bronze last time. It wasn't a Nobel Prize. But at least then he wouldn't be a total loser, right? Late twenties, no girlfriend, dull desk job, tiny house, lots of video games—and a race medal.

The future looked bright!

His lips quirked into a self-deprecating smile. Hmph. Maybe he'd finally ask out that barista at Starbucks. "Hi there. Yes, this medal's bronze. Do you like tiramisu?"

Or maybe not. He didn't want to be that *dude. And getting a "no" would suck doubly since he'd have to find a new coffee place.*

And yet the way she always ran her hand through her hair and smiled when they spoke . . . ! Was it just—?

—immense impact. His mind failed utterly to wrap itself around what his body felt. But he did perceive that he was tumbling through the air, watching a whirling collage of pink and green and grey, and something red speeding away.

Motion abruptly stopped. Brightness battered at his eyes. Was that the sun? Or . . . ? He tried to discern if his eyelids were closed, and he couldn't tell. So bright.

Time passed. Then: "Proto! Proto!" A familiar voice. The light dimmed. Someone was leaning over him. He couldn't see the face, but he was close to recalling that voice. He struggled to remember.

The voice stopped saying his name after a moment. There was a pause. Then it was saying something about a "dark red car," "didn't get the plate," something something. Proto wasn't really listening to the words. Just trying to figure out that voice.

And then it dawned on him: Yemos! Of course it was his voice. This was Cherry Blossom Lane, after all.

And with that delirious insight, Proto's awareness sank from mirky indistinction into a black void dotted with far off lights.

There, he tarried for some indefinite amount of time—somewhere between hours and an eternity, he supposed—before vague voices started to intrude upon the starry silence.

He struggled to hear them, but only snippets came through, like fish flitting briefly above the sea's dark waves: ". . . body's failing . . . two options . . . painless way to go . . . could try . . . still experimental . . . induce a coma . . . indefinite time . . . need to decide . . . "

Time passed. Things were said and done.

And all Proto knew was that, suddenly, he was cold. So very cold. How could he possibly be so cold . . . ?

"And . . . I think that's enough to give you the gist!"

Somnus' voice blew through the memory like a gust through a house of cards. In a blink, the memory collapsed back into the present.

Disoriented, Proto shook his head and scanned his surroundings blearily. The lounge. Everyone in the room, staring at him. Astrid, Lilac and Dahlia, all smiling sadly with sympathetic concern.

"To put it simply," Somnus said, "you suffered an accident. You were placed into a coma. You spent a long time dreaming. During that time, your Spirit found its way here. As for the other details, you'll learn about them if you go back up there."

" . . . who else knew all this?" asked Proto.

The Lord of Dreams winced a smile. "Everyone, Proto. Don't hold it against them, though. I forbade them to tell you. I'll take the blame for that."

"Of course," he went on, "*someone* tried to spill the beans early. She didn't openly defy me. Instead, she thought it'd be clever to shadowcast Yemos while you were there, so she could 'accidentally' tell you about your accident and how Yemos found you. And—to top it all off—she would blame poor, innocent *Lady Luck* for this so-called lucky coincidence!" He gave Dahlia a pointed look. "Well, Miss Shadowseer, it's a good thing Yemos' shadowcasting stayed vague about this subject, or I might be a bit peeved!"

"I tried." Dahlia smiled apologetically to Proto, then turned to Somnus. "And it's a good thing I did too, or else we might never have saved the world! Think what we learned from Yemos."

"Beside the point!" boomed the Lord of Dreams, waving a hand dismissively.

Meanwhile, Proto's head was whirling. He struggled to make sense of what he was hearing and work out its implications. But there were so many new facts. "Wait. You said I'd learn the other details '*if* I go back up there.' 'If' I wake up. 'If' I go back to the breathing world, as you call it. So . . . does that mean I can choose to stay here?"

"That's not up to you, I'm afraid!" Somnus shrugged commiseratively. "No living humans allowed here. Rules are rules. I don't make them, I just follow them."

" . . . okay," sighed Proto. "So, I guess it's time for farewells, huh."

"Well, yes. Unless something very unusual happens!" added the Lord of Dreams.

Proto raised his brow at Somnus and regarded him levelly.

"Alright, alright!" waved Somnus. "Yes, there's a way you can stay. We wouldn't have bothered with this whole mentorship and evaluation rigmarole, if we'd known for *certain* you'd be leaving today."

"And what would happen if I stayed?" asked Proto.

"Well, first," said Somnus, "you'd get that promotion. A full visitor! Just tap those slidey white doors, and they'd slide right open! And you could visit dreams on your own! Though I find having company is nice. Then, in 29.5 years—your next Saturn Return—if you'd decided you'd have enough and wanted to leave, you could leave! Or not. Up to you."

"So, if I don't go back today," Proto replied slowly, "I'll be stuck here another 29.5 years? So I'll be an old man when I eventually do wake up?"

"Old man? At 59? Why, at 59, life has just begun!" retorted Somnus. "But no, you needn't worry about that. No matter when you return to the breathing world, you'll be hardly a day older than when you came here."

"Wait, I don't get it." Proto's brow furrowed. "Time passes for everyone up there, but *not* for me? Even though my body's alive up there? How does that work?"

Somnus gave an exasperated sigh. "Of all the weird and wonderful things that've happened here, *that's* the one you finally demand me to explain? Look, I promise: If you go back up there, you'll understand *very* quickly why you're no older."

"I should mention, though," he went on, "everyone else up there *would* be getting older. So, if you wait here for 29.5 years, they'll be rather greyer and wrinklier."

"Also, you probably realize this, but I'll say it anyway," continued Somnus. "Whenever you *do* leave here, whether it's today or 29.5 years from now or whatever, it's farewell to all this. Forever, most likely. Of course, we'll come visit you every now and again, as we visit everyone. In dreams. But it will be brief and fleeting, as most dreams are."

"Fair enough," Proto managed. He tried to wrap his mind around the enormity of the choice that lay before him. But he didn't feel up to the task quite yet. "So . . . if I stay here, I can live forever?"

"Oh, let's not get carried away," laughed Somnus. "We're all bound for the Mists eventually. At least, those of you who aren't already there." He held up a hand and smiled wistfully at it. It wisped away to white mist, then re-solidified. "But I think it's safe to say you could spend a very, *very* long time here. Maybe even as long as Astrid!" He waved at the silvery-blue haired woman.

"Of course, if you eventually got bored of life here and wanted to awaken, it'd be a little tough, waking into an unfamiliar future. But at least you could take a friend with you," mused Somnus. "That is, *if* you could stay here at all. As I said, that'd require some very unusual circumstances."

" . . . wait, what?" said Proto. "Take a friend? What are you talking about?"

The Lord of Dreams turned to Astrid, Lilac and Dahlia. "Which one of you three would like to explain?"

They stared at him in seeming shock.

"Somnus . . . " said Lilac.

"I know, I know I ordered you not to share this earlier!" he replied. "Well, now you have your chance! Speak up!"

"Somnus . . . what are you doing?" asked Dahlia.

"Why, I'm the Lord of Dreams! I daresay, whatever I'd like to do!" he retorted, turning back toward Proto. "Anyhow, since there are no takers, I'll explain. I'll be the mentor, for once!"

"To begin with, let's start with who we are. I'm Somnus. You're Proto. And everyone else here"—he spread his arms across the room—"is a Lost Spirit."

"Generally," he explained, "when new human life is being made up there, Spirit rushes into the body. That Spirit lives out some span of years on Earth, short or long, and then goes to the Mists. Occasionally, however, the process goes awry and some Spirit never has any body to go to."

"Many of those Lost Spirits end up here. You could think of my Palace as a sort of orphanage for Lost Spirits that don't find a home in a human body. Astrid, Lilac, Dahlia and the rest—even Paunch, down in the kitchen!—all Lost Spirits."

"Remember how Lilac dipped her whole arm into the River Lethe and was fine? Didn't lose any memories of life?" recounted Somnus. "Of course she didn't! She had no memories of *life* to lose!"

"Now, mind you, I said my palace is like an *orphanage*. Not a final resting place!" said the Lord of Dreams. "I am allotted a limited number of living bodies to bestow on Lost Spirits. Alas, I have nowhere near enough to go around. So I've devised a few ways to divvy them up fairly. Breath Tokens and so forth."

"But one hard rule I've always followed—as these three ladies all know well—is that I never break up true love," said Somnus. "If you were to tell me truthfully that *someone* here were your true love, and she felt the same way, I'd allot one of those living bodies to her. Should she desire it. In other words, I wouldn't separate you two by making only you leave."

"You can thank my mother for that," he shrugged. "She made the rule and the one exception—no living humans down here, *unless* true love requires it. Hopeless romantic, the Queen of Heaven! But then, deep down, perhaps I am too."

"There's just one problem," he continued. "I'm fresh out of bodies right now. Fully committed, no takebacks. So no one's leaving with you today, true love or not! But you could leave together in 29.5 years on your next Saturn Return. Or a later one. Much later, if you two wanted. I'm not about to use up one of my few bodies on someone who doesn't want it yet!"

The implications of Somnus' words seeped through Proto like an anaesthetic shot—first warmth, then numbness. "You mean, during all those talks I had with the others here"—he looked at Dahlia, Lilac and Astrid—"all those times we had together, each of them knew that if I picked her as my 'true love,' you'd give her a shot at living a real life up there?"

"In a word," replied Somnus, "yes. But don't be too hard on them! As I said, I made them promise not to tell you. Until now."

Dahlia reached for Proto, pain in her eyes. "Proto, it's not—!"

She abruptly went silent and motionless. Beside her, Lilac looked shocked and dumbstricken—and similarly motionless. Astrid was facing him with wide and earnest eyes, her mouth half-opened—and motionless.

Indeed, the whole room had frozen in place, except for Proto and the Lord of Dreams.

"I'm sorry," smiled Somnus at Dahlia, "but I'll have to insist that no one interrupt this part. I made a bet a long time ago, and I'm not about to have it spoiled! Not after all this! But don't worry, Proto, they can still hear us talking. They'll hear exactly what you have to say. We all will!"

"What *I* have to say?" Proto's head was swimming. Mists had started rising from the floor, and he found himself remembering more by the moment—things he'd forgotten he'd forgotten, and people too. *What . . . ?*

"Indeed! Isn't it clear what I'm asking you?" The Lord of Dreams seemed to grow before Proto—nay, greaten. His wry facade was flushed with glory, and his robed frame was exalted into something more-than-manlike. Eminence welled about him. "Have you not suspected, for quite some time now, that this choice would lie before you? Have you not brooded on this choice with almost every waking moment in this place of dreams? Have you not *dreamt* about this choice?"

"I . . . " Proto struggled to sort his feelings into coherent words. But the moment of the moment was swelling within him, and it swept coherent thoughts away.

Unready to answer Somnus' question, Proto asked a different one. "But what about the pandaemonium up there in the breathing world? The fire, the ruin. How does that play into all this? How can I help fix it?"

"Well, that's up to you, isn't it!" answered the Lord of Dreams. "You can stay here and keep doing your part here, together with us, whom you've come to know. One dream at a time! Or you can return whence you came, and make the breathing world a fairer place from within its bounds."

"But no more questions now!" he boomed. "Now is your moment, Proto. The time is come, ready or not! Certain choices, certain possibilities, lie open before you. We all can think of a few. Perhaps you've thought of more. Perhaps you've opened more possibilities for yourself! Or perhaps not. In any event, you choose among them now."

Recoiling from the zeal in Somnus' gaze, Proto's eyes strayed to Astrid, Lilac and Dahlia—those three with whom he'd had such times here at Somnus' Palace, here in the realm of dreams. Even now, he smiled as far off memories winged through his recall, like silhouetted birds against the skyline.

And yet a new weight hung upon his smile, making it wistful, making it sad. Was each of them just using him as a way out of here? A way of getting a real body and a real life? Things he'd already had up there and taken for granted?

When Proto had arrived here, he'd thought he was dreaming, and he'd deliberately lived his life here like a dream. It'd made him happier. He'd come to suspect that, if he'd only lived life that way up there in the breathing world—like a dream—he would've loved it as much as he loved life here.

Was that the lesson of all this? That what he really loved was life itself, lived properly? Or . . . ?

"*You can keep what you love, if you give up everything else.*" The quote echoed through his mind from somewhere unremembered. Who had told him that? And why did it feel so important?

"So, Proto!" The Lord of Dreams faced him as a tidal wave faces the shore. "What will it be? Will you be waking up today? Or have you found your true love here?"

Even as Proto beheld this frozen world, the mists of memory swirled through him. All that he'd seen and done and felt, here at Somnus' Palace, rushed through him warmly and fleetingly—like smoke rising from a fire, mingling and consuming life that'd come and passed. Or perhaps like springtime clouds, more laden by the moment and ready to warmly rain new life into being.

Out of those swirling memories, something new started forming. Soon, he discerned it clearly.

Yes. He knew now.

Seeing the gleaming zeal of Somnus' gaze upon him, he met it squarely. And Proto gave his answer.

PART II
POSSIBILITIES

"So be it!" decreed the Lord of Dreams. He snapped his fingers, and the screech of steel on stone split the air.

Mists swirled up from the lounge's floor. They lapped their way up the legs of chairs and tables, and of Astrid, Lilac and Dahlia, and of Proto himself. And they whirled about Somnus like this whole dreamy realm were his dervish.

"I hope you meant it! There's no undoing it now!" declared the Daemon of the dream realm, even as the mists rose above Proto's head and thickened to grey opacity.

Lights glinted into being—a thousand points of far off light, piercing through the fog like beacons. The shores they shone from were beyond sight.

The lounge was lost in this starry grey. But, somehow, Somnus still showed clearly at its center, like the world had just showered and wiped only his spot on the bathroom mirror.

" . . . where are we?" Proto squinted at those mirky points of light. They spun and tilted in parallax, as though he were gyring in a maelstrom. Yet all felt tranquil and unmoved.

"I'm glad you ask!" said Somnus. "We're in Chaos. Let's have a bit of Order, shall we?"

That wand he'd wielded in Fyrir's dream misted into being in his hand. He waved it lightly, and branching veins of blood red suddenly flamed through the void. "I'm not as good at this as my mother is; but she's taught me a bit. I won't be creating any worlds for all of humanity to inhabit; but my *job* is to create worlds for one. We call them dreams. So, I daresay I can create a world for two."

Interspersed with pulsing red arteries, the mists began to rearrange themselves. They remained amorphous. And yet their formlessness started hinting toward forms, like cells in the womb.

"So, first things first," said Somnus. "They all heard your choice back here. None of them can hear you anymore."

"Now, there's something *I* have to tell *you!* I hope you're listening, because this is awfully important."

POSSIBILITY 1
LIFE AND THE STARS

Proto stared at the Lord of Dreams, hovering in a mirk of whirling stars. His words echoed in Proto's head: *"Now, there's something* I *have to tell* you! *I hope you're listening, because this is awfully important."*

"There's something I have to tell you about Astrid." Zeal gleamed in Somnus' eyes. "I'd mentioned that, if you picked her—if she were your true love—she could leave this place with you. She could finally receive that human body she'd yearned for these last few millennia. And she's known that all along, throughout all you've done and seen and felt together."

"What I didn't mention was," winced Somnus with a smile, "she could've left a couple weeks ago. It was *her* Saturn Return. And she'd collected enough Breath Tokens to finally depart. 777,777."

"That's what they're there for, you see," he explained. "I only have so many living bodies to dole out to my Lost Spirits. If anyone's determined enough to collect *777,777* Breath Tokens, why, clearly drawing breath means a lot to her! And so I make it happen."

"It doesn't happen often," he shrugged. "It took Astrid 3,000 years! She's been gambling for Breath Tokens since before cards existed!"

"Then, when the long-awaited day came for her to leave, what did she do?" said Somnus. "She chose to stay here! She wanted to be here when *you* made *your* decision. Maybe you noticed she seemed a little shaky recently? Hard to blame her, maybe?"

"In other words," the Lord of Dreams explained, "she wasn't using you to get out of here. She didn't even need you for that! No, what she needs you for"—he held his hand over his heart—"is something quite different."

Proto recalled that gaze of violet earnesty, frozen upon her face, as she and the others stood unmoving back in the lounge. Abruptly, he felt ashamed to his core that, even for a moment, he'd doubted her.

"Pardon me for misleading you about her," shrugged Somnus with an apologetic smile. "But if you'd believed me—if you'd believed she was using you to get out of here—well, I'll tell you what, *that's* not true love! And I had to be sure. I can't hand out my few bodies willy-nilly!"

As Somnus spoke, the mists were dwindling down. What their absence revealed, however, was not the lounge. It was the darkling heavens, fraught with nebulae and galaxies.

And it was a bedroom. At the center of the starscape, there stood two wardrobes, two nightstands, two starry lamps—and one huge bed.

"Ahh," admired Somnus, tapping his wand on a shooting-star-shaped bedpost. "I even impress myself sometimes."

"Sometimes?" mused Proto, taking it all in.

"Touché, Provisional Visitor!" acknowledged Somnus. "I mean, *Visitor.* A thousand pardons, Visitor Proto. You've lost your Provisional!" He leaned on the bed and eyed it. "I wonder, what else will you lose today?"

" . . . very funny. I'm 29.5, not 18," replied Proto.

"You think 29.5 is a long wait? Try 3,000 years!" admonished Somnus.

Proto blinked. His eyes went wide.

Somnus beamed. "Well, anyway, at least you're dressed for the occasion." He waved at Proto's robe. "I know you all gibe and jeer at my raiment. But doesn't it just *work* in a place like this?" He spread his arms toward the glow-spangled empyrean.

Looking down at the grand robe of blue and yellow falling down his form, Proto couldn't help but agree—even if he did look like he was going to a formal dinner hosted by Gandalf and Saruman.

"Anyway, I've talked enough." Somnus opened the lone door hovering in the nightscape. Light streamed in from beyond it. "Hope you like the couple's suite! Love's about finding that space where two people intersect. I did my best. Have a good time!" With a genial wave, he strolled out and slammed the door.

At that instant, Astrid blinked into being in front of Proto, abruptly unfrozen. Her mouth continued opening toward the words she'd been about to speak in the lounge—then stopped. She blinked and looked around.

"And . . . she's back!" observed Proto.

"What . . . ?" she managed, squinting at the unbounded starriness.

He supposed this must seem a little odd. "I can explain—"

"No." She shook her downcast head, so silvery tresses hid her gaze. "First, *I* have to explain. What Somnus said earlier. What he made you think about me." Words rushed out breathlessly. "Do you know those Breath Tokens—?"

"I know. I know," he interrupted, holding up a hand. "He told me just now."

She looked up at him. "Did he explain . . . a couple weeks ago . . . ?"

"He explained." Proto clasped both her hands.

She nodded. Her violet eyes shimmered. "You gave me the last two, Proto. The two Breath Tokens that added up to 777,777. The two that would've let me leave," she recalled tremblingly. "That was the moment I knew—I wasn't going to use them. One way or another, I wasn't going to use them.

Proto started to smile, but his brow furrowed. "One way or . . . another?"

She looked away, silent for a moment. "Most of us Lost Spirits never get bodies. We spend some span of years here. Then, once we've had our fill of life—or at least, this life-like existence—we can choose to go to the Mists. You know. The same place all living men are bound for."

"I'd longed for life. And it'd finally come within reach," she recalled. "But it was that moment, when you handed me those Breath Tokens, that I decided I'd never use them. I decided, if I couldn't have life with—if you hadn't felt the same way that I . . . "

Astrid blinked and faced away, wiping her eyes. When she lowered her hands, they glistened.

"You see"—her voice was wobbly, but her lips curved up—"I'm a *very* old lady after all. I'd had quite enough of everything from life, except life itself. And if I couldn't have that with you, then . . . " She looked toward the swirling mists of far off nebulae and smiled wistfully.

Proto drew her toward him, his hand sliding up her arm. Her violet eyes were suddenly wide and blinking up at him, impossibly young and innocent.

He leaned forward and kissed her. As his eyes closed, the violet fire-fraught cosmos in her pupils, reflecting him, gave way to a glory of swirling stars within his mind's eye and his tingling breast. It felt unbounded.

Indeed, it lingered after their lips and eyelids parted. It glimmered in their gazes.

"Well," managed Proto. "What a start."

"Yes!" blushed Astrid.

They stared upon the starry nightscape for a while.

Well, she did, and he did at first. But he found his gaze falling to some silvery-blue tresses, and the way they spilled over a grey jumpsuit. And how its stripes of purple and blue followed her form, outward and inward, and again. And how . . .

Smiling, he returned his gaze to the night sky. "I wonder where the Earth is out there."

"Right there." She pointed instantly, and he eyed her in bemusement. "What? Surprised? People were really into the stars when I was young. My name even *means* star, you know!"

"And you want to go down there to Earth," he mused. "Not just stay here in starry dreamland."

"That's right!" she affirmed. "We'll be leaving here and heading there ASAP. You can give me a tour."

"Somnus' Palace isn't cutting it for you anymore?" he asked.

"Oh, I've liked it here," she said. "But 3,000 years is a long time. And there are . . . things that can be done down there but not here." Her cheeks pinkened, and she spoke carefully.

" . . . wait." Proto's eyes went wide. "You're saying that while we're here, for 29.5 years, we can't . . . um." His gaze fell upon that huge bed.

She was red now. "*We* can just fine! But *we're* not all I'm concerned about, Slow Bro!"

At first, his eyes went even wider, if that was possible.

Then, a memory flashed through his recollection:

A little girl sprinted in front of them . . . Her feet were bare, and she looked skinnier than she should. Her hair bounced behind her in a rudimentary braid. She glanced behind her fearfully . . .

Astrid opened her mouth and started to hold up a hand, a look of infinite tenderness on her face.

Like an echo, another memory followed:

"What do you need all those Tokens for?" he asked.

"Oh, I don't know," she mused absently. "I've just always dreamt of having a little girl, and—"

She blinked twice, then gave Proto a violet-eyed glance.

Proto felt himself smiling. "Once we're down there, will we soon be expecting a visitor?"

"Well, I sure hope so!" she mumbled.

Proto hugged her.

She blushed. "So! I hope we're on the same page about what's going to happen in 29.5 years and nine months!"

"Golly. That's a lot of pressure," he observed.

"Yes! A lot will be riding on you," she agreed.

"What, 115 pounds or so?" he asked.

She tilted her head at him.

Then, violet eyes flaring, she swatted at his head, mussing up his hair. "This is not a joking matter!"

"Agreed, agreed!" he laughed. "We'll, ah, need lots of practice for this very serious matter."

"Well." She looked away. "We have 29.5 years to get good at this." She blinked twice, pinkening.

"How soon do we start?" asked Proto.

"Well." She glanced at him, then looked away. "A matter like this is too important for any procrastination!"

" . . . now?"

She flushed. "Are you really going to make me say this more clearly, Proto? After 3,000 years of modesty?"

Laughing, he lifted the back of her hand to his lips. As he kissed it gently, she was all blinking violet innocence. Turning toward the bed, her hand still enclasped, he led her to the edge.

Then, he paused. "Question, Astrid."

"*Yes*, Proto?"

"Um," he said. " . . . what if it's not . . . "

"Not *what*, Proto?" she sweetly replied. "Don't ruin this moment!"

" . . . not a little *girl*," he finished.

She blinked.

Then, laughter bubbled from her. "Is that all? What, you think I'm loony? Like I'd hold it against you? Of course not! We'd just have to *keep going*. And going and going and . . . you know. Like that old battery commercial with the rabbit. Yes, like rabbits."

"Now you're speaking my language, Nastrid!" he enthused.

She flushed. "I'll have you know, I'm very modest! Let's see you wait *3,000 years* for . . . " She trailed off, somehow reddening further.

"Really?" he marveled. "3,000 years . . . ?"

"What are you *really*ing me about!" she chided. "It just so happens there's one girl out there who believes in true love. And she's standing right in front of you!"

Proto looked at Heaven and laughed.

"I hope you're not laughing at me, Proto!" she cried.

He clasped her arms again and smiled with everything he had. "Astrid, you're one of a kind."

"Lucky you!" She leaned her head against his breast. "But luckier me."

They stayed that way a while. Then, together, her hand in his, they approached the bed.

Space unbounded sprawled above them. Worlds whirled about their stars, and stars swirled themselves to galaxies unnumbered.

And yet, for one night, for one star-crossed pair, it felt like all of this—all those shining heavenly revolutions—dimly revolved around what blazed between them.

POSSIBILITY 2
A SEA OF DREAMS

Proto stared at the Lord of Dreams, hovering in a mirk of whirling stars. His words echoed in Proto's head: *"Now, there's something I have to tell you! I hope you're listening, because this is awfully important."*

"There's something I have to tell you about Lilac." Zeal gleamed in Somnus' eyes. "I told you I never break up true love. You could be a way out of here for Lilac. She could leave together with you. And she's known that from the moment she poured your first drink. Everything I said was true. Technically."

"But . . . there is one thing I neglected to mention," winced Somnus apologetically. "Lilac doesn't *want* to leave this place. Never has, probably never will. She loves her job! She loves my Palace! Life here is all she ever wanted. Well, almost." He smiled. "So, yes, I hope *you* like this place, Proto."

"I may have given you the impression she was just using you to get out of here. Probably misleading of me," observed Somnus. "But what am I saying? You didn't *really* think Lilac, the Lilac you knew, would do something like that, right?

I mean, really: That black mug? The crack she mended? Holding it against her heart? *That* Lilac? If just a few words from me made you lose faith in her—well, I'll tell you what, *that's* not true love."

Proto might not have lost faith, but he still felt abashed. *"Yours to break and mine to mend. . . . But try not to break it too badly."* How could he have doubted her even briefly?

"Pardon me for putting you to the test, but I had to be sure," Somnus went on pleasantly. "I care a lot about Lilac—about everyone here, but especially Lilac. She's like a daughter to me. And, before I invited you here for an eternity, I wanted to make sure things would work out. I feel good about it now!"

"Of course, I had a good feeling from the outset. Remember when I predicted what drink would be a match for you? My prediction was—well, ask her!" Somnus smiled. "Why do you think she's the one I shared my prediction with?"

Proto stared at the dusky-haired, long-robed eccentric and, not for the first time, wondered what must pass through his head.

"But before we get to that, let's spruce this place up a bit, shall we?" The Lord of Dreams waved his wand, and the red-veined mists began dwindling.

Out of the mirk emerged a scene from nature. Cliffs rose tall on their left and right. To their fore stood a single tree—a sakura, pink petals fluttering in the faint breeze. A few were always falling.

A path wound down beside the cliff toward a sandy shore, where waves were lapping. In the distance, mists drifted over the waters.

Proto found himself ambling a few steps toward the water with a faint smile. This, he recalled well. "Just like the original."

"Is it though?" questioned Somnus from behind him.

Proto turned to look—and his eyes widened at what he saw there.

What he recalled was a cave, which he and Lilac had emerged from on their first odyssey together.

What he saw, instead, was a spacious open-air grotto. It had two wardrobes, two nightstands, two cat-shaped lamps—and one very well-stocked bar.

And a big bed, of course. The quilt was a swirl of black and white, like coffee when you first pour in the cream.

A tingling warmth in Proto's breast thrilled through him.

"Ahh." Somnus grinned at their surroundings, basking in the sea breeze. "Makes me wish *I* could stay here and get some sun! In fact."

The Lord of Dreams abruptly lifted his robe and pulled it off.

Proto blinked and stepped backward, arms raised before his face protectively, like someone had tilted a spotlight at him.

Through this vain self-defense, he could see Somnus—every bit as pale as Lilac—was wearing swim trunks.

"I think I'll swim home!" declared the Lord of Dreams, facing the sea with his hands on his hips. "Mind bringing my robe back to the lounge, whenever you're done here? Door's back there." He thumbed toward the grotto behind him. "But no rush. Definitely no rush!"

"I . . . suppose so," replied Proto, still blinking out sunny afterimages of Somnus. "I guess I owe you that."

"You guess! Well, that's good. Enjoy your paradise." Somnus strolled down to the beach. "Alright, Visitor Proto. You two have fun!"

Then, he dove in.

"Wait! What about—?" began Proto, as Somnus disappeared among the waves and mists.

He was interrupted by a gasp behind him. He spun—and there was Lilac, blinking at the sun's glare, her pallor shining with it.

For a moment, she looked disconcerted. Then, she spun to Proto, and her eyes widened.

"Proto!" she half-cried, half-whispered. "Somnus didn't tell you everything. He—"

"He did." Proto clasped her hands. "He did."

Lilac blinked twice at him, her curved black eyes uncertain and reflecting him back whole. "So you know now. How I want to stay . . . " A tear slid down her cheek. "He should've told you *before*. You can take it back. You can still leave today."

"Take it back?" He smiled and, turning, tugged her by the hand. After an instant's hesitation, she let herself be led to the sakura tree.

The wind blew a cloud of petals from its boughs. He deftly caught a handful and, one by one, he placed them in Lilac's hair, pinkening the flowing blackness.

"Proto?" She tilted her head and blinked at him. "What are you doing?"

But he kept placing the petals, right down to the last one. He nodded in satisfaction.

"Are you done?" she chided with tender exasperation.

"Done? No. Not as long as flowers bloom, and you and I are here," he replied.

She touched her hair. " . . . that long?"

"That long." He clasped her hand, and they saw eye to eye. "But . . . maybe we can take a break now." He eyed the cerulean waters.

"Agreed!" She squeezed his hands, her black gaze shimmering. "Come!" She pulled him along the path toward the beach. Her black hair billowed inches from his face. Its sunny glimmers beckoned him along.

He halted at the shore, while she waded knee-deep into the water. Hiking up her yukata and holding it with one hand, she dipped the other into the waves. Eventually, she grasped and lifted a corked green bottle. She tossed it backward onto the dry sand.

Then, she reached into the water again.

"What are you doing?" he asked.

"What I do best!" she answered, reaching for another bottle.

Holding her yukata up while leaning down was awkward, with the waves' continual ebb and swell. She often had to go tippie-toe to keep her clothes dry. At one point, she gasped and stepped backward as some spume sprayed over her waist and soaked through the fabric.

"You know," he mused. "It *is* just us here. If the outfit's in the way—I mean, what's the difference, really, between a two-piece swimsuit and—"

"Don't rush this, Proto!" she chastised sweetly.

"Okay! Okay." His lips curved up.

After she'd gathered a minibar's worth of bottles, she bundled them in her arms—then paused. "Oh. I don't have any cups, do I?"

"Sure we do. Back at the bar." Proto pointed up the sandy hill.

"The bar? Back in the lounge?" She blinked twice in dismay.

He laughed, then decided to go with it. "What, were you planning to make drinks in the sand?"

She looked so sad her bottom lip was out.

Proto laughed again. "Come!" He led her up the path, and she followed wistfully.

Her eyes went wide upon beholding the grotto-bedroom—which, till now, she hadn't seen—rather than the dismal cave she'd expected. She took it all in, gaze settling on the well-stocked bar.

Then, she turned to face him chidingly with hands on hips. "I see."

He chortled.

"I suppose you forgot to tell me you'd freshened the place up!" she admonished.

"I can't take all the credit," he replied. "Or, really, any."

"This *is* downright home-like though!" she marveled, wandering into the shady grotto. "A forever home."

"Literally," mused Proto.

"Hm!" She brushed back one of the two black tresses casting shadows on her face. "I feel like I've just woken from reality into a dream."

"It's getting hard to tell the difference," observed Proto.

"True!" She gazed upon the Sea of Dreams—then blinked. "Oh, right!" She gathered up the bottles again and set them on the bar.

Then, she promptly started mixing.

"I don't think I've seen you make this drink," noted Proto, as she poured the cocktail into two glasses. They seemed to have a faintly pink tinge. But maybe that was just the sakura blossoms she'd garnished them with.

"Oh, it's something I dreamt up a long time ago." She handed him a glass. "I'm just glad I finally got to make it."

"Mm." He started lifting it to his lips—then paused. "What happens if I drink it?"

"Oh, you'll grow fairy wings, and flowers will blossom beneath your feet," she answered.

"Ah, well, as long as we're in this together," said Proto.

With black eyes sparkling, she raised her glass to him. *Clink.* And they both drank.

"Hm," mused Lilac as he swallowed, "what if the River Anima is like the River Lethe and only affects you, not me?"

Proto's eyes widened. "You . . . were being serious . . . ?" A hand rose toward his throat.

"Too late! Once you drink, you're flappy and pink!" she cried.

He hacked a cough out.

"Just kidding!" she laughed. "I want a Man Proto, not a Fairy Proto."

Even in the midst of his now-receding terror, he couldn't help admiring the cocktail's tasteful perfection. Those light notes of flower and sea and springtime. He smiled, his gaze drifting from the grotto's shadow toward the seaward sun.

"So . . . ?" Lilac looked hopefully at him, then the drink, then him.

Proto pondered her creation for a moment.

Then, he leaned in toward the pale woman, clasping her light-robed arms—as, faintly, she drew breath, her curved black eyes going wide—and kissed her.

She blinked up at him twice, her sealed lips touching his.

Then, like a snowflake in hand, she melted into the moment.

Her eyes shut. Her lips parted. And in that kiss was all of Lilac—light and subtle, dark and bright.

Of that, she had enough for only one. But for Proto, there was enough and more. It was unending.

Breathless, she withdrew, looking up at him. "Well! That's one way of telling me what you think."

"It was . . . hard to find the right words." Proto felt rather loopy himself.

"I think you put it right exactly," she breathed. "But . . . you're welcome to try again."

"Hm." He looked at the cocktail. "Yes. Here's what I think." He lifted the cup, admiring its contents.

Then, he tossed the whole thing back.

"Proto! That's not what I meant!" gasped Lilac. "What are you doing?"

"What I do best!" declared the Visitor.

"What, be a flamboyant lush? You're Proto, not Somnus!" she rebuked.

"Lilac, Lilac, give me my rye back!" He held his glass out toward the cocktail shaker.

"There's no rye in there, you dipsomaniac playboy!" she scolded. "But . . . there is enough for seconds." She poured another serving. "Suppose I'd best start making thirds, Proto-Somnus!"

"Call me Minor Underlord of Dreams!" He sipped his cocktail.

"As you command, Minor Underlord!" she said. "You can call me Lilac."

"Lilac!" he repeated. "Is that all, Madame Bartendress Lilac?"

"Mm. I don't think I've ever been as happy as when you said Lilac earlier." She looked fondly afar. "At least, not until ten minutes later." She blushed, pursing her lips.

"Hm," replied Proto carefully. "Do . . . you think we can set three records in one day?"

She studied his face.

Proto double-gunned her hopefully.

"Don't rush this, Proto!" she chastised sweetly.

"I don't know what you're talking about!" He innocently sipped his cocktail.

"Mm-hmm!"

"This drink." Proto tapped it. "It's the one Somnus predicted, isn't it?"

"Somehow, yes," she replied. "Even though you're the first to taste it, besides me. . . . And you'll be the only one."

He looked at her, lips quirking up.

Her ears flushed faintly. "What! You wouldn't share, like, a love letter you wrote."

"A *love* letter!" He tapped the glass again.

She flushed more. "What! Don't laugh at my romanticizing!"

Proto laughed and squeezed her hand. "Anyway, it seems like Somnus always wins his bets."

"Yes, he and Lady Luck have a thing," affirmed Lilac.

"Oh? He is always talking about her, isn't he," said Proto.

"Isn't he! Long story, those two." She poured herself another cocktail. "But I guess we have all the time in the world, huh?" She strolled out from behind the bar.

"Literally," mused Proto, sipping his drink. *Not a bad thought at all.*

Smiling absently, he scanned the bar. His eyes fixed upon a black ceramic object with two white-lacquered cracks. "Oh, look. It's my Lilac-style coffee mug."

"Good! You're going to need it by tomorrow morning," noted the bartendress from behind him.

"Oh? How many rounds are we doing here?" asked Proto, eying his third cocktail—then, blinked and turned.

For Lilac had placed a slender hand upon his shoulder, her black eyes sparkling up at him. "As many as you'd like." Her yukata's belt was untied and hanging loose, and its shoulders were slipping downward. "As many as you'd like."

Hair, face and eyes—black and white and sparkling bright. His gaze fell over her like a falling star, yearning downward in a heavenly burning, fulfilling wishes on its way. Hair, face and eyes, and more.

Slipping an arm around her waist, where her blue-and-yellow primrose belt had been, he led her to the bed.

And at their backs, the Sea of Dreams swelled and sounded, misted and swirled, borne by the warm breeze from form to form, as it always had and always would, as changeless as the changing seasons.

Possibility 3
Chasing Our Future

Proto stared at the Lord of Dreams, hovering in a mirk of whirling stars. His words echoed in Proto's head: *"Now, there's something I have to tell you! I hope you're listening, because this is awfully important."*

"There's something I have to tell you about Dahlia." Zeal gleamed in Somnus' eyes. "I gave you the impression that Dahlia hoped you'd be her chance at life. She hoped you'd declare *her* your true love. And then she could join you up there in the breathing world."

"And guess what? That was 100% true! She's hoping you'll help her get a human body. And, boy, what a body that'll be!"

"But . . . there is one detail I left out," winced Somnus with a smile. "This isn't the first time Dahlia had a chance to leave here."

"About a century ago—yes, she's *that* old and more, there's a reason she loves Victorian robes and literature!—a century ago, we had another longtime visitor who was finally leaving this place. Reginald. Fine chap. Loved armagnac, wore a robe, and played a mean game of Euchre. My kind of man!"

"Well, Reginald had gambled his way to 777,777 Breath Tokens. So he was all ready to trade them in and head up to the breathing world," recounted Somnus. "That's what the Tokens are there for, you see. I only have so many bodies to dole out. And if anyone's determined enough to collect *777,777* Breath Tokens, why, clearly he ought to be given breath!"

"The thing is, Reginald had a thing for Dahlia. He invited her to join him when he left. And . . . she turned him down." Somnus shrugged. "Fine chap, but true love just wasn't there. Not her fault! It's not one of those things you can control. Or should control!"

"And . . . it gets a little sad here," recalled Somnus. "Reginald's heart broke. He didn't want life without Dahlia. And—even more—he wanted *her*, a woman with such life in her, to have a shot at life. So, he took his 777,777 Breath Tokens, left them at the old Shadowcaster, and went to the Mists." He looked away wistfully. "In other words, he went to the place where all men go when life ends."

"So, Dahlia found the Breath Tokens. She'd been dreaming of life for some time. Now, she could have it! Go up there to the breathing world and seek her fortune!" said the Lord of Dreams. "But . . . no. She wouldn't let the story of her life be written that way. Dahlia gave the Tokens to a couple here who'd been in love for a long time, but had no way out. She gave them their way out."

"As for Dahlia, she decided she'd wait here until true love gave *her* a way out. She was ready to wait here for eternity to see if that would happen. You know her. All those old romantic novels and such!"

"And to think," mused Somnus. "She picked *you!*"

"Anyway," he shrugged, "long story. But it seemed relevant."

" . . . yes, that does seem relevant," said Proto.

"Oh, don't be *too* vexed with me, Proto!" urged Somnus. "If you'd lost faith in Dahlia based on a few sentences from me—after all the times you'd had with her—well, I daresay *that* wouldn't have been true love! In my view, there's no true love unless you've hit such heights of bliss together that the memory alone lifts you above all doubts."

"But there I go, spouting off like one of those romantic poets that Dahlia likes!" waved Somnus. "I hope you like poetry. It comes with the package. But, boy, what a package it is!"

Proto scanned the red-laced mirk surrounding them. "So . . . speaking of that."

"Yes, I suppose I've rambled, haven't I? Here, let's get this going." Somnus waved his wand dramatically, and the mists started swirling. "Ah. I feel like Prospero, bidding farewell to Ferdinand and Miranda. . . . Eh. Dahlia would appreciate that."

The mists began solidifying into forms, tall and wall-like, curved and winding. They were bookshelves, Proto discerned after a moment. About fifty feet tall, and stuffed with books from top to bottom.

Within moments, they stood within a grand gothic library. Colored light streamed in through stained glass high overhead. Amid the literary abundance stood occasional ornate chairs and tables, even some sofas.

Proto blinked. "Um . . . what is this?"

"It's called a *library*," Somnus patiently explained. "And it's yours! Well, hers and yours." He scanned what he had made in satisfaction—then yawned. "Hm! That took a lot out of me. But I suppose ordering Chaos into an endless library will do that."

"Endless?" repeated Proto. "Like . . . it goes on forever?"

"Interesting philosophical question! For your purposes, yes, more or less." The Lord of Dreams admired the boundless literary abundance. "I've created some fine bedrooms in my day. But, I have to say, I've *really* outdone myself on this one. Library of Babel, eat your heart out!" He slapped his hands off and started strolling toward the door behind Proto.

"A bedroom?" repeated Proto. "I mean, this is great. But I do have one question, Lord of Dreams."

"Hm?" Somnus craned his head inquiringly.

" . . . where's the bed?"

"Proto," sighed Somnus with a smile. "Do you really think that will stop *her?*" Proto blinked.

"Find it together, Proto! I have faith in you," declared Somnus, walking out. The door slammed shut behind him.

Abruptly, a woman's voice was crying, "—not what it sounds like!"

Proto spun toward the sound.

There stood Dahlia—her eyes going wide even now, her hand thrown up in shock, her form bouncing dramatically beneath her robe as she did so.

"Oh, you made it, Delphinium," he greeted her.

She placed a hand on her breast and took two breaths. "Sparky," she spoke with studied calmness, scanning the towering walls of books. "Have I died and gone to Heaven?"

"Interesting philosophical question," replied Proto. "You should probably ask Somnus."

"Bugger philosophy, I have *books!* Books, books, and more books! Tastefully *and* functionally arranged." She turned back to Proto. "And, better yet."

Faced with Dahlia's glowing smile and blue gaze, he felt like the clouds had parted to let the sun shine solely on him.

"When you said my name—well." Her radiant hair spilled over her, curving over her figure, like a hilly sunlit field. "I'd never thought I'd be—I mean, I'd *hoped*—I guess I felt I'd been cast as Lilith against Eve, or Milady against Constance, or Acrasia against Una, or—you know, the romantic comedy who wandered into a comedic romance—oh, I'm not sure what I mean!" She was blushing. "Pardon, this is very un-Dahlia-like, isn't it!" She fanned her red face.

"Hot in here?" asked Proto.

"Yes! Quite!" she cried.

Then, she brushed her eye. "Hmph. Look at me, going all Victorian maiden. Catch me if I faint, would you?"

"That's understandable, given that you *were* a Victorian maiden," observed Proto.

Dahlia blinked at him. "Georgian, actually. But how would you . . . ? Oh." Her face took on a far off look. "Somnus told you about all that, didn't he. The Breath Tokens and . . . the rest."

"And the rest." He clasped her hand and squeezed it gently.

"Well." She sniffed and brushed her eye again. "Yes, well, I'm glad you saw through that nonsense of his. The idea that I would *do* that—! After all these years of—ugh!"

She smoothed her face and robe. "And the thing is, I'm not even in a rush to leave here." She tried to firm up her voice but it still came out wobbly. "Someday, likely, but no rush. There's still plenty to explore right here. Especially now!" She gestured toward the bookshelves. "And all I really wanted was the right person to explore it with."

"Who would've thought?" mused Proto. "Dahlia, deep down: the romantic."

"Yes, well, it's literally true, you lovable twat!" she cried. "I'm a born romantic. Born in the Romantic Era!" Her voice was round and full with feeling. As round and full as . . .

Eye contact, Proto. "Lucky me," he managed.

"Yes! To start with, I promise I'll never be needy," she vowed. "I mean, I need my books. And food and water, I suppose. But besides that, I'm a girl of few needs. And, between the two of us, I think we can meet the rest." Her lips curved up. "That will take some long, hard work. But I *love* long, hard work."

"I think this will be a good match," he declared.

"Yes, well, true love usually is!" she said. "Even if, alas, you're a visitor and I'm a shadowseer. You're an orange and I'm an apple. 'Thou art thyself, though not a shadowseer.'"

Proto shrugged. "'That which we call an apple, by any other word would taste delicious.'"

"Ooh, that's quick!" she praised, curling her fingers around his hand. "Well, rest assured, this apple's *very* tasty."

"I'd love to find out what that means," said Proto.

"This." She stood upon her tiptoes and kissed him.

One moment, bantering about apples and oranges, Romeo and Juliet.

Then, all was flush and flesh and blonde abundance—her parted lips on his, her breasts against his breast, the sun's dispersion through her hair.

He felt like he'd been given leave to taste forbidden fruit. Its fullness left him sated; its flavor left him starved. Like life, the more he had, the more he craved. And she was oh-so-happy to give it.

Or was she taking it? Was this kiss given or stolen? Or was it planted? Would it grow and bear fruit for them both?

That was love, supposed Proto—that which, being given and taken, somehow grows and makes more.

But these thoughts were just glints of light upon a sea. And the sea itself was *them*, touching and tasting and knowing each other.

Their lips separated. Dahlia sank from her tiptoes, even as her hand rose to her breast. She heaved a breath that lifted her hand, then let it sing out in a sigh.

"That about sums it up, huh?" agreed Proto.

"Yes, how strange!" she breathed. "The longer it goes, the more I long for more. 'The giving famishes the craving.' Hmph! You make me wax poetic, Proto."

"Strange," said Proto. "It almost feels guilty that we can just . . . do it again."

"Quite!" Her pale gaze gleamed. "Well, I've always said, the guilty pleasure wins in the end. That's literary history in a nutshell, you know! Yesterday's guilty pleasures become today's high arts, by winning young romantic people's hearts."

"You're waxing poetic again, Dahlia," observed Proto.

"Quite!" she sighed, fanning her flushed face. "Pardon. It's the heat, I think."

"It's awfully hot in here," he concurred.

"You feel it too then?" She lifted the neck of her robe and fanned beneath. "Glad it's not just me."

"Awfully hot," repeated Proto. "Of all the days for me to wear my robe."

"Strip down to what's beneath, like I do," suggested Dahlia. "Here, I'll do the same, if you want."

"I wish," said Proto. "But I have nothing underneath."

"That's funny. Same here!" she replied.

Proto blinked.

Dahlia beamed.

"I guess the apple's finally fallen on my head," he mused.

"Well, she *will*," assured the gleaming-eyed blonde. "If that's the way you like it, Spunky."

Proto blinked.

Dahlia beamed.

Then, hiking up her Victorian robe, she turned and jogged away, her footfalls translating through her bouncing figure.

"What . . . ?" Proto stared.

Pausing, she craned her head at him, so golden tresses strayed over her face. "Hint: Chase chase chase!"

Then, she ran away. "You'll never take my apple!" she cried melodramatically, rounding the corner and vanishing.

A moment later, a Victorian robe flew into view from ahead and crumpled against the bookshelf.

Proto laughed. He felt a warmth from his breast thrilling through him from top to bottom, and everywhere in between.

"You can't hide!" he menaced. "The apple will be mine!" He ran after her, reaching for the sash of his robe.

And off they went into the endlessness, exploring in the many-colored light of Heaven, chasing a future and making it theirs.

POSSIBILITY 0
INTO THIN AIR

Proto stared at the Lord of Dreams, hovering in a mirk of whirling stars. His words echoed in Proto's head: *"I hope you meant it! There's no undoing it now!"*

He felt sick. Doubts rose in him like bubbles from a rotting swamp. But he'd meant it. Every word of what he'd said to Somnus back in the lounge:

"When I came here, I thought all this was a false dream. Now, I'm not sure if it's a dream. But I was right. It's false. I haven't found true love. How could I in a false place?"

False, and yet it'd felt so real. Even now, sinking into effervescing memory, his lips curved up as he recalled it:

How Astrid had scowled and smiled at him with fiery violet eyes, and swatted at him, and adventured through farflung dreams. Beneath her hardness, she'd always seemed to be hiding something fragile and beautiful that, someday, might come to dazzling light. Like a geode.

Or how Lilac's black gaze had sparkled even as she hid her smiles. Who would have expected such playful whimsy and elliptical humor from the quiet bartendress? They'd gone on odysseys together. It'd always felt like they were leading somewhere. It'd felt like there would always be more.

And how Dahlia, amid her banter, had given him those gleaming glances. She'd always overflowed with life—from the wit that laced her words, to the ardent play that warmed her smiles, right down to abundance of her figure. She'd seemed as undeniably true as life.

False, false, false. Living life like a dream, together with them, he'd thought he'd found something realer than reality. It almost seemed absurd now. *One of them? With* me? *Please.*

No, in reality, he'd just been a way out of here. A one-way ticket out of this place for three people to fight over.

Or maybe he'd been right at the outset—this all was just a dream.

Either way, it'd all been false. *They'd* all been false.

Then again, was he any better? Had he picked one of them as "true love," would the others not be feeling what he felt now? *False, false, false.*

Shaking off the brooding, Proto glanced up at the Lord of Dreams.

"As I said, I hope you're listening," repeated Somnus, smiling sympathetically. "As you saw earlier, you had an accident."

As he spoke, the red-laced mists surrounding them began to swirl into forgotten but familiar scenes.

"You were running on Cherry Blossom Lane. You were hit by a car. Your body was broken. Your friend Yemos found you. He dialed 911. You went to the hospital," recounted Somnus. "The device used to treat you was . . . experimental. A prototype."

"First, you were put into a medically induced coma. Your battered body just wasn't up to keeping your brain alive."

"Next, the doctors repaired what they could. Which was a lot, but not everything. The brain damage was just too much."

"Well, too much to fix at *that* time. But medicine advances quickly—believe me, I've been watching from the start!—and they knew what was irreparable today might be a routine procedure tomorrow. Or in a few decades or centuries or what have you."

"So . . . they put you into cryogenic hibernation," winced Somnus with a smile. "Kind of sci-fi, isn't it? Then again, not long ago, smartphones felt like sci-fi. We're living in the future! Even if it's not flying skateboards and robot housemaids like we hoped for."

"The idea was, you and the others there would be retrieved when medicine was up to treating you," said Somnus. "You'd be a sort of proof of concept. If it worked, they'd start deploying this technology more broadly."

"Then . . . Fyrir's crew woke up my brethren. The Elements. They soared across the skies raining fiery ruin, leaving the world fragmented, leaving civilization in wreckage, and sending humanity spiraling back toward the Dark Ages. So much for cryogenics, eh?" shrugged Somnus. "Maybe next civilization."

As Somnus spoke, Proto watched all this playing out hazily in the red-laced mists. But now, those mists were dwindling down, and soon he found himself standing in the lounge again.

Everyone there was still frozen. Dahlia was still mid-sentence with her hand outstretched. Lilac was still staring in mute shock. And Astrid's earnest violet gaze was still upon him.

"Now, obviously, all this is a problem for you. No doctor from the future's coming to heal you anymore!" said Somnus.

"So . . . I took care of it. Not that *I* can do much up in the breathing world. But I called in a favor. I have friends in high places!" mused the Lord of Dreams. "In short, you're good now. Fit as a fiddle! Right as rain! Bright-eyed and bushy-tailed! Minus the tail. This is cryogenics, not a cosplay convention."

"I'm . . . grateful," Proto managed, his head whirling with everything that'd happened in the last few minutes.

Somnus shrugged and waved dismissively. "I felt I owed you that much. You've done a lot for us! I'd hoped you'd get something out of it. And, if nothing else, you'll get this."

"If nothing else," he went on, "I think you've learnt about life here. It can be a dream, if you choose to live it that way. You'll wake soon. But now you know the dream doesn't have to end with waking."

Proto nodded slowly. All this might be false. But he still felt there was something true beneath it.

"By the way, you're absolutely right. You haven't found true love here. Of that, I'm sure," the Lord of Dreams assured him. "And, given that, you've absolutely made the right choice. It's time for you to search elsewhere! I have faith you'll find what you're looking for."

"But it won't be here." He waved his wand lightly.

The lounge began to evanesce like mist in sunlight: first, the elegant wooden bar and chairs and tables, then the happy crowds.

Somnus smiled wistfully at that painting of the old man watching the two young lovers by the sea. "'These our actors, as I foretold you, were all spirits, and are melted into air, into thin air.'"

Abruptly chuckling, he thumbed over his shoulder. "Now I sound like *her!*"

Following his finger, Proto saw Dahlia, her pained face fixed on his, her mouth open, his name upon her lips.

"But that's silly, isn't it?" Somnus said. "Saying I sound like a dream. Gets things backward, don't you think?"

And, with that, Dahlia, Lilac and Astrid all melted into misty nothing.

That left Proto alone with the Lord of Dreams, who now was strolling toward the downward staircase, still present behind the vanished bar. He descended into mirky depths, even as the world melted all around him. And Proto followed.

Down they went, passing the many floors and doors of Somnus' Palace, which dwindled into nothing in their wake.

Proto felt like he was wandering through a dream—so numb and absent that, upon reaching the ground floor, he kept descending toward the caves below. He was down half a flight before he realized he was alone.

"Where are you headed?" called Somnus from the top of the stairs. "Off to have an odyssey? With whom, I wonder?" He turned and walked out the door to the grand foyer.

Proto climbed back up the stairs and followed. And all behind him melted into nothing.

The Lord of Dreams led Proto through the blue foyer, where silvery ceiling patterns swirled into a Milky Way, and pairs and trios in diverse costumes roved and chatted. All melted into nothing in their wake.

On they went through the courtyard, wending past trees and bushes, past the twelve fountains with twelve different shapes—the Ram, the Bull, the Twins, and so forth.

Idly, the Lord of Dreams picked some flowers as they passed, admiring them. He still held them even after the plant they'd come from had dissipated, even as the garden itself evaporated.

"Lovely flowers! Such a hue! Almost as violet as . . . hm." Somnus smiled. "Forget it." He cast the flowers aside. And before they hit the ground, they'd melted into nothing.

Out the two went through the grand gate of Somnus' Palace.

Moments later, they stood at the cliff, where Proto once had watched the slumbering shades rove. Lone in the sky, a gloamy star was shining.

"Well, here we are! This is where, alas, we part ways." Somnus faced the misty plain below. "I've never been much for long farewells, and I know you've places to be. I'll just say it's been a dream, Proto."

"It has." Proto glanced behind him. Already, the last traces of Somnus' Palace were wisping away. He felt like part of him was wisping away with it.

"In fairness, I should mention. My prediction was wrong," sighed Somnus. "Remember? I made a bet what drink was a match for you? I had a few second guesses too. But, in the end, *none* of them was right! Congratulations! You've won!" he praised. "Or, at least, I've lost."

Unsure what to say, Proto took a deep breath, then let it out. "Will I see any of you again?" he finally asked.

"Well, certainly, you'll still dream. And perhaps you'll dream of us," replied the Lord of Dreams. "As for what you choose to make of those dreams—what reality you choose to give them—that's quite up to you."

Proto nodded. He watched the shadowy figures roving aimlessly below. "So . . . what now?"

"Why, it's obvious, yes?" said Somnus. "You may not be the Lord of Dreams. But we all know there's one sure way to wake up from a dream."

Proto looked down the precipice, its depths obscured by swirling mists, then back up at Somnus. " . . . really? That?"

"What? So concerned? About a mere dream?" Somnus smiled lightly. "Go on!" He waved Proto forward. "You have a whole *real life* ahead of you!"

From his clifftop prospect, Proto turned back toward where Somnus' Palace had stood. Not anymore.

Now, there was only Somnus—his robe and long hair billowing in an unfelt wind, zeal gleaming in his gaze.

"Go on!" commanded the Lord of Dreams.

Proto turned to face his plunge into the future. Mists hid what waited there.

"You can do it, Proto. I know you can," urged Somnus gently.

He stepped forward—

"Just take it one dream at a time, Proto!" called Somnus. "One dream at a time."

—and by the time the words were out, Proto was plummeting back toward where he'd come from.

Possibility 34
Flap Flap

Proto stared at the Lord of Dreams, hovering in a mirk of whirling stars. His words echoed in Proto's head: *"Now, there's something I have to tell you! I hope you're listening, because this is awfully important."*

Learning Astrid, Lilac and Dahlia had been false with him had hurt a bit. It reminded him of when a girl in high school had pretended to like him so he'd give her his second ticket to a Muse concert.

Vexing. But it hadn't come as a surprise. In fact, he'd suspected something like this for some time. Hadn't he said so?

"Sometimes, I feel like all my friends have some secret that I'm not in on. And they're all leading me along toward doing something for reasons they're not telling me. And I wonder, 'Can they be trusted?'"

Well, he had his answer now. Those three thought they were playing a love game, and he—the dupe who didn't realize it was just a game—would be picking the winner. His "true love."

Heh. The joke was on them. He had no interest in picking any true love. He wasn't sure true love was even real—and if it was, it sounded boring.

But they were right about one thing. He'd pick the winner. And what he'd pick was far more exciting than love.

Weeks ago, something had happened that'd changed him. It'd only lasted for a moment. But after that moment, life itself seemed less than life. What was life without *that?*

A pale reflection? A muffled echo? The metaphors leapt toward that feeling and fell short.

This was the moment his life's B.C. became A.D.

This was his nirvanic enlightenment—the moment so full of meaning it made all else meaningless, except for how it'd led him here.

All he wanted to do was *that.* It was sort of like that song about the guy who didn't want to sleep and just wanted to keep on lovin'. Except . . . not lovin'. At least, not that kind of lovin'.

. . . I think? He wasn't quite sure, actually. All he knew was, he needed it.

His relationship with Muse Concert Girl, rather improbably, had taken off. She'd become his *first.* Not the night of the concert, but a week later. They'd broken up soon after. But he still remembered something she'd said to him that first time:

"It's like you filled a place I never knew was empty." He had supposed he'd never know exactly what she meant.

Well, now he knew. Now, having felt full—deliciously, gloriously full—all he'd known since then was emptiness.

But not for long.

Zeal gleamed in Somnus' gaze. "There's something I have to tell you—"

"Just a minute." Proto held up a finger. "There's something very important *I* have to tell *you.*"

"Oh?" blinked the Lord of Dreams, zeal turning to confusion. "Well, let's hear it."

He'd already told Somnus, of course, that he'd found no true love here. He'd been polite about it. After all, who could blame those three dream-girls for hoping to live? He wasn't going to act all brokenhearted and make them feel bad. They'd been nice enough. If false.

False—and yet they'd led him to something true. Some*one* true. There was one here who'd shared her true feelings with him, who'd truly sought to take him under wing.

Unlike those three, she had absolutely no need of anything he had to offer. Indeed, she was far beyond him in every way. And yet that glimmer in her pink gaze . . . ! It'd seemed to hint that, maybe, just maybe . . .

He hadn't *maybe'd* himself so much since Muse Concert Girl at age 18!

Meanwhile, the red-laced mists had dwindled down. They now were back inside the lounge. Everyone there was still frozen.

"As I said," Proto replied, "I haven't found true love here."

Somnus rolled his eyes and tsked. "Yes, well, no need to rub it in. I tried! I knew this was a possibility. I can't say it's the one I guessed, or the one I hoped for. But if there's no true love, there's nothing for it. You'll have to leave, I suppose!"

"But that's the thing," replied Proto. "I'm not sure I will."

"The rules, Proto! I don't make them, but I follow them," shrugged Somnus helplessly. "And if you don't have someone here—"

"But I *do* have someone!" rejoined Proto.

Somnus tilted his head. "But . . . you just told me, two times now . . ."

"Someone who's always been open with me about all she wanted from me," Proto went on. "I felt it at first sight."

The Lord of Dreams stared in bafflement, then chuckled. "I confess, Proto, I don't know where you're going with all this! Is it Uberta? Those Velma-sweaters of hers?"

Through Proto's recollection, glory passed. And it was red and purple, with a matching little dress. And it was flapping.

"Somnus, the one I'm meant for is Anima," he declared.

Somnus' jaw dropped. His *wand* dropped.

Apparently, he was so shocked he let his room-freezing enchantment slip. Because, abruptly, everyone in the lounge was moving again.

"Anima? My sister?!" Somnus turned to Astrid, Lilac and Dahlia. "Well, you've gone and done it now, haven't you?"

"Oh, no," Lilac was murmuring, her hand on her face. "This is all my fault. I never should've had him carry those Breath Tokens for me!"

"You took him to meet *Anima?!*" Dahlia was flabbergasted.

Astrid threw up her hands. "What in the world were you *thinking*, Lilac?!"

Lilac cringed. "I'm sorry, I wasn't thinking!"

"Like taking Mister Moth to meet Miss Flame!" said Dahlia.

"Like taking Mister Moth to meet Miss Pretty Butterfly Wings!" said Astrid.

"I'm sorry!" cried Lilac.

"Well, what's done is done. No point crying over spilt fairy dust." Somnus turned to Proto. "So, I'll tell you what, Proto. *I* can't help you here. Forget the whole get-a-body-from-Somnus-and-go-live-together thing. Giving Anima a body is quite beyond even my power!"

"Her body's quite enough as-is," shrugged Proto.

"Oh, try to restrain yourself, you ponce! She's my *sister!*" scolded Somnus. "Anyway, maybe she'll have some way of keeping you around her domain. Or maybe not! She has to follow the same rules as me. But you're welcome to go find out."

Proto nodded. "I'm grateful for all you've done. Even if it turned out differently than expected."

"Yes, well, as they say," shrugged Somnus, "sometimes it's not the journey's end, but what you see along the way that matters."

"'It's not the catching, it's the chasing,' right?" mused Proto.

The Lord of Dreams sighed. "Yes, you do sound like her. Birds of a feather, I suppose. Or fairies of a wing? Anyway, you two have fun. Come visit sometime. She may have an elysian paradise, but I have better drinks." He held his hands forth winningly.

Proto saluted farewell and strolled down the stairway behind the bar. The Lord of Dreams waved. And the three would-be true lovers just sighed and shook their heads.

Down Proto went, passing the many doors and floors of Somnus' Palace, until he reached the grand foyer. He hastened through that blue room, brushing past the colorful passersby, barely noticing the Milky Way overhead.

Out hurried Proto through the courtyard, scarcely seeing its trees and flowers and twelve fountains as he left them in his wake. No, he had a mind for only one thing now.

And he was nearly flapping with excitement!

Out he went from Somnus' Palace toward the cliff that overlooked the wandering shadowy dreamers. Down the cliffside path he hied, until the cave mouth yawned pink before him.

He felt a tingle at the sight.

Into the mirk and mystery he advanced. He deftly followed the path he'd learnt upon his odyssey here with . . . what was her name? Some flower or other?

Already, his old life's inessentials were falling from his memory. But he remembered the way through this cave. He'd never forget the path that led to Her.

Whatever that girl's name was, he'd have to thank her for their odyssey. It hadn't led where she'd wanted, but it'd sure led him to what *he* needed.

As a boy, his dad had read him that children's version of the Odyssey a dozen times or so. The ending was happy enough, he supposed. But his mind always went back to an earlier scene—where Calypso had offered Odysseus eternal life beside her in an island paradise.

He'd always thought it was a darn good offer. He'd always suspected that, later in old age, lying bald and decrepit, aching as he creaked about in bed, Odysseus must have recalled that goddess he'd rejected—and mused to himself, *What the F was I thinking?!*

Well, Proto wouldn't make the same mistake!

On went Proto toward his destination and his destiny. He hopped the dazzling river of pink. He climbed The Cliff. Reaching the four tunnels, he dashed into the one She'd taken, wending and bending through the mirky pink.

It felt so near, so soon, and yet so faraway!

But in time, finally, the gloam gave way to the dim glow of day. It streamed around the corner ahead. He raced into the light.

And there she was, flapping in the grotto, her gaze of pink upon him.

His mouth fell open, but no words came.

No, he was too busy admiring her from top to bottom. From those shimmering pools of pink, now blinking at him curiously, to . . . *wow.*

Rude as it might be, he couldn't help but trace those curves—those luscious red-and-purple curves—of her gossamer wings. They sparkled as they slowly flapped. Their luster sparkled through him.

Anima smiled. "Do you see the satyrs playing yonder?" She gestured toward the field outside the grotto.

There, some goat-legged men were prancing about merrily, playing pipes, laughing raucously, rubbing their horns, and drinking to excess.

And they were chasing fairies. The winged creatures flitted to and fro, glimmering purple and yellow, blue and green. And at their winged backs were horned satyrs.

"There's a lot of wisdom in satyr play," mused Anima. "It may look like frolicking wastrelry. But in the end, they do what needs doing in life. And they do it much more than most of us." She eyed them fondly. "And those horns! Those long, curved, lovely horns."

Proto looked at her. " . . . um."

"Yes." She turned back to him. "Welcome, Proto. I knew you'd be back. You keep coming back."

"How did you know?" he wondered.

"Oh, just the way you looked at me when I . . . mm." She flapped and said nothing.

"When you what . . . ?" he asked.

"Never mind that. What matters is, you're *here!*" Her pink eyes sparkled dazzlingly.

"So, about that." That gaze made it hard to focus. And those *wings*, and the way they were . . . He shook his head. "Somnus says I have to ask you whether I can stay here. It's not allowed unless I meet some exception to the rules, right?"

Anima waved dismissively. "Oh, you let me worry about the exception. I'll make sure it's satisfied. I leave nothing unsatisfied." Her eyes widened, and her lips parted.

Suddenly, the air about her wings was dustily glowing and swirling, as when a breeze brushes pollen from a flower. And it blew toward him.

Proto opened his mouth to ask a question—then squinted, struggling to remember the question.

"Now, now, no more boring, technical questions," she chided. "I'm *Anima*, not Somnus! We do things differently here."

Part of him thought these questions were important. But she was a heady brew. And, as he drank deep, he found a different part of him shouldering its besotted way into the conversation. "Not Somnus? What, you don't wear robes, drink absinthe, and wax philosophical about the nature of dreams?

"Bleagh!" Anima made a face. "You know he tries to make me *drink* that when I visit? Says I'll like it someday. How many more aeons before he gives up!"

"How about his eighty-year old armagnac?" suggested Proto lightly. "Does that do it for you?"

"Eighty? Why? You are what you drink!" she pointed out. "Do I want to look eighty? Do I want to act eighty? Do I want to feel eighty? Then why would I drink eighty?" she reasoned. "No, I make him stock something pink and fizzy for when I visit. It's how I wash down his drek."

Come to think of it, Proto *was* feeling a bit parched. "What drinks do you stock here?"

"Something *much* better. I make it myself." Her pink gaze shimmered. "Here, let's go get some!"

Taking the lead, she fluttered to a plant pod with a leaf overtop. It looked like a lidded cauldron that'd grown from the foliage. She removed the leaf-lid.

The clear pool of liquid inside had a pinkish tinge. It was dazzling, somehow throwing off far more sun-sparkles than water would have.

And he was so thirsty. He felt like Merry and Pippin looking on the ent-draught.

"May I?" asked Proto, cupping his hands.

"May? I insist!" Anima cupped some in a curved leaf and handed it to him.

Proto lifted it to his nose, swirled it and inhaled, as Somnus had taught him. The aroma was alluring. Roses. Honey. And . . . something. "Is this as strong as absinthe?" he asked absently.

What is *that smell?* It was tantalizing.

"Strong? I like to think it's delicate," mused Anima. "But then, maybe strength can be delicate. What do you think?"

"I think . . . I want it." He lifted the cup to his lips.

She sparkled with pleasure. "Yes, that's what matters, isn't it?"

Some pinkish sweetness. But something savory too. Like . . . *like what?* Something familiar. He felt it seeping through him as he sipped. He felt it fill a part of him he'd never known was empty.

Proto shivered. "This is like nothing I've ever drunk."

"Well, I should hope not! I put a lot of myself into that drink." Anima blushed and fanned her face.

He chuckled at her winsome modesty.

Well, maybe modesty. Or maybe just the fact that it was hot out here. He hadn't noticed it earlier. But now, he could feel a sweat sheen forming underneath his robe. He was probably flushed himself.

"Yes, I agree," affirmed Anima. "You do look hot."

Proto blinked and wondered if he'd accidentally spoken. It was possible—he was feeling a little liquored up.

"Here, let me help." She flapped her wings at him and squinted. He seemed to see her pollen-dust swirl toward him. But maybe that was just a trick of sunlight in his bleary eyes.

Then, his Somnus-robe started misting away.

He gasped and covered up.

"Oh, no need to be concerned!" she laughed musically. "I'm not indecent. Look!" She pointed.

He saw that, beneath the dissipating robe, he now had on—well, something.

It looked like what a 1500s Vatican seamster might have fashioned if he'd been ordered to make a ceremonial loincloth. It was blue and yellow and white. And—indeed—it had a Saturn emblem.

"Ooh, that suits you!" she cried.

A sort of leafy garland was also strewn about him decoratively, and he had on a laurel crown. It was like what all the male fairies were wearing, he realized.

"Wha—what are you doing?" Part of Proto found this distressing. But another part just wanted to drink more of that Anima-draught, whatever it was. He found himself doing so.

"It's not that Somnus' tastes in clothes are *bad*," she observed. "Just a bit stuffy. We can do better. Also, your robe won't work anymore, for obvious reasons."

" . . . obvious reasons?" Proto felt so thirsty, so hot and bothered, that he couldn't seem to understand anything she was saying. That *drink!* What was that familiar flavor?

He shifted his weight, feeling a prickling and a tickling underfoot. Glancing, he saw that he was standing on a patch of springy blue and yellow primroses. *When did those get there?*

"Yes, drink up!" she urged. "There's more where that came from."

Proto dipped his leaf-cup to refill. "At this rate, I'm going to drink you dry!"

"Oh, my! You're welcome to try!" She fanned her face again.

Yes, try he would. "I take it this isn't eighty," he observed, savoring the liquid's life and freshness.

"No, not eighty. Hm. It's aeons, I suppose!" she mused. "But what's age but a number?"

Proto wasn't sure what she meant. Probably something about nature being ageless and eternal, blah blah. He just wanted more of it.

"What is it, anyway?" he asked absently. "Some sort of herbal liqueur . . . ?"

"Herbs? Liqueur?" She double-blinked her pink eyes. "I told you, I made it myself."

Proto tilted his head. "But where it did come . . . ?"

"Myself." She smiled.

Proto's eyes widened.

Anima's smile widened.

Proto's shoulderblades widened.

What—! He tried to look, but couldn't look back that far.

At least, not at first. But they kept growing and—*wait. Those aren't shoulderblades. They're . . . !*

Flap flap.

He gaped behind him. Two big fairy wings were flapping there, in gossamer hues of yellow, white and blue. He gaped at Anima.

"As I said," the smiling Daemon went on, immersed in swirls of shining pollen, "you let me worry about the exception. Mother's rule is, no living *humans* down here, unless true love requires it. Somnus found one exception. Me? Another."

Proto continued his—what to call it? Transformation? Metamorphosis? Apotheosis? Whatever it was, with every second, he felt less human and more . . . *flap flap.*

"Yes, my brother's 'one true love' bit is sweet and all that. I feel it, I really do," Anima mused idly. "But, honestly, after an eternity, it'd get a little . . . *old*, don't you think?"

"What we do is older than love. And yet it keeps things young. We have more fun. Fun's not in what you do; it's how you do it," explained the flapping fairy. "And now you, too, will do what we do. And we'll explore the *hows* together."

"What? How?" Warm intoxication seeped through Proto. "I don't understand . . . "

"Who said anything about understanding?" she chided. "Were you even listening to what I was talking about?"

He struggled to recall through the haze. "Fun?"

"Me." Cloudy radiance swirled from her wings, curling about him alluringly. Her pink lips parted, and her pink gaze widened. Their shimmers lured him into rapture. And that aroma! Roses and honey and . . . "*Me!*"

He couldn't help himself. *Flap flap.*

The red-and-purple-winged Being beamed back. *Flap flap.*

"I suppose I should've told you before you drank," she mulled. "But—I'll be candid—I didn't want you saying no! All's fae in love and war, yes? I hope you don't mind."

Proto was too absorbed in the manifold new sensations thrilling through him to answer audibly. But the *flap flap* of his wings, and the blossoming of blue and yellow flowers at his feet, said all that needed saying.

"I didn't think so." Anima's smile was roses and honey. "Yes, I'm the sort of girl who throws fairy dust to the wind. I just . . . go for it!" From her flapping wings there wafted glowing dust, which swirled about him.

Roses, honey, and . . . He shivered and drew breath.

"And, in that respect," she concluded, "I think we're two pixies in a pod!"

"We will be soon." Proto advanced toward her.

"Ooh! Will we?" She touched her lips.

"All we need is the pod," he affirmed.

"Oh, you leave that to me!" Anima flapped her wings at a nearby plant, sending a stream of shining dust swirling about it.

In seconds, the plant had burgeoned into an enormous leafy thing with room-sized hollow pods, their vertical lips parting faintly, alluringly. It looked like something a free-love-hippie fairy godmother might've conjured forth when Cinderella asked for somewhere to go after midnight.

"Yes, you leave everything to me," urged Anima. "All you have to do is . . . catch me."

Proto thrust his hands out and seized both of hers. "But I already have."

"Are you sure?" Her pink gaze shimmered. "Or have I caught you?" She flapped, and shining pollen swirled about him.

Breathing in, he was suddenly in a whole new world. And the way he'd be flying through it was *not* by magic carpet.

As he smiled dumbly, his eyelids drooped, and absently he let loose her hands.

"Mm-hmm," she murmured happily.

Proto needed more. His eyes fixed back upon her. He flapped forward.

"What's this?" the fairy innocently asked.

He held his open hands toward her.

Hand to her breast, she breathed in. "Oh, my!" She flap-flapped backward, her eyes gone wide and gleaming.

He flap-flapped after her.

She pointed a delicate finger at him. "Stay back, you lascivious winged satyr horn!"

"*Your* lascivious winged satyr horn!" he replied.

"Oh, my!" exulted Anima, her fearful fingers to her lips. She turned and winged away, her red and purple curvature spraying sun-glimmers. *Flap flap.*

Lured along by the curling wisps of shining fairy dust that wafted from her wings, he chased the eternal creature fleeing him. *Flap flap.*

And in a land of bliss, the sun shone, and petals fluttered in the breeze, and two beings of wing and spirit flapped their way toward bliss still greater.

. . . *Flap flap!*

Epilogue

And so, Proto completed his journey through Somnus' Palace. He'd saved the world! He'd been confronted by a choice to end all choices! And now he'd reached a clear, definitive ending.

Was it a happy ending? Reasonable minds could disagree on what was happy—especially when more than one ending was possible, and picking one meant giving up the others. Choosing wrong is rarely happy. And it's even less happy when what *you* would've chosen isn't a choice!

Still, setting aside whether it was happy or not, all could agree on one thing—there *had* been an ending.

So when Proto found himself hurtling through a grey void, with faraway stars streaking in parallax as he tumbled, without any recollection of having just visited a dream, he felt confused.

Did I fall asleep without realizing it? Have I forgotten where I was?

Galaxies swirled as he pondered his plight. He was quite sure he was misunderstanding something. And yet, on a deeper level, he also felt sure—the answers to his questions were *yes* and *yes.*

How, though? None of this made sense. How had he ended up here? And by "here," what did he mean? The starry greyness he was hurtling through? *Or...*
?

Before the misty ambiguity in his mind could finish coalescing toward an answer, Proto reached something.

Everything changed. Everything was dim blue light. And pervading it all was dreamy music, its strains welcoming him back to something he'd once known.

But what? What is it...?

AFTERWORD

If you'd like to help me write more books about Proto and his adventures, I'd earnestly ask you to consider rating or reviewing Somnus' Palace on **Amazon** or **Goodreads**. As Yeats said:

I, being poor, have only my dreams;
I have spread my dreams under your feet;
Tread softly because you tread on my dreams.

I'm flattered you've given your time to reading this poor work. I hope that in return it's given a few smiles and good thoughts; or, if nothing else, perhaps a good dream.

Till next time,
C.V.